T0033423

ALSO BY KATE DRAMIS

The Curse of Saints

THE

CURSE

OF

SINS

THE
CURSE
— OF —
SINS

KATE DRAMIS

sourcebooks
casablanca

Copyright © 2024 by Kate Dramis
Cover and internal design © 2024 by Sourcebooks
Cover design by Amanda Hudson/Faceout Studio
Cover images by tuk69tuk/Getty Images, Kozlik/Shutterstock
Map illustration © Sally Taylor represented by Artist Partners Ltd.
Internal artwork © Chloe Quinn/Astound US Inc.

Sourcebooks and the colophon are registered trademarks of Sourcebooks.

All rights reserved. No part of this book may be reproduced in any form or by
any electronic or mechanical means including information storage and retrieval
systems—except in the case of brief quotations embodied in critical articles or
reviews—without permission in writing from its publisher, Sourcebooks.

The characters and events portrayed in this book are fictitious or are used fictitiously. Any
similarity to real persons, living or dead, is purely coincidental and not intended by the author.

Published by Sourcebooks Casablanca, an imprint of Sourcebooks
P.O. Box 4410, Naperville, Illinois 60567-4410
(630) 961-3900
sourcebooks.com

Originally published in 2024 in the United Kingdom by
Michael Joseph, an imprint of Penguin UK.

Cataloging-in-Publication Data is on file with the Library of Congress.

Printed and bound in the United States of America.
LSC 10 9 8 7 6 5 4 3 2 1

For those who are afraid to show their worst…and to the ones who dare to see it and love us anyway.
(And to Po, who always loved me despite mine.)

The Order of the Visya, as decreed by the Nine Divine and recorded in the Conoscenza, the Book of the Gods

The Order of the Corpsoma:
Physical Affinities

Zeluus: Strength Affinity
Anima: Life and Death Affinity

The Order of the Dultra:
Elemental Affinities

Incend: Fire Affinity
Caeli: Air Affinity
Terra: Earth Affinity
Auqin: Water Affinity

The Order of the Espri:
Mind, Emotion, and Sensation Affinities

Sensainos: Sensation and Emotion Affinity
Persi: Persuasion Affinity
Saj: Studiers of Magic

There's something about the sound of a blade tearing through flesh and bone. It lingers, its vibrations echoing in the mind long after the blood has finished seeping from the wound, like a dark symphony crescendoing toward madness.

It draws them all from sleep:

A reluctant saint.

A young king.

A treasonous enforcer.

United by blades and blood and the brewing of war.

Prologue

MATHIAS DENIER WAS NO STRANGER TO THE DARK, DANK crevices of Dunmeaden. He had made those corners his kingdom, the bars and brothels and seedy establishments he patronized his own royal court of sorts.

He was used to the brutality of his life, the bartering and the blood. Sometimes, he even found it quite beautiful.

Darkness was the King of the Crooks's friend. Which is why he was...*surprised*...to find a cool shiver working up his spine as he surveyed the five Dyminara who waited on the docks where he stood.

He wasn't fearful of Queen Gianna's elite force. While most Visya—those blessed with one of nine gods-given affinities—used their powers in service to the kingdom, Gianna's Dyminara had been trained to use theirs ruthlessly under the guise of protection of their queen and Tala's citizens. For years, Mathias had taken credit for more of the Dyminara's dirtier deeds than even he personally would have liked, but as such, his own unfavorable doings had gone unpunished.

They had a symbiotic relationship of sorts, he supposed.

Typically, the Dyminara prided themselves on remaining unseen.

To be here, so *visible...*

An inexplicable foreboding settled in Mathias's stomach.

He had noticed the subtle changes in town. The increase in the Royal Guard's presence in public spaces, the rumblings of the ongoing recruitment for Her Majesty's forces. All preparations for a war that now seemed unavoidable.

"They've been here since the news broke, Boss," a slick voice sounded from his left. Mathias tore his gaze away from the warriors standing sentinel and arched a brow at Dobbins. The stout man's ruddy face reddened as he ran a hand over his wiry brown hair, betraying his nerves.

Horribly conspicuous, Dobbins was. But he didn't mind getting his hands, quite literally, dirty, which was surprisingly hard for Mathias to find in a kingdom of warriors. Mathias supposed it had something to do with *honor*. A petty thing.

"Well, don't keep me waiting with bated breath, Dobbins," Mathias drawled, his tone conveying his boredom. "What news do you speak of?"

Likely something far from thrilling. Another pirate attack, perhaps.

"King Dominic is dead. Killed at the hands of his nephew for partnering with Kakos and capturing the Second Saint."

Mathias felt his other brow rise, both now inching toward his slicked-back silver hair. A dead monarch was no small thing, yet he could hardly focus on *that*, not with Dobbins's second piece of information.

"And what zealot shared this news with you?" Because truly, only the most devout would believe a *saint* walked among them. He knew of the prophecy. Utter hogwash.

Dobbins shook his head. "They say the news came from Zuri, the king's advisor."

Mathias barely contained his snort. A brilliant alibi, no doubt spun from Trahir to paint the rest of the court as innocents to avoid the wrath of the realm once news of their king's treason broke.

And Gianna will let them prey on her piousness, Mathias thought.

Dobbins continued to prattle on about which brothel he'd been in when he'd heard the gossip in the early hours of the morning, but Mathias's mind was already spinning toward plans of his own. Strings he could pull. Deals he could make. People he could exploit. Political upheaval was a prime time to reap reward if one was prepared for it.

"The general has been released," Dobbins was saying.

That caught Mathias's attention. Tova had been arrested months ago under suspicion of treason. She was reportedly found with orders for weapons—orders from the two trades-men in Trahir who were killed for buying on behalf of Kakos. Such acts were illegal after an embargo had been placed on the ostracized southern kingdom for their experimentation with dark magic.

"They say she was framed by Kakos," Dobbins continued. "Means the supplier is still out there. Interesting, ain't it?"

Mathias rubbed a hand across his jaw as he watched the Dyminara. Interesting indeed. He'd never quite known what to make of the decades-old suspicions that Kakos wanted to resurrect the Decachiré—the forbidden practice that had Visya reaching to be gods by making their power limitless. It had *supposedly* been abolished by the War and outlawed by the gods.

But the Dyminara had captured a dark magic practitioner in Tala just months ago. A Diaforaté, the realm called them: a Visya who had siphoned magic from another to create corrupted raw power. They were found just after the Trahir tradesmen were caught trying to buy weapons for the south-ern kingdom.

Mathias hadn't become the most notorious crook without learning how to watch for signs. Even he couldn't ignore how everything was pointing toward Kakos preparing for war.

And with the supplier still on the loose, perhaps they'd gotten their weapons after all.

"Does anyone know who it is? This presumed *saint*?" The word sounded like the butt of a horribly poor joke.

"They say it's Gianna's Third."

Mathias couldn't contain his scorn now. "Now I *know* this is no more than gambling gossip. There's no way the gods would choose that…" Mathias didn't even have the words to describe what the spymaster was. A pain in his ass would be a good start.

He'd had enough interactions with the young spymaster's vitriol to know the woman was no saint. Her dagger had found enough precious parts of his body to prove it.

Dobbins shrugged. "Just what they're saying, Boss. Apparently, the general took the fall for her first display of power. Was protecting her, she was. Either way, I imagine the queen will get to the bottom of it all. The saint and such. Quite dedicated to the faith, she is."

Mathias muttered a noncommittal sound.

The entire bloody kingdom was dedicated to the gods. Even Mathias made it a point to attend the key services in the town's main temple. Of course, the blessings *he* sought weren't from any deities, but from the patrons whose secrets he could trade as easily as the delicacies from Trahir.

Mathias rolled his shoulders back as he tore his gaze away from the warriors. "Enough gossip, Dobbins. We're late."

The man spluttered his apologies as he scrambled into motion, leading the way toward the gambling den. Mathias was owed another delayed payment—the establishment's second this quarter. It was exactly why he'd brought Dobbins along for this particular visit.

Mathias sighed, the day already weighing on him, and cast a glance back at the Dyminara as he strolled away.

They were clearly waiting for someone.

He hoped she was ready.

PART ONE

Deikosi

1

THE CHILL OF THE MARBLE FLOOR WAS ERASED BY THE warmth of blood. It stained the surface red as it crept under her cheek and she slipped toward death.

She blinked, the edges of the bright room blurring further. Screams of terror echoed off the walls as she struggled to lift her chin, her eyes seeking that ever-present anchor. The room fell into a loose focus as she blinked again.

There. A slumped figure was on the floor beside her, his hand outstretched slightly, as if reaching for her.

No.

No.

No.

Denial pounded through her head, as loud as the screams that echoed off the walls.

He couldn't be dead. He *couldn't* be dead, because someone was still screaming, still roaring, still begging.

Her gaze settled on his face.

His gray eyes were lifeless.

The screams reached the pitch of the deepest sort of despair as a burning sensation ripped through her throat.

Only then did she recognize them as her own.

"A stubborn saint," a voice murmured from above her. She dragged her eyes up, up, up, searching for the man responsible for her agony.

But a soft face stared down at her.

Golden hair. Brown eyes. A white gown.

The corners of the woman's heart-shaped mouth were turned down in pity as she glanced at the lifeless body. Will's hand was outstretched, still reaching, even in death.

"Perhaps *now* you'll behave," Gianna mused. "What do you think, Aya?"

Her name echoed across the room, a dull beat to the terror clawing at her chest.

Aya.

Aya.

AYA—

"AYA!"

Aya gasped, salt-tinged air searing her lungs as she sucked in a panicked breath. She barely registered the shadow of a figure above her before she was moving, her hand reaching for their throat.

I'll kill her. I'll kill her. I'll kill her.

But warm fingers caught her wrist, pinning it by her head as a firm body pressed against her own.

Aya wrestled against the weight, but her other arm was pinned as well, and she couldn't move, she couldn't *breathe*, her mind too panicked for her to wrangle her power, and—

"It's me," a deep voice rasped, tension lining the baritone of it. "It's me. You were dreaming."

There was a note of familiarity just beneath the surface of her panic, but her adrenaline was still climbing, her fear a visceral thing that clawed up her throat and choked her breaths into shallow pants. The unmistakable presence of a Sensainos affinity slammed through her shattered shield, cool peace buffeting against the sharp edges of her panic. The affinity wrapped itself around the sensations inside and *tugged*, urging her pulse to slow and her lungs to open. It was enough to force the lingering visions from Aya's nightmare out of her sight.

She blinked, and brown eyes became gray.

"Will." His name was a whispered relief as his face came into focus, even as her breath stayed locked in her lungs.

"Breathe, love."

Another wave of his affinity, gentler this time, brushed against her remaining panic. Aya felt her muscles relax into the mattress beneath her, her chest loosening slightly. Will's thumb stroked the inside of her wrist, his head ducking as he brushed his lips across the space just below her ear.

A silent reassurance.

She could feel his own heart pounding against her chest, and he let out a shaky exhale as he murmured against her skin, "You're safe." Another brush of his lips, and he said it again—as if he needed to hear the words, too. "You're safe."

It took another moment for Aya to register the creaking of the ship. Her gaze darted around the small stateroom, her eyes adjusting to the darkness and aided by the moonlight streaming through a sizable porthole on the right. It cast flickering shadows across the tanned skin of Will's chest as he carefully released his hold on her wrists and sat back on his heels.

Safe.

Aya sat up and braced her arms on her knees. She let her head hang as she forced another, deeper breath into her lungs. Will's affinity brushed against her again, a mere caress, and that small feeling of peace settled further into her, as if his very essence curled around her bones. It helped to pull her heartbeat further from her throat, enough that she could mutter a soft thank-you, her voice raw from her screams.

Safe.

No.

They weren't safe.

And it had been foolish to let herself pretend that they were anything close to it.

Five days. Five days at sea that Aya had spent distracting herself with training, *gods*, with Will, if only to bury the fear that crept into her dreams at night. It had been so simple to convince herself that they deserved a moment's reprieve after everything that happened in Trahir.

Aya lifted her head, taking in his disheveled black hair, curled slightly from the humid sea air. His eyes were alert.

"You were awake."

Will carded a hand through his strands. "I was."

Just as he had been each night before when her dreams hauled her out of the few minutes of peace she'd found in sleep.

A full silence followed the admission. He never pushed her. Never forced her to talk about what drove her screaming from sleep, just as he didn't share why he was awake when she did. It was as though they'd come to an unspoken agreement to bask in their stolen relief for as long as possible.

Gods knew it was going to be short-lived once they returned home to Tala.

Aya swallowed as she took in the exhaustion lining Will's features—the exhaustion he pretended wasn't there when they sparred on the main deck during the day, just like the pain in his side he ignored. Her gaze flitted to the scar now, the jagged line still an angry red from where King Dominic's Second, Peter, had buried his knife in that godsforsaken throne room.

"You've hardly slept since we left," she said softly.

Will gazed out the porthole for a long moment, his brow furrowing slightly. "I can't," he finally admitted, a heaviness brought on by far more than a lack of sleep thick in his voice.

It wasn't just a confession.

It was a surrender.

And it was enough to have Aya moving, her legs strad-dling his as she settled into his lap, arms locking around his neck. Will's hands found her hips as he tugged her closer to him, his grip warm through the fabric of her shirt—*his* shirt, that she had stolen to wear at night, letting his burnt-ember and spiced-honey scent wrap around her fully, just as his arms did now.

She could feel some of his tension release as his forehead fell against hers, a long breath escaping his lungs.

For a few long moments, they simply breathed each other in. Will's eyes stayed locked on hers, as if he could read her thoughts through her gaze.

"Talk to me," he finally murmured.

Because apparently, five days were enough avoidance.

Aya's jaw shifted. It was still so new—this thing between them. Or, at least, her acknowledgment of it. She still wasn't used to letting herself share her fears with him. Gods, she hardly shared them with Tova, and Tova had been her best friend since they could walk.

"She killed you," Aya admitted softly. "In my dream."

"Gianna?"

Aya nodded, and Will fell back into his patient silence. He offered no platitudes, no empty promises of ease for what lay ahead; just his steady presence as an anchor while she sorted through the emotions that hung heavy in her chest.

"Ever since I learned of my power, it's like I can't catch my footing. Like I'm always one step behind," she continued slowly. Will's hands took up soothing strokes up and down her back as Aya forced a steadying breath. "Going home like this...not knowing what's ahead of us..."

A broken body.

An outstretched hand.

Vacant gray eyes.

She swallowed the rest of her words as she tilted her head

up so she could see him fully, her eyes tracing his features in an attempt to erase the visions of her nightmare. "I need to know if Lorna is right. If Gianna truly intends to use my power to tear down the veil and call in the gods."

"I know," Will murmured softly, tension lining his features. "I trust Lorna about as much as I trust Gianna, which only complicates matters."

Aya wasn't surprised that Will placed his mother in the same category as their queen. He'd thought Lorna dead for years until she'd approached him on one of his trips to Rinnia. She was a Saj, gifted with the Sight, and her ancestor had been the one who foretold the prophecy of the Second Saint.

Should darkness return, the gods hath not forsaken us. For a second of her kind will rise, born anew to right the greatest wrong.

Lorna had faked her own death and fled to Trahir to make sure Gianna never learned of her connection to the prophecy, or her own vision: that the veil, the gods-created divider between their realm and the beyond, was weak. Torn. Vulnerable.

What was it that Lorna had said?

What better way for your queen to enact vengeance on those who spit on the name of her gods than to call down the wrath of the gods themselves?

Aya wasn't sure what to think. Gianna was devoted to the gods, yes. But the gods had promised that their return would mean destruction of their realm. To risk the wrath of the Divine, to risk the entire *realm*, to stop Kakos from recreating the Decachiré?

It hardly made sense.

Yet Aya's trust in her queen had died in Trahir along with other parts of herself she'd yet to examine too closely. And Lorna…she had abandoned her son, her *life*, because she believed so fully in Gianna's zeal.

They couldn't simply ignore that.

Aya took a steadying breath before she continued. "My

position as…a saint"—gods, she could barely get the word out—"is beneficial to us. The more Gianna believes I'm gods-sent, the more I play into her piousness, the more she will confide in me. If for no other reason than to feel as though she has a unique connection to the Divine. I can get us answers."

Will's eyes were hard, but his sigh was one of resignation. "I knew you'd arrive at such a conclusion."

Aya cocked a brow. "Do you have a better plan?"

He cleared his throat, his hands flexing where they'd settled on her hips once more. "Lorna may not be trustworthy, but she was right about one thing: Gianna *does* have her way of getting answers."

Aya frowned as she recalled Lorna's insinuation—that her own son would be used against her. That Will would willingly hurt her in service to his queen. To get Gianna's answers.

She opened her mouth to argue, but Will continued before she could. "It's true. I left Tala with a certain reputation. I'll need to continue it when we return."

Aya turned his words over slowly. They both had reputations to uphold. She was Gianna's Third, and Will her Second, the Dark Prince of Dunmeaden, Gianna's Enforcer and…

"No." Aya was surprised at how hard her voice sounded. But the meaning behind his words, the realization of why his face looked so grave, finally dawned on her, and she could feel her pulse ratcheting up as it did.

He couldn't be serious. He couldn't actually mean—

"It is what she will expect."

"*No.*" Aya shoved herself off the bed, her thumb swiping against that scar on her palm—a marker of all they were to each other.

"It's not as though I'm returning under her good graces," Will pressed as he followed her. "I didn't respond to the last letters from Lena." The Persi, a fellow member of the Dyminara, had not only taken up the search for the supplier on the continent, but had also been responsible for corresponding with Aya and Will when they were gone. "By the time we arrive home, the last Gianna will have heard from me will be over a month ago. It's naive to think I won't face punishment for that alone, even with Zuri's missive explaining what transpired."

"You expect that to help convince me you should get *closer* to her?" she asked incredulously. "To pretend to be her…"

She couldn't bring herself to say it.

Gianna's Second. Her Enforcer.

And her rumored lover.

A lie—a mask he'd spun to stay close to his queen and keep her attention from Aya.

"I do," Will confirmed. "We both know I'm going to have to deploy every one of my talents to get back into her favor. This is one that has served me well. She will expect it of me, Aya. And me being close to her means we have information." Will was speaking, but Aya could hardly hear him over the roaring in her ears. To hear those whispers, to watch as Gianna raked her eyes over him as if she couldn't wait to undress him behind closed doors…

The queen's plaything. The queen's whore.

"It doesn't have to be you," Aya hissed. "It *shouldn't* be you."

"Aya—"

"She wants *me*. That's what you said. She wants my power, and we need to know why. So letting her think she has the weapon she's longed for in her pocket is the right move. She will confide in me."

"Aya—"

"And that means you don't have to do this again. Regain her trust as her Second, fine, but don't… You don't have to…"

Her frustration was rising as she fumbled over her words.

Will didn't have to ruin himself for her. Not this time. Not when Aya could use her position to their advantage. She could manipulate Gianna just as Gianna had manipulated *her*. She could use the tools Gianna had given her—the training Gianna had afforded her—and play Gianna's loyal saint. And in doing so, she could get them answers about what, exactly, Gianna wanted with the Second Saint.

But Will wasn't deterred. "This isn't just about getting information, Aya!" he snapped.

"What the hells *else* is it about?"

"Protection!" The word rang long into the silence that followed. Will shook his head, something like pain twisting his features. "Dominic knew," he rasped. "He knew what we are to each other, and he used *me* to get to you. I won't let Gianna do the same. I will not be a weapon she gets to wield against you. If she knows what we are to each other, that's exactly what I will become."

"Once she sees my power, she will know not to trifle with me—"

"She suspected your power, and that didn't stop her from using Tova." The words were soft. Low. But they sliced through Aya's argument like a knife. Her mouth snapped shut as she glared at Will, but he didn't retreat. He met every bit of the anger in her stare with his own stubbornness.

"She kept your best friend in prison knowing she was innocent. She had Tova take the blame not only for your show of power in the market, but for those fucking weapon orders that she *knew* Tova had nothing to do with. Gods, for all we know, Gianna had them planted on her to set you up the same way Dominic did. Whatever protection you could afford me would be diminished the moment she realizes she can use me to motivate you into doing her bidding!"

Aya's breath became unsteady as she shook her head. "Stop it."

9

But Will took a step toward her anyway. "She will dangle me in front of you like a carrot just like Dominic did—"

"*Stop* it—"

"*And I won't have it,*" he finished, the words coming through gritted teeth. He was in front of her now, his hands cupping her cheeks as he tilted her head up to his. His eyes scanned her face, reading every ounce of obstinance written there. "*Why* are you so against this?"

"Because..." Aya forced out. An aching sadness was clawing its way up her throat, thickening her voice as she fought against it.

Frustration flashed in Will's eyes. "You know it's not real. And I know you better than to think this is about petty jealousy or an aversion to keeping what we have between us. So *why*? Why would you expect me to not use *everything* in my arsenal to help us now?"

His frustration took on a sharper edge as she continued to bite back her words, his voice dropping low as he swore. "Dammit, Aya—"

"Because it is yet *another* sacrifice you are making!" The truth burst forth like water from a broken dam as Aya tore her face from his hold and took a step back. "And you have sacrificed *enough!*"

Yes, she could see the reasoning in it—both keeping their relationship a secret and Will using his charm to sidle back into Gianna's attention. But he had donned that particular mask for *her*. For years, he had honed his abilities into something brutal and enchanting. He had fought his way to becoming Gianna's Second, and he had led Gianna in a chase to keep her attention on him and away from Aya.

Despite Aya's hatred. Despite the whispers that followed.

And he was mocked and hated for it. Feared, even. But never seen for who he truly was. And perhaps the realm would never see the Will she knew now, but she could spare him this one thing.

Gods, she had the power to spare him this *one* thing.

Slowly, Will closed the distance between them. His hands found her hips, his grip firm but gentle as he tugged her in to him. "This is no sacrifice," he said quietly. Aya shook her head, but Will's hold tightened. "It isn't," he insisted. "I don't need the world to know the truth about me. As long as you do, that's enough for me. That will always be enough for me."

Aya blinked back the burning in her eyes. "What about your protection?" she breathed. "Who protects you?"

The corner of Will's lips twitched as he grabbed her hand and placed it flush against the scar on his abdomen, where she'd healed him. "You do."

Now this—this was familiar. They were mirrors of each other, after all. For every bit of stubbornness she threw at him, he threw it right back. But while before, it had led to an all-out brawl, usually by her hand, now Will's forehead fell against hers as a shaky breath left him.

"Please don't make me a danger to you," he continued, his voice rough. "I won't survive it."

Despite the anger pounding through her, despite the terror and the frustration and the stubbornness that she wasn't sure she'd ever part with, Aya closed her eyes and let herself sink into his hold.

She hated that beneath that tidal wave of emotion inside of her, she could see the logic in this, and not only because they were desperate for answers regarding Gianna's motivations for her power. This *was* how Aya could protect him—by letting him make Gianna think there was no reason for Aya to care about his fate.

"Fine," she whispered. "But only until we uncover what she plans to do with my power. Then we…we figure something else out."

Will pressed his lips against hers, warm and smooth and steady, just like him. There was no heat beneath it, just a solid devotion that made her tight muscles loosen as she sank further into him, her hands sliding up his chest and locking behind his neck.

He pulled away once she was thoroughly breathless, a whispered murmur in the Old Language she couldn't quite make out ghosting across her lips as his skimmed hers once more. "So it's agreed then," he said, his voice soft but clear this time. "When we return, we'll both use our unique connections to Gianna to garner what we can. And as for us...we'll present any change in our formerly hostile relationship as...us growing to be allies." Aya couldn't help but scoff at the word, but Will only grinned. "Surely you won't struggle to act annoyed with me every once in a while."

"I'm sure I can manage that," Aya muttered.

His grin grew as he ducked his head, his nose brushing hers. "How *will* my ego manage your torment?"

Aya rolled her eyes. "You'll survive."

His lips coasted across her jaw and her head tilted back.

"On the contrary, Aya love," he rumbled against her skin. "I'm sure you'll be the death of me."

Gods.

There was enough heat to his words that Aya tugged his head up, caring only that his lips met hers, their kiss filled with urgency. He devoured her, kissing her until her breath came in uneven pants and her hips unconsciously shifted against his.

"Have you changed your mind about the extent of our physical exertion?" he murmured against her mouth as he backed her toward the bed.

There was enough arrogance in the question that she pulled back, intent on making him suffer, but Will trailed his mouth down her neck, clearly determined.

Five days at sea, each of which they had spent training and distracting one another, *learning* the different parts of one another, if only to avoid the fear, the apprehension of what was to come. If only to escape the visions that lingered from their nightmares.

And yet…they still hadn't crossed that final line together.

It wasn't as if she'd ever cared to wait before. Aya certainly didn't deny herself the pleasure of others' company in bed.

But…

Not like this.

Not when terror choked their words and fear drove them from sleep. Not when their wounds had barely begun to scar and heal.

Aya bit her lip as she forced the obvious lust from her voice. "I believe it was *you* who mentioned you didn't want to taint the experience with your injury."

Will huffed a laugh against her throat, a groan of resignation following the sound.

"The death of me, I swear it."

2

Will had never much considered the concept of home. His childhood town house had been a cold place, wrought with bitter disappointment from a father whose expectations could never be met. It had hovered over Will like a cloud, growing ever darker, especially in the years after his mother had left.

He supposed the closest he'd come to finding a sense of comfort anywhere was the Quarter, but even that had its undesirable traits. The narrowed gazes of his fellow Dyminara. The whispers they thought he couldn't hear. The hungry looks from those he seduced to try to find something that felt like belonging.

At least there, he'd earned his judgment.

No, Will hadn't much considered the concept of home. The only place in Tala he'd felt truly settled was in the mountains—in the isolated inclines he roamed with Akeeta, his bonded Athatis wolf, away from the stares and whispers and masks he'd chosen to wear.

But as the towering Mala mountains grew closer, their imposing figures looming over the ship's deck like something straight out of the seven hells, Will had never felt more unsettled by their presence.

And as they drifted into the bay, the docks of Dunmeaden finally becoming visible from where he and Aya stood on the deck, that sense of dread only grew.

The port was typically full of boisterous noise, especially with its proximity to the Rouline, Dunmeaden's entertainment district. But today, there was a muted hum to it, and Will was willing to bet it was thanks to the five guards that stood sentinel at the edge of the docks.

Even from this distance, Will knew exactly who they were.

Five Dyminara, each dressed in battle black.

For once, Will cursed the messenger skiffs that raced across the Anath with the help of the Caeli and their wind-wielding affinities. Zuri's missive—and courtly gossip, for that matter—would have arrived far earlier than he and Aya had. And while that was supposed to have been helpful to them... it did not appear to have done them any favors.

"How lovely," Will murmured, his gaze moving to Aya. She stood with her shoulder just close enough to graze his. "A greeting party."

Aya let out a scoff. Her eyes cut to him, the blue in them piercing, before she looked back toward the port. "They're making a statement."

Will hummed in agreement. "I have several working theories as to what that statement is," he muttered. "None of them fill me with pleasure."

Aya's jaw shifted. He didn't need his affinity to feel the tension roiling off her the closer they approached those waiting guards. And perhaps it wasn't the time, but he couldn't help but reach for the familiar goading that had always been so effective at getting Aya out of her head.

"You, on the other hand," he continued, his voice lowering to a purr as his eyes scanned the black wool sweater that hung loose on her frame. *His* sweater, given to her because

15

her wardrobe from Trahir was useless this far north when the lingering chill refused to loosen its grip on Tala until the late summer months. "Have I told you how arousing seeing you in my sweater is?"

Aya's jaw remained tight, her stare still fixed on the Dyminara. "You think this is the time for such sentiments?"

It wasn't. But her shoulders were still tense enough that he shrugged. "I have mere moments to lavish you in compliments before I have to act like I don't want to prove you'd look even better *out* of my clothes. Surely you can't blame me for taking advantage of each and every one of them."

Her tension eased, but only just. He could tell by the twitch of her lips as she turned to look at him fully. "You're impossible."

His hand grazed hers as he ducked his head, his lips nearly close enough to her ear to brush against her skin as he whispered, "You mispronounced *perfect.*

He got a low laugh for that, and despite the unease that had weighted itself in his bones, something in his chest lightened at the sound. He leaned away from her, his gaze following the crew as they readied the gangway. He let his fingers brush the scar on his palm—the mark of the oath they'd given to each other.

No matter how far the fall.

The words anchored him as he forced his face into that mask of subtle insolence he knew his peers would expect while the dockworkers caught the ropes and began to tie up the ship. They were close enough that he could identify the waiting Dyminara:

Liam and his twin Lena. A young Sensainos named Cleo. Phillip, a brutal Zeluus. And an Anima Will couldn't remember the name of.

Liam and Lena waited until the gangway was lowered before they stepped out of line, the Persis' strides quick as they walked toward the ship. In moments, they were aboard and making their way across the deck to where Aya and Will stood.

The last time Will had seen Liam, his black hair had been cut into a high-top fade. Now he wore it cropped close to his head. His square jaw was locked as he took them in, his arms crossed over his chest. His twin stood at his side, her coils pulled into a tight bun. A scar marred the dark-brown skin of her cheek—a new addition since Will had last seen her.

"What a welcome," Will drawled, his brows lifting.

"It's good to see you too, Enforcer," Lena retorted, her hands braced on her hips. Will didn't miss the way her fingers skimmed the pommel of her blade. Lena had always been confident, but today...there was an arrogant air to her that put his teeth on edge. He clocked it in the set of her shoulders, the jut of her chin, the glint in her brown eyes.

Lena wanted arrogance?

Will would show her arrogance.

"Ah, Lena, I wish I could say the same," he drawled. "If only you weren't greeting us like criminals."

Lena rolled her eyes, but Liam took a step forward, his gaze flicking to Aya. "It's for her safety," he replied tersely. There was something beneath his explanation—something Will couldn't yet place. "We're to escort you both to Her Majesty."

Aya cocked her head. "A bit conspicuous, isn't it?"

Liam's jaw shifted as his eyes darted to the docks and back. "It is," he muttered, his voice low enough that the words barely reached them. "But better safe than sorry."

Lena raised a brow. "Any other complaints, or can we go?"

"Someone's testy," Will smirked.

Lena took a single step forward. "I wonder why that is. You suddenly disappear—stop responding to every inquiry—and next thing we know, news of the Second Saint has spread throughout the realm. News that puts *our people* at risk, now that they know she exists and resides here!" Lena leveled him with a glare, which Will met unflinchingly.

She wasn't wrong. It was the same argument Aya had made to Aidon in Trahir before all hells broke loose. Keeping Aya's identity a secret was supposed to have given them an advantage in war. But that ship had sailed, and Will did not need Lena's lecture.

He was Gianna's Second, and Aya her Third. Yet here they were being treated no better than fledgling recruits in the Dyminara.

"Surely you've put the pieces together, Lena," Will muttered. "I stopped receiving your damned missives. I take it you stopped receiving mine as well? You *do* know the late king was partnering with Kakos, don't you? I *wonder* where our letters must have gone."

It was a plausible excuse but even so, Lena raised a brow. "I would have expected more from the Dark Prince of Dunmeaden."

Will's grin was sharp. "And how did your search for the weapon supplier fare, Lena? Have you found the one responsible for trying to supply Kakos in the first place?"

It was a petty blow, and perhaps dangerously foolish, but Will couldn't help the rush of satisfaction as Lena's eyes flashed with anger.

Liam shook his head and stepped between his sister and Will. "Enough."

Lena turned on her heel and made her way to the gangplank, her movements crisp.

"Come on," Liam said quietly. "Gianna is waiting."

Time seemed to warp as Will followed Liam to the palace. It shifted between rapid and slow stretches that made the journey up the winding path feel too short and too long at the same time.

He'd been dreading this meeting with Gianna ever since they'd left Dunmeaden four months ago. For a few spare moments in Trahir, Will had dreamt of taking Aya away from here and never returning. But as he had often come to learn, hope was a dangerous thing. It muddled the mind and weakened the defenses.

They trudged through the iron gates that marked the entrance to the queen's grounds, and Will didn't miss the curious glances the Royal Guard, dressed in their crimson livery, shot them. They were similar to the looks they'd received in town. Will suspected it was in part due to the news that Lena had alluded to. But perhaps it was also because of how the Dyminara were positioned around him and Aya: one on either side, two at their back, Liam in front.

A prisoner escort.

Aya remained silent for the entirety of the walk, but Will could feel her tension rise as the palace came into view.

It had always been a formidable structure, with its towering stone turrets made of the same granite that formed the Wall of Dunmeaden, which encircled the structure and the grounds beyond it. But as they stepped into the palace's looming shadow, Will couldn't help but feel a heavy sense of foreboding seeping from the stones.

They filed into the palace, and Will rolled his shoulders back as he slid his hands into his pockets. Liam led them deeper into the palace, bypassing the long hallway that would lead to Gianna's quarters, where their queen usually met with her Tría, and heading for the heart of the castle.

Will's jaw clenched as he realized exactly where the Persi was headed.

Gianna's throne room. The place she reserved for only the most serious of business.

Another message.

But Liam veered to the left, bringing them instead to a small antechamber that sat beside the towering double doors that marked the entrance to the throne room.

Seven hells.

Trahir had rendered Will paranoid.

They entered the circular room, its gray cobblestone floor and rough stone walls typical of the castle architecture. But while most of the palace's rooms were filled with flickering torchlight, this one was lit by rays of sun streaming through the arched stained-glass window on the far wall. It depicted a meeting of the Nine Divine on the highest peak of the Mala range—the day they created the Visya.

Beneath the window, her white dress dancing with flickering reflections of reds and yellows and oranges and blues, stood Gianna, a crown of iron adorning her golden-brown hair.

They stopped in the middle of the room, and as smoothly as the day he left, Will dropped to his knee with the rest of the small procession, his thumb skimming his new scar as he brought his fist to his chest, his gaze fixed on the floor.

"Praise the Divine," Gianna breathed as she rushed forward. "I was so worried."

From the corner of his eye, Will saw her grasp Aya's arms, tugging Aya up from her kneeling position. "When we stopped hearing from you, and the rumors started, I feared the worst. Even with Advisor Zuri's letter, I wasn't sure if Trahir was telling the truth about your safety, or if they were spinning lies to cover their king's heresy and keep me from retaliating immediately."

Will cut a glance to Liam. The remaining Dyminara, including Will, were still kneeling, as they had not been given the command to rise. But the Queen only had eyes for Aya, it seemed.

"Are you harmed?" Gianna asked, her soft voice tense.

"No, Majesty."

"You are certain?"

"Yes. We're fortunate to have friends in Trahir. The new king will be instrumental in the war. I'm sure of it. Just as he was in our escape from Rinnia and the defeat of his uncle."

"Rise," Gianna commanded, her attention still fixed on Aya.

Slowly, Liam rose and Will followed suit, the other Dyminara likewise behind him. Finally, Gianna's gaze settled on Will.

"So it's all true, then? King Dominic was partnering with Kakos?" Will dipped his chin, but it seemed his confirmation was not enough. "And what about what Zuri wrote of your power? Is that true as well?" Gianna pressed, turning her focus back to Aya. And while her face was wrought with relief as she stared at her Third, Will had spent years reading his queen. Her slender shoulders were rigid, and there was a tightness in her round face—in her eyes, her lips.

He glanced at Aya. He couldn't see her expression from where he stood, but her movements were smooth and purposeful as she lifted a palm and extended it toward the stained glass.

"Yes," Aya murmured. There was a hiss and pop as the window began to frost, ice crawling up the decorated glass like a spider's web. Liam swore softly behind Will as the ice thickened until the depiction of the gods was a mere blur of color beneath a cloudy ivory surface.

"My gods," Gianna breathed. Aya curled her hand, and the ice melted easily, water dripping down the panes like rain.

A Persi no longer, but the Second Saint—not bound by the Orders of the Visya created by the gods, but with pure, raw power that rivaled that of Saint Evie.

For a moment, Will wondered if Gianna would fall to her knees. She swayed slightly, her hand resting at the base of her throat as she stared at Aya. There was a long silence before Aya dropped her hand and dipped her chin slightly.

"I apologize for our delay," Aya finally said. "In order to confirm that I am indeed the one the prophecy speaks of, I needed to be able to wield the power. That took far longer than either of us expected. But I knew I could not return until I could control it. Until I could be of use to you, Majesty."

Aya's explanation was smooth, her voice ringing with that quiet confidence that Will had often witnessed in Tría meetings.

"But you can, now? Control it?" Gianna pressed breathlessly.

Aya nodded her head once, and Will watched as relief, and perhaps joy, flickered across the queen's face.

"Praise the gods," Gianna exclaimed, her eyes bright as she rushed forward and grasped Aya's hands. But a small frown marred her golden brow as she flipped over Aya's left palm. "A blood oath?" the queen asked as she took in the marked skin.

"I hope you don't mind," Aya replied without missing a beat. "The Dyminara... It's my home. Serving this kingdom, serving *you*..." Her voice trailed off, and Gianna's mouth lifted into a soft, gentle smile.

Aya's lie was so effortless that even Will couldn't detect the falsity in her words. Perhaps it was because she coated them with a layer of truth. The Dyminara *was* her home. Even with all he'd shared about Gianna—all he'd suspected of their queen—it would not change that Aya was driven by a sense of duty, and she felt a strong one to Tala, to its people.

Maybe, deep down, even still to its queen.

Will shoved the thought away as Gianna pressed a kiss to the back of Aya's hands. "As I've told you once before, Aya, I am proud to have you defend my kingdom. I cannot imagine someone more loyal, more *true*, for the gods to have chosen to lead our people through the dark times to come. You are a blessing," she whispered, reverence coating her voice as she dipped her head, her forehead pressing against Aya's knuckles.

Will's jaw shifted, but he kept his face blank as Gianna stepped away from her Third and finally turned to him. "And yet, it sounds as though darkness has found you both already."

The words were pointed, and heavy with meaning he didn't dare try to unpack. Instead, he waited under Gianna's gaze, which stayed inexplicably soft as she said, "Please explain what happened in Trahir."

Will slid his hands into his pockets again as he gave Gianna a small accommodating bow. "Certainly, Majesty."

He kept his explanation focused on their discoveries of the Trahir Court's corruption, explaining how they learned Dominic was loyal to Kakos, and how Aidon not only saved their lives, but saved the realm from a much worse fate.

Because Kakos, with the Trahirian army...

That would surely spell destruction.

As for Aya's power, he let her own explanation suffice.

Gianna nodded once when he had finished, her hands clasped in front of her. "And yet you did not suspect the king?"

"He hid his tracks well," Will reasoned. "Even the crown prince did not suspect the depth of his treason until it was almost too late."

"A crown prince who, any day now, will be king to a people who doubt him, if the talk that has made it to our shores is to be believed."

"Aidon will lead his people well," Aya interjected. "And he *will* help us in this war, Majesty. I am sure Advisor Zuri assured you of it."

But this time, Gianna did not pay her saint any mind. Her attention remained fixed on Will.

"You understand," she finally said softly, "how disappointed I am. I sent you to gain allies and protect the *one* chance we have at winning this war. Not only did you allow yourselves to be captured, but Trahir is now in upheaval over the death of their king."

Quiet, steady disappointment punctuated every syllable.

"Dominic's death was a necessity, Majesty," Will said. "With the king partnering with Kakos—"

"A crime a proper trial would have found him guilty of and would have easily swayed support to our cause in taking a stand against Kakos," Gianna cut him off. "Aidon now must focus on gaining the support of his people. How do you expect him to come to our aid when his own citizens might not follow?"

"There was no chance of a trial. We had been compromised. He would have killed us."

"A fate you both could have avoided if you had done your job," Gianna answered gravely.

"Majesty—" Aya started, but Will held up a hand.

"I do not need your defense," he said sharply. Aya bristled, and he couldn't tell whether her affront was real or forced. He didn't particularly care. He was too focused on Gianna, too confused as to why she was still looking at him not with anger, but a sad sort of disappointment—something nearing regret. What was he missing?

"I gave you specific orders, and you failed me," Gianna continued.

Will frowned. "Forgive me, Majesty," he muttered. "But you have your saint. You have your allies. *Those* were your orders, were they not?"

The words worked exactly as he'd intended. Gianna's eyes flashed with anger, her voice seething as she snapped, "*You forget yourself!*"

As did she.

It was rare that she lost her temper, that every word that came from her mouth wasn't one of careful calculation.

Gianna inhaled, her spine straightening as her features cooled into the steadiness the kingdom equated with their ruler. As if she, too, knew that she'd given something away. When she spoke again, her voice was back to that level calm. "You can also understand why I suspected the worst." She took a single step toward him, the sunlight glinting off her iron crown as she tilted her head. "Imagine my dismay when I suspected my second-in-command guilty of treason."

Will stiffened, and despite his years of training, he wasn't quick enough to hide his surprise. There it was. The missing piece—the heaviness, the sadness beneath her disapproval.

"I understand your disappointment, Majesty," he said slowly. "As the situation in Trahir became more volatile, I stopped receiving your letters. And I thought it safer not to continue to attempt to contact our forces here, lest our missives be intercepted and decoded. The consequences were far too great to take such risks." His eyes flicked to Aya for a breath before meeting the queen's again. "It was a miscalculation, and I accept whatever consequences you must bestow upon me for my actions."

"You left us in the dark," Gianna continued. "I had no idea what had become of you two until the rumors began, until I received a letter from the new king's advisor, and even then, I wondered if it was all a lie to cover their tracks. To cover *your* tracks."

Will couldn't hide the way his brow furrowed. He'd expected her frustration at his lack of response these last several weeks, but *treason*? He'd been so careful when it came to Gianna and ensuring she never questioned his loyalty. The only risk he ever took in that regard was when he showed up in Tova's cell and begged her to help him get Aya away from Tala.

I don't know what, exactly, she wants with her. But I know our queen well enough to know that this is dangerous for Aya...

For Gianna to jump to *treason* over a lack of communication? It didn't make any sense.

Unless...

Unless Tova had told her of how he'd pleaded for help that day in the dungeon.

"I remain ever loyal to you, Majesty," Will said finally, his fist finding his chest. He could feel his heartbeat through his clenched fingers. It raced in time with his thoughts.

Tova had agreed to help him; she knew just how dangerous Gianna could be. She would never betray Aya like that. She couldn't have. She'd agreed.

She'd *agreed*.

"Even so," Gianna said softly. "I cannot afford to let mistakes go unpunished. Not when we are at the precipice of war. You mishandled the situation in Trahir, William. The news that the Second Saint has arisen, that she is my Third, puts both Aya and our people at risk. There are consequences for such failures."

"I understand, Your Majesty," he replied steadily. "As I said, I humbly accept whatever consequences you bestow."

Lena appeared at his side.

A slender black whip hung in the Persi's hand.

There was pain in Gianna's brown eyes as she softly said, "On your knees, Enforcer."

3

THE WORDS FELL LIKE THE FIRST SKIPPED STONE ON A STILL lake, the meaning taking a moment to settle in Aya's raging mind. She took in the whip, cold dread washing down her spine as she realized just what Gianna intended.

"Majesty…" Aya began, but Will's eyes cut to hers, a storm building there.

"If you're asking for a test of loyalty," he interjected, his words directed at Gianna, "surely you know I'll comply."

Aya had seen warriors punished before. She had seen Sensainos use their power to keep the elite guard in check. This was no normal exercise in obedience. To wield a whip over an affinity was an archaic punishment, and a purposeful one.

This was humiliation.

Retribution for the embarrassment they'd brought their queen.

And perhaps Will was right. Perhaps it was more than a punishment. Perhaps it was a way to ensure he remained loyal, even in the face of harshness such as this. After all, Gianna had suspected him of treason while they were away, a suspicion Aya didn't have time to sort through now. Not as Will was shrugging off his jacket, his hands steady as he unbuttoned his white shirt and tossed it on the floor.

No.

Aya made to reach for him, but she'd barely moved before a hand was grasping her bicep tightly. Liam stood at her side, and he was tugging her backward to where the other three Dyminara stood, his face grave as he watched his sister unravel the whip.

Slowly, Will lowered to his knees, and the image was so like the nightmare that had sent Aya screaming from her sleep that her stomach clenched. She tried to swallow, but her throat was utterly dry.

"Surely you know I take no pleasure in this," Gianna said softly.

And gods, the words were so sincere, Aya nearly believed them.

"Understood, Majesty. I took an oath," Will intoned. And though his gaze was fixed on Gianna, Aya knew the words were for her.

No matter how far the fall.

It was a reminder—not to interrupt, not to intervene, not to jeopardize either of their positions. To let him face his punishment and work his way back into Gianna's good graces.

Aya clenched her fists as anger, cold and sharp, pierced through her. It crackled beneath her skin, stirring her power awake so brutally, she had to force a steadying breath through gritted teeth.

He couldn't ask this of her. He couldn't expect her to stand here and watch him be brutalized. But Liam's grip tightened on her arm to the point of pain, and Lena drew her arm back, and suddenly—

The first crack of the whip exploded through the space. It had Will jerking forward, his hands bracing on the cobblestone floor.

Don't react.

The second crack of the whip brought blood to his skin.

Don't react.

The third tore a grunt of pain from his lips.

Don't react.

The brutality echoed throughout the room, the agony of it barely settling before the next chorus began.

Inhale. Crack. Pain.

Inhale. Crack. Pain.

Inhale. Crack. Pain.

Aya's jaw ached, her muscles screaming as she held herself stiff enough to avoid flinching as the whip sounded again. She had seen brutality. Had even taken part in it and had learned how to keep her face expressionless in the midst of such things.

But this...this tested every part of her control. She was going against every instinct screaming inside of her to *move*. To reach him. To stop this.

The whip cracked again.

And again.

Will's arms trembled, his hands flexing on the floor as another strike rocked him forward. Blood ran in rivulets off his back, and it flew from the braided leather as it soared through the air.

The next blow had Will's arms giving out, a strangled sound escaping him as he hit the floor.

An image of Will dead on the floor flashed in Aya's mind, lingering there like the cold that refused to loosen its grip on the mountains.

He's not going to survive this. She'll kill him.

Aya wrenched her arm out of Liam's hold, but Gianna's soft voice cut through the room before she could take a step out of line. "Enough."

Lena let the whip fall immediately.

Will's wet rasps filled the tense silence that rippled

throughout the room, each labored breath sawing into Aya like a blade. Her own chest rose and fell rapidly, her breath shallow as Gianna approached Will. "Let this be a warning, William," the queen said softly. "Fail me in such a way again, and you will lose your position entirely. Understood?"

Will didn't move from where he was sprawled the ground. "Yes, Majesty."

Aya could hardly make out his response. Pain punctuated every syllable.

Gianna looked at the rest of them. "And let this be a reminder to *all* of you of the seriousness of what we face. War is approaching—the fate of our realm relies on us. There is no room for error."

She turned to Lena. "Take him to Suja."

Aya felt Liam push past her, his steps clipped and posture stiff as he helped his sister haul Will up from the floor. Aya couldn't tear her gaze away from his ruined flesh. His back was a gruesome canvas, all blood and flayed skin.

His head hung limply, his black hair slick with sweat as the twins half dragged him toward the door, as if unconsciousness was a breath away.

I'll kill her.

The thought was the only clear thing against the roaring in Aya's ears. Her palms tingled as she watched Will disappear, her hands trembling with fear, with *rage*, with—

"Aya."

Her gaze snapped to the queen, whose hand was outstretched toward her. That graveness still lined Gianna's face, but her eyes had softened, as had her voice as she said, "Come. I'll accompany you to the Quarter. Tova is waiting for you there."

Tova.

Aya couldn't move. She couldn't *breathe*.

Gianna had suspected Will of treason. A suspicion only *one* person could have sown in her mind. But…Tova couldn't

30

have… She *wouldn't* have told Gianna about how Will suspected their queen was not to be trusted. She had agreed to help him; that's what Will had said.

And yet…that had been months ago. Perhaps Tova had changed her mind during her time in prison.

Aya nodded once. The only reset she would allow herself. *Let them see what they want to see.*

It was a tenet of her training, one Aya excelled at.

Deception. Masking. Lies.

Her arms twined behind her back, her hands grasping her forearms to stop their trembling as she walked that distance to Gianna. Her steps were steady, her posture not faltering once.

Not even as she stepped through Will's blood, her steps leaving a rich crimson path toward the door.

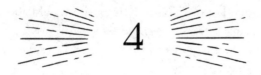

4

W HEN AYA WAS YOUNGER, HER FATHER HAD TAUGHT HER a trick to soothe her anxious mind.

"List what you can see, *mi couera*," he'd say.

It would stop her hands from trembling, her limbs from tingling, her breath from burning in lungs that didn't seem to want to open.

Towering pines.

Part of the Wall.

Stones on the dirt.

"I am sorry your reception had to be tainted by such unpleasantness," Gianna murmured as they made their way toward the Quarter.

A raven.

A broken tree branch.

Moss.

It wasn't working. Because even though Aya appeared at ease, her head dipping in understanding, she felt utterly detached from herself, an intruder in her own body.

Aya glanced behind them, if only to hide any potential flicker of emotion that she might not be able to keep from her face as she forced a slow, silent breath through her nose.

Cleo followed them at a respectful distance, along with six members of the Guard, whose crimson livery was as dark as the blood on Aya's boots. She swallowed the bile that rose in her throat as Gianna followed her gaze and said, "Cleo has been a welcome addition to my personal escort now that a threat is imminent."

A murmured noise of understanding was the best Aya could manage. It made sense that the queen would not be without a member of the Dyminara. Not now that war was breathing down their necks.

A Sensainos was a wise choice.

Would it be Will once he was healed? Would Gianna trust him after suspecting him of treason, even if only for a moment?

And what will you do if it was indeed Tova who raised the queen's suspicions?

"Two guards have been assigned to you," Gianna was saying, distracting Aya from the vicious thought. "They're to meet you in the Quarter this afternoon."

Aya's shoulders stiffened, her fingers twitching at her sides. Her every move would be monitored. She fought to keep her voice even as she said, "That's not necessary, Your Majesty."

One of Gianna's golden brows rose. "You think I would leave the Second Saint unprotected?" Her lips tightened as they passed through the arch that separated the queen's grounds from the Quarter. "I will not make mistakes with your safety again."

"I am alive because of Will," Aya retorted steadily. Her heart clenched as her lips formed his name. Gianna's gaze felt like a brand, but Aya kept her eyes forward.

Wildflowers.

Stones.

The training complex, where Will and I sparred months ago in front of the young Visya students.

33

"You seem to have warmed to him," the queen remarked.

"Grudges feel childish in the face of war."

Gianna made a soft noise of agreement, stopping as they rounded the bend and stepped into the clearing. Aya stilled beside her, something in her chest aching as she took in the stained-glass windows of the small stone palace that glinted in the sunlight.

The Quarter. Her home.

She tried to picture the room she'd left four months ago, tried to remember what it felt like to sit with Tova on her bed, a fire crackling happily in the grate as her best friend teased her for choosing to stay in another night rather than join her in town.

It felt like peering into a different lifetime.

"When was she released?" Aya asked, her brow furrowing as she took in the lush gardens. The Terras used their earth affinity to coax beauty from the grounds in all seasons, but especially the spring. Splashes of pink and red and purple and yellow filled the space, the flowers swaying in the ever-present wind. Aya resisted the desire to burrow further into Will's sweater at the bite of cold the wind brought with it.

"As soon as I received Advisor Zuri's letter. The whispers of what had transpired in Trahir had already begun in town. When the news of the Second Saint broke, we issued a formal proclamation that Tova had been framed by Kakos and was cleared of all charges—and that in taking responsibility for what transpired in the market, she protected your identity. She was never truly a prisoner, Aya. She knew that, and so did you."

And yet, Tova should never have been imprisoned in the first place.

Aya's jaw locked, and she took a steadying breath as she met Gianna's gaze. "And the weapons supplier? Were they found?"

The queen's lips tightened, her golden brow furrowing as displeasure rippled across her features. "There has been no sign of them. But we can discuss this more tomorrow when we review your new duties."

"New duties?"

Tendrils of Gianna's golden hair swirled in the breeze, but her skin was warm as she took Aya's hands and squeezed. "Our people will need hope, Aya. *You* will be the beacon of light in the dark times ahead." Aya opened her mouth to retort, but Gianna continued with a sigh before she could speak. "We have not known war in centuries. I know the gods have prepared us...but I do wonder if we've taken our peace for granted."

The words were soft, thoughtful. There was a weariness in her queen's face that felt like staring into a mirror of the past. Aya's own reflection had looked like that for months in Trahir, when the weight of what was ahead of her was almost too much to bear.

Months ago, Aya would have seen this softness, this vulnerability from her queen, as a sign of trust. But now, she could only see that whip and drops of blood like rain as Lena struck Will again and again on Gianna's orders.

Gods, how had Aya been so deceived? Everyone had thought Will was nothing more than Gianna's chess piece. But they were wrong. Aya had been the worst of them. Because she hadn't questioned her devotion, her loyalty, until it was too late. She manipulated, and threatened, and killed whenever her queen commanded it, because Aya had trusted Gianna. She had *believed* in her.

"Go," Gianna urged, nodding toward the Quarter. "Tova is waiting in her room."

The queen was several paces back down the path before Aya spoke. "Dominic told me you offered to marry me off to Aidon for an alliance. Would you truly have done so?"

It wasn't wise to be so transparent, to show the wound that had continued to fester with bitterness ever since she'd discovered the truth in Gianna's letter to Dominic.

35

And yet…

She needed to hear Gianna say it. And perhaps she needed Gianna to know that she was no longer naive to her doings. That she was someone to be reckoned with now.

Gianna frowned. "It was merely an attempt to see how hard we'd need to push Dominic."

It wasn't an answer. Or perhaps it was. Because Aya knew her queen. Gianna would have done whatever it took to get Trahir's support in the war. If it meant selling Aya only to snatch her back, or perhaps leave her there to do whatever it was the Second Saint needed to do, Gianna would do it.

And back then, Aya would have let her.

5

AYA HAD IMAGINED THIS MOMENT FOR MONTHS. AND YET for every scenario that had played through her mind, every conversation she'd run through again and again, unable to find the words to adequately fix what she assumed was broken between them, she'd never imagined *this*.

Doubting her best friend. Anger toward her, and confusion, because she wasn't even sure Tova was to blame, and guilt, because if anyone deserved someone's fury, it was Aya who deserved it from Tova.

If Tova had truly betrayed Will, could Aya blame her? Hadn't she given her friend every reason to think they'd abandoned her here?

Tova had been in prison for months because of Aya. She had taken responsibility for a crime she did not commit. For *deaths* she did not commit. And even now the truth was out that the orders for the weapons and the Decachiré book were planted on Tova—hells, even the truth that she had been protecting Aya—it did not immediately erase the months her troops had spent doubting their general, the months her friends and her own *family* had spent doubting her.

Aya glanced down, her teeth grinding as she tried to

steady herself, but the sight of blood on her boots had her sucking in another ragged breath.

Enough.

She set her shoulders before rapping swiftly on the worn wood, and then she was pushing her way inside before she could convince herself otherwise. Aya paused just inside the threshold as the door clicked shut behind her.

It was as though she hadn't been gone a single day.

There was Tova's mirrored vanity, its surface littered with blushes and brushes and coals. Garments were scattered across the floor, lining an imperfect path to the floor-length iron-rimmed mirror that sat next to the stone hearth. And across from it, on a silk comforter of the richest purple, sat Tova, a book hanging forgotten in her hand as she gazed at Aya. Her pillows were skewed, as if she had been lying among them just moments before, her silvery-blond hair messy in its ponytail.

The silence between them seemed to stretch for an eternity.

And then they were both moving, a broken sound wrenching itself from somewhere deep in Aya's chest as she lunged for her friend. Tova launched herself off the bed, the book hitting the gray rug beneath it with a soft thud.

They collided in the middle of the room in a tangle of limbs, and Aya swore her legs almost gave out, or maybe they had, and it was Tova's vise grip holding her up, always holding her up, even when the world around her was fracturing.

"You're home." Tova said it again and again, the words whispered against Aya's hair, and it took a moment for Aya to realize her friend perhaps meant it as a reassurance, because Aya's body was shaking, her breath coming in sharp inhales through clenched teeth as she clung to Tova.

She could feel tears wetting her cheeks, but it didn't matter, because Tova was *here* and she was safe, and she was hugging Aya as if she loved her despite all that had transpired.

"I'm home," Aya finally managed to say.

Because this—this warm embrace and cinnamon scent that soothed her better than any tonic from a healer ever could—this had long been the only place Aya had ever felt still.

Felt peace.

"Gods, I missed you," Tova huffed into Aya's hair, her hold tightening around her. Aya's fingers dug into the soft fabric of Tova's gray shirt.

"I missed you too." She stepped out of Tova's hold to see the tears coursing down her friend's cheeks, that ever-present flush of pink turning a deep red as she sniffled. Aya scanned her friend, taking in the healthy glow of her round face. Her loose shirt showed off the toned muscles of her arms, her maroon pants hugging her lean legs.

She looked fine. Perfectly fine. As if Gianna had kept her word in keeping her not only safe, but comfortable.

"You're safe? You're okay?"

"Me? Hepha's flame, Aya, what about *you*? When Lena said Will had stopped responding to the missives, I thought…I thought something horrible had happened."

Aya stilled as reality came rushing back to her.

I suspected my Second-in-Command guilty of treason.

Tova frowned. "What is it?" Her gaze roved over Aya as if checking for wounds. "Is that blood?" Tova's eyes had gone wide as she stared at Aya's boots.

"Not mine," Aya muttered, her hands curling into fists at her sides.

Tova didn't seem any less concerned. "Whose the hells is it?"

Aya's nails bit into the palms of her hands as she tried to force away the echo of Will's grunts of pain.

"Will's." She rubbed a fist across her chest, as if it would somehow ease the ache there. "Gianna had him whipped. She said it was for his failings in Trahir, but…"

I suspected my Second-in-Command guilty of treason.

"She said she'd suspected him of treason before he

returned. I expect the punishment had more to do with that," Aya finished, her own suspicions heavy on her tongue.

Tova stilled, her face going slack. Slowly, she lowered herself on to the edge of the bed. "She… Gods, I knew she was upset, but a whipping?" She let out a breath before giving her head a vicious shake. "Pathos help him."

Aya raked her eyes over her friend, as if she could uncover the truth without asking. But Tova was lost in her own thoughts, her bottom lip pulled between her teeth as she stared at the floor.

"Tova," Aya began, a slight tremble in her voice. "Did you…did you say something to Gianna?" Tova's hazel eyes were sharp as her gaze snapped to Aya. "I understand if you did," Aya continued, holding out a cautious hand. "But I need to know what—"

"You think I'm at fault?" Tova interjected, and there was enough bitterness in the question that Aya faltered. "You blame *me* for the fact that she took a whip to him?"

"No, I—"

But Tova was standing, her face flushing as her eyes narrowed. "Will has spent *years* making his bed with his impertinence and arrogance," she hissed. "I can't believe you'd accuse *me* of being the one to rouse suspicions of him. Especially when I was *tortured* because he couldn't deign to respond to a fucking missive!"

Aya's lips parted, her eyes wide as her hands went slack at her side. "What?" Her question was a mere exhale, hardly a whisper as a distant roaring began in her ears.

Tova's jaw shifted as she ran a frustrated hand across her face. And though her voice was softer, it was still lined with bitterness as she said, "This wasn't how I wanted to tell you."

Aya could feel her anger stirring, that same rage that she'd buried in the palace chamber starting to burn in her veins again.

"Gianna thought Will was up to something," Tova continued. "As the only remaining member of the Tría, she suspected I might have a hand in it. Or at the very least, know something I hadn't shared. So she had me questioned."

Bile burned the back of Aya's throat.

Twice.

Tova had been tortured because of her twice.

Tova huffed a short, dark laugh. "Seriously, Aya, what did either of you expect? What would *you* have thought if your Second-in-Command disappeared with the presumed Second Saint? You're lucky *you* weren't whipped right along with him."

And the words were so bitter, so full of betrayal that Aya jerked back as if Tova had slapped her.

Tova paled, her face falling as she reached for Aya. "I didn't mean that."

But she had. Aya could see the resentment in her friend's gaze, and it had her stepping out of her grasp, her arms folding across her chest as she dipped her chin once. "It's fine," she assured Tova quietly. "It's true. I am equally responsible."

"No, you're not," Tova gritted out, her eyes bright. "You were dealing with something unimaginable. *He* was responsible for keeping our queen apprised of updates. He was responsible for keeping you *safe*." She shook her head. "I all but agreed with Gianna's doubt of him until seeing you walk through that door. But even so, I never said a word against him. What would I even have had to share?"

Aya shifted her weight between her feet. "That he asked you to fake your questioning, because he…"

Aya's voice trailed off, her brow furrowing as she took in the confusion and then disgust that twisted Tova's features. Her friend laughed again, the sound cold and harsh and so unlike the vibrancy she typically felt in Tova's presence.

"Is that what he told you? That he came to me and tried to find a way to spare me pain? Is that how he's trying to assuage his guilt for torturing one of his own, even though he knew I was innocent?"

Aya could feel the growing silence pressing against her skin, clinging to her in the same way that the heavy humidity had in Rinnia.

Tova shook her head. "You should've known he was lying to you as soon as he made it sound like he gives a shit about anyone but himself."

Aya's lungs tightened, and this time, even her tightly clenched fists were not enough to stave off the tingling in her hands.

No.

Will couldn't have lied to her.

He *wouldn't* have lied to her.

Aya had felt his pain, his guilt, when she'd accidentally broken through his shield in Trahir. And afterward, he had told her the truth: that he had told Tova he was worried about what Gianna wanted with Aya's power, and wanted to help Aya escape Tala.

That he had asked Tova to fake her questioning, but had to torture her anyway when Gianna arrived with Cleo, who would be able to sense Tova's sensations.

Will wouldn't have lied to Aya. Not about this.

And yet Tova was still staring at her, something like pity in her gaze as her voice softened. "I know that you hate that I was questioned that day. I know you heard…everything. And I get that you had to work with him in Trahir, and pretending he's not a monster made that easier. But Will is…" Tova shook her head, as if she couldn't think of a bad enough word to describe him. "Let's talk about something else," she urged softly. She stepped back toward her bed, the firm mattress bouncing as she plopped down on it. "You haven't told me about Trahir."

And though Tova's voice had lightened, her closed-lip smile didn't meet her eyes.

He wouldn't have lied.

Aya cleared her throat, her hands twisting in the sleeves of Will's sweater.

He wouldn't have lied.

She silently repeated it again and again, as fervently as any prayer.

"Right," Aya said. "It's a thrilling tale."

And though the tension between them was still notice-able, Tova's shoulders dropped slightly, her plastered-on smile becoming something more genuine as she shrugged. "You know what I always say," she said lightly. "The more dramatic the better." She patted the spot next to her on the bed. "Come. Tell me everything."

6

WILL HAD ALWAYS IMAGINED THE SEVEN HELLS WOULD be cold. He had been wrong. The heat set his skin on fire, the burning so intense he couldn't bear to move. Somewhere, someone was hollering. Another tortured soul, most likely.

Hold him still.

I'm trying. *He's thrashing around like a fucking fish.*

Something tight wrapped around his arms, pinning him to wherever he lay. He didn't—couldn't—open his eyes.

Not that it would matter anyway.

Fire was fire, and Will didn't need to see it. He could feel it on every inch of his sweat-soaked skin. And just when he thought the pain couldn't get any worse, a searing sensation ripped across his back, the feeling so intense, he thought he might die all over again.

His throat ached as he registered that the hollering was his own.

Will's eyes wrenched open, but everything was a blur. Dark shapes surrounded him, two of which pinned him to a table, while a third barked instructions, each order bringing another wave of pain.

You're going to be alright, the third shape said, their voice softening as it muttered to him beneath his screams. *You're going to be alright.*

Will's vocal cords strained to the point of snapping before darkness swooped in again.

The next time consciousness found Will, the dark was cool and soothing. And yet he yearned to leave it, the urgency of his desire so intense, he couldn't make sense of it.

No, it would be far better to stay in this comfort, asleep in his and Aya's shared cabin at sea, would it not? Perhaps he could convince Aya to skip training today. They only had so many peaceful moments left before they returned home.

He made to reach for her, his left arm shifting to pull her body closer to his, but a burning pain radiated across his back at the slightest of movements.

"Fuck." The word croaked out of him, his throat as dry as the sands in the Preuve desert. His eyes blinked open to take in a room he didn't recognize. The flickering light of torches set in sconces bathed the rough stone walls in a soft shade of gray. Dim light entered the room through a window behind him, casting long shadows on the small table beside the narrow bed where he lay. A basin of water and bloodied washcloth sat on top of it. And at the foot of the bed was an old wooden chair that seemed far too small for the lean warrior who sat on its weathered surface.

Liam blinked at Will, but he didn't move from his lounging position: arms folded, legs stretched out before him, feet crossed at the ankles.

Will's jaw locked as the memories came rushing back to him. Gianna and her anger, Lena and a whip and a pain so intense, Will was surprised he hadn't blacked out sooner. The look of horror that passed over Suja's face as Lena and

Liam dragged him inside the healing quarters, before blessed darkness gave him brief relief.

"Fucking finally," Liam murmured, his baritone voice weary as he looked Will over. "I thought you were dead." He didn't sound particularly bothered by the possibility, but at least he wasn't gloating.

"How long have I been out?" Will rasped.

Liam stood and stalked toward the table, where a small cup of water sat. He crouched down next to the bed as he handed it to Will. "Four hours. You passed out just as Lena and I got you here."

Will didn't bother to sit up as he took a sip of the water, letting it soothe his raw throat. Simply moving his arm was agonizing.

"You were in and out during the healing until Suja finally forced another dose of pain tonic down your throat," Liam continued. "You were kind of a dick about it but"—he shrugged—"I suppose you're consistent, even on the brink of death."

It was coming back to Will. He'd tried to refuse the tonic, unwilling to be pulled into its dreamless depths. He'd wanted to stay awake—stay alert—so he could get back to Aya.

Aya.

Where was she? What had happened after Lena and Liam dragged him out of that room?

Liam's eyes narrowed as he settled back into his chair, his arms crossing once more as he scanned Will. "How are you feeling?"

Will grunted. "Wonderful." He shifted his arms to push himself up. Sweat coated his bare skin, his back burning worse than any fire. The new flesh was taut like a bowstring. "You didn't have to stay," he said, sucking in a breath through his teeth as he prepared himself to move. Liam simply shrugged.

Perhaps he felt some modicum of guilt for what his sister had done to Will.

Been ordered to do, Will grudgingly corrected himself.

Not that Lena had seemed to wrestle much with the task.

His vision blurred, pain ripping down his back as he pushed onto his forearms. An agonized groan escaped him before he could stop it.

"*Fucking hells.*"

"And that's why I told you not to move," a warm voice chided from the doorway. Suja bustled into the room, her arms filled with various bottles and tins, which she deposited on the bedside table. Her long silken hair was tied into a braid that ran down her back, and her white healer's tunic was smeared with blood—his, if Will had to guess. A frown marred her face, pinching wrinkles in her otherwise smooth brown skin.

Will had wondered in his agony-induced haze if Suja had known he'd be under her care today, if Gianna had ensured the best healer of the Dyminara was nearby. Clearly, Suja hadn't expected *this*, but it was telling that she'd been here at the ready.

"Was I conscious when you gave those instructions?" he gritted out as he sat all the way up. His head swam with the movement, the pain intensifying before it slowly ebbed back to a steady burn. The healer didn't bother to answer as she laid a hand on his bare shoulder and gently forced him forward so she could inspect his back.

"You'll need to be careful with your movements for the day. The new skin is tender."

"I'd noticed." Will hissed in pain as Suja prodded one of the particularly tight areas. She straightened and reached for a tin of salve. It was cold as ice, with a sick, sweet smell, and Will fought to hold still while she smoothed it over the wounds. "You'll need to apply this twice a day for the next week. It will accelerate the healing and help with the scarring." Suja's large brown eyes were solemn as she met his gaze. "I tried to limit it as much as I could, but some wounds…"

"I am grateful to you, as always, Suja." He knew healers had their limits. Their works could be just short of miraculous, but Mora, the goddess of fate, would never have given them the depth of her true power. To even have been able to encourage his skin to regrow like this...

Well, it spoke of Suja's extraordinary prowess with her Anima affinity.

One of Suja's dark brows rose. "Flattery won't get you out of taking another dose of tonic for the pain."

"No." His response was curt, but he didn't care. There was no way in hells he was losing himself to the lull of the tonic again. He'd already wasted hours. He had no idea where Aya was, or what she had faced while he'd been unconscious.

And then there was the matter of Gianna. Will had known he'd face consequences for his failings in Trahir, but he suspected this punishment was more about her momentary suspicions of treason, and he didn't buy her reasoning for said suspicions for a second. Delayed correspondence, while not ideal, wasn't enough to cause such doubts. Not when he'd spent years building trust with Gianna.

"You need rest, Enforcer," Suja pressed.

"I can rest when I'm dead."

"Which you will be if you don't *listen* to me," the healer snapped. "You will spend the night here. Rest will accelerate your healing. On Mora's favor, you'll be able to leave tomorrow and return to your duties, *if* you rest."

Will swallowed his retort. He doubted the patron goddess of the healers and death bringers was paying him much mind.

If she were, I wouldn't be in so much fucking agony.

Suja thrust the tonic toward him, and Will bit back a curse as he relented, downing the bitter liquid in two gulps. She leveled him with a fierce look. "*Stay in bed.* I mean it. If you tear the new skin in your impatience, don't call on me to heal you again."

Will couldn't help the small smirk that tugged at his

mouth. Though she may spew fire, Suja was born with the temperament of the truest Anima. She was kind, and warm, and would never turn away an injured warrior. She knew it as well as he did.

Her lips tightened, some emotion flashing in her gaze. It was almost as if she were fighting against saying more. But she looked between Will and Liam, and whatever she saw there must have had her deciding against it, because she turned on her heel and left without another word.

"Such a lovely woman," Will murmured, aware of Liam watching him carefully. The Persi pushed himself out of the chair with a sigh.

"Careful," Liam warned. "That impertinence is what landed you here in the first place." He made his way to the door, his hands bracing on the frame as Will called after him.

"Where's Aya?"

"With Tova, I assume. Why?"

Will fought against the instant drowsiness that settled over him. If Tova had indeed turned him in to Gianna, what awaited Aya, then?

She won't harm Aya. She loves Aya.

Liam was still watching him, his gaze calculating. "I can think of at least five people in my drug-induced haze that would want her dead, Liam. She needs protection, lest she be killed before the war truly starts."

Annoyance flashed across Liam's face. "Gianna's assigned her guards to her."

Aya would hate that. As did he. They'd need to be even more careful than he'd thought in their interactions with each other. "Besides," Liam added darkly, drawing Will's attention back to the door. "The war has already begun."

7

I T WAS GROWING DARK BY THE TIME AYA LEFT TOVA'S ROOM. Sitting there, talking until her voice was hoarse, all while Tova's words were swirling in the back of her mind, joining the echoes of the whip and the grunts of pain she hadn't been able to shake…

It had been another type of torture.

Aya had felt only half in the room with her friend, even as she told her of all that had unfolded in Trahir. About her power, and how it fed on her. About Natali, and the darkness they sensed in her. About Aidon, and how she'd stolen his tonic and used his information about the Vaguer.

She even told Tova about the desert, and seeing her mother in the Soul Trial and facing the belief that she'd killed her all those years ago.

"Why did you never tell me you thought you were responsible for your mother's death?" Tova had asked, her eyes glassy with unshed tears.

"It was hard enough to admit it to myself," Aya had replied.

And when Tova had asked her if Aya could use her power now, Aya had held out her fist, her palm facing toward the arched ceiling, and slowly uncurled her fingers, revealing small flickering flames.

Tova's lips had twitched, her hazel eyes glassy as she met Aya's gaze. "Mine are prettier."

Aya had managed to laugh then. But as she closed the door to her bedroom—the two guards Gianna had promised, Lamihr and Kahn, on the other side—an overwhelming heaviness swept over her. It sent her slumping against her door, her eyes falling shut as her head hit the wood.

She had told Tova everything, save for Aidon's Visya power, of course, and Will's involvement in, well, everything. She couldn't stand to see that disgust twist Tova's features again at the mere mention of Will, couldn't stand for a seed of doubt to be planted in her own mind.

But it was there regardless, along with guilt, because gods, he had withstood his own torture, torture he had willingly walked into for her.

Aya let out a breath as she opened her eyes and stepped further into her bedroom, her gaze sweeping across the large space. Like Tova's room, it looked exactly as it had the day she left it. Except Aya's had an abandoned feel, as if she'd meant to return, but simply forgotten.

Her bed, with its white comforter and assortment of pillows, faced the iron-grated fireplace, where an Incend attendant must have already set the fire going. The old wooden chair that Tova had dragged to Aya's bedside while she recovered from the Athatis attack was still sitting there, as if her friend had only just left it.

Aya swallowed hard as she turned in a steady circle, her eyes landing on the door she'd just walked through.

Paranoia bit at every thought.

Treason.

Guards.

Torture.

Lies.

"No." The word slipped between her clenched teeth before she could stop it. Because the doubt wasn't just prodding at her now, it was twisting her insides, even though she couldn't let herself fully believe, *wouldn't* let herself fully believe, that Will had lied to her.

He had been trying to let Aya go, trying to convince her that Aidon was the better choice for her, when he'd confessed the full truth about what had happened with Tova. There was no reason for deceiving her, not then.

And yet...

I have made horrible choices to get what I want. I always will, when it comes to you.

Will had confessed that too—had used it as a reason Aya should be with Aidon instead of him. Because Will was dark, and selfish, and would willingly let the world burn if it meant she survived. The look of self-disgust on his face as he told her as much was a blurred memory that got clearer and clearer the more she turned their conversation over.

Aya took a shuddering breath.

The stone walls seemed to be closing in on her, crushing like the weight of the thoughts that spun in her mind. She ran a trembling hand through her hair.

Could *Tova* be lying? Had Gianna somehow gotten to her?

Treason.

Guards.

Torture.

Lies.

Aya could feel her chest tightening, her breath aching in spasming lungs. She pressed a hand against her heart, feeling its racing rhythm as she bowed over. Her room became nothing but blurred colors and hazy edges.

She tried to breathe, tried to push away the panic clawing its way up her throat. She was all too aware of the guards on the other side of the door, a mere extension of the queen who had always had Aya firmly pressed under her thumb.

Even now.

Aya knew what her queen was capable of, and yet here Gianna was, still able to sow doubt in Aya. To manipulate her into feeling alone, and betrayed, and questioning of the ones she thought she trusted most.

Aya hated her for it. Her fury pounded through her blood, making her skin tingle and her ears ring and something roil beneath her skin, begging for release. Her anger, her power— she wasn't sure which. She wasn't sure if it mattered.

Her arms flung outward, a shield of hard air encasing her room, blocking the sound from prying ears as she tilted her head back and screamed.

Aya wasn't sure how long she stayed on the floor, her knees aching as she stared unseeingly ahead of her, her thoughts swirling. But when she finally stood, her stomach growling with hunger, the sky outside of her window was fully black.

Tova had offered to sneak a plate to Aya when she'd gone to dinner, as if she knew Aya wouldn't want the attention of the dining hall. But Aya had waved her off. Even now, she doubted she'd be able to keep a single morsel down.

Her anger was far from gone. But it had a muted feel to it now, allowing her focus to sharpen.

Aya rolled her shoulders as she weaved through the trunks of luggage an attendant had dropped off. She stopped at her oak dresser and tugged at the top drawer, her heart clenching as she found what she was looking for.

Her black fighting leathers were folded in a tidy square, exactly how she'd left them.

She ran a finger over the smooth material, letting that bitter ache that had descended on her as soon as she saw the Mala mountains radiate through her, before she pulled them out and changed.

She quickly plaited her hair before wrapping a scarf

around her neck. It would come in handy should she need to mask herself entirely. She sheathed a small knife at her thigh and made her way to the two arched windows on the far side of the room.

She glanced back at the door, her shield of air long forgotten, before she slowly, silently pushed one window open.

The torchlit path beneath her was empty, and she was high enough above the Incend flames that anyone at a distance wouldn't be able to see her in her black ensemble.

Her room faced the thick of the forest. She doubted anyone would be coming to the remote side of the Quarter, anyway.

Aya pushed herself onto the ledge, the cold night air biting her face as she scanned her route: through the trees to the servants' entrance of the palace.

She took a steadying breath, the rough stone of the sill digging into her palms as she swung herself off the ledge, letting her body hang into the night. Slowly, she let go of the ledge with one hand, reaching for the pole of the sconce next to her. Despite the flames, the iron was cold in the night air. It bit against Aya's palm as she gripped it tight and brought her other hand to meet it before shimmying her way further out toward the torch—just far enough so that the fall wouldn't send her careening against the stone of the castle.

She and Tova had learned that the hard way. They'd snuck into the Quarter once, before they were Dyminara, and they'd had to sneak out of one of the second-floor rooms to avoid being caught. The scrapes on Aya's arms from slamming into the rough stone wall burned for days.

Aya nearly grinned at the memory as she let herself drop.

She landed with a soft thud on the path, the vision of Pa's bemused expression when she and Tova had shown up scratched and covered in dirt lingering in her memory before another stab of guilt washed it away.

Tova had asked Aya if she was off to see Pa this evening.

She'd dismissed her friend's innocent question with a simple, "Not tonight."

Pa was used to Aya disappearing. She hadn't been as far as Trahir before, but she'd vanished on enough missions for him to at least know to expect it. It was the part of her role with the Dyminara he hated most.

But now...now Pa would have heard the rumors. Not only that she was home, but that she, his only daughter, was said to be a saint.

She wasn't ready to explain what had happened in Rinnia. To share what the visions of the Soul Trial had shown her. To confess that she still wasn't sure if her persuasion had made a difference in her mother getting on that godsforsaken ship.

In her death.

To look at Pa, to watch the warmth in his brown eyes fade as he realized what his daughter could be capable of...

No. She wasn't ready to see him yet.

Aya took a deep breath before she scanned the stretch of field that led toward the forest.

Besides, she had more pressing tasks tonight.

8

THE PALACE WAS QUIET ENOUGH THAT AYA COULD HEAR HER pulse in her ears. It pounded in time to the guards' footsteps as they surveilled the long hall she peered into. She kept her back pressed against the wall of the cross hall as she monitored them, their hulking forms mere shadows except for when they passed through the splashes of moonlight let in by the arched windows.

The Royal Guard changed their routes every so often, as well as the timing of their rotations, but Aya knew this palace like her own breath. She had memorized its long halls and winding staircases long before her job required it of her, when Tova pestered her into sneaking in on more than one occasion, mostly to steal dessert from the kitchens.

Aya watched them approach the far end of the hall, her body hugging the wall as she crept around the corner. She had known it was foolish to hope the rotations were the same as when she'd left months ago.

At least she could follow behind them. Any route would take them in a loop, and—

The sound of boots on the cobblestone cut off the thought. Aya ducked her head back around the corner to see two more guards approaching down the hallway she'd just come from.

Godsdammit.

Gianna had increased the presence of the Royal Guard.

The queen had grown paranoid, then, since the news of the Second Saint broke from Trahir. Aya nearly scoffed. As if Kakos would be able to reach Gianna with the Dyminara present.

Aya quickly tugged her black scarf over her head. The fabric masked her neck, her mouth, her nose, leaving the smallest slit for her eyes. She dashed toward the first window and somersaulted across the cobblestones, counting on the echoing of the guards' footsteps to mask the ruffle of her leathers against the floor. She moved through the sliver of shadow that sat below the windowsill before righting herself in the next long swatch of shadow. She made it to the next window just as the first set of guards turned the corner and the second set stepped into her hallway.

Aya fused herself to the stone wall and flipped her palms as she called her power forward, endlessly grateful for the affinity training she'd done with Will in Trahir. Creating a shield of air that sealed her against the wall, she held her breath and stood utterly still.

Ten paces.

Six.

Three.

The guards passed by her without a second glance.

Aya waited until they were on the far side of the hall to release the sound barrier, her breath leaving her lungs slowly, silently, as she watched them turn in the opposite direction from the first guards.

She'd be following them, then. Excellent.

Aya crept after them, her footsteps silent as she moved slowly. She sent up a silent prayer of thanks to Mora as the guards turned a sharp corner that took them out of eyesight of the door she needed.

She held her breath as she pushed it open slowly and stepped into the wide empty hall.

The south wing. One of the most remote parts of the palace.

She wove through the long wooden worktables that marked the space, hooking a left into a long hall lined with doors. Aya peered through the small windows of those that were closed until she found the one she was looking for.

Her knife was in her hand in an instant, the small blade slipping into the lock as she held her breath and waited for that near-silent *click*. The lock gave, and Aya slipped into the room, careful to close the door softly behind her.

She blinked once, her eyes taking a moment to adjust to the low Incend flames that burned in the sconces on the wall as she scanned the room.

"I should have known you'd sneak in here."

Aya turned, her heart twisting at the rough rasp.

On the far-right wall, on a narrow bed under a small square window, was Will.

His black hair was disheveled, his smirk missing its usual sharp edge.

And despite the doubt and guilt swirling in her mind, dizzying relief rushed through Aya at the sight of him, the feeling so overwhelming that her knife clattered to the floor as she moved toward him as though on instinct.

"No trouble with the guards, I assume?" Will grimaced as he pushed himself into sitting position, the fire casting flickering light across his sun-kissed skin. Aya reached the side of his bed and froze.

She thought she had been prepared for it—the proof of what Gianna had done to him. But now that she was beside him, the low light of the flames illuminating it...

She laid a hand on his shoulder and gently pushed him forward, the world growing quiet as her eyes took in the rich canvas of reds and purples and blacks where the wounds were the deepest. It was as if even the gods were focused on the brutality, that reminder from Gianna of the power she held and was not afraid to wield.

Aya willed herself to breathe, to keep control of the rage that was starting to climb through her veins like wildfire, once again threatening to devour every single thing in its path.

Your fault.

This is your fault.

She could have shielded him, or taken away his pain, or demanded that Gianna grant him leniency. She should have done something other than *stand* there and watch as he was hurt like this.

Distantly she was aware of Will saying her name, but it was a dull hum against her fury.

And then he was in front of her, his shoulder level with her eyes, but Aya kept staring, and staring, and staring, lost in the storm inside of her. Something brushed her chin—his hand—and it tilted her face up, forcing her to meet his gaze.

"They're just scars, *mi couera*," he murmured, his thumb stroking her cheek once. *My heart.* A term of endearment he saved only for the worst of situations. He pressed his lips against hers, soft and warm and coaxing her out of her head and into the room with him.

He's alive.

He's alive.

He's alive.

She repeated it silently with every move of his lips.

Will pulled back, his forehead resting against hers. "Just scars," he repeated. "More to add to the collection."

Aya's jaw ached as she ground her teeth together.

It was too much. He was asking too much of her.

She jerked her chin out of his hold as she took a step back. "*Don't.*"

"Aya—"

"Do not make light of this." She was trembling, her voice

quiet to avoid detection, wavering with the force of it, and she wasn't sure if it was anger or agony that was welling up inside of her as she stared at him. She wanted to scream, or hit something, or cry, or burn the entire palace to the ground.

"We knew we weren't walking into a warm welcome," Will said warily, his brow furrowed as he stared at her.

Aya was well acquainted with bitterness and anger and guilt. They had lived inside her, cold and steady, for nearly her entire life. But this…this wasn't the chill she was accustomed to. This was hot and vicious, and it painted the room red as she shook her head.

"You think that was merely a cold welcome?" Aya scoffed in disbelief. "Gods above, Will, she suspected you of treason. She *tortured* Tova because of it!"

The words flew from her lips before she could stop them, before she could think if this was truly the way to start this conversation, to try to get the confirmation she hated that she needed because *he couldn't have lied to her*, not after everything they'd been through, not after what he had endured from Gianna because of it.

Will went utterly still. She could see the way his muscles tensed as if bracing for impact, as his hands fisted at his sides. For a moment, the only sound in the room was the crackling firewood in the grate. There was a look in his eyes that Aya couldn't name; it was reflected in the rough rasp of his voice as he finally asked, "What did Tova tell her?"

"Tova didn't seem to think there was anything to tell."

Will frowned as he scanned her face, as if he were searching for his own answers there, confusion darkening his features. Aya inhaled slowly.

"'I have made horrible choices to get what I want. I always will, when it comes to you.'" Recognition flared in Will's eyes as she repeated his words back to him. "You told me that."

He took a step toward her, his hand twitching, as if he

wanted to reach for her but thought better of it. "Aya." Her name was released on an exhale as he shook his head.

Will was an expert at wearing masks. Cold, disinterested, pompous, calculating—Aya had seen them all, had cataloged them for far longer than she'd once cared to admit. But his face was completely open now, dread then desperation flickering across his features in such rapid succession that she wondered if he even knew how open he had made himself to her, how clearly she could read him.

Perhaps he simply didn't care.

"You tortured her to save me," Aya continued, fighting to keep the tremor from her voice. "You were willing to lose me to Aidon to save me. And now...now Tova is saying you didn't come to her and tell her to fake her questioning—"

"Aya—"

"Tell me you didn't do this. Tell me you didn't lie to me about what happened in the dungeons that day so that I would trust you. So that I would let you help me." She could feel something aching in her chest, some piece of her that wanted desperately to believe that she hadn't been deceived, not again, not by him. Her voice wavered, then broke, as she rasped, "Tell me you didn't do this to save me."

He did reach for her now, his hands grasping her shoulders and pulling her to him. "I did not lie to you," he swore, his eyes wide and earnest in the low light. "On my oath, I did not lie to you."

An oath not to a queen, or a kingdom, or its citizens, but to her.

To each other.

No matter how far the fall.

"Everything I told you about our encounter was the truth," Will ground out, his hands sliding from her shoulders to her cheeks. "I went to Tova and begged her to help me. I told her I thought Gianna was after you. I told her to fake her questioning, and—"

"Why would she lie?" Aya hated the way her voice cracked.

"Why would *I*?"

Will's grip tightened on her face as if he could will the truth into her skin and make it settle in her bones. "After everything, why would I...?" His throat bobbed as he swallowed his words.

His eyes darted between hers, desperation settling in the gray of his irises. Those flecks of green she'd grown used to seeing, present when Will was at his lightest, were nowhere to be found.

"Read me."

Aya blinked, his command taking a moment to register. But when it did, something cracked in Aya's chest.

She had made the same request of him just weeks ago, in another dark and desperate room. Had uttered that exact command when she realized there weren't any words in any language that would be enough to convince him of what she felt.

The memory ached now, guilt and shame painting it a different color in her mind. She'd known then their history was too much for him to believe she could have felt differently. And here they were again: doubt tugging at the fragile threads of what they'd built.

But their love was one made in terror and desperation, in battling enemies and courting death. It was fast, and desperate, and a part of her wondered, or maybe feared, that it was not enough to stand on.

"Use your Sensainos affinity and read me," he repeated roughly. "You'll feel the truth. I have nothing to hide from you."

She wanted to say she didn't need to. She *needed* to say she didn't need to. But Will was drawing her closer, his lips pressed into a firm line. "I have nothing to hide. So read me."

His eyes fluttered shut, and despite the tic in his jaw, his hands slid further back on her cheeks, his touch soft and gentle and so unlike the tension lining his features.

Aya swallowed hard. And though it twisted that thing that writhed in her stomach even further, she called her Sensainos affinity forward.

Will's shield was already down, and it was easy, really, to feel him. To feel his truth, bone-deep like his very essence that tinged his sensations with a feeling that was uniquely his.

On Will, the truth felt like the certainty of the sun rising every day. It washed over her now—sure and solid—filling in the cracks of her doubt.

But there was something else there. Something hollow, and pained, and aching. Something she'd put there by doing *this*. By trusting her affinity to show her the truth instead of trusting him.

Aya cut off her power with a sharp inhale. She stepped out of Will's hold, her eyes blinking open to find that same pain lingering on his face.

"I…" she breathed. "I should have—"

"Don't," Will muttered. "It's fine." His movements were stilted as he lowered himself to the mattress. He braced his arms on his legs, his hands clasped between his knees as he stared at the floor. "It's not like I haven't earned your doubt."

"Will."

He shook his head, his voice sharp and weary all at once. "I understand. Why you'd need help trusting me." He ran a thumb across his lip, his jaw shifting as he glanced toward the fire. "As for Tova…I don't blame her for lying to you about our conversation in the dungeons. Especially if she did tell Gianna something of value."

His eyes were distant as they met hers. "Yet I imagine if she truly had, I would be dead, not injured. I can't imagine where else the treason accusation came from though, if not her. It's too severe to be brought on by a few missed missives."

"Tova said she was questioned *because* Gianna thought

63

you were up to something. If that's true, then the suspicions of treason didn't start with Tova."

Will tugged a hand through his hair, further mussing the strands in his frustration. "I'll talk to Tova. We'll get to the bottom of it." Aya went to interject, but Will cut her a look. "This is my mess, Aya. The truth about our conversation aside, it doesn't change what I did to her. It doesn't change that I still…"

His voice trailed off, as if he couldn't bring himself to repeat what had transpired in that cell. What Gianna had made sure had happened by bringing Cleo with her to monitor Tova's questioning.

"Let me handle it," he finished.

An uneasy silence fell between them, so full that Aya couldn't decide where to go next. Will, with all his masks, reached for one of the most familiar as he jutted his chin toward her abandoned knife on the ground. "Was the knife for me?"

The question was light. Teasing. But with what had just unfolded between them, it left a bitter taste on Aya's tongue. That hollowness that she'd felt in Will had settled in her, his disappointment and hurt echoing in her chest. She stared at him for a long moment, the flickering light dancing across the scars that crept over his shoulders.

"I should have shielded you." The words slipped out of her on a breath, a quiet confession that had any trace of humor vanishing from Will's face. He stood, closing the distance between them in two slow strides.

"You and I both know that with Cleo in the room, it was too much of a risk. If she sensed you were helping me—"

"I don't care," Aya interjected. Gods, she'd failed him twice in the mere hours she'd been home. First in the palace chamber, and just now, when she'd trusted in her power more than *him*.

"You should care," Will hissed, his voice hushed.

"Shielding me in front of Gianna, directly defying her orders of my punishment, would have been foolish."

"One could say the same about kidnapping a saint," Aya shot back. "Or was today not enough evidence of that for you?"

Will didn't balk at the bite in her words. Instead, his lips twitched toward a smirk.

"One could," he conceded. "But as we've already established, I'm selfish when it comes to you. Let's not model my behavior."

There it was again, that forced levity. It tangled with her frustration, with her *anger*. He had asked the impossible of her, was *still* asking the impossible of her—to act like she didn't care, like she wasn't screaming on the inside, hadn't been since the moment Gianna's command registered in her mind.

"I thought she was going to kill you," Aya bit out. "I thought she was going to kill you, and I was just going to stand there and watch."

"Aya—"

A tear slipped down her cheek, and Aya brushed it away angrily. "I walked through your *blood*. And I pretended I didn't care. I went to see Tova as if nothing had ever happened, as if I hadn't just watched Gianna have you maimed, and stood by while she did it. What is the point of *this*"—her arms flung wide, her gaze raking down her body as if she could see her power—"if I can't use it to protect those I care about?"

Will's hands found her waist once more as he tugged her closer to him. "Breathe for me, Aya love," he murmured. His eyes stayed locked on hers as he took his own deep, intentional breath. Aya followed, forcing her lungs to open.

She was drowning, and the warmth of his hands on her waist and the steady rise and fall of his chest were the only things keeping her from going under entirely.

Gianna had had him whipped. She'd nearly *killed* him, and even then, Aya still had come here and questioned him, had let the past taint her mind as if everything he'd done hadn't been because of their queen.

Gianna was still twisting, still manipulating, still *hurting*, and it carved something out of Aya as she pressed her head against Will's chest and bit back her rage. She fought the urge to scream again, to unleash some of the fury that seemed to still want *out* despite her episode in her room.

He's alive.

He's alive.

He's alive.

For now, a traitorous voice whispered in her mind.

"I can't let her do this," she swore into his skin. "I can't stand by and let her hurt you."

"You can," Will muttered into her hair. Aya leaned back to meet his gaze. "I will apologize to her. I will make it right. I *have* to make it right. Gianna's trust in me is invaluable."

He was wrong, though. There was a price Aya wouldn't pay, and she was looking at it.

"This is the role I chose to play," Will continued. "I told you once before that I knew there were consequences for the choices I've made."

The vise that seemed to be wrapped around Aya's chest tightened further. That hurt she had felt as she read him, mixed up in his solid truth and bitter understanding, was nowhere to be found on his face now, but it lingered in Aya's mind anyway.

Will's fingers gripped her chin, tilting her head up toward his. "I would do it again, every time, if it meant being here with you now."

Aya blinked against the wetness in her eyes.

"I'm sorry."

She wasn't sure what she was apologizing for specifically. Perhaps for all of it. For doubting him. For reading him. For the horrible things he'd done because he'd wanted *her*.

The corner of Will's mouth lifted slightly as he tangled

his fingers in her hair, his thumb pressing against the pulse point at the back of her head. Slowly, he let their foreheads fall together.

"I'm not," he whispered.

Aya let her eyes close, let Will anchor her there in the middle of the room. His breath was steady, calm, and she let it drag her own down to its pace.

"You should go," he finally said softly as he drew back and glanced at the clock on the wall. "The healers will be making their rounds soon."

Her fingers grazed his cheek. "You'll have something for the pain?"

He shook his head. "I need to be alert."

He *needed* sleep. But Aya knew it was fruitless to argue with him. So she pressed her lips to his instead, trying to convey all that had been left unsaid in that kiss.

"Go," Will murmured as he finally pulled away, his forehead pressing against hers. There was something stilted to his words—something left unsaid. But he pushed her away gently, his fingers lingering on her cheek before falling to his side. "Go."

So she did.

9

PATIENCE WAS KNOWN TO BE A QUALITY OF THE PERSIS, A virtue passed on from Saudra herself. Aya had been taught in school that her patron goddess knew persuasion wasn't about pushing, or forcing, but waiting. It was a matter of setting up the pieces, priming a person until the persuasion would actually stick.

And though it was supposed to be engrained in Aya, that had not stopped Galda from honing Aya's patience into something not unlike a weapon when Aya had spent her childhood training with her.

After all, Galda had trained Aya not just as Persi, but as a spy.

She'd taught Aya to bury the things that made her rash, or vulnerable. The things that threatened her careful control, that made her show her hand before she'd meant to.

It was that training she leaned into as she stepped into Gianna's chambers the next morning and dropped to one knee, her fist pressing against her chest.

The queen greeted her with a warm smile from where she was seated at the low oval glass table as Aya rose. The table was dotted with pastries, as it typically was for early meetings with the Tría, but instead of Will and Tova filling the other seats, Hyacinth, the High Priestess, sat in Tova's ornate, high-backed armchair, and in Will's spot on the velvet-green love seat was…Lena.

Aya stilled, just for a moment, as she noted the Persi's presence. Lena had always been a valuable spy, but clearly, she had made herself even more important to Gianna in recent months.

Aya tucked the information away and met her queen's gaze. Gianna's smile faded as she looked at Aya more closely. "She told you," the queen remarked solemnly.

It was easy for Aya to let her resentment show. Easier still to have just a note of it bleed into her voice as she replied, "She did." Aya took a single step forward. "I'm curious as to why you didn't, Majesty."

"Tova asked that it be left to her to decide when, and how, to tell you that she was questioned. I felt it was the least she deserved." Gianna's head dipped. "I know you must be angry with me, Aya," she continued, "but you also know that as queen, I must make difficult choices for the sake of Tala's protection, especially in times of war. If there was any chance that Tova knew—"

"I understand," Aya interjected.

She was a good warrior.

An exceptional spy.

A loyal member of the Dyminara and Tría.

Gianna would expect her anger; but she would also expect her obedience. And Aya planned to give it to her.

"'We all have duties, Majesty. I understand yours comes with its own difficulties," Aya said as she sat beside Lena on the love seat.

Gianna's relief was evident as she leaned back in her own chair, a show of emotion Aya realized was for her benefit. Another tool to gain trust. A manipulation to show Aya exactly what she wanted to see.

"Yes," Gianna breathed. "It certainly does. And I have no doubt we both will face more in the days to come."

Gianna trailed a finger around the rim of her white teacup. "You asked about the supplier yesterday. I've asked Lena to be here to update you."

Lena pivoted so she was facing Aya. "I traveled to the Midlands myself, stopping in the key merchant centers on my way toward the southern border. Ezé, Colmur, Vezekol—there was no sign of anyone fleeing, nor reports of any suspicious travelers making their way through the region. I had made it about halfway to the border when I learned our sources there had gone dark, and the Midlands were preparing to secure their borders due to the growing threat of Kakos. There were rumors that Queen Nyra was sending the bulk of her forces to Sitya."

Aya frowned. The city of Sitya was the closest Midlands port to Kakos. As such, it had always been more heavily defended than others. But to send the bulk of the Midlands army there...

Queen Nyra must have anticipated Kakos would move, and soon.

"Queen Nyra wouldn't grant us access?"

Lena cut a glance to Gianna before she said, "We were worried such a request could risk burning our assets."

Aya braced her elbows on her knees, her frown deepening as she considered the risks. They had spent years building up their sources across Eteryium. And while the Midlands had long been an ally, if only because they needed Tala's support, it didn't mean Tala hadn't cultivated assets there: important sources who provided key information when needed.

"I didn't want to risk our sources or my own cover. So I returned home," Lena continued. Gianna gave Lena a curt nod before turning to face Aya.

"We've renewed the search here and will continue to try to make contact with our sources in the Midlands to see if they know of where the supplier might be, but we expect they're wary to communicate on such matters," Gianna explained. "We have not known war in centuries, and no one is eager to hasten its arrival."

But they already *had*. The revelation of the Second Saint's existence could be the very thing to goad Kakos into action, especially if they had a supplier in their pocket who was giving them weapons. War was closing in on them from every direction, every action leading them closer to the battlefield.

"I tapped my best sources in town this winter," Aya mused as she straightened. "The Rouline was the most likely place to find a lead, but nothing came of it."

The entertainment district was the heart of secrets, and they hadn't heard a whisper.

"But if our supplier knows that we'd have the Rouline covered, then they'd likely resort to alternative measures," she continued. "I can try the avenues I hadn't—"

"No," Gianna interrupted Aya's planning. "Lena will continue to lead the search."

Aya's gaze darted between the Persi and queen, the insinuation rankling her. "With all due respect, Your Majesty, as your Third and spymaster—"

"As our realm's only chance at survival, you have other responsibilities. Lena can keep you apprised of her findings. The entire realm has heard whispers that the Second Saint has risen. In Dunmeaden, those who know of my Third know your face. We must act quickly." She motioned to Hyacinth, who was still studying Aya carefully. "We've planned a Sanctification ceremony for this evening; a chance for you to claim your role before the gods and the people of our city. To formally become the beacon of hope so many will see you as. It will be an opportunity to truly celebrate your homecoming and show gratitude for how the gods have blessed us."

Dread replaced Aya's irritation, flooding through her like the waters of the Loraine River as Hyacinth smiled.

"This evening," Aya repeated slowly. She met Gianna's gaze, readying to bury her feelings, to hide any indication of vulnerability.

But this…this was an opening, an opportunity to press Gianna a bit further, to see if she would give any indication of her plans for Aya and her power.

So Aya clasped her hands on her lap, letting her shoulders fall forward. "Is that wise, Majesty? I still am unsure *how* I am to right the greatest wrong, as the prophecy says. No one knows how the remainder of the prophecy is to be fulfilled."

"Which is why I asked Hyacinth to be present for this meeting."

The Priestess leaned toward Aya, her eyes warm beneath her sheer veil. "As you know, the prophecy states that the greatest wrong will be righted once the Second Saint arises. It could be possible that once you are formally recognized as a saint, the gods will make the answers available to us. It is also possible that it's a path the Divine will *only* reveal to the chosen."

Aya cocked her head, her brow furrowing. "So I'm waiting until the gods speak to me?"

She'd felt the presence of her patron goddess, but never once had she heard Saudra's voice instructing her. She'd never heard the voices of any of the gods.

Hyacinth chuckled. "There are ways to open yourself up to the gods, Aya. How do you think we priestesses lead worship? We study the Conoscenza. We commune with the gods daily. We purify our spirits and ensure we can be holy vessels to share the blessings of the Divine with Visya and humans alike."

Aya fought off a shudder. The last time she'd attempted to get to know her soul, she'd almost died.

"When you displayed your power in the market, I instructed a few of our most dedicated Saj of the temple to gather the most ancient of texts surrounding the gods and the First Saint. The queen and I believe that through study, especially in regards to Saint Evie, and training with the priestesses, the gods will make the path forward clear to you."

Aya frowned. "Why aren't such texts in the Maraciana?"

Gianna and Hyacinth shared a bemused look. "The Saj of the Maraciana may study power, but their rejection of the Old Customs renders them blind where religious texts are concerned. We expect they never truly thought a Second Saint would arise, so..." Gianna gave a shrug. "It's not as though they truly know what they're missing. Tala has long not felt the need to point it out to them."

Ridiculous. Here they were, on the brink of a war that could destroy the realm, and the kingdoms still worried about petty things such as who controlled what knowledge.

Aya struggled to keep the tension from her voice as she said, "I see."

Hyacinth leaned in eagerly. "I am confident the gods have answers for you, Aya. We are prepared to welcome you to the temple to study and train alongside us."

Aya bit back a bitter retort. She didn't like the prospect of spending hours in the temple with the Saj priestesses. She could be of so much more use doing what she knew how to do—spy, manipulate, fight.

But Hyacinth continued, oblivious to Aya's discomfort. "Studying the texts is part of opening your mind to the Divine, but there is also much more our people will expect of the Second Saint. You will be a representation of faith, Aya. A direct line to the gods. There are customs and...behaviors... one must practice when acting as a representation of divinity."

"Would it not make more sense, then, to wait on a Sanctification ceremony until after I've completed such training?"

Gianna shook her head, and this time, her voice was edged with impatience. "No, it would not. Not when the entire realm has heard a saint has arisen."

Aya held her queen's gaze. She had claimed her title in

Rinnia to help Aidon and ensure Trahir would lend their forces should Kakos attack. She would do it again if it meant helping her friend. She owed Aidon that at least. And while she no longer believed what she once did—that her power was fueled by the darkest part of her, brought on by the sins of her past—Aya knew, better than anyone, that darkness still lingered in her.

Both live within you; as they do in all of us, Lorna had said. *Your power does not decide—you do.*

She was trying to make better choices, to stay anchored in the light, like Lorna had instructed. But to be sanctified? To deem herself holy before the gods and the people of Tala?

It was wrong.

"I've also arranged for you to train with Galda," Gianna continued, "so that you can continue to develop your power."

"And what of my regular training with the Dyminara?" Aya asked. "Am I not to be a member of the force?"

Giving up such a position would not come without its losses. Her proximity to the queen, for starters. But there was something deeper Aya would mourn. Because despite what she knew of Gianna, the Dyminara had been her home, the first place she truly belonged. Yes, she had taken an oath to Gianna...but it was also an oath to her people. To her gods.

She wasn't willing to abandon it entirely.

Gianna's face softened. "You remain my Third, Aya. You are a crucial member of the Dyminara." Her gaze flicked to Aya's left hand, as if looking for that new scar on her palm. "I would never abandon one with such loyalty to their oath. But *this* is how you serve Tala now. Learning how such power is to be applied to rid us of darkness is what the gods have planned for you. I do not want you distracted."

Aya went to argue, to shove against the isolation she could already feel closing in on her, but Gianna set her teacup down in its saucer with a note of finality. "This morning, you'll meet the priestesses who will be helping you and see where your studies will take place. Hyacinth will review the schedule with you, and you can begin in earnest after the ceremony tonight. Hyacinth will prepare you for what to expect."

Gianna stood and smoothed her hands down her pale-blue dress.

"One more thing, Majesty," Aya said before she could leave. "The guards."

A golden brow arched. "What of them?"

"I'd like them removed."

"Absolutely not."

Aya stood, forcing her body to remain relaxed as she held her queen's gaze. "If it would make you more comfortable, Tyr can accompany me whenever I am in town. I won't be at risk of being approached if he is with me."

Gianna cocked her head. "You're sure he remains bonded to you? The wolves have never experienced power like yours. Even if he recognizes you, it is possible Tyr will not be able to fight beside you. That your raw power will be...a distraction. A threat."

Aya stilled, her body going cold.

The Athatis and the Dyminara were said to be bonded by their magic. Like called to like, creating a unique connection between wolf and Visya. Aya hadn't considered that hers might be broken now that her power had changed. To even imagine a world where she and Tyr weren't bonded...it felt like carving out a piece of her very soul and wrenching it from her body.

"He will," she gritted out. "And when he does, he will be a far better guard than any you could assign me. Unless there's another reason you want someone stationed outside my door?"

Gianna cocked her head, her brow furrowing slightly as she contemplated Aya. "I admire your confidence in your bonded, Aya. But I do worry. So much has changed since Trahir," she murmured, the words loaded with meaning.

Aya kept her face blank.

Had she pushed too hard? It was Tova, after all, who typically pushed back in Tría meetings. Who let her fire guide her. Aya more usually adopted a position of quiet calculation.

But she hadn't been able to keep quiet—to keep still—as Gianna stirred that already simmering anger that threatened to burst from her.

Gianna let out a long breath. "You can train with Tyr after we get through the Sanctification. If he remains your bonded, perhaps I will consider a reduction in the guards. For now, Kahn and Lamihr remain. If their location outside of your room is bothersome, then they can be stationed at the entrance to the Quarter. It's not as though the Dyminara aren't looking out for your safety."

Aya tensed at the reminder.

Her *safety*. As if she was truly safe anywhere.

The queen smoothed her hands down her dress once more, her face softening slightly. "The Divine will not fail you, Aya," she reassured her, as if the hesitation on Aya's face had anything to do with the gods and not the queen sitting in front of her. "And I know that you will not fail me."

Those words had once felt like trust, a confirmation that Aya knew her place. Had chosen her path well.

But now, she couldn't help but see them for what she suspected they truly were:

A threat.

Perhaps they'd been that all along.

10

W ELL, AT LEAST YOU LOOK LESS DEAD."
Will looked up from where he sat on the edge
of his bed to see Liam leaning against the doorframe, his
brow cocked in subtle amusement. A pile of fresh clothes was
tucked under his arm.

"You're too kind."

The warrior huffed a laugh before chucking the bundle
at him. "Get dressed. I'm to get you caught up on your next
assignment. Then Gianna wants to see you."

Will's jaw shifted at the order—and Gianna's continued,
subtle condescension. Sending another to brief him on her
behalf before she could be bothered with him...

Apparently, his whipping hadn't been enough punishment for her.

"Can it wait?"

He'd love to bathe, or hells, even just sit on his own bed.
Besides, he'd forced down the sludge Suja said was porridge
this morning, but he was hoping to sweet-talk Elara, the
head cook of the royal kitchens, into allowing him to steal
something less...beige...to eat.

"No," Liam said flatly. He ducked out of the room and shut the door, giving Will privacy.

Will sighed, wincing as he stood and began to change. His entire body felt stiff, the skin on his back itchy and tight. Suja had tried to force another dose of pain tonic down his throat, but he'd refused.

"I have work to do," he'd told her.

"It can wait," Suja had snapped.

"War waits for no one."

She'd stopped arguing then.

Will gritted his teeth as he tugged on the long-sleeved black shirt Liam had brought. Fucking hells. The fabric felt like it was flaying his skin all over again.

Will went to the small bedside table and grabbed the tin of ointment, his eyes flicking to the mirror. He looked like shit. His hair was disheveled, his face pale, his skin tinged with sweat from the simple exertion of changing.

He shook his head as he stalked to the door and wrenched it open to find Suja standing with her arms crossed, a stern look on her face as she surveyed Liam. Her gaze cut to Will. "Remember, no affinity use today," she said.

"Understood."

"And you'll need to apply the ointment—"

"Twice a day for the next week," he finished for her as he held up the tin. Suja's expression warmed slightly.

"So the Dark Prince *does* listen every now and again."

"I like to keep people guessing," he muttered, sliding the tin into his pocket. "Thank you, again, Suja. I am further indebted to you."

The healer waved him off. "I am simply using the gifts Mora has blessed me with." She looked back and forth between the two men, and Will was again struck by the notion that she wanted to say more. But she merely dusted her hands on her tunic and excused herself.

"Ready?" Liam asked.

Will gave a dramatic bow. "Lead the way."

"Am I to be detained as well as whipped?" Will drawled over the scuffing of their boots, which echoed throughout the dark, dank halls of the palace dungeons. The last time Will had been here, he'd been desperate to get Aya out of the kingdom—away from Gianna. He wasn't keen to be back in this godsforsaken place, especially not when he could still hear the echoes of Tova's screams as he'd been forced to question her.

Liam muttered a curse beneath his breath and shook his head. "Stop being an asshole for five minutes, would you? It might enable you to see that I'm trying to help you."

Will didn't actively *dislike* Liam. In fact, he'd always preferred his company to Lena's, and that preference had only grown in the last several hours. A whipping would taint anyone's perception, he supposed.

But even without active resentment, Liam wasn't a friend, per se. Will didn't have many of those in Dunmeaden. Not true friends, anyway. There was always a certain allure, he supposed, that came with being the Dark Prince. But there was a danger there, too. Most people regarded him as some sort of challenge or conquest, a wild animal to be tamed, but never fully trusted.

Yet Liam had never treated him as such. They'd trained together, even gone into town for an evening of debauchery a time or two.

But it didn't mean Will trusted him.

"Why would I need your help?"

Liam scoffed. "I know your ego is nearly insurmountable, but even you aren't that thick." The Persi's eyes swept the dungeon once before his voice dropped to a murmur. "Things have changed since you left. Drastically."

Will cocked a brow, his hands sliding into his pockets. "A

saint has arisen, Liam, and we are on the brink of war. Of course things have changed."

Liam nodded his head down the corridor. "Just wait."

Will bit back his irritation, brought on by the sense of foreboding that was settling in his stomach. He hated being caught unaware. And this whole entire godsdamn return home had been one instance of it after another.

They stalked through the prison, deeper and deeper into its cold, dark corridors. Will was used to the murmurs— even the shouts. But what he wasn't accustomed to was the pressing silence that felt like a physical weight. It began in the deepest part of the dungeons, where the last hall stretched toward the center point beneath the palace.

"What the hells?" Will muttered. He frowned as he stepped past Liam, his eyes scanning the rows of wooden doors. Several were closed, the typical sign of occupancy. Yet there wasn't a whisper of sound coming from them.

No shouting, no muttering, no pleading, no *breathing*.

The air was heavy, and not just with the wet cold that often frequented these halls. There was something *else* here.

Will cut his gaze back to Liam. The flickering Incend flames, set high in the torches on the wall, made his brown eyes gleam. "What the hells is this?"

Liam crossed his arms as he leaned a shoulder against the wall. "A Caeli is down here every hour to reinforce the shield of air. Apparently, the constant yelling was aggravating the prison guards."

"Who are these people?"

"Lower merchants, mostly. Apprentices to weaponsmiths she's deemed suspicious. A few ship workers." Liam's jaw shifted as he took in the long hallway behind Will. "They're being rounded up slowly enough to not cause alarm, but steadily. I doubt we've seen the end of the arrests."

"Why?"

Liam glanced over his shoulder, as if to ensure they

were truly alone. "She's looking for anyone with a connection to the supplier who met with the Trahir tradesmen this winter."

Will frowned. It had been months since Aya apprehended the two tradesmen, months since Will questioned them and realized they were buying weapons on behalf of Kakos. The supplier had escaped arrest, but only because Ronan, the Royal Guard who was on duty with Aya, hadn't been at his post.

He was found dead shortly after, killed days before their assignment.

"I had assumed when Lena's search was fruitless, it was considered a lost cause," Will finally admitted slowly.

Liam's gaze was steady. Unblinking. "As did I."

What, then, was Gianna hoping to find? Proof of the supplier's whereabouts? Surely, she could not think they had stayed in Dunmeaden. Not after all this time.

Will frowned as he stared at the row of cells. The tradesmen he had questioned had sworn there had been no supplier at the meeting. And when the papers were planted on Tova, and Will's search in Trahir came up empty...

He'd started to wonder if his queen had more of a hand in the missing supplier than he'd originally suspected. But there was too much unfolding in Trahir then, and he'd been on the other side of the realm, unable to act on it.

Now, irrefutable evidence of Gianna's innocence seemed to be staring him in the face. Why redouble her efforts, why make arrests, if she knew someone could tie her to the tradesmen?

And yet Will couldn't help the nagging in his gut that something was off.

He rubbed a hand across his jaw, his back aching with the movement. He wasn't used to feeling so *behind*. He'd always been the one with the information. With Gianna's ear, and with the inside tracks to the best knowledge. And now, when he truly needed it most, he was on the outskirts, begging for scraps.

"Who knows about these people here?" Will bit out.

He knew better than to show his frustration, but his back felt like it was on fire, and the only damn peace he'd felt was in those stolen minutes with Aya last night, and even that had been shattered as quickly as it came.

Tell me you did not do this.

He could still hear the pleading note in her voice.

Liam shrugged. "Me, Lena, Gianna. She hasn't wanted to raise alarm."

"Keep it that way," Will muttered, his eyes scanning the cells once more. "Surely you could've told me this in the healing quarters. I don't see why Gianna felt a demonstration was necessary."

Irritation rippled across Liam's face. "You're fucking impossible, you know that?"

He did. Which is exactly why he'd reached for that arrogance that was like a second skin.

It's what they expected. What they'd be watching for.

"What's wrong, Liam? Does Gianna's trust in you only extend so far?" Will goaded.

Liam took a step toward him, his chin jutting forward. "That's rich. We both know your anger is because you find yourself out of her confidence. Is the queen's whore jealous?"

Will reached for his power without a second thought, but the Persi was ready for him. Will's affinity, already weak with his injuries, didn't make it through Liam's shield. Will's body spasmed, Suja's warning ringing in his ears as he let his power drop, his hand clutching his chest, his breath coming in sharp, pained pants.

"Saudra grant me patience," Liam hissed. "I thought—" He bit off his words, hands tightening into fists. "Fucking forget it," he continued with a shake of his head.

Liam turned on his heel and stalked toward the hall that would begin the winding journey out of the prison, his movements tight with anger.

"The queen is expecting you," he snapped over his shoulder. "You better bathe."

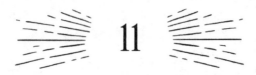 11

WILL DIDN'T THINK HE'D EVER SEE THE DAY HE'D LONG for Trahir. But he'd been home now for approximately a day, and suddenly, the cliffs of Rinnia, hells, even the blinding colors of the Old Town buildings, seemed more enticing than the utter shit of a situation he found himself in currently.

He'd even take a round of cards with Aidon over this.

Will had left the dungeons shortly after Liam, returning to his room to bathe and change into his fighting leathers. The black material clung to his skin, and while it chafed against his tender back, he had a point to make. It couldn't hurt for the rest of the Dyminara, for the rest of Tala, to remember who exactly had returned.

The Dark Prince of Dunmeaden.

He loathed the title. But he'd wield it like a fucking knife if he needed to. And if Gianna's welcome had been any indication, he needed to.

He nodded at the guards stationed outside of Gianna's office. He found the queen standing behind her desk, her teeth digging into her bottom lip as she scanned a sheaf of parchment.

He knelt. "Your Majesty."

"Will." His name was an exhale of relief, but he kept his eyes fixed on the floor, his head bowed, as silence stretched between them. Her footsteps shattered it, and then there was a hand on his arm, and she was gently tugging him to standing. "How are you feeling?" she murmured.

Will couldn't help the way his brows rose. "Wonderful," he retorted.

Gianna ignored his sarcasm, that hand remaining on his arm as she guided him to the chair. She waited for him to sit before she took her place across from him. "I had Suja at the ready," she murmured, her eyes bright with worry as she scanned him. "She was able to administer something for the pain?"

This had to be some sort of trick, or manipulation, or *trap*. That couldn't be actual concern on his queen's face. Not after what she'd done to him.

Gianna leaned forward, her hands clasped on the table. "You must understand...I had to punish you. Even though you returned, I could not act as though my earlier doubts, while wrong, meant nothing. Nor could I excuse the mess you created in Trahir. There must be consequences for the Dyminara. They must *know* what is to be expected, especially with the threat of Kakos looming over us."

Will was careful to keep his movements smooth, to not give her the satisfaction of seeing even a hint of the dull pain that radiated throughout his body as he settled back in his seat. "So I was to be an example."

Gianna's jaw shifted. "Unfortunately, yes. The outcomes of your actions remain the same, William. We are at a significant disadvantage in the war now that word has spread about Aya."

Will cleared his throat, forcing his voice into a solemn tone as he said, "I understand. Despite the obstacles Aya and I faced there, you trusted me to do the job smoothly, and I failed you. Not only that, but I instilled doubt in you because

85

of an error in my judgment. It was the gravest of mistakes—mistakes which, as you pointed out yesterday, we cannot afford."

It was easy to let her see the resentment he held toward himself for his shortsighted thinking. Easier still to hold her gaze and make a vow. "I will never make such a mistake again."

Gianna's lips were pursed as she considered him, a small furrow wrinkling the space between her brows. "I must admit, of all people's loyalty I've had to question, it was most disappointing that it was yours," she finally confessed softly.

"I can assure you, Majesty, that it was the focus on the mission *you* gave me that guided my actions. Perhaps I was too singularly focused on protecting the Second Saint, but..." He bowed his head in regret. "I would rather commit myself to the seven hells than betray this kingdom. Than betray *you*."

Truth and lies, all woven together into exactly what she wanted to hear. He could see it in the way some emotion flickered behind her brown eyes, lightening her irises just a shade. Gianna swallowed.

"I doubted you too quickly. But I trust you'll continue to prove yourself."

It was a question, a demand, and, gods willing, perhaps even the start of forgiveness, all rolled into a single statement, which she delivered with a note of finality.

And it was far, far too easy.

"Let's put it behind us," she continued. Her eyes scanned him, her lips quirking at the corner. "Perhaps we can rebuild other parts of our relationship as well."

Something in Will's stomach twisted. Gianna wasn't the sort to move on so quickly, to let bygones be bygones.

"I would be considered lucky, Majesty, for such a second chance," he replied carefully.

"I'm glad to hear it. I'll have need of you tonight."

Will stiffened in his seat. She couldn't possibly mean...

"We're holding a Sanctification ceremony for Aya."

Vicious relief rushed through him. "A Sanctification ceremony," he repeated. Gods, Aya must be furious. He dreaded to think of how she received the news this morning.

Gianna's smile was sharp. "Surely you understand the disadvantage at which we find ourselves now that news of the Second Saint has spread. It's important that Tala and the realm know the truth."

Will nearly scoffed. The truth. What did Gianna know of the concept?

He propped an ankle on his knee. "Certainly, Majesty. What does the ceremony entail?"

Gianna waved a dismissive hand. "Hyacinth is attending to those details. I'd like you and Tova to attend with me, in the worship. Other members of the Dyminara will be there throughout for additional protection."

For you, or for Aya?

It felt foolish to point out that simply parading Aya around was asking for danger, now that news of her identity had spread, but apparently Gianna trusted the most devout of the realm. Besides, with the rest of the Tría and the Dyminara in attendance, as well as the Royal Guard, no one would dare make a threat against her.

And then there's Aya herself, Will thought, biting back a smirk.

"I humbly extend my service to you, Majesty."

Gianna's brows lifted, as if to say she'd never seen him show a hint of humility in his life.

Good. Humor, amusement—those were good. Even if those alarm bells were still ringing as he stood.

"If that's all, then I'll take my leave," he murmured as he stood.

Gianna's lips tipped up, her grin tugging at something familiar in his mind. "Not just yet," she said lightly. "I trust Liam showed you the work we've been doing in your absence."

"He took me to the dungeons, yes."

87

Gianna trailed a finger across her desk. "The arrests... We've been keeping them quiet, so as not to alert the merchants. We wouldn't want the supplier to catch wind of it if they're still out there."

"Certainly..." Will said slowly, unsure of where this was going. Gianna tilted her head as she looked at him, and it dawned on him then what that expression on her face reminded him of. She looked like his bonded Athatis, Akeeta, right before she went in for the kill.

"Sit down," Gianna commanded. "Let's discuss how you can help with our search for the supplier."

Will stalked through the training complex of the Dyminara, his gaze fixed unseeingly on the labyrinth of halls he wandered through. He didn't bother to acknowledge those he passed, nor did they acknowledge him. They simply stared—and he was used to it.

The stares had followed him for years, both here and in town. Stares of hatred. Stares of fear. Stares of lust. They were all the same, in a way. All seeing what he wanted them to see rather than who he truly was.

It chafed today, but he stifled his irritation. He had one more task before he could perhaps find Aya ahead of tonight's ceremony, and that was finding the blond-haired warrior Lena had said was training here. Will peered into the various training rooms, stopping only when he found her.

She stood alone in one of the larger sparring rooms, her sword whirling through the air as she threw vicious combinations at a wooden post. She was dressed in her own fighting leathers, her long hair pulled back into a high ponytail. From the sweat shining on her face, Will could tell she'd been at it for a while. Yet her movements were still swift, the swish of the blade the only sound aside from her steady breaths as she struck the post over and over.

"Tova," he murmured, breaking the trance she often slipped into while fighting. The general whirled to face him at once, strands of her hair sticking to her face. She stared at him for a moment, her eyes flicking across him, before she raised a brow.

"What?" Her voice was flat—bored even.

Will stepped further into the room, but Tova stayed exactly where she was, her hip cocked, sword point resting against the ground.

"I need to speak to you."

"Why?"

To apologize. To learn the truth. To know what, exactly, Gianna knows.

He dragged a hand through his hair and let out a heavy breath. "You know why."

But she was already turning away from him. She flipped her ponytail over her shoulder as she faced the post.

"I'm not interested in anything you have to say." She began drilling again, her sword glinting in the light streaming through the window. Will let the steady swish and thud of her blade fill the silence between them. He could wait her out, he supposed. She couldn't train forever. But he knew Tova. She was proud, and stubborn, and hardheaded, and there was a particular way they'd dealt with their issues in the past.

So Will sighed, his body loosening as he strolled around to the back of the pell, forcing her to meet his gaze. Tova glared at him, her sword falling to her side.

"I said," she gritted out between pants, "I'm not interested."

"I heard you. Shall we fight it out then?" Tova's gaze narrowed, and Will smirked. "Come now, Tova. I know you don't want to miss an opportunity to get your vengeance."

There.

Her eyes flashed as if the flames Hepha had blessed her with lived in her hazel irises. He had her, and she was too enticed by his offer to care that she knew it. Tova chucked her sword to the floor.

"Fine," she growled. "But it's hand-to-hand. Affinities allowed."

Will shrugged. "Fine by me."

Tova turned on her heel without another word, leading them toward another room within the training complex. It was small and square and sparse, with three windows lining the outer walls, a bench underneath one, a table with a pitcher of water on the other. A large circle was drawn in the middle of the room with chalk—the sparring ring.

"You had to pick the worst room, didn't you?" Will grumbled, his boot toeing the dirt as he took his spot in the ring.

Tova's grin was as sharp as a knife. "It's the furthest. Less chance of people hearing you scream." Will huffed a laugh, but Tova merely crouched down, her fists raised. "Don't you dare hold back."

"Wouldn't dream of it," Will muttered. And then she was in front of him, her fists aimed for his head. Will ducked, turning to keep her in front of him. His body felt stiff, the skin on his back straining with each movement, but he kept any hints of pain buried as he let Tova take the offensive.

If he could wear her down, then perhaps she'd listen.

Perhaps she'd give him some indication of what had truly transpired when they'd left.

A stream of fire came for him next, and he sidestepped it, biting back a grin as Tova huffed in frustration. She lunged for him again, and Will blocked her punch, managing to land one to her side. She hardly winced as she twisted, her elbow jamming into his shoulder.

Will grabbed her arm and twisted, but Tova didn't even wince.

She wrenched her arm from his hold. Will ducked under her next jab, but he couldn't miss the next flare of flame that seared his side. But his shield held tight, and Tova's jaw shifted as her anger increased.

"Fight me, you fucking coward," she spat out.

"You and I both know I don't need to hit first to win," Will panted, ducking under the hook she sent sailing toward his head. He landed a punch to her gut, and Tova doubled over, giving him space to step back.

"The situation in Trahir was too turbulent. If I had—"

"I don't care," Tova hissed as she straightened, sending another spear of flame coming for him. "I was tortured." Another. "And it was because of *you*." Another.

Will retreated, his back screaming as he ducked out of the way of her flames. His shield wouldn't hold for long. Not with the intensity of Tova's fire, not with the injuries currently depleting his energy with each and every movement.

Sure enough, Will let out a hiss as her next round of fire caught his shoulder. His flesh seared, and he twisted in pain, his gaze leaving Tova for a breath.

She was on him in an instant.

Suja's instructions be damned. Will sent a pulse of his power for her, slipping through the shield she hadn't kept tight in her anger. But it hardly mattered.

He was too weakened from the whipping, and Tova was too angry, and her palm was hot with fire as she grabbed the back of his neck and brought her knee into his stomach. Will doubled over, and Tova swiped his feet out from beneath him, bringing him down hard.

He rolled, but she was right there. She pressed her boot to his chest, her eyes bright with rage as she stared down at him.

Will let his shield drop as he took in her fury, her *hatred*. It wasn't forced. Not a single bit of it was forced.

"I'm sorry," he panted. Everything hurt, and he didn't bother to hide the way he gritted his teeth as he held her gaze. "I am sorry. I didn't think Gianna would suspect—"

"Save it," Tova snarled as she leaned over him, fire dancing in her palms. "No matter what you say to me, you're still a worthless piece of shit. Don't think I forgot what you did to me in those dungeons."

There. They had finally arrived at the true matter at hand. "Enough, Tova," he hissed. "You agreed to help me that day."

Tova just blinked at him, her heel digging deeper into his chest. "I don't know what the fuck you're taking about."

There was that anger, that hatred—she didn't bother to hide it from him. It muddied her sensations, making it impossible for him to find a ripple of a lie, or the resounding weight of truth that he'd spent years tugging out in those he questioned.

"Tova," he urged through heaving breaths.

But she merely lifted her boot from his chest, disgust twisting her lips as she snapped, "Stay away from me." Her boot collided with his ribs, and Will couldn't stop the groan of pain that wrenched itself from his chest. "I mean it."

And then she was gone, her flames vanishing as she stalked out the door.

 **12**

Aya hadn't spent much time in the Synastysi, the most ancient of temples in not just Tala, but all of Eteryium. It was one of the only places of worship to survive the War, and today, it served as home to the most devout of the priestesses and the High Priestess, as well as a historic place to honor the Divine.

It would also be where she was sanctified this evening, it seemed.

Aya could count on one hand the number of services she'd attended at the temple, which sat at the far back of the Relija—the quarter that served as the center of worship in Dunmeaden.

Her mother had always preferred the small dockside temple, with its stained-glass windows and old creaking pews. It was perhaps the only piece of her mother Aya had let herself continue to indulge in after her death.

Aya stared at the square stone structure, which was topped with a dome of granite just a shade lighter than the mountain the building stretched into. Two cylindrical towers stood like guards on either side of the main structure, their iron spires twisting intricately toward the Beyond.

"Come," Hyacinth said as she nodded toward the towering double oak doors. "The priestesses are eager to meet you."

Aya followed Hyacinth into the temple, but Kahn and Lamihr stopped at the doors, turning to stand guard outside. "Weapons are not allowed in the Synastysi," Hyacinth explained, following Aya's gaze as the heavy doors slowly swung shut.

And yet they allow me inside.

The thought was tinged with bitterness as she followed the High Priestess further into the entry hall. The large space was dimly lit with torches, the reflection of their flames flickering across the surface of the shallow rectangular pool in the middle of the room. Evenly spaced around the pool were nine altars, each representing one of the Divine. Aya followed Hyacinth around the pool for the customary worship, kneeling at each altar to thank the Divine for their blessings in the realm. At Saudra's altar, Aya pressed her palm against the rough stone carving of her patron goddess and called her power forward, letting a drop of power seep into the stone like the Persis before her.

It's a symbol of gratitude to our patron divinities, Pa had explained to Aya when she was old enough to make the customary sacrifice. *We pour a piece of ourselves into them, as they did for us Visya by giving us kernels of their power.*

"The priestesses who will assist us are waiting on the second level," Hyacinth murmured as Aya rose from Saudra's altar.

"How many levels are there?" she asked as she followed the Priestess through the entry hall. They entered the worship section of the temple, their footsteps echoing off the cavernous stone walls that were carved from the mountain. Aya glanced up, taking in the two windows set in the mountain face on either side of the pulpit.

To let the light of the Divine shine down on us, Aya remembered her mother saying the first time they'd attended a ceremony here.

Would her mother be watching tonight from the Beyond? Would she be smiling down at her, or would that concerned frown be marring her dark brow as Aya stood before Dunmeaden and proclaimed herself a saint?

"Five," Hyacinth replied as they made their way to the far side of the room, where a small door was carved into the rock. The High Priestess opened it to reveal a wide winding staircase made of stone. "The first floor is open to the public, but the four below are restricted," she explained as she led the way down. "The second and third floors contain a library, offices, and private gathering rooms. The fourth and fifth are living quarters."

The staircase gave onto the center of a large open room with smooth marble floors. Sconces were attached to the rough stone walls, enough that the entire space was bathed in light. As in the Maraciana, there were rows and rows of bookcases separated by small nooks and study areas. But here, Aya could clearly see where the library ended and the offices and private gathering spaces began. That section of the room became a long dark hallway that stretched even further back into the mountain. Aya couldn't see where it ended.

"I didn't know the Synastysi was so large," she remarked as she followed Hyacinth toward that hall.

"Most do not. To see the depths of the Synastysi is a privilege few are granted. The texts kept here are sacred, and some are the only copy in existence," Hyacinth explained. "You will be one of the first to touch them who is not a priestess." Hyacinth stopped at the edge of the library, where a group of three priestesses, each of them dressed in the traditional maroon robes and sheer veils, sat tucked away at a round wooden table. They stood immediately, and Aya shifted awkwardly as they each gave her a small bow.

Hyacinth quickly introduced them, their names flitting out of Aya's mind as quickly as they muttered them. The priestess on Aya's left leaned toward her, a soft smile on her face. "It is an honor to meet you," the priestess said. Her eyes shone with reverence as she placed a hand on her chest. "We thank the Divine morning and night for sending you to us."

Aya swallowed, her brain scrambling to come up with something to say in response. "Thank you," she finally said. She cringed at how it sounded more like a question, but the priestess didn't seem to care.

"As I mentioned in our meeting with the queen," Hyacinth said as she paced around the table, "I have gathered some of our most trusted Saj who study the righteous law and word of the Divine to help guide your studies and training, and to answer any questions you may have. Most of the ancient texts are in the Old Language, and they are working on translating as many as they can."

Aya tilted her head as she studied the piles and piles of books between them. The leather covers were faded, the bindings worn and fragile. The Old Language was the language of the gods, given to the Visya in addition to the language of the humans. It had mostly faded after the Great War once the Visya were scattered, but some families still taught it to their children.

"There's no need," Aya said softly, trailing a finger across one of the diaries. "I speak it."

For some reason, seeing Hyacinth's surprised blink filled Aya with a petty sort of pleasure. Aya had been the one caught off guard since she arrived. It felt good to finally throw someone else off-kilter.

Hyacinth recovered quickly. "Excellent! Then we can spend our time searching the archives for additional reports of Evie and the gods that may prove helpful. You'll study here with us, splitting your time between the texts and training with me."

Aya kept her face blank. She didn't want Hyacinth to see the unease that was choking her.

I will be watched every moment of every day. A prisoner—I'm no better than a prisoner.

A prisoner.

A puppet.

A pawn.

Aya supposed the title didn't matter. The outcome was the same.

"And tonight?" she asked.

Hyacinth gave her a kind smile. "There is nothing to fear about tonight's ceremony. As it is the first of its kind, we suspect any formality will bring our people peace. In the same way you honored Saudra upon entering the temple, you will honor all Nine of the Divine."

Aya blinked. She supposed she *should* present her power to each of the Nine, given it now encompassed all of the affinities. But Aya had spent her entire life believing Saudra was watching over her; guiding her whenever she used her persuasion. She did not welcome the thought of abandoning her patron goddess so publicly.

Besides, in their studies in Rinnia, Will had discovered that Evie claimed Pathos as her patron god, and that was before the Visya were bound to one of nine affinities. If the First Saint could have a patron divinity, then Aya didn't see why she couldn't as well.

But she didn't press Hyacinth on it. She merely nodded, her eyes scanning the ancient texts on the table. "Is that all?"

"There will be some recitation from the Conoscenza. And after your ceremony, we'll have a celebration in the center of the Relija," Hyacinth explained, referring to the main square that sat at the center of the religious quarter. "It will be a chance for those who cannot attend the ceremony to pay their respects to their saint."

Aya's mouth went dry, a vision of Evie's altar from the Dawning coming to mind. Would they make her stand before their citizens? Let people fall to their knees before her, as if she deserved such praise?

"And for you to display your power," Hyacinth added.

Aya's chin jerked up, her gaze as sharp as her tone as she stared at the High Priestess. "What?"

"People will need some proof, Aya, that you are who you say you are. It does not need to be a large display. Something similar to what you showed Queen Gianna is perfectly fine. Only..." Her voice trailed off, the first signs of hesitation showing on her face.

"Only what?" Aya gritted out. She could just make out the splotches of red on Hyacinth's cheeks as the High Priestess fiddled with her sleeves.

"Perhaps you can display light, like you did when you first showed your power."

Aya stared at the woman, her body tense. Surely the High Priestess was not referring to the time she'd uncontrollably burst into light to save Tova, striking four guards dead in the span of a single breath.

Hyacinth at least had the courtesy to look sheepish, her fingers twining together as she clasped her hands in front of her. "It sends a message, Aya. That you have come to defeat the darkness."

Aya's jaw clenched. Her fingers brushed the empty holster at her thigh, instinctively searching for the worn handle of her knife, for a touch that would ground her as the floor seemed to ripple beneath her. Hyacinth took advantage of her silence, recovering quickly as she pressed on. "The ceremony will take place at dusk. That gives you a few hours to refresh yourself. You're welcome to use my quarters on the third floor."

Aya thought she might be sick. "I didn't bring any clothes."

Hyacinth waved her off. "I've taken care of everything. Tova will be here later to help you get dressed."

The words had Aya drawing up short.

Had Tova known? Had she known about this ceremony and said nothing to her?

"Any other instructions?" she finally managed, all too aware of how carefully the priestesses were watching her.

"No," Hyacinth said calmly, looking around the table. The other priestesses shook their heads. "Come. I'll escort you to my chambers."

It's fine if she knew. Tova has every right to be angry. To be reserved.

And even though Aya kept repeating the silent assurance as she followed Hyacinth, it didn't stop the sting of bitterness that settled in her as she wondered, yet again, what else Tova was keeping from her.

13

Waiting for the Sanctification felt something like waiting for the Vaguer to start the Soul Trial in the desert of Trahir. Only this time, instead of being confined to a small clay hut, Aya was hidden away on the second floor of the Synastysi, unable to mark the passage of time due to the windowless halls where she wandered.

She knew they were getting close when Tova arrived to help her get ready. Her friend looked resplendent in a satin dress of dark red, its thin straps and neckline twisting into a deep V where the bodice scrunched. The skirt was floor-length, with a long slit up one side.

The gown Hyacinth had picked for Aya, on the other hand, was far more subtle. It was long, with flowing sleeves that widened at her wrists and a bodice that cinched at her waist. The fabric was a pale gray, with a subtle sheen that caught when the light hit it.

Tova frowned at it, her head cocked to the side as she looked over Aya's shoulder in the floor-length mirror. "It's not very you," she remarked.

Aya merely shrugged, her throat already too tight to

express that she wasn't particularly sure what constituted *her* anymore—or if Tova would even recognize it.

She didn't bother to ask Tova if she had known about the ceremony. She wasn't sure she wanted to hear the answer.

"Will Danté be accompanying you to the celebration after?" Aya asked instead, shooting Tova a suggestive smile that felt tight on her lips. The merchant had been smitten with Tova when Aya had last seen him at the Dawning festival. But Aya's grin faded just as quickly as it came as Tova stiffened behind her.

"No," she said softly. "Danté didn't wish to resume our relations once I was released."

Aya felt as though she'd been doused in cold water. She turned from the mirror, her brow furrowed as she looked at her friend. "Even though he knows the truth of your innocence now?"

Tova lifted a shoulder, her face solemn as she brushed her hands down her dress. "It doesn't replace the months he spent not knowing it."

An awkward silence settled between them, interrupted only by a priestess coming to fetch Tova away.

Aya wished she'd asked Tova to stay. Because as she stood in the stone stairwell a short time later, listening to the murmurs of the crowd, a low rumble like thunder as they entered the Synastysi's worship hall, she could feel her breath shortening as the reality of what was about to occur set in.

Not right. This is not right.

"Ready?" Hyacinth smiled back at her, her head nodding toward the shut door.

No. Aya wasn't ready. Aya would never be ready for this. But she nodded anyway as she followed Hyacinth up the winding stairwell and into the worship hall. A hush fell over the crowd, hundreds of faces staring at her, mere smears of beige and brown and gold and black, like paint on one of Josie's canvases. Her friend would laugh at all of this. Would roll her eyes and wave her hand in that unbothered way that Aya would never be able to channel.

Aya forced herself to swallow and her gaze to sharpen.

The cavernous space flickered with dim firelight from the torches burning on the walls and the candles set on a large wrought-iron chandelier that hung in the center of the mountain slope of a ceiling.

Was Pa here?

Had he come to witness his daughter be proclaimed something she'd never thought she'd be?

She tried to find his face among the worshippers, but there were too many stares, too many whispers. So she focused on the front row instead, where Tova and Will sat on either side of Gianna, her guards flanking them. Aya could read the tension in Tova's face as easily as she could see the flashes of her drop earrings in the flickering firelight. Her round jaw was tight, her back ramrod straight as she scanned Aya, then Hyacinth, then the row of priestesses that stood behind them.

Aya risked a glance at Will. He was dressed as he usually was for such events—a fitted black jacket, a white shirt beneath it. Black pants and black boots.

Dunmeaden's Dark Prince, returned home at last.

His posture was loose, relaxed even, as he leaned back against the wooden pew, one arm propped on the back. His face was set in that unfeeling mask that one might even think meant he was bored as his eyes swept the gathering before him. But they paused as they met Aya's, and together, they allowed themselves that small moment, just one breath to find peace in each other before their gazes shifted, Will's roaming the hall and Aya's turning to the High Priestess.

Hyacinth stepped forward and held out her arms, the loose sleeves of her maroon robes draping like wings as she regarded the worshippers. A hush fell over the crowd at the motion.

"Welcome," she called, her voice echoing across the hall.

"Welcome to this most blessed occasion. We have gathered today to witness a miracle of the Divine—proof of the Nine's mercy. For the prophecy of the Second Saint has been fulfilled! A second of her kind has risen, and she has been born anew to right the greatest wrong!" A wave of murmurs rippled through the hall, the cavern amplifying the sound as Hyacinth gestured to Aya. "Her power has been confirmed by the Saj of the Maraciana, those who know godly affinities best. And tonight, you all will see what we have: that she has come to defeat the Decachiré for once and for all."

The crowd voiced their approval, their shouts of praise to the Divine a deafening roar. Aya was grateful for the billowing sleeves of her gown. They allowed her to hide the way she curled her hands into fists to control their shaking. She let her eyes find Will again. He hadn't moved from his lounging position, staying customarily seated with Gianna, even as rows and rows of people stood behind them. But she could see the way his jaw had tightened, the way tension settled in his body as the roars grew louder, a zealous chorus to the Nine.

Hyacinth raised her arms again and the crowd settled, but most stayed on their feet, necks craning to see.

"Just as you have paid respects to your patron gods and goddesses, so too will our Second Saint. Bear witness as she gives back to the Nine who gave to her, while she pledges herself to the Divine and their righteous promise that darkness will reign no more!"

The shouts of praise rose again. Visya worshippers called to their patron gods and goddesses, while humans echoed the names of all Nine Divine. Hyacinth urged Aya forward toward the nine makeshift altars that had been made to replicate the ones outside. They had been planning this for some time, if the carvings were any indication. That, or Gianna had recruited some Zeluus and ordered they work quickly upon hearing of Aya's return.

Aya stood beside Hyacinth, her eyes fixed on the first altar, for Nikatos, the god of war. A rough depiction of his legendary sword was carved into the stone face. She waited for Hyacinth to begin the recitation from the Conoscenza—a typical passage of devotion to the Divine, but adapted for the prophecy and spoken in the Old Language.

Hyacinth began, her voice stronger than Aya had ever heard it as she read the first devotion. Aya closed her eyes and reached into her well, the stirring of her power nothing compared to the pounding of her heart as she pressed her hand against the rock and let a minuscule pulse of her raw power flow into it.

"*Y promentomai,*" Aya responded, the words nearly choked in her throat.

I promise.

It was the same for every Divine. A vow, followed by a promise, an infinitesimal bit of her power flowing into the rock, unseen by the worshippers but felt in the tingling of Aya's skin.

Why not just display my power fully when pledging myself to the gods? Aya had demanded. But Hyacinth would not be swayed. The true proof of her power was to be saved for the particular display they had requested of her.

By the time Aya reached the final altar—Sage, the goddess of wisdom—her mind was buzzing, Hyacinth's words a distant murmur. But she kept her face impassive, leaning into her years of training as she sent that final pulse of power and faced the worshippers once more. The High Priestess raised her hands, her voice ragged with fervor as she led them in a prayer to the gods.

"Praise the knowledge of the Divine, who knew evil might grow once more."

"Praise the mercy of the Divine, who delivered one to us who might finally right that which is wrong."

"Praise the goodness of the Divine, for they have granted us hope and a promised fulfilled."

The crowd almost seemed to swell with every praise Hyacinth shouted, their responses growing louder and louder, made worse by the echoes of the hall.

"Lodaréste tous!"

Praise them!

"Lodaréste tous!"

Praise them!

"Lodaréste tous!"

Praise them!

Aya's control was slipping, her body becoming restless as her desperation to escape grew. She felt dizzy and nauseous, and like her lungs were failing her. Perhaps that's why she nearly lost her footing when Hyacinth grabbed her wrist and tugged her forward. She looked at the High Priestess just in time to see Hyacinth pull a knife from her robes and slash it across Aya's left palm, just above the scar of her blood oath.

Aya couldn't stop the hiss at the sting, the gash far deeper than any she'd made.

They hadn't planned this, hadn't discussed anything like it when Hyacinth had walked through the ceremony. But Hyacinth didn't seem to care. She was lost to her shouts of supplication, and she jerked Aya forward roughly as she yanked up her bleeding palm for all to see.

"The second of her kind pledges herself to the gods and seals her oath with her blood, all for you, those who will uphold the light and dispel the dark!" Hyacinth bellowed.

The worshippers didn't wait for any confirmation from Aya—for any agreement to such a blood oath. The shouts reached a fever pitch, the crowd exalting and stomping as Hyacinth continued to hold Aya's palm up, her grip like a vise around Aya's wrist.

Aya looked toward Will again, but his gaze was fixed on her hand, his eyes following the blood as it streamed from her palm down her exposed arm. He hadn't moved from his position, but his fist was curled, his knuckles white.

"Follow us now!" Hyacinth commanded, dropping Aya's wrist but keeping her arms aloft. Aya locked her jaw, keeping the pain from her face as her hand throbbed. "Follow us into the Relija and bear witness to the miracle of the gods!"

Hyacinth stepped off the platform, the splotches of red on her cheeks and the brightness of her eyes visible beneath her sheer white veil. Aya could feel the priestesses closing in behind her, ushering her forward, but before she could move, Suja appeared at her side and caught her arm, her hold gentle.

The healer covered her palm with her hand, a tingling sensation rippling across Aya's skin as the severed flesh knit together under a soft flare of white healing light. Suja met Aya's gaze, her full lips pursed as her eyes flicked across Aya's face. She squeezed her hand once, the touch so light Aya barely felt it, before gently pushing her forward.

Aya's feet moved of their own accord, the raucous noise of the worshippers swelling over her like a wave. Even so, her heartbeat was louder. It thundered in her ears, her throat constricting with every slam of her pulse as she moved toward the double doors that would take them into the street.

Hyacinth led Aya through the entry hall, and she felt Kahn and Lamihr at her back, their presence oddly settling as the High Priestess pushed through the doors and into the night. Kahn and Lamihr immediately fell into step beside her, their shoulders close enough to brush hers. Aya risked a glance behind them, to where the priestesses followed like a wall of maroon in their robes. Aya could barely see Gianna, Tova and Will, and Gianna's guards behind them.

Those who had come to witness the ceremony were close behind, forming a procession of sorts that spilled out into the already crowded streets of the Relija.

There was a hum of energy that Aya had never witnessed in the religious quarter. It prickled against her skin as they walked, making the hair on the back of her neck rise. She kept her eyes fixed firmly on Hyacinth's back, her focus on putting one foot in front of another. Her mind felt hazy, her thoughts tripping over one another.

As they grew closer to the center of the Relija, Aya made out the steady beat of drums, the rhythm almost in sync with the thundering in her chest.

She had heard the processional before—at the Dawning, marking the beginning of the ceremony that celebrated Evie. Aya had always found it to be a joyous rhythm. But tonight, there was something haunted to it, something dark.

It didn't feel like a Sanctification.

It felt like an execution.

They stepped into the enormous square that marked the heart of the Relija, a towering stone statue with symbols for each of the Nine Divine stretching toward the Beyond at its center. A string quartet sat around the base of the statue with the drummers, their instruments ready for the night of celebration that would follow Aya's demonstration.

On the far side of the large space stood a small raised platform. Hyacinth led Aya through the crowd, nodding to those she passed, her hands skimming a few who reached out to her.

Aya's body buzzed, that familiar numbness settling further into her as she climbed up the stairs after Hyacinth and onto the platform. She scanned the square, watching as it filled with people who seemed to press in from all directions.

The noise in the square grew louder, and Aya's nails bit into her palms as she tried to steady herself. Her mind was blank, her throat tight as she stared out at nothing.

Aya had never been one to enjoy being the center of things.

To be put on display like this, to be so visible...

She wanted to crawl out of her skin.

Wrong. This is wrong.

Hyacinth stepped forward and the drumming stopped, the crowd quieting as she began to speak. She was saying something—exalting the gods once more for the mercy they had bestowed upon them through the prophecy. But her words were a mere humming in Aya's ears as she stared unseeingly at the crowd of people, the sheer number of humans and Visya who had packed themselves into the Relija's main square and surrounding streets to witness this "miracle" overwhelming her entirely.

Her vision blurred.

Where was Tova? And Will?

Was Pa here?

"Breathe," came a low, raspy command. She cut her gaze to her right, to where Galda stood beside her in gray pants, a matching blazer buttoned at her sternum and showing off the black skin of her collarbone. The trainer's dark-brown eyes were fixed forward, her hands clasped behind her back, her full lips pressed in a thin line, but Aya could feel her attention on her. Aya hadn't even seen her arrive. She'd been too lost in her panic, too overwhelmed by all that was occurring.

She could almost feel Galda's displeasure. She had trained Aya herself—had taught her how to not lose herself within her own mind, her own emotions, when it mattered most.

It mattered now.

"Your queen is counting on you," Galda muttered, her lips barely moving.

The words did nothing to soothe her. If anything, they sparked a flame of anger as Aya's jaw clenched, her teeth grinding together.

Her queen was the reason she was standing here like a godsdamn puppet.

She scanned the crowd once more, finding Gianna at the corner of the platform, her guards standing before her on the ground. Her eyes were wide as she nodded along with Hyacinth's praise, her lips moving in uttered worship of her own.

"Watch now!" Hyacinth shouted, her arms spread wide. "Bear witness to the miracle of the gods!"

Hyacinth turned to Aya and motioned for her to come forward. "Show them," she urged. "Show them the light that will banish darkness forever!"

Aya's anger sharpened.

Darkness had not been defeated. The war was still coming, whether Aya had power or not. People would still die. The realm wasn't safe or even *saved* merely because she existed. To act otherwise was the deepest sort of betrayal to these people—the people she had sworn an oath to protect long before the Sanctification. And yet here they were, prostrating themselves before her as if she were one of the gods herself.

The familiar taste of anger coated her tongue and cleared the clouds from her mind, sharpening her focus like a knife as she stepped forward and reached inward toward her well.

Aya had only ever called her power forward in this way in desperation.

In pain.

When she was trying to save Tova, when she was lost to the lull of the visions in the desert with the Vaguer, when she had seen Peter drive that knife into Will and watched him fall to the ground with a note of finality.

And now they were asking her to call forth a weapon and use it as a party trick. Not just to prove to the masses that she had raw power, but to prove it in a way that made a statement. To show her citizens and, through them, the realm that *she* was the one who would abolish the Decachiré for good, even when she didn't know *how*.

A lie.

This entire celebration was a carefully crafted charade. Political posturing disguised as an act of devotion to the gods. And though Hyacinth was at its head, it was Gianna's doing. Aya was certain of that.

Gods, it was selfish. And cruel.

And yet what choice did Aya have? She needed Gianna to trust her. To believe her saint was loyal to her cause through and through.

So Aya opened her arms, sending a gust of wind over the square and extinguishing the torches, plunging the crowd into darkness. Startled cries burst forth, but Aya was already moving, her arms reaching toward the sky as she called her power forth. It zipped across her skin, across the blood that had crusted from where Hyacinth cut her, in webs of bright white light, weaving up her arms as it raced toward where she forced it: up into the sky.

Gianna wanted her to send a message? Fine. Aya would also send one to *her*.

Aya tilted her head back as she poured her power out, and out, and out, the light spearing up again and again, until she was no more than a lightning storm, crackling with energy and fire and a light so bright, it was almost blinding.

Pulse after pulse, flash after flash, her power flowed from her, its crackling sound lost among the growing noise of the crowd.

Slowly, Aya turned her gaze to the queen as shouts rippled across the square, into the side streets and beyond, where others could not see her, but could see her light.

"Deikosi! Deikosi!" they shouted.

Divine. Divine.

Gianna stared at that light, her fingers pressed against her lips.

"Deikosi!"

"Deikosi!"

Aya turned her gaze back to the square as the shouts grew louder. She scanned the faces before her, and this time, she found him immediately, like metal to a magnet. Will stood off to the side, his hands in his pockets.

But unlike the others, he wasn't looking at her power.

He was looking at her.

His eyes bored into hers, his stare fierce in a way she had seen it only once before: in a cave in the desert of Trahir, when he placed her hand over his heart so she could feel the way it pounded in his chest with want.

With longing.

With love.

He'd once called her dangerous. And he had been right.

Aya was not a pawn.

She was a spy.

A warrior.

A weapon.

She held Will's gaze as she sent one more pulse of light into the sky, letting it ripple outward through the square. It shattered the windows of the closest buildings, sending glass cascading down like rain.

14

Will's arm flew up to shield his face as the windows around him exploded. He didn't have time to react, to think about what, if anything, he could do about the falling glass. But as he lowered his arm, his coat sleeve was dusted in a layer of powder, as soft and fine as sand.

Gods. Aya hadn't just exploded the glass. She'd obliterated it.

Utter chaos had never looked more beautiful. It was the only thought Will could conjure after seeing Aya become a living storm, that righteous rage shining in her eyes as glass rained down upon her. It should terrify him—the display she had just made. The consequences she was bringing to herself.

But all he could think was how much he loved her.

Gods, he loved her.

The people were right.

She was divine.

But while there'd been a flash of vicious triumph on her face while she did it, he looked to her now to see that Aya was pale, her eyes widening as she took in the shock of the crowd.

There was a groundswell of noise, a steady roar that dissolved into the chaos of the devout. Some fell to their knees, tears streaming down their faces as they shouted their praises to the gods. Others lunged for Aya, their hands outstretched in a desperate attempt to touch some part of the Second Saint.

Will was moving through the crowd in the next instant. He roughly shouldered through the worshippers, a · chill snaking down his spine as they prostrated themselves before the Divine and before Aya.

"Deikosi! Deikosi! Deikosi! Deikosi!"

The shouts were deafening, even as the string quartet started to play.

Will reached the base of the platform, shoving through the line of Royal Guard and Dyminara who stood at its base, keeping the crowd at bay.

For now.

Aya stood between Hyacinth and the queen, both of whom stared at the worshippers with rapt delight. Gianna's cheeks were flushed, her eyes bright in the torches someone— Aya? Some of the Incends?—had relit.

Will vaulted onto the platform, all too aware of the growing chaos behind him. "Perhaps it's time for Aya to retire," he said over the noise of the crowd. Aya blinked, her hollow gaze focusing on him. He tore his eyes away from her, making a point to address Gianna and Gianna only. "After such a display, I worry about our ability to control the crowd. It would be safest for her to slip away now, before the revelry truly begins."

Whether Hyacinth had intended for Aya to remain at the celebration or not, he didn't know, but he was sure Gianna would not want to risk her precious saint. The queen nodded. "Very well. Will you escort her back, William? Kahn and Lamihr will follow and will remain stationed at the Quarter entrance."

The queen gave Aya a kind smile. "You did marvelously today, Aya."

For a moment, Will was afraid she wouldn't answer. Her face was still bloodless, her eyes distant and lost. But she blinked again, and some of that fog cleared, even though her voice remained flat. Distant. "Thank you, Majesty."

Gianna didn't seem to notice. She merely turned back to the crowd Hyacinth was addressing, the High Priestess shouting some words from the Conoscenza over the music and growing mayhem. Will grabbed Aya's arm and tugged her to the back of the platform. They were down the steps in the next instant, the guards closing rank as they quickly walked toward the back of the square.

"Thank you," she murmured.

Will dipped his chin, his gaze scanning the crowd, but he didn't risk saying another word as they slipped between the tables of refreshments set up for the celebration. He kept his hand on her bicep, steering her through the guards, and sent up silent thanks to Pathos that the crowd was thinner here, and even with those who lingered, there was enough distraction between the shouting and the music and the praise that they were able to make it to the edge of the square without interruption.

But Aya lurched to a stop, the movement so abrupt that Will accidentally yanked her forward.

"What is it?" he asked sharply. There was no threat that he could see, just the last few feet to the street that would take them to the outskirts of the Relija.

Aya didn't respond. She simply stared off to the side, and Will followed her gaze, desperate to see what had caused her to blanch even further.

There was just a table of wine…

No. Not just a table of wine. A man was standing there, a man with olive skin and black hair and a warm expression on his face.

Aya's father.

Will felt Aya trembling beside him, her eyes bright with

unshed tears as she looked at her father. Will glanced behind them. They needed to go, and they needed to go now.

"Aya," he warned as gently as he could.

"I know." She dipped her chin at her father, and he nodded once in return before turning back to the drink table, careful not to bring more attention to his daughter.

They'd barely made it two strides before another figure appeared before them.

"Mathias," Will growled.

It had been months since Will had seen the crime lord, but as Mathias stepped in front of them fully, blocking their path forward, he noted Mathias Denier looked just as he had at the Dawning, down to his silver-threaded black jacket.

"Leaving already?" he asked. He took a step toward Aya, but Will stepped forward, his hand latching onto Mathias's arm.

"Back up," he ordered, a soft promise of violence woven through his tone.

"Easy, Enforcer. I simply came to pay my respects to our *saint*." Mathias slipped into a drawl on the word, his smirk as sharp as his features as he tore his arm from Will's grasp. His silver brows flicked toward his hairline. "I must confess, I was skeptical when I heard the rumors. I thought it no more than drunken diatribes and gambling gossip when Dobbins came babbling to me about you. But seeing this...*spectacle*...tonight..." Mathias chuckled softly. "You might make a believer of me yet."

Aya lifted her chin, her eyes narrowing at the crime lord. "Is there something you want, Mathias?"

Mathias's grin was a slash of white against the dark of the night. "Merely to confess my doubts to the savior of the realm and beg your forgiveness," he answered smoothly. Aya's brow furrowed, her eyes searching his face for some hint of...something. Something that would tell her why he had approached her, what he hoped to gain. If anyone knew that the King of the Crooks did not waste his words, that every syllable was as curated as his clothing, designed to distract, mislead, or in rare cases, inform, it was Aya.

But Mathias merely sighed, picking a piece of lint from his sleeve as he gazed off in the distance toward the refreshments.

"Though I suppose you cannot blame me too harshly. Even those closest to us can surprise us."

His gaze returned to her, and there was something in the smile he gave her that made Will reach for the blade sheathed at his hip. But then Mathias was stepping aside in the next moment, giving them a dramatic bow before strolling off into the night.

"What the hells," Aya breathed.

Will shook his head. "Not now."

Because Kahn and Lamihr were behind them, and the crowd was growing, and they needed to leave before he truly lost control of this situation. "Let's go."

Aya didn't argue.

15

AYA COULD FEEL WILL'S GAZE FLICKING TO HER EVERY SO often as they walked back to the Quarter. But he remained silent, walking close enough that she could feel the warmth of him against her arm, as if he knew that numbness was spreading and his subtle heat was the only thing tethering her here.

What have I done?

The words were a steady refrain in her mind that echoed in time to the heartbeat that pulsed through her like the drums she swore she could still hear, even as they passed through the palace gates.

The celebration would likely to last until dawn.

What have I done?

People would be praising, and shouting, and prostrating themselves in the name of a saint who did not know what the gods asked of her, who was no closer to solving the prophecy than she was when she'd first burst into light in the city's Artist Market.

What have I done?

Aya could feel her composure starting to crack as they rounded the bend and stepped into the clearing for the

Quarter. Her control was slipping, that numbness spreading throughout. She tried to retreat into her mind, but it brought no relief. She could count and breathe and name what she saw as much as she wanted, but nothing silenced the thoughts ravaging about in her conscience.

What have I done?

She had made it worse with her display of power; with the way she'd let anger take control, her fury at Gianna. In doing so, she had furthered that same hope that she was disgusted with Gianna for giving in the first place.

No better... She had acted no better than her queen.

Aya was hardly aware that they'd made it inside the Quarter and up the stairs. But suddenly, Will's hand was in hers, and he was pulling her gently to her room.

It was dark inside, the light spilling in from the hall casting long shadows as Aya walked to her fireplace. Her body felt weak, a tingling sensation weighing down her limbs. But she lifted her hand anyway, forcing her mind to focus as she reached toward that seemingly endless well of power within her to light a fire.

Will's hand was on her arm in the next moment, his fingers gently curling her hand closed as he lowered it to her side. He walked to the mantel, grabbing a box of matches, and lit a fire in the grate himself. Aya watched numbly as he walked around her room, lighting the various candles until the space was basked in a glow that should have felt comforting, but for some reason, Aya couldn't quite access the feeling.

Any feeling.

Will closed her bedroom door, his footsteps the only sound aside from the crackling fire as he walked back toward her and took her face in his hands. For a moment, he simply held her, his thumbs stroking her cheeks, eyes boring into hers as if he could see straight into her soul.

"Tell me what you're feeling," he finally rasped.

Aya swallowed, her unformed words heavy on her

tongue, as if her mouth wasn't the right shape for speaking. "Nothing," she murmured.

She felt nothing.

Not comfort.

Not relief.

Not even anger or guilt, even though she knew it was brewing somewhere inside her, somewhere she could not reach, not now.

Will didn't seem fazed by her response. He kissed her softly, only for a moment, before taking her hand again and leading her into her bathing chamber, where he pushed her down gently on the edge of the tub. Then he grabbed a washcloth from her sink and ran it beneath the faucet before he crouched down before her and took her left hand in his.

"I thought I might kill her," he confessed quietly as he started to wipe away the blood that had dried on her palm. "I didn't care that she was the High Priestess, or that we were in the Synastysi in front of hundreds of people. When she cut you like that, I thought I might kill her."

He brushed his thumb over the scar of their oath to each other before slowly pushing up her sleeve with a gentleness that was so at odds with the rage that flickered in his eyes as they tracked the streaks of blood that had crusted on her skin. His fingers trailed over them lightly, leaving goose bumps in their wake. He followed the path of his fingers with the cloth, his brow furrowed as he washed the red from her skin.

Suddenly, Aya was back in her chambers in Rinnia, on another night she'd been covered in dirt and blood. Will had taken care of her then, just as he did now. Had let her sit in silence as she ruminated over what Dominic had told her that night—that her queen had offered her up in marriage to his nephew in exchange for an alliance.

Will hadn't pressed her, hadn't forced her to speak. He'd merely wiped the grime from her skin, soothing her in the ways he knew how to until she had the words to express what was roiling inside of her.

Aya covered his hand with hers, stilling the washcloth and drawing his gaze up to her face. His eyes were that storm-colored gray, a hurricane of emotions reflected in his irises.

"I can't do this," she croaked, her throat raw. "I can't... I will only disappoint them. When they learn that I can't save them, I will only disappoint them."

Will considered her for a long moment. "No one could ever think you a disappointment, Aya love." Slowing, as if he were afraid of startling her, he moved a hand to her cheek, his thumb swiping against her skin. "You're magnificent." His lips brushed the pulse point of her throat, and Aya let her head tilt back, let him bleed warmth into her as he murmured against her skin. "Strong." Another kiss, this time beneath her ear. "Beautiful."

His hand shifted into her hair, and he drew her forehead against his. "You're a godsdamned gift that none of us deserve. And yet selfishly, I keep letting myself believe I can have you."

Aya let out a shaky breath, her hand moving to the base of his neck, her fingers threading into his hair. There was a desperation burning inside of her, one she hadn't known before him. And while it had simmered in her for weeks now, tonight it seared her very veins.

Perhaps it was the thought of something ruining *this*—the thought of them finding each other only to not have a life together—that terrified her.

So much had threatened it already. So much that they still hadn't sorted through.

But she didn't care. Not tonight.

She wanted him.

Perhaps that made her selfish, too.

"Then have me," Aya breathed as she closed that last sliver of distance between them, savoring the warmth of his lips on hers and the way it seemed to spread throughout her as she kissed him softly.

Slowly.

The washcloth fell into the tub with a wet smack as Will's hand moved to the small of her back, steadying her as he deepened their kiss. He nipped at the seam of her lips, and Aya opened for him, a soft moan escaping her as his tongue tangled with hers. Her legs wrapped around his waist, and Will hoisted her off the tub easily. Her back hit the wall in the next instant, his fingers digging into her thighs as he kissed her like a man who was suffocating, and she was his air.

Aya's hands reached for the lapels of his jacket, yanking the fabric off his shoulders. He kept one arm on her, his body pinning hers to the wall as he helped her slide his jacket off the other. It was mere seconds until his other arm was free, and then Aya's fingers were undoing the buttons of his shirt as he licked and nipped and sucked his way down her neck. Will let out a sharp breath as her nails dragged lightly down the bare skin of his chest, and before Aya could blink, she was off the wall, his strides quick and smooth as he brought her to her bed, where he laid her down with a tenderness that had her breath catching.

Will paused, his arms bracketing her head on the mattress as he hovered above her. His shirt hung open, his hair mussed, the flecks in his eyes looking like green sparks in the light of the candles he'd lit around her room. He stood slowly, his fingers bunching in the skirt of her dress, his eyes never leaving hers as he pushed the fabric up at a glacial pace. The slow brush of the fabric and his fingers against her sensitive skin had her writhing, her fingers digging into the mattress as she lifted her hips. Will chuckled, mischief glinting his eyes as he nodded at her to sit up.

"Arms up," he ordered.

Aya raised her arms, her teeth digging into her lip as Will's thumbs skimmed the undersides of her breasts as he pushed the fabric over her chest, then her head, finally, *finally* letting it drop to the floor.

For a moment, he simply stood there, his eyes scanning her body, the hunger on his face making her stomach tighten with need. Aya reached up, her hand cupping his face. She pulled his lips down to hers, her hands pushing his shirt off his shoulders. She heard the rustle of the fabric hitting the floor, the shuffle of his boots following. And then her hands were on his belt, tugging the leather out of its loops and dropping it on to the floor. Soon there was nothing at all between them but feverish skin and desperate touches as Will hoisted Aya further up the bed, his hands memorizing every inch of her they could reach.

"Fuck," he muttered, his lips moving down her chest. He slid a hand down her stomach, his finger swirling against that sensitive spot between her legs as he licked and sucked at her sensitive flesh. Aya's hips bucked at his touch, a desperate whimper leaving her as he slid two fingers into her.

"*Fuck*," he rasped again, his lips pressing into hers.

He didn't kiss her. He devoured her.

"I swear this isn't what—" He cut himself off with a groan as Aya moved against his hand.

Aya's eyes nearly rolled back into her head with pleasure. "Please, gods, don't stop," she whimpered.

Will chuckled, the sound dark and seductive as he grinned down at her. "*Will* is a perfectly acceptable way to address me, love," he murmured, his fingers curling until they hit that spot that had her breath coming in short gasps.

Aya moaned, her fingers digging into his arms. "Fuck you," she snapped back, but the words were breathy and desperate.

Will laughed again, his thumb brushing that spot between her thighs lightly. "Is that a request?" he asked as he continued to tease her there. Aya bit her lip, her back arching as pleasure raked through her.

Gods, this was unlike anything she'd felt before. Her skin was flushed and tight, the pleasure of his touch seeming to stretch through her entire body.

She put a hand on his wrist, and Will stilled, his fingers leaving her immediately. "What is it?" he asked, his brow furrowed. "Did I—"

"Yes," she cut him off, her chest heaving. She swallowed, trying desperately to catch her bearings. "Yes, it's a request."

Will stared at her for a moment, and she thought he might be the most beautiful thing she'd ever seen with his swollen lips, his flushed face, his mussed hair. "Are you sure?" he rasped, all trace of teasing gone from his face. His body stayed still, his muscles trembling, as if it took every bit of his control to restrain himself.

As if he couldn't believe she truly wanted him.

She supposed she had instilled that doubt in him just last night.

Aya's fingers found his left hand and she lifted it to her lips, pressing a kiss against the scar of their oath. "Undoubtedly," she whispered as she placed his hand on her hip.

Will let out a shuddering breath, his palm skimming down the side of her leg, fingers digging into her flesh as he hooked her leg around his waist. Aya bit back a moan at the feeling of the tip of him against her opening. Her grip tightened on the back of his neck, but she resisted the urge to tilt her hips and take him inside her.

She kept her eyes locked on his as she said, "I want you."

It was the last bit of confirmation he needed.

Will slid into her, and Aya's eyes fluttered shut, a low moan escaping her as he filled her.

"Fuck, Aya," Will groaned, his head falling against hers as he pushed in further. He stilled once he was in to the hilt, his heart a thunderous beat against her chest. "You feel incredible."

And he felt perfect.

Aya rolled her hips, and Will hissed in pleasure.

His fingers dug into her hip as he pulled out slowly, the drag of him inside of her pulling a breathy noise out of Aya that made him grin. He thrust back in, harder this time, his kiss muffing his moan.

Slowly, they built a steady rhythm together, each thrust of his hips met with a roll of hers. His lips found her neck again, his muttered words half lost against her skin.

"Waited so long…"

"Like you were made for me…"

"Better than I ever…"

Aya tugged his head up, desperate to feel his lips on hers. But he withheld his kiss, the flecks of green flaring in the gray of his irises as he snapped his hips harder, her body trembling with the pleasure he wrung from her with every thrust.

And gods, the way he was looking at her…

It obliterated every wall she'd ever built, destroyed every barrier she'd ever put between them as he thrust into her again. Again. Again.

Will pressed a tender kiss to her mouth as he rolled his hips once more.

Aya gasped, her back arching. The pleasure inside of her was building, pulling so tight she swore that when it snapped, she'd break with it. It intensified with every thrust of Will's hips, his motions sharp and hard, as if he knew the exact way to pull the most ecstasy from her body.

"Will," she panted, his name the only word her mouth could form. She said it over and over as he brought them barreling toward that cliff.

"Magnificent."

"Strong."

"Beautiful."

Each word was murmured against her skin as he wound her tighter and tighter. The tightness inside her snapped, and Aya let out a hoarse cry as her body shuddered around him, pleasure coursing through her in waves so big, she thought she might drown in them. Will continued moving, dragging every bit of that blessed feeling from her as he held her through it.

And then he followed her over that edge, his body stilling, a choked-off groan tearing from his throat as he came.

Will dropped his head on her shoulder, his warm breaths tickling her skin as they fought to catch their breath. Aya dragged her fingers into the back of his hair, the strands damp, as she let herself melt beneath him, the tension bleeding from her bones.

He lifted his head, that tender happiness that he rarely showed the world on his face, and like a prayer to the gods themselves, he whispered one final sentiment.

"*Divine.*"

16

I T WAS RARE THAT WILL AWOKE AND WONDERED IF HE'D DIED and ended up in the Beyond. Mostly, he thought of the seven hells, convinced as he was that his actions had earned him an eternal sentence in its layers.

But as he opened his eyes to see Aya's head resting on his chest, her dark hair fanned out across her bare back, legs tangled with his, he could conjure up no other explanation.

Because this...this was heaven.

No. This is real.

He ran his fingers through her hair, her body warm and soft against his as he tugged her closer. The need to feel her, to touch her, to prove that this wasn't some cruel dream given to him by the gods was almost overwhelming.

This is real.

His fingers skimmed the small of her back, his lips whispering across the top of her head. A thousand mornings like this wouldn't be enough for him to get used to the feeling of her naked body pressed against his, to the fact that she was *here*, in *his* arms, her lips having been pressed against *his* skin.

Aya shifted slightly, and those lips brushed his chest as she muttered, "I can hear you thinking."

Will grinned down at the top of her head. One morning—it had only been one morning since he'd heard the husk in her voice that lingered after she slept. He hadn't realized how much he missed it.

"Would you care to know *what* I was thinking?" Will drawled, his fingers tracing circles as they trailed down her spine. Aya lifted her head, and the quiet joy in her blue eyes made his entire world go still.

Her lips tipped up into a small smirk, her hand trailing down, down, until he was biting back a groan as her fingers wrapped around his already stiff arousal. "I'd rather you show me."

And so he did.

It was still relatively early by the time Will left Aya's room to bathe and change his clothes. He was pulling a black sweater from his armoire when there was a knock on the door, her head peeking in moments later.

"I figured you needed help with that ointment Suja made."

"You putting it on would be far more effective than me," he admitted.

Aya frowned, her head tilting to the side as he grabbed the balm and sat on the bed. "How have you been managing without me?"

"I haven't."

She shot him a look, her brow furrowed as she snatched the tin from his hand, murmuring something about his character he chose not to hear. But her touch was gentle as she laid a hand on his shoulder, pushing him forward slightly so she could reach the expanse of the scars.

"How does it feel?"

Will shifted under her touch. "Tender." He tilted his head to meet her gaze as he gave her a wry grin. "I may have overextended myself."

She rolled her eyes, but a smile pulled on her lips regardless. Will inhaled sharply as she prodded a particularly sensitive area. "What happened after you left Suja's yesterday?" Aya murmured, her thumb coasting across his shoulder in soothing strokes, as if to help with the pain.

Will's jaw shifted. He had been dreading this conversation.

"I spoke with Tova." Aya's hand paused on his back, and something churned in his stomach. But he forced himself to look her in the eye as he continued. "It's safe to say she's not keen to forgive me. It's just as you said: she acted like we never had that conversation in the dungeons." Aya's face was unreadable, and it was enough to have Will nervously stammering on. "I should have told you last night. Before we—"

"No," Aya interjected, her gaze sharpening. "Gods, Will, that's not... I'm just... Why is she lying? If she *didn't* tell Gianna anything, what's the point in pretending you two didn't even speak?"

Will shrugged, something hollow still lingering somewhere behind his sternum. "Tova has always been headstrong. She's angry, and she has every right to be. Perhaps she'd just rather believe I'm horrid through and through. Maybe it's easier to hate me that way." The words felt as heavy as they sounded when he spoke them.

"And Gianna?"

Will tried not to shift as Aya began smoothing the ointment over his scars once more. "Gianna seems more than willing to put her anger aside. Which leads me to believe Tova truly didn't tell her anything. If she had...well, one of us—Tova or me—would be dead."

"Her forgiveness came too easily," Aya murmured. Of course Aya would say that. It was her job to read people, and Aya didn't always need to be in the room to do it. Will made a noise of agreement, carefully turning his next words over.

"It did. But she's redoubling her efforts to search for the

supplier who was willing to trade with Kakos, and she wants me involved."

Aya frowned. "I thought Lena was leading that charge."

"I *am* still her Second, you know," he countered. Even if Lena seemed keen on edging both him *and* Aya out of the positions that kept them close to their queen. Aya squeezed his shoulder harder than he deserved, a whisper that sounded awfully like *ass* leaving her in a huff.

"Why double her efforts in it now?" Aya pressed.

Will drummed his fingers on the bedspread. "I don't pretend to know the inside of Gianna's mind. But I plan to find out. She's given me the perfect opportunity to do so by involving me in the investigation."

There was more to tell her—gods, there was more to tell her about what Gianna had tasked him with, and he had promised himself that he would after the Sanctification, but the words were lodged somewhere in his throat, held there by the memory of Aya's shaking voice in the healing quarters.

Tell me you did not do this.

Aya placed a tender kiss on his shoulder, drawing him from his thoughts. "I had the same thought this morning about the Synastysi."

Will's hands found her waist, tugging her to stand before him as he gazed up at her. "And here I thought you'd hate the orders to study with the priestesses."

"I do," Aya retorted darkly. "But reviewing the texts could help me learn about the veil. If it's truly damaged, like Lorna thinks, perhaps I could repair it."

The thought made something in Will's chest tighten. Toying with the veil had killed Evie. He loathed to think of Aya interacting with it at all.

"Aya…" he started to argue, but she merely pressed on.

"I have a favor to ask of you."

Will hesitated for only a moment.

Later, he supposed. They could discuss this later.

"Anything."

She bit her lip, her eyes darting across his face, unsure of herself in a way she didn't often show. "Would you come see my father with me?"

Will blinked. Of all the requests he expected her to make, it wasn't this. She must have felt the way his hands stiffened on her hips, because Aya rushed on, her fingers fiddling with the sleeve of her dark-blue sweater. "I know we agreed to keep this between us, but I don't want to go alone, and I–I want him to meet you." Her eyes flicked up to his. That quiet joy still lingered in her irises. "To know you."

Will swallowed, his fingers flexing on her hips. "Will he not be…concerned, that you're with me?" he asked, hesitation written in each of his words. Aya frowned, and Will sucked in a steadying breath. "I am the queen's Enforcer. My reputation is one most parents would find unsavory. And it is not entirely undeserved."

Aya's frown deepened, that light in her eyes vanishing as something like determination replaced it. She cupped his face, forcing his gaze to stay fixed on hers as she said, "I choose you. There is not a single part of you that I don't choose. Not one."

It was instinct to lean in to that familiar crutch—to mask his uncertainty, his insecurity, with insolence. But his smirk felt forced as he drawled, "I believe you've used the word *insufferable* quite frequently to describe me."

Aya didn't give in to it—not this time. She didn't smile, or roll her eyes, or even snap back. She merely stepped closer, nothing but unwavering truth on her face. "And I choose you."

Why?

The question unsettled him as it came roaring to the front of his thoughts, as if it had been fighting to break free from the depths of his subconscious. As if he already knew what was about to change between them. But as Aya kissed him, his mind went blissfully blank, his sole focus the feel of her lips against his.

His fingers tangled in the thick strands of her hair, and *gods* he would've said yes to anything she asked of him in this moment.

After. I'll tell her after. Because that soft joy was back in her face as she pulled away and gave him a smile edged with mischief.

"We're sneaking out the window, though. I don't want any guards following."

Will barked a laugh.

"Whatever you say, love."

Aya's childhood home was a small farmhouse that stood alone in a vast field, a wooden fence separating it from the path they walked. Will could just make out the neighboring homes in the distance, dotting the valley like the cyclamen that spread between them.

Aya squeezed his hand, her other hand reaching for the gate. "Ready?"

He had a feeling the question was more for her than it was for him. Because the closer they'd gotten to the farmlands, the quieter she had become, that *V* appearing between her brows just as it always did when she started to lose herself to the endless thoughts in her head. Will squeezed her hand back.

"It's going to be fine."

She nodded, the motion tight and stiff, but she pushed through the gate anyway, leading them up the path that would take them to the front door.

Aya stilled just before they stepped on to the front porch, the pale-blue paint chipped and peeling. Her hand went slack in his, and for a moment, Will thought that perhaps she'd changed her mind. He turned to reassure her once more, but her gaze was fixed on a patch of flowers that lined the porch, their stems broken and crooked, as if they'd been stomped on. A few of the petals littered the soil, and Aya stared at them, her body going as rigid as a board.

"What is it?" Will asked, his brow furrowing. Aya didn't answer. She merely pulled her hand from his and reached for her knife, her face pale as she scanned the front of the house. Tension radiated from her, thickening the air until he could feel it pressing against his skin.

"Aya?"

"Something's wrong," she muttered, already heading toward the front door. He stayed a step behind her, his own body stiffening as he drew his knife. "The flowers... Pa's a Terra... He cares for his garden like it's his child..." Her voice trailed off, her face set in concentration as she pushed the door open.

Will tensed as they stepped into a small sitting room, his eyes sweeping the space. The walls were a faded yellow, the furniture worn but in a comforting way. For a moment, Will could almost envision what Aya would have looked like in their younger years, curled up in the leather armchair by the stone hearth, a carving knife in her hand.

He took another look around the room. Nothing was out of place—at least from what he could tell. He cut a glance to Aya, watching as her shoulders dropped slightly, a breath leaving her lungs in a whoosh. "Pa?" she called. She frowned at the silence that greeted them, her head cocking as she glanced up at Will. "I thought he'd be here."

Will scanned the room again, the skin on the back of his neck prickling. His body was still tensed, as if waiting for an attack. He paused as his gaze landed on the small kitchen. He could only see part of it from where he stood—just the stone floor, the edge of a table, one of the wooden chairs. The chair was skewed, as if someone had pushed it aside in haste. Will started toward the kitchen without another word. He could feel Aya behind him, could feel her energy shift back into that place they'd grown far too used to—the suspicion. The dread.

The dread only worsened as he stepped into the kitchen fully.

It was spotless. The copper pans were stacked neatly in the sink, a towel resting on the countertop, as if her father had just finished doing the dishes. A mug of tea sat on the old table that bore more signs of life than most people Will knew.

It was spotless.

Except for the blood.

He reached out his arm to block Aya, as if he could save her from the hurt awaiting her. But she was too fast, and they had been too *slow*, and the next thing Will knew, she was ducking under his arms and crashing to her knees, a broken wail that Will could feel in his very bones echoing through the kitchen.

Because there, on the floor, was Aya's father—lying in a puddle of his own blood.

PART TWO

The Rotting of Flesh

 17

THE WESTERN CLIFFS OF RINNIA WERE BATHED IN SUNLIGHT, making the rocks sparkle as though diamonds hid within them. The alcove, set a fourth of the way up the cliffs, gave a perfect view of the half-moon bay and eastern cliffs rising above it, that sandstone palace a blinding beige in the bright light.

It would be a gorgeous view if it weren't for the gallows.

The old wooden structure was angled so it ran parallel to the eastern cliffs. *So the spirits of the seven hells could claim them upon the first rising of the moon,* Aidon had once heard a priestess say.

He was fairly certain the gallows were constructed here to keep the executed baking in the hot sun for as long as possible. To quicken the rot and bring forth the bones.

But no sun would be hot enough to decay the bodies before the coronation tomorrow. What a ghastly backdrop the dead would make.

Deceiver. Usurper. Murderer.

A hand, warm and soft, rested on his arm, drawing his attention away from the looming structure. Aidon glanced to his right to see his sister's concerned face. "I'd ask how you are," Josie murmured. "But I know it would be a waste of words."

They had an unspoken agreement anyway, it seemed. To put on brave faces. To bury themselves in their duties. To pretend they weren't both screaming on the inside, both reeling from their uncle's betrayal.

But the signs were there. Aidon could see it clearly in his sister.

It showed in the hollowness in her cheeks. In the way her dress—a modest black thing—hung loosely on her frame, the fullness of her figure beginning to whittle away. In the way her brown skin had darkened just beneath her eyes.

Aidon swallowed, his arms twining behind his back. "I'm fine," he muttered in response to the question she wouldn't ask.

He had to be fine. *They* had to be fine. Because their kingdom was not.

Deceiver. Usurper. Murderer.

News of Dominic's treason had spread far and wide these last three weeks, and yet, even in Rinnia, there were those who doubted.

Doubted his uncle's partnership with Kakos.

Doubted the existence of the Second Saint.

Doubted Aidon had any agenda other than ascending the throne prematurely.

And yet as Aidon stared at the half-moon beach, a crowd beginning to form there, he couldn't help but notice that despite the whispers that followed him, many were eager to participate in today's activities.

It sends a message, his mother had said after Aidon returned from another particularly long interrogation with one of the treasonous guards who had sided with Dominic. *It should take place before your coronation, so we can celebrate the change in Trahir. A true king at last.*

But he wasn't a true king. And not because he'd ascended

the throne far earlier than any of them anticipated, but because he was breaking the holiest of laws. He was occupying a seat the Nine Divine had expressly forbidden his kind from taking.

Visya weren't allowed to rule, not after the War. It was an ordinance that hadn't been broken in over five hundred years, and yet here Aidon was, shattering it like glass.

His people didn't know it, but Aidon did. And it left a bitter taste in his mouth, especially as the threat of war with Kakos drew closer. There was already little tolerance for heretics, and Aidon didn't fancy being looped in with the likes of Kakos for disobeying the gods in this way.

"Things would be so much easier had Aya and Will stayed," Aidon muttered. "Our people wouldn't question us so much."

Josie made a noncommittal sound. "Perhaps. Or perhaps they'd want to see her hanged as well." The thought of Aya's corpse dangling from the gallows made Aidon's stomach turn. He was already haunted enough by the lingering visions of him slamming that blade into her chest.

In his nightmares, she never woke up.

"I miss her," Aidon admitted quietly. Not in any sort of romantic way. Perhaps they could have grown to love each other in time, but…no. He had been certain of his decision there. Had not once regretted choosing something for himself, just this once. But he still longed for her company as a friend. As someone who understood, even in the smallest ways, what it was like to be different.

"So do I," Josie agreed.

Even so, she had a point. His people had not witnessed any of it: not Dominic's betrayal, nor Aya's power. Already, there were grumblings about Tala's interference, enough that Aidon knew he had an uphill battle ahead of him in getting his people behind lending their support in the war.

He felt Josie's eyes on him, but he couldn't bring himself

to look at her. He was too raw, too close to not being able to keep his composure.

And, gods, did he need his composure.

"It does not matter if they believe in her," Josie said quietly. "It's you they need to believe in. It's you they'll ultimately follow into battle."

And yet his own sister hadn't even believed in him, had she? Josie swore that she didn't hold Aidon at fault for what had happened to Viviane, and that she understood what he'd tried to do. What he'd tried to stop.

And yet…

She'd immediately rejected his offer of becoming his Second-in-Command without a moment's hesitation, or reasoning, or even an excuse.

I'm honored, Aidon. But the answer is no.

A priestess came up beside him, drawing his attention away from the beach and Josie. The woman was young, her white robes fluttering in the breeze. For a wild moment, Aidon wanted to ask her if *this* is what she'd expected when she took her vows to the Divine.

Overseeing executions. Leading the rare coronation. It was the extent of a priestess's celebrity in a kingdom where the Old Customs of honoring the gods were considered outdated.

"The prisoners are beginning their procession, Majesty," she said quietly, her chin jutting toward the beach.

He hadn't needed her to alert him to it. He could already hear the swell of noise that came from Old Town. Citizens had been lining the main thoroughfare that stretched all the way toward the western cliffs—toward the gallows—all morning.

The Procession of Penance, they called it. A chance for those who had committed the most atrocious of crimes to meet their misery at the hand of those they'd wronged before their execution.

More like a trail of torment.

Aidon had stood in that virulent crowd only once. Had watched as the City Guard struggled to hold the line—to keep the chaos contained to curses and spitting and the occasional throwing of rotten food. Those who managed to break free— to get their hands on a prisoner—talked about it for ages. As though it was a point of pride.

Those that couldn't join the procession, whether from the crowds or some other obstacle, took to the beach to witness the execution. There was debate on which role was better.

It was barbaric.

And yet...

Duty.

Responsibility.

Loyalty.

Aidon owed his people this, did he not? He had taken away their chance to bring his uncle to justice. He had wielded a sword on behalf of his kingdom, and in doing so, he had denied thousands their retribution.

And so they shall have it.

Aidon glanced to where his mother and father stood on the other side of the gallows. Their faces were solemn as they gazed toward the procession, not that they could see much of it from here. Aidon had been surprised his father was willing to stand up here at all. What was it that Enzo had said when he stepped down as Lead Councillor?

My presence will only bring you more strife, Son.

Aidon had almost laughed. As if Enzo's abandonment hadn't left yet *another* hole for Aidon to fill—a task he'd complete after his coronation. As if it hadn't caused even more difficulties.

Own father won't even sit on his Council.

Deceiver.

Usurper.

Murderer.

Aidon's Second-in-Command and new general to the

Trahir armies, Aleissande, stood beside his parents. Her back was ramrod straight, her blond hair pulled into a low bun. She was dressed in the traditional brown fighting leathers of the forces. Come to think of it, Aidon wasn't sure he'd seen her in anything else these last few weeks. As if she knew war was just on the horizon.

At least someone here did.

The noise grew louder the closer the procession drew to the gallows, and Aidon felt his heart begin to pound as the prisoners came into clear view on the main thoroughfare. Already bloody, and battered, and bruised. Already getting justice for a crime some refused to believe had been committed.

Aidon swallowed as the prisoners turned the bend to begin the climb up to the alcove. It was nearly time. The beach was packed to the brim now, and some had even taken to their boats to witness the prosecution. Aidon caught sight of a white sailboat, and his heart twisted as he thought of Peter. His childhood friend, Dominic's Second, would have been among the prisoners, had Aya not killed him in the throne room.

He still wasn't sure how to grieve Peter's death. Or if he even should.

Nevertheless, he was grateful that he would not have to look upon Peter as he pulled that lever today. It was hard enough to see Sion, one of his uncle's favored attendants, limp up the path, his lip gushing blood.

Sion, who had grated on Aidon's nerves endlessly, but had made it a habit to sneak Aidon the lemon-flavored candy he loved so much whenever his uncle's scolding became particularly harsh.

Sion, who had turned the other way when Aidon and Josie snuck out of the palace on so many occasions.

Aidon had known these people for nearly his entire life. Gods, he'd *trained* two of the City Guard who now stood in shackles.

And yet he hadn't truly known them. Because if he had, he would've become wiser to their plan. He would've seen their betrayal before it was nearly too late.

Bile burned the back of his throat as Aleissande approached the gallows. Typically, it would be his Second conducting the execution alongside the priestess. But the worst of the crimes were saved for the king.

The City Guards dragged the prisoners up the wooden steps, their chains clanking steadily as they climbed. Aidon made himself watch as Aleissande stepped behind each one and fastened the ropes around the prisoners' necks. He waited until she stepped back before he strolled forward, his steps unnervingly steady as he walked onto the platform.

He faced the prisoners, the shouts from the beach reaching fever pitch as the anticipation grew. He raised his arms for silence, but he still needed one of Aleissande's Caeli, who stood behind him, to manipulate the air so that it carried his voice over the crowd.

"You stand convicted of treason against your kingdom!" Aidon paused, letting the angry roar of the crowd give him a moment to swallow, to meet each prisoner's gaze. Sion was last, and Aidon held it as betrayal and bitterness and agony settled in his gut. "Your penalty is death by hanging."

Another wave of sound from the crowd. Some chant he couldn't make out—wouldn't try to make out—had begun, and his heartbeat pounded in time to it.

"Priestess," Aidon called as he tore his eyes away from Sion. "Please begin."

The priestess stepped forward from where she stood off to the side of the platform with Josie, her hair whipping around her face as she raised her arms to the Beyond and closed her eyes.

"Nine Divine, hear us as we cry out to you! We place in your hands the souls of these who stand committed of treason, so that they might await your judgment! While we carry out their mortal sentencing, may you meet each of them in death and enact your justice as you see fit!"

And though Trahir would never claim to be the most devout of the kingdoms, though they had long deviated from the Old Customs of worship, one wouldn't have known it from the righteous roar that rose up from the crowd.

That was the interesting thing about it all, Aidon was coming to realize. Human or Visya, devout or faithless, it didn't matter. All mortals had a penchant for violence. Some masked it as justice, others as devotion, and others as vengeance, but it was all the same, really.

They were all the same.

And today the people of Trahir wanted pain. They wanted blood. They wanted death. And it didn't matter that it would happen again by Aidon's hand.

Deceiver.

Usurper.

Murderer.

The priestess nodded to Aidon as two of the prisoners began to shout, their hands clawing at the rope around their necks. The third and fourth were crying silent tears, their pants already soiled in their fear. But Sion—godsdamn him, Sion—stood stoically, awaiting his fate.

The noise on the beach was deafening, so loud that Aidon couldn't separate the roaring in his ears from that of his people. His hand shook as he laid it on the lever, his eyes finding Sion's once more.

Was this what awaited him as king? The continued death and decay of a nation that he called home?

No. I will change it. I will save it.

Because *that* was what it meant to be king. What his father had prepared him for. What Aidon would vow to be when he took the crown under the eyes of the Divine tomorrow.

Deceiver.

Usurper.

Murderer.

Aidon pulled the lever.

The five bodies dropped like puppets from a string.

18

Josie wondered if it was selfish to feel the way she did—to look at the two dormitory towers of the Maraciana and be full of dread. She kept trying to remind herself that Viviane was the one who needed to mourn, the one whose entire life had been changed in mere moments.

She was the one locked away here. The one who couldn't tell a single soul what had happened to her. The one who closed in on herself, abandoned her friends, her *life*, because she did not know how to lie about this.

Viviane needed her.

And yet Josie couldn't help that traitorous thought, which had haunted her steps every time she'd climbed up the godsforsaken hill to the Maraciana in these last three weeks.

In some ways, Viviane had made her own bed.

She had betrayed Josie's trust, had taken the secret of Aidon's Incend affinity, and had nearly used it to cost Aidon his crown.

Josie hadn't thought about any of that when Dominic's soldiers had dragged Viviane into the dungeon. She had only cared that her partner survived—even if it meant being turned into a Visya so Dominic could prove Aya's power was legitimate.

And though Josie was grateful, so incredibly grateful, that she had not had to watch Viviane's body hang from the gallows mere days ago, she couldn't rid herself of betrayal's sting.

Of course, Josie wasn't naive enough to think Aidon had spared Viviane just for Josie's sake. Viviane had raw power now, and though it wasn't limitless like Aya's, it was *something* that could be of use in this godsforsaken war. If only he could convince Viviane to use it.

Josie wondered how long Vi had until Aidon forced her hand, until he made her choose between fealty or death.

Josie sighed as she made her way into the first tower and began the long climb to the rope bridge that connected the two dormitories. It was slow going in her coronation outfit, an emerald green gown of tulle that swished with every step she took. Surely there would be a lecture from her mother about creasing it before the ceremony, but with the day so full, Josie hadn't wanted to risk being late, or cutting this time short with Vi.

Her nightmares had made her restless last night, visions of Aya's power flowing into Viviane while Vi screamed in agony, making Josie toss and turn until she gave up on sleep entirely. The dreams had left her anxious and restless and eager to see Vi, despite everything.

Josie stepped onto the open-air bridge that connected the two buildings. The breeze tore at her dress, the scent of the sea settling something in her as she paused to take in the waves, lit by the pink dawn sky, crashing against the cliffs where the Maraciana was settled.

She could at least say this about Viviane's new home: it was peaceful.

Josie ducked through the archway and continued up the staircase until she reached the top floor. Viviane's room was at the far end of the second tower, giving her a splendid view of the Anath Sea.

As soon as the guards outside Vi's driftwood door let Josie into the room, Josie's eyes tracked to the small window seat. Vi was curled in on herself, her knees hugged to her chest and her chin resting on top of them. Her black hair, normally cropped close to her head, had grown out to her cheekbones, and its limp strands fluttered in the breeze that came through the open window.

Vi turned her head at the sound of the door closing, and she gave Josie a closed-lipped smile. "Hi," she said softly. "You look nice."

Josie grinned. "Thank you." She smoothed her palms down the layers of her dress before meeting Viviane's gaze, which was resting on the delicate silver crown on her head.

Josie shifted uncomfortably.

"It's Aidon's coronation today," she needlessly explained.

"I know." Viviane offered another smile, but her eyes, usually a piercing blue that Josie once jested could see layers beneath anyone's foolishness, were dull. It was as if the sickly pallor that had come over Vi's peachy skin was leaching color away from every part of her.

Josie crossed the room, dropping into one of the chairs at the small wooden table across from the bed. "It'll have me occupied the rest of the day, but I didn't want to miss out on our time together. That's why I'm here so early. You know I typically wouldn't be caught dead out of bed at this hour, but gods, my mother has completely lost her mind about today. You should see the chaos in the palace. Everyone's in quite a state."

She was rambling, her fingers toying with the folds of her dress, and she knew she should stop but she just couldn't, because Viviane was still staring at her with an expression that felt foreign, her eyes flicking to that godsdamn crown every so often.

"Has there been any news about Avis?" Viviane finally asked, her voice a quiet rasp.

Josie swallowed. "No. He's still awaiting sentencing." Aidon didn't seem to know what to do with the Bellare member.

Vi's gaze sharpened. "You know he's innocent."

"I know that he didn't kidnap you or Helene. That does not make him innocent. He's confessed to other crimes."

Like vandalism. Knowledge of the attempted murder of Will and, in her refusal to leave him, Aya. But Viviane had heard Josie's reasoning over and over since Avis Lavigne was arrested. Vi didn't care. She was too consumed by her anger, too scarred from what had happened to her because she, too, had been a member of the rebel group. And though Vi had apologized, time and time again, for what she'd nearly done to Aidon—what she'd nearly cost him—it didn't erase the fact that Viviane had bonds with these people.

Avis included.

"Being a member of the Bellare is not a crime," Viviane hissed, her voice low and bitter.

"It is when their activity is illegal. They could have killed my friends."

"And your uncle killed mine!" Viviane spat out.

Josie closed her eyes, forcing a steady breath in through her nose.

She gets to be angry, Josie reminded herself. *She was changed against her will.*

But what about Josie's anger? Didn't she have a right to it as well? Didn't she deserve to be furious at Viviane and her plan to utilize the rebels to remove Aidon from his throne for something he couldn't even control? He hadn't chosen to be born Visya. It wasn't his fault.

Josie opened her eyes and forced herself to swallow. "I don't want to argue with you," she said quietly.

Not about this, not again.

But arguing seemed to be the only times that Viviane was more herself. For a moment, that fog would lift from her, and Josie could see a glimpse of the woman she loved beneath it. The one who laughed fully, and teased wickedly, and found beauty in the most rugged, untamable of things, like the mountains in Tala.

Viviane scrubbed a hand over her face, her head falling back against the edge of the window. "Neither do I," she finally muttered. "I'm sorry. I'm still figuring out how to… be. Being locked up here, with no one to talk to but Natali… it's weighing on me."

Natali was one of the best of the Saj of the Maraciana. They were also the most discreet. They were the only one outside of Josie's family, save Aya and Will, who knew what had transpired in the throne room. And they had earned Aidon's trust by helping him save Aya from Dominic.

Josie fought to keep her face soft. Understanding. But inside, that flicker of irritation was growing into a full-grown fire.

Viviane had refused to come forward and testify about her experience, which meant they'd lost a key way to prove to the kingdom that what had transpired was true, both Dominic's betrayal and Aya's power. Josie understood, in some way. She truly did. Vi didn't owe it to anyone to share her trauma, not even Josie, and definitely not the kingdom or the realm at large.

But it did not change the fact that Viviane was unpredictable, not just because of her prior allegiances, but also because of her power. The only thing that could even come close was the Decachiré practitioners putting unstable, mutilated affinities into humans.

Viviane's power was raw and pure, and given by a saint.

It was like comparing acrylic paintings to watercolors.

So when Aidon, unsure of what to do with Vi, had come to Josie, Josie had suggested that Vi stay at the dorms of the Maraciana, and take the tonic to hide her power from the Saj, and let Natali help her understand what it was she was facing.

It wasn't prison, but it wasn't freedom either.

"I'm nothing more than an experiment," Vi had spat out the first day Josie had visited her. Her anger had cooled, but only just.

Meanwhile, Josie's continued to build.

Tell me how to fix this. Please, gods, just tell me how to fix this.

That heavy awkwardness settled between them once more, and Josie scraped her nail across the wood of the table.

"You don't have to come here every day, you know," Viviane finally murmured.

Josie's head snapped up. "I like coming here."

Vi lifted a shoulder. "I know. But surely you have more to do than this." Her eyes flicked to Josie's crown once more. "Duties to abide by."

Josie wasn't sure if the remark was truly caustic, or if it was her own irritation that made it not just sting but burn, the words settling on her flesh in a way that made her shift in her seat.

Perhaps it was because she *didn't* have duties. Not now.

Sure, these last three weeks had been spent by her family's side, aiding in the political posturing that was necessary to smooth the transition between kings. She took meetings with prominent merchants, soothed those closest to the nobility, and even helped her mother with the correspondence to foreign allies to assure them everything was fine.

But these responsibilities—this tumultuousness in Trahir—would not last forever.

Aidon was king, and she knew her brother well enough to know he would not be like Dominic. He would not force them into the positions that their births demanded; he would not tell Josie what she could and could not do.

She'd always thought she'd feel free when this day came. But now she just felt...purposeless. Directionless. Empty.

You could have been Aidon's Second. That could have been your new purpose.

Josie shut out the thought immediately. She'd meant what

151

she'd told her brother: she *was* honored that he'd considered her. But that was a responsibility she could not be trusted to have.

Not when she'd missed what had been happening right before her eyes.

Not when she'd nearly cost Aidon his crown because of it.

Maybe one day, she would have the words to explain it to Aidon, to sort through how foolish she felt, how betrayed, how angry, not just at Viviane, but at herself for causing him that strife.

But for now, she settled for a simple refusal. Aleissande was much better suited to the task, anyway.

But then, what *did* remain for her? She had wanted something for herself, hadn't she? Before she'd settled for what Dominic had made available to her?

A life with Viviane.

Perhaps children, one day.

To be happy. Content. Loved.

The words echoed hollowly in her mind, and Josie swallowed, aware of how Viviane was still watching her, as if waiting for some sort of response.

"Perhaps you're right," Josie finally breathed, her gaze moving past Viviane to the horizon, where the sun had finally risen fully. She'd be due back in the palace soon to join the procession to the temple, where Aidon would be coronated. And then...

What? What would her days look like then, when her brother, her entire family, moved on to their new responsibilities?

She looked back to Viviane, something twisting in her chest at the dullness in her partner's gaze.

See me, she wanted to scream. *See that I'm not free either, see that I'm struggling too.*

Josie stood, her hands smoothing the folds of her dress. "You're right," she said again. She forced a smile to her face.

"I do have duties to attend to. Mother will kill me if I'm not back in time for the procession." Her smile faded as she stared at her partner. "But you're important to me, Vi. I don't mind coming out here. If not every day, then at least as much as I can. As much as you want me to. I love you. I want you to be okay."

I want us to be okay.

Viviane stared at her for a moment, and Josie nearly held her breath, wondering if this time, Vi would *truly* talk to her. Hells, she'd even take yelling, arguing, *anything* over this strange silence that had settled in the space between them.

For a moment, she half expected Vi would argue with her. Because there was a glint in her blue eyes, and a straightening to her posture, and her full lips parted as she inhaled, as if she couldn't contain the words.

But then Viviane paused. Breathed. And it was like watching the sun disappear on the horizon, the way the light faded from Viviane's eyes, the fight seeping out of her. She deflated, her body curling in on itself once more as she scooted closer to the window.

"I know," Viviane said softly. She turned her head back to the window, her hair fluttering in the sea breeze. "I love you, too."

19

"Y OU HAVE TO ADMIT—FOR SOMETHING SO HASTILY THROWN together, it turned out rather lovely."

Aidon nearly choked on his wine as he whipped his head to Lucas. His friend smirked as he sipped his wine, his white slacks and purple jacket, marked with the golden swan sigil of his merchant house, perfectly pressed for the occasion.

"Surely you could have said that more quietly," Aidon retorted. He nodded to a group of merchants as they passed, and Lucas merely shrugged, mischief dancing in his brown eyes.

"Surely *you* could have pointed it out instead of me." Lucas's grin was a slash of white against his brown skin, and Aidon couldn't help the chuckle that rumbled through him.

Perhaps Lucas had a point. Three weeks *was* a miserably short time to organize a coronation celebration, and that was without the added strife that came with this peculiar event. Yet his friend had risen to the task marvelously. As Aidon looked around the large outdoor balcony, full of the richest and noblest of Rinnia's citizens, he couldn't deny Lucas had conjured up a splendor that made today seem as though it had been planned for years.

Of course, a version of it had. The traditions were clear: the coronation was to take place with the priestess in the main temple, and the celebration in the ballroom of the palace.

But Aidon had taken one step into that ballroom and hadn't been able to breathe. Not when he could see himself handing Will that champagne diluted with tonic. Not when he could remember Dominic summoning him from the ballroom to the dungeons, where he found Vi chained and beaten.

Lucas hadn't pressed Aidon when he'd asked to have the celebration somewhere—*anywhere*—else. His friend had simply taken to the task, and he'd outdone himself.

They stood next to several tables loaded with food and drinks and more flowers than Aidon could name. High-tops dotted the balcony, giving guests a place to settle if they didn't want to participate in the dancing that was taking place on the far side of the balcony, where a string quartet was playing a merry song from a raised platform.

Behind Aidon, the terrace gave an unobstructed view of the crescent-moon beach, where celebrity fires were being lit along the sands.

"You're right," Aidon finally said. He clapped his friend on the shoulder. "Thank you, Lucas. It's truly incredible."

No one could look at the celebration and see what Aidon knew existed at its center:

A broken family.

An imposter of a king.

It did its job marvelously in distracting the people, if only for a moment. But Aidon, for all his forced smiles, couldn't forget—as he couldn't forget that just beyond those celebrating on the beach, a fourth of the way up the western cliffs hung five bodies, dead by his hand.

"Now *this* is certainly more enjoyable than the yawn-fest in the temple," a voice drawled from behind them.

Clyde, dressed in the same purple jacket as his husband,

155

strolled forward, a glass of wine in his hand. His olive-toned skin had darkened with time spent in the sun, and Aidon found himself jealous that they'd been out on the barge and he had not. Clyde swung an arm around Aidon and Lucas's shoulders, his black hair brushing his collar as he tossed his head back and let out a noise of contentment.

"Careful, you're touching a *king* now," Lucas chided. "Don't spill wine on his royal attire."

Clyde fixed Aidon with an exaggeratedly solemn look. "My apologies, Your Majesty." He swayed slightly, and Aidon felt his lips twitch. Clyde and Lucas could always be counted on to squeeze every bit of celebration out of an event.

"I'll forgive you as long as you don't make me a subject of my mother's wrath," Aidon retorted. The three of them looked over to where Zuri stood by the edge of the dancing area, her eyes narrowed at them while a merchant prattled on in her ear.

"Zuri loves me," Clyde scoffed, raising his glass toward Aidon's mother. And though she rolled her eyes, turning her focus back to the merchant, Aidon didn't miss the way her lips quirked in amusement.

Everyone loved Clyde.

It was why he'd make a perfect Lead Councillor.

Clyde, for all his love of entertainment, was smart, and strategic, and charismatic in a way that reminded Aidon of Josie.

Or at least, reminded Aidon of how his sister used to be. *Before*—the clear divide for everything in Aidon's life as of late.

He took a sip of his wine. He had planned to ask Clyde prior to this evening if he would be interested in the position, but he'd hardly had a chance to breathe in the last three weeks. Perhaps tonight would be the perfect time.

And then there'd be just one seat remaining for Aidon to fill: Avis Lavigne's.

"Seriously though," Clyde said as he let his arms fall from their shoulders. "How you didn't fall asleep standing up there for so long today, Aidon, is beyond me."

Aidon rubbed the back of his neck, his head aching under the weight of the crown he was now forced to wear at all occasions. "I was more afraid of passing out from the nerves, to be honest."

His heart had been pounding so hard, he was afraid he wouldn't be able to hear the words he was supposed to repeat to the priestess, let alone actually be able to speak them. And when the priestess had read that verse from the Conoscenza—the one that spoke of the gods demanding only a human could rule, and thus *Aidon* was chosen by the Divine to be their king—it had taken everything in him to keep his face emotionless, to not let them see the doubt, the fear, the guilt on his face.

Deceiver.

Usurper.

Murderer.

"What do you say, Aidon? Will you be able to join us on the barge this summer, or will you be too busy with your kingly duties?" Lucas asked, drawing Aidon's attention back to the present.

Aidon refrained from mentioning they'd likely be at war by the summer. Instead, he took another sip of his sparkling wine and cleared his throat before fixing his gaze on Clyde.

"Speaking of duties, there's actually something I've been meaning to ask you."

"I'm sorry to interrupt, Your Majesty," a deep voice interjected from beside him. Aidon turned to see a tall man with tawny skin and silken black hair standing before him. He wore a beige linen suit, the white shirt beneath it unbuttoned to his sternum. "I was wondering if I might have a moment of your time."

Aidon forced what he hoped was a genuine-enough smile

to his face. "Certainly." He cut a gaze to Clyde and Lucas. "I'll see you two later. Try to behave, won't you?"

Clyde smirked, but Lucas looked almost affronted. "Honestly, it's as if you think we have no decorum," he grumbled as he pulled his husband away. Aidon turned back to the man, who motioned toward the far end of the terrace, where several high-tops stood empty.

"Perhaps we could speak in private?"

Aidon nodded and followed, aware of how his guards tracked his every movement as he and the stranger stepped away from the revelers. His guards remained by the balcony doors, however, having been instructed by Zuri not to attract too much attention for the sake of maintaining a welcoming atmosphere.

The man stopped at the furthest table by the balcony, his posture loose and easy as he smiled at Aidon. "Congratulations, Majesty. I must say, I never thought I'd attend a coronation."

Aidon tried to place the stranger's face, but he couldn't. Perhaps he worked for one of the established merchants and had received an invitation as payment for good service.

"Thank you," he replied. "Forgive me, but I don't believe we've met."

The man shook his head. "My apologies," he said as he shifted to pull off his jacket, leaving him in his short-sleeved shirt. "The heat has made me forget my manners." He folded the garment once, laying it on the table before he slid his hands into his pockets and turned to face Aidon fully.

Aidon stilled, his eyes tracking the lean muscles of the man's arm.

Because there, just below where the sleeve of his shirt stopped at his bicep, was the bottom of a rose tattoo.

The marking of the Bellare.

"It's a pleasure to meet you, Your Majesty," the man said. His full lips tipped up in the corner. "My name is Ryker Drycari."

20

ONCE, WHEN AIDON WAS YOUNGER, HE'D SNUCK OUT OF the palace with Josie to go sailing even though his parents had expressly forbidden them from doing so without an adult present. But Aidon had been through hours of lessons, and he'd even manned the small skiff with Peter and his father, and really, he'd thought, how hard could it be?

He could still remember the feeling of icy dread as he'd lost control of the rigging, sending the ship tilting to its side and careening dangerously toward the rocks. Josie had screamed, and Aidon had just barely regained control of the sails and avoided a crash.

That same feeling of icy dread was slipping through his stomach now as he stared at Ryker, amusement glinting in the rebel's hooded brown eyes.

He doesn't know anything. Pull yourself together.

Aidon braced his forearms on the table, his fingers drumming a steady beat on the polished wood as he surveyed the young man. His eyes flicked purposefully to the rose tattoo before meeting Ryker's gaze again. "I must say, I'm relieved that you show your affiliation so…honestly."

It was rare, especially with the increase in activity from

the rebel group. They'd existed for years, but recently they'd made their opposition to Visya not being limited to the roles detailed in the Conoscenza quite known.

Ryker shrugged. "I have nothing to hide, Your Majesty. As far as I know, being a member of the Bellare isn't a crime…"

He left the statement hanging, an unspoken *yet* lingering between them. Aidon's brows flicked up.

"Ah, but one might argue your actions are."

We must keep peace, Zuri had advised. *If we let it be known that Dominic framed the Bellare for several of the attacks on the city, we will lose further trust with our people.* You *will lose further trust with our people.*

Aidon hadn't argued the point. It wasn't as though the Bellare were innocent. They were still behind some of the attacks, one of which had almost killed Aya and Will.

They were still a threat to Aidon's crown.

Ryker held up his hands in a gesture of innocence, the melting ice in his crystal tumbler of whiskey clinking against the glass. "I'm not here to discuss accusations, Majesty. Unless you'd like to turn this celebration into a hearing?"

Aidon's jaw shifted. Impertinent bastard.

Nonetheless, he was aware that people were watching him. Partygoers glanced in his direction every so often, no matter where he was or who he was speaking to. He shifted onto one arm, letting his gaze scan the party casually. His mother, dressed in a gown of the emerald green of the royal livery, was in conversation with a councillor. But she eyed him, the look on her face clear.

Do you need help?

Aidon gave a subtle shake of his head and kept his tone bored. "Proceed."

He could almost *hear* the smirk in Ryker's voice as the rebel said, "I'd like to request Councillor Avis Lavigne's seat on the Trahir Merchant Council be given to me."

Aidon trailed a finger around his wineglass, his gaze still

fixed on the party. He watched as his sister waved off Clyde's request to dance, a smile that didn't meet her eyes fixed on her face.

"Avis Lavigne is still awaiting trial for his crimes in aiding the Bellare in their attacks," Aidon said finally. Negligible, really, when compared to the acts Aidon's uncle had committed in their name. Not that his people knew that. Aidon still hadn't quite decided what to do with the man. Avis was a valued member of the rebel group. Perhaps if Aidon bestowed some consequences on him, it would temper their activity.

"You're quite eager, aren't you?" Aidon added as he turned back to Ryker.

Ryker shrugged. "I'm not naive enough to assume Avis will be returning to the Merchant Council, even if he proves the Bellare weren't responsible for all of the attacks of late. Although I assume you've put those pieces together. Avis is many things, but to kill his own daughter? To organize the kidnapping of another Bellare member?"

Guilt, heavy and unrelenting, pooled in Aidon's gut. Helene Lavigne's murder wasn't his to own, and yet...

If I had been faster to catch on to Dominic's plan. If I had been faster in that courtyard, before she'd bled out...

Aidon frowned, choosing to ignore the first claim and focus on the second. "Viviane vows it was the Bellare who took her once she denounced your ways."

Another lie in an endless list of them.

Ryker just laughed. "Interesting. Where *is* Viviane these days? I haven't seen her around lately."

Aidon met the rebel's gaze, forcing his face into the bored look he'd often observed on his uncle when he tired of people's company. "Viviane must be avoiding the likes of you, if I had to guess. And that's beside the point. Council seats are reserved for leaders of prominent merchant houses." He scanned Ryker once. "Forgive me, but I don't see a sigil."

Ryker's eyes glinted with annoyance, but he wasn't

swayed. "I think you'd be surprised how well-connected the Bellare is. Avis has made it a point to keep us apprised of his dealings. And, well, given he now has no heir..." Aidon didn't move a muscle as Ryker's voice trailed off, the rebel's gaze piercing.

"Is that all?" Aidon asked as he pushed himself off the table. "Because if so, I should get back to my guests—"

"Let's make a bargain," Ryker interjected. "Our people value trade and prosperity, yes? I assume bargaining is a language you speak."

Aidon paused, unable to hide his curiosity. "And what could you possibly have to offer me?"

Ryker grinned.

"Your crown."

"Pardon?"

"Give me Avis's seat on the Council, and I'll ensure the kingdom doesn't learn their new king is Visya."

Aidon stilled, his mind going blank as he stared at the rebel. There was a tingling in his hands, a swaying in his head, as if the entire terrace was moving beneath him.

Ryker couldn't possibly...

How...?

Aidon swallowed, his face hardening as he recovered himself. "Your lies are as good as treason," he growled. But the words felt thick on his tongue, his voice hollow against the ringing in his ears.

Ryker toyed with a thread on his discarded jacket. "Interesting then that Viviane has not been hanged," he mused. "She was the one who passed the knowledge on to me." Ryker's eyes flicked past Aidon to where Josie stood, her fingers toying mindlessly with the tulle of her dress. "Though perhaps Vi is afforded certain...privileges...due to her association with the princess."

Aidon felt his jaw tighten.

Seven hells. This...this would destroy Josie. Because

Viviane had promised. She had looked them in the eye and promised she had told no one, and Aidon had believed her, had *wanted* to believe her, because his sister was in love, and she had watched her partner nearly die, and if he could do something, *anything*, to spare Josie more pain, then he would, even if Viviane had been intent on taking his future from him.

Aidon turned back to the high-top, his arms braced upon the surface as he forced his body to relax—to appear casual—as he regarded Ryker. "How many people have you told this to?" he muttered. Ryker didn't answer. "I could just have you thrown in jail." Aidon's eyes flicked to his guards. "Or killed."

Ryker didn't look too concerned with the threat of death. In fact, he slid his hands into his pockets, his posture loose and easy.

"You could," he mused. "But that would cause quite a scene, would it not? And then people would get curious and… Well, I assume you know better than anyone how the rich and royal *love* their gossip."

Aidon was going to kill him.

"But I imagined you'd make such threats, regardless of our company. You ask how many I've told? One. As a show of good faith. You give me Avis's seat, and I promise neither of us will breathe a word of your affinity. None will know you have broken the holiest of laws—not from us." Ryker's smirk faded, his impertinence replaced by something far more serious. "But if I don't return this evening, my confidante is set to share your secret not just with the Bellare, but with those who will make this news citywide by tomorrow morning."

Aidon's mind whirled, sorting through various strategies. Ruling could be similar to battle, he was learning. It was about people, and places, and timing the strikes perfectly.

He cocked his head, his brow furrowing. "What do you have to gain from all of this?"

Riches, if he had to guess. Or perhaps the lad was simply attracted to the potential of power. Everyone knew the Merchant Councils were the closest thing to nobility. And Ryker could say what he wanted about the Visya, but humans were just as selfish, just as greedy. Aidon had seen that firsthand.

"We're facing a war of your kind's making," Ryker growled. "Visya once again aren't satisfied with the power they've already been given by the gods, and humans will pay the price with their lives. They deserve a voice on the Council."

"They have several voices on the Council." Over half the councillors were human. But Ryker wasn't placated.

"Not one like ours. Say what you want about the Bellare and our methods, but we are the only ones in the kingdom who hold human interests above the Visya." He gave Aidon a pointed look. "Especially now. When Avis is removed from the Council, which we both know he will be, the Bellare will lose a valuable place of power. The *humans* will lose a valuable place of power. I'm here to ensure that doesn't happen. Besides, don't we ordinary citizens deserve to have our voices heard? Shouldn't we have a say in the tariffs and laws of trade?"

Aidon let out a bitter laugh. He'd long thought so. But the reasoning rang hollow when it came from the man before him. *This* was not how Aidon wished to accomplish such change.

"You have no proof of your accusations," he said, his voice dropping low.

"Unless you intend to kill Viviane along with me, she is all the proof I need," Ryker shot back. "Her name will be tied to the rumors of your power."

And then she would hang right alongside him.

Aidon could see exactly how this would escalate—exactly how he would have to play it, should this come to light, and exactly how that would break Josie, who was already trying too hard to pick up her broken pieces. But to fold under such pressure, and from a rebel no less…

It went against every instinct that had etched itself into Aidon's very bones from his years in the forces.

He needed Ryker to give up *something*. There had to be some exchange that mattered enough to Ryker that he would feel the sting of sacrifice, that he would remember who was truly in charge.

Aidon ran a finger across the wood of the table.

"I'll bargain with you," he finally said slowly, the outlines of a plan forming in his mind. "I'll give you Avis Lavigne's seat on the Merchant Council. And in exchange, you will ensure the Bellare don't retaliate when Avis is convicted for his crimes."

Ryker's brows rose. "You think you're in a position to make demands of me, Majesty?"

Aidon shrugged. "I suppose we could find out. But how difficult would it be to turn public opinion against the Bellare? To paint your accusations as a calculated attempt to use my uncle's treason to garner more power for yourselves? One might even think you're trying to overthrow the throne entirely." Aidon glanced around the party as he let out a *tsk* of disappointment. "And at my coronation, no less. What *would* the people say?" Ryker's hands curled into fists, but Aidon wasn't done. "Between the attacks, then turning on one of your own, one who's stepped away from the Bellare's ranks?"

The words tasted like poison as Aidon spoke them, but he didn't let a single bit of the lie show on his face. Instead, he let Ryker see his steadiness. Ryker stared him down, but Aidon let the silence between them grow. He knew how to wait out an opponent. He would not strike first. Not now.

Slowly, Ryker's fists unclenched as his shoulders dropped. "Promise not to kill Avis," he muttered. "Promise me that, and you have a deal."

Aidon opened his mouth to respond, but there was a hand on his arm, and suddenly his mother was beside him. "Your Majesty," she said, giving a small bow. Aidon nearly jerked out of her hold. It was jarring to hear his mother address him so formally. "I'm sorry to interrupt, but your sister is requesting a dance."

Aidon glanced past his mother to where Josie stood on the edge of the dance floor, an inquisitive look on her face as she observed him and Ryker. She frowned slightly at the rebel, as if trying to place his face.

His mother gave Aidon's arm a light squeeze, and while her smile was warm, her eyes were fierce as they darted between him and Ryker, who was careful to keep his body slightly turned so his tattoo was out of Zuri's view.

Even so…

They had been speaking too long. She must have noticed the tension if she'd come to interrupt.

Aidon forced a smile onto his face as he stepped out of his mother's grasp. "Certainly, Mother. We were just wrapping up some business, weren't we, Ryker?"

Zuri didn't bother to hide her confusion. "Business? Today?"

Aidon shrugged. "It was pressing," he said lightly, before extending a hand to Ryker.

"Welcome to the Merchant Council."

21

THERE WOULD BE HELLS TO PAY FOR LEAVING HIS OWN coronation early. If Lucas didn't kill him for it, Aidon was sure his mother certainly would.

But as he'd watched Ryker sauntering away, the soft hiss of his mother's *"What did you just do?"* in his ear, Aidon could only think one thing: he had to get out of this godsforsaken crowd.

He hadn't even known where he was going as he stormed out of the palace. But he supposed he shouldn't have been surprised that his feet had led him here to his favorite sparring room in the training complex.

Gods, when was the last time he'd been in this building? One week ago? Two? He used to spend every single morning here. Back when he was just a general, and his mother was just his mother, and his family wasn't splitting apart at the seams.

Or maybe they were, even then. Maybe they'd always been on this path, and he just hadn't realized it.

Aidon let out a hard breath as he took off his crown and threw it as hard as he could at the wall, right where the tally he and Josie had kept of their fights was carved.

He hadn't even made it a fucking *day* as king before he'd been embroiled in some scheme.

What did you just do?

He kicked off his shoes and tugged off his jacket and shirt, crushing them into a ball as he tossed them on the floor. Then he stalked to the sparring post and let himself loose upon it.

What did you just do?

One fucking day. One *fucking* day, and already he was manipulating those who tried to manipulate him—moving them around like chess pieces, thinking only of the grander consequences.

Was this the life he was destined to live?

Lying, manipulating, scheming so that his people did not learn the truth about him?

You've been lying every day of your godsdamn life. What's the difference?

The thought was bitter in his head. Because there *was* a difference. He was king now, and the weight of those lies was so much heavier than he'd once thought. It kept growing, becoming something he could not carry upon his shoulders with everything else.

Dominic's betrayal.

Josie's misery.

His family's fracturing.

The fucking *war* that was haunting him every time another day passed and he received no news of battle, or movement, or *anything* that indicated it was actually happening.

Sweat began to bead along Aidon's skin as he threw another combination at the post, his muscles aching with that initial burn that came from days of disuse.

He wanted to feel *more*.

He had always known that in accepting the crown, he would be going against what the gods decreed. But even though his parents had reminded him each and every day of his coming duty, it had still seemed a distant thing. Besides, he had never touched his power, not until that day he had burned the assassins masquerading as the Bellare when they attacked him and Aya and Will. And that had been accidental.

Did it matter, then, that he was Visya if he chose not to live that way?

Yes, that voice murmured in the back of his head. *Because you...you were never meant to be king. You wouldn't even be here now if it weren't for the disgrace of your uncle.*

The sparring post blurred in front of Aidon as he hit it again and again and again, his teeth gritted against his rising frustration as he took it out on the rattling wood.

His chest heaved, heart pounding in time with his doubts, his fears.

Ryker has made you a pawn.

Hadn't he *always* been one?

"Fuck!"

Aidon unleashed himself on the post, hitting it as hard as he could. He could almost smell the way the wood burned the flesh of his knuckles, could almost feel the heat of the wood itself as if it were on fire, could almost—

He stumbled back, his breath coming in a choked *whoosh* as flames raced up the old sparring post with a roar, devouring it within seconds. Time slowed as he looked down at his hands, panic racing through his veins as he saw fire coating his palms.

"Fuck," he panted, his vision blurring once more as the flames climbed up his arms, the sensation tickling his skin. Something was wrong. He could feel it in the way something was pressing against his insides, begging to be released. Aidon stumbled backward, his breath punching out of his lungs as he tried to find some way to cut off his affinity.

He'd taken his tonic today, hadn't he? It had become such a part of his routine, he hardly thought of it. But...

He'd taken it the day he'd used his power to save Aya, too. But he'd *meant* to use his power then. This was accidental, and inexplicable, and...

Godsdammit.

Aidon gritted his teeth as he fell to his knees. His very veins were on fire, he was sure of it. The flames were burning him alive from the inside out as he tried to contain them, tried to stop them from devouring more of him, more of the training room, more of *everything*.

He braced his hands on the training room floor, his body trembling against the strain of whatever he was keeping inside as he let out a hoarse yell. It burned his throat, and he swore he tasted ash. Distantly, he registered the rush of running footsteps.

His guards.

He couldn't convince them to stay at the palace, but he'd ordered them to stay outside, and they'd likely heard his holler...

"*Fuck*," he swore again, his body trembling as he dug his fingers into the floor. He had to stop this, had to stop it now, before he ruined everything. Aidon closed his eyes and imagined a knife cutting across that something inside of him, that tension he could feel pressing against his skin.

Aidon sucked in a breath as the fire vanished, not an instant too soon. He swiped his hands across the ground, burying the ash in a fine layer of dirt.

"Your Majesty!" Two of his guards rushed into the room, their swords drawn.

"I'm fine," he ground out, his hands still braced on the floor. He should stand—should look more like a king. But his head was swimming and his hands were shaking, and he was sure he might vomit if he moved too fast. "I'm fine," he repeated, sitting back on his heels. He took a deep breath. "Too much sparkling wine to be indulging in calisthenics." He shot his guards a wry grin.

He was banking on the fact that no one sparred in this room save him and Josie so that his excuse would not be questioned. And by the way his guards relaxed, their swords lowering, it seemed he'd gotten away with it.

"Do you need anything, Your Majesty?" one of them asked.

"Yes, actually." Aidon's breath was coming in uneven pants as he stood. "A carriage. I need to go the Maraciana. Now."

"I was wondering when I would see you." Natali didn't even look up from the thick book they were stooped over, not even as Aidon forced himself to take a seat on the other side of their desk, his limbs shaky and hollow after his unexpected flare of power. "I have to say, I didn't expect it to be today of all days."

Neither had he. But the Maraciana was blessedly empty at this hour, the Saj who remained too engrossed in their studies to care who walked among them.

It seemed Natali would remain engrossed as well. They merely turned the page, their amber eyes narrowed as they scanned the text before them.

"Yes, well…it's urgent," Aidon muttered. His foot tapped a nervous rhythm on the floor, filling the silence that stretched between him and the Saj. Natali glanced up, their chin-length silver hair swaying with the movement.

"The girl still refuses to let me her study her," they said flatly. Aidon blinked, his panicked mind tripping over their words.

Viviane. They thought he was here regarding Viviane.

He almost laughed. Vi was the least of his worries in this very moment, and gods, wasn't that saying everything?

"I'm not here about her." One silver brow rose. "It's my affinity. I think something is…wrong with it."

Natali slowly flipped the book closed and took a seat, their elbows resting on the desk, palms pressed together as they surveyed Aidon. "Explain."

He forced a calming breath through his clenched lungs, his fingers loosening their hold on the arms of the wooden chair as he did so.

"I was sparring," he choked out, ignoring Natali's bemused look. "And it…it just…came out of me. Uncontrollable and *burning* like I was on fire, too."

Any hint of amusement vanished from Natali's face as they stared at him, unblinking. "Did you take your tonic today?"

Aidon felt his face grow warm. "I don't…I don't remember." Their sardonic look had him bristling. "As you may recall, today was full of its own distractions. Besides, I've overridden the tonic's control before."

Natali's eyes narrowed. "Intentionally?"

Aidon nodded. "The night Helene was killed, when my uncle's assassins attacked me, Aya, and Will. I didn't think. I just reacted. I killed one of the attackers with fire."

Natali pursed their lips in contemplation, a strained silence filling the space between them. Aidon couldn't stop fidgeting, couldn't contain the restless energy building inside of him.

"It's possible you've built an immunity to the tonic," Natali started slowly. "That after all these years, your affinity has been wearing it down inside of you."

"And how would we know for sure?"

It had taken the Saj in the Maraciana over a year to develop the tonic that masked his power. He didn't have that sort of time.

"I'd need to see you use your affinity," Natali began. A huff of irritation left them as Aidon started to stand. "Don't be foolish. Not *now*."

Aidon bit back his frustration as he slowly lowered himself back into his chair. He wasn't one to wield his title, but if Natali didn't stop looking at him as if he were no more than an asinine child, he just might become such a person.

"It's too risky for you to frequent here without drawing suspicion," Natali snapped. "Kings have no business loitering in the Maraciana. And this won't be a matter we solve overnight. I need to do some research before we test my theory. As you may recall, any of my musings on the tonic are simply that—*musings*. I don't test before I study, Majesty."

Aidon rubbed a hand across the back of his neck, an exasperated sigh leaving him. His muscles felt like lead, his head heavy, not just with the weight of the crown that adorned it, but with a thick fog that seemed to press against the back of his eyes. Too much. Today had been too godsdamn much, and that was before he'd stepped foot in the training room.

He should have stayed at the celebration. A king did not run. A king did not cower. A king did not lose control.

"We can meet at the palace," Aidon intoned, his back straightening as he met Natali's gaze. He needed control—some sort of control. "It would be far less conspicuous, and if anyone asks, you're there to help prepare us for Kakos. It would not be unusual for me to call on the advice of a Saj to help us prepare to face dark magic."

Natali's brows flicked up. "So it's true, then. The king chooses war."

Aidon didn't bother to keep the heaviness from his voice as he pushed out of his chair again. "No one chooses war, Natali. It chooses us." He made his way to the door.

"I'll need a few days to prepare for our meeting," Natali called after him. "There is research to be done."

"A week," he said, letting the authority ring in his command.

He didn't bother to wait for them to confirm before he left.

22

IT WOULD BE TOO MUCH TO ASK THE GODS THAT HIS PARENTS *not* corner him when he returned to the palace, Aidon supposed.

It was why he rarely bothered to pray. The Divine never did listen to him.

Even so, he'd been hopeful when he made it into his family's private wing—the one they'd lived in since Aidon was born, him having refused to move after Dominic's death—without interruption. The hallways were quiet, the sound of his boots on the marble floors making it impossible to hear his parents' soft murmurs until it was too late.

He'd stepped into the small dining room they used for informal occasions to see if the attendants had refilled the bowl of fruit that was usually kept at the center of the small wooden table that had just six chairs.

His parents sat in two.

Aidon froze as their heads whipped to him, their silhouettes illuminated by the candles in the golden chandelier that hung above them. For a moment, the only sound was the sea crashing into the cliffs, the roar carrying through the windows that lined the outer two walls facing the sea.

Aidon's shoulders tensed at the look his mother was giving him. His father, on the other hand, still in his tan linen suit from the festivities, that crown of silver he saved for state occasions adorning his head, masked his anger beneath bitter disappointment. It tugged on his gray brows, pinching the wrinkles in his pale skin into deep creases.

Luckily, Josie was nowhere to be found.

The silence was as heavy as the exhaustion that had settled over him, and he was desperate to break it. Perhaps that's why he leaned against the wall, his arms folding across his chest, and said, "Let's hear it, then."

His mother's eyes, typically a warm, open, bottomless brown, were narrowed, the light of the candles dancing across her black skin. And while she barely moved from the way she sat, straight-backed and ever poised, Aidon could feel her disapproval growing like a wave. "I don't think you need to, do you?"

"You clearly have thoughts. So please," he said, motioning toward the table. "By all means, share them."

That silence returned, but this time, it was tense and full. Zuri kept her eyes fixed on Aidon, the frown still marring her brow as she considered him.

"There are proper ways to do things, Aidon. Proper ways to *behave*. You are king now—"

"I do not need the reminder," Aidon bit out, but Zuri was unmoved.

"You gave away a Council seat as if it was nothing! And that's not to mention you storming out of your own celebration like some petulant child—"

"He knows," Aidon hissed as he pushed off the wall. He stalked forward, his hands bracing on the table as he leaned across to face his mother. "Ryker Drycari knows about my power. He threatened to expose me if I did not give him Avis's seat on the Council."

Shock rippled across his mother's face, smoothing her furrowed brow. "How?" she breathed.

"Viviane," Aidon ground out. "He's a member of the Bellare, and they know each other."

Zuri laid her palms flat on the table. "You said she told no one. You said you were confident that she was truthful in her interrogation—"

Aidon straightened, his hand pressing his chest as if he could rub the tension from it. "Do you think I'm *happy* about this? That I'm proud she lied to us again? That I'm glad someone else has knowledge that could ruin our family's legacy?"

"I think you were foolish not to order her imprisoned with Avis!" his mother snapped.

"By the gods, she was *tortured*! She was imbued with power that could kill her!" His heart was hammering, the worries about his own affinity sharpening his breath until it burned in his lungs. "Forgive me, Mother, for wanting to extend a sliver of humanity, of decency to Josie's partner." The words settled into a heavy silence, tense and full and as tight as the pain in his chest as he regarded his parents.

Gods, he used to love this room. Loved the boisterous dinners that were always filled with such laughter. It had been a time to shed their duties, and responsibilities, and loyalties, and focus on the simple pleasure of being in each other's company. A time to avoid Dominic, too.

Aidon had insisted his family continue to take dinners in the small private dining room, thinking it would give them all a sense of normalcy.

Now he wondered if that had been the wish of a dreamer.

Nothing was normal anymore.

Nothing.

"Who else knows?" his father asked, his baritone voice sharp with tension.

"Ryker said he'd told one other person as assurance he'd return tonight. If I didn't meet his demands, he was prepared to spread the news. If I arrested him, his contact would do it for him."

Zuri kept her eyes fixed on Aidon, her disapproval still evident as she considered him.

"It was not worth the risk," she said finally. "He is a member of the Bellare. To have such a member on the Council..."

"Avis is a member of the Bellare," Aidon interjected. "And he served the Council for years."

The gold wedding ring on his mother's hand glinted as she waved her hand dismissively. "The boy is manipulating his *king*. He should be hanged, not rewarded."

Aidon's fists clenched at his side. "You think I made the decision lightly? That I acted without a plan?" he demanded. "Aleissande is my Second. She will oversee the Council. I will give Clyde the remaining seat and name him Lead Councillor."

"This is not just about the Council!" Zuri cut him off. "It is about *appearances*, Aidon. Plan or not, you now appear weak to a member of a group that is threatening your kingdom. He manipulated you into giving him what he wanted."

"I made Ryker ensure the Bellare would not retaliate when we sentence Avis—"

"It is not enough!" Zuri exclaimed.

"What would you have had me do?" Aidon ground out. "Kill him, and let my secret come out?"

"You could have painted it as a lie!"

"And he would have dragged Viviane into it! We would have had to hang her for treason right alongside him if he framed her as the source!"

"Then she would hang as well!" Zuri hissed.

He had never seen his mother like this. His even-tempered mother, who had advised a selfish king and anchored her place as the voice of wisdom between two arguing brothers. Who had taught Aidon the value of patience, of timing the strike just right.

Zuri was furious, her kind eyes glinting with such rage

that he wondered if, like the fire that had burst from him earlier, she had been burying it for years.

Aidon shook his head, his breath settling into a shallow rhythm. "That is Josie's partner—"

"Who has committed treason not once, but *twice* against her king—"

"Have you not noticed!" he yelled, his hands slamming on to the table. "Have you not seen how Josie is wilting away? She is crumbling, and yet you sit here and tell me to kill the *one* person keeping her tethered to some sense of life!"

Gods, what had happened to his family? What had happened to the closeness they'd once had? The way they'd once been able to read one another with a simple glance?

Maybe we never could. If we'd been able to, I would've known they're suspicious of Dominic. The thought was bitter and vicious, and it had Aidon's blood boiling within his veins.

"You could have *lied*," his mother was saying again. "You could have told him you'd give him the position and used Viviane to infiltrate the Bellare under threat of hanging!"

"That suggestion, Mother, is worthy of Dominic himself." The words were out of Aidon's mouth before he could stop them, and Zuri reeled back as if she'd been slapped. His father leaned forward, his green eyes narrowing into slits.

"Watch your tone," Enzo warned. Because here, in this room, Aidon was not king. He was a son and a brother, and he'd *wanted* that. So why, then, were the words kindling to his temper? "Your mother is right, you have a duty—"

"You," he snarled, pointing at his father, "have no right to lecture me on duty." Aidon stood and pushed away from the table, his chair catching against the edge with a loud bang. "You want to berate someone for being a coward?" he asked his mother, jerking his head toward Enzo. "Try the man beside you."

Enzo stood up so quickly his chair fell over, but Aidon was already turning away, his long stride taking him to the entryway before his father could even speak. He paused at the threshold, his jaw tight as he looked back toward his parents. "Josie is not to hear a word of this. Not of the Bellare knowing about my power, and not of Vi's involvement." His mother opened her mouth to argue, but Aidon pressed on.

"That is an order from your king."

Aidon had fifteen minutes of blessed silence in his room—just enough time to change out of his coronation attire and into cotton pants and a loose shirt and pull his sketch pad out of his desk—before someone was rapping on the door.

He let his head fall into his hands, not bothering to hide his groan. Technically, he could tell them to go away, he supposed. He was the king now.

Aidon sighed and pushed himself up from his desk, his bare feet padding across the marble floor. He took a steadying breath before pulling the door open, his frustration vanishing as soon as he saw who was on the other side.

"We need some sort of code so I know it's you," he told his sister as he stepped aside to let her into the room. "I almost ordered you away."

Josie chuckled knowingly as she made her way to his bed—a large mattress set in an ornate golden frame—and flung herself onto it. "As if I'd listen to you."

"As if you'd have a choice," Aidon retorted. He closed the door and turned to face his sister, forcing his face into a mocking look of severity. "Haven't you heard? I'm king now. My word is law." She snorted as she settled back among his many pillows. She still wore her dress from the coronation, and the tulle settled over his navy bedspread like an overzealous blanket.

"Did you come to lecture me about leaving my own coronation celebration?" Aidon asked teasingly as he settled into the chair at his desk. His body ached as he propped his feet on the wooden surface, as if the fire that had burned through him had bludgeoned his muscles in the process.

Josie shot him a roguish smile, the light of it not quite meeting her eyes. "I was actually coming to apologize for my early exit. Seems I don't need to, though. Where did you run off to?"

Aidon trailed a finger over the sketch he'd started as he forced an easy shrug. "Needed some peace and quiet. You?"

He glanced at his sister to see her frowning at him. She knew him well enough to know that while Aidon didn't need to be the center of attention, it was rare for him to pass up a good time. Especially when Clyde and Lucas were there.

But she didn't press him on it. Perhaps she knew the events of the other month had changed him, just as they had her.

Josie sat up, tucking her feet beneath the folds of her skirt. "I just needed a breath. I did some painting. I went to visit Viviane this morning and it was…a lot," she remarked quietly, her gaze focused on the tulle of her gown.

"Ah."

An awkward silence followed, not quite tense, but not easy either. Aidon hadn't judged Josie for keeping her relationship with Viviane. Not once. But that didn't mean he'd known how to feel about the situation. Vi had been intent on destroying his claim to the throne. And yet…she had suffered terribly at Dominic's hand for it.

But now that he knew she'd lied again…

It was further muddied, what with her rare power and the use she could be to them.

Sometimes, Aidon wondered if it made him just as bad as his uncle that he looked at Viviane that way—as someone to be used. Someone he could manipulate when the benefit was greatest to him.

Aidon rubbed the back of his neck, that spot where tension always built, as he searched for something else to say. He was afraid he'd give himself away if he discussed Vi much more tonight. Luckily, it seemed Josie wasn't keen to share more about the visit. She had a faraway look on her face, the type she got when she was lost in thought and was not to be interrupted.

He waited her out, his fingers tapping a steady rhythm on the paper. Finally, she sighed, her expression solemn as she met his gaze.

"I wanted to ask you something."

There was enough seriousness in her voice that Aidon found himself straightening, his feet smacking against the floor as he dropped them from the desk. "Anything."

Josie shifted, her hands digging into his comforter. "I was wondering if you might...write me a contract." Her throat bobbed, but she raised her head, her voice steady as she met his gaze. "For the Royal Army."

Aidon blinked. "Aleissande oversees the Royal Army and City Guard," he replied automatically.

Josie nodded, her jaw shifting with determination. "And you and I both know that Aleissande, or any general for that matter, would not accept a princess in her forces unless mandated by the king."

He could spot the logic in her argument instantly, and yet Aidon still found himself hesitating. Josie was an incredible fighter. Hells, he had been telling Aya mere weeks ago that his uncle was wasting Josie's talents. But that was before war was breathing down their necks.

"Josie..." Aidon stood up. But she was already off the bed, her stride purposeful as she closed the distance between them.

"I am not naive about the risks, Aidon. I know I will likely find myself on the battlefield before the summer is out. Let me serve our kingdom. Let me serve you."

He had wanted her to. He had *asked* her to. As his Second—the most trusted position in his court. She had rejected the offer without a moment's hesitation.

He couldn't pretend that it did not sting.

"This is not a decision I'm entering into lightly," Josie pressed as he paced away from her, giving himself a moment to breathe, to think. His fingers pinched the space between his brows.

Aleissande wouldn't be happy about him going over her head on this. And yet Josie was right. It didn't matter how great a warrior she was. There was no way in hells the general would contract her to the military, not with the years Dominic had spent crafting a reputation for Josie of political posturing, which was more sweet-talking nobles and entertaining foreign diplomats than anything else.

"Please, Aidon."

The request was soft and tinged with a desperation that made Aidon draw up short. He glanced over his shoulder to see all trace of the levity he'd been so relieved to see on her face earlier today wiped thoroughly from her gaze.

The stoicism that had hung heavily over his sister had returned, and it made her vibrant gaze dull as she whispered, "Please."

She needed this. And perhaps…perhaps it would be good to have another member of the royal family in the force. Especially if his newfound affinity issue would prevent him from being as involved as he once was.

Aidon's stomach tightened at the thought. He'd managed to push it from his mind for a few moments, but the dread came roaring back as he continued to stare at Josie and assess his options.

"Fine," he said finally. "But it's up to Aleissande to place you within the forces. I make no guarantees that she'll allow you to join the front lines, or any prominent units for that matter."

It was telling that Josie merely nodded with no hint of dissent.

Gods, when was the last time he'd seen Josie's inner fire? When she'd fought against the guards in that godsforsaken dungeon?

No. It was when she'd thought Aidon was truly aiding Dominic and had punched him so hard across his jaw he'd sworn the bones had cracked.

He'd known it was bad, that her desolation was deep. But only because he'd spent twenty-one years learning to read his younger sister. She'd always been such an open book, but now…

Secrets. They both kept so many secrets.

Josie stepped toward him, her arms circling his shoulders as she pulled him into a hug.

"Thank you," she murmured against his shoulder. "You won't regret this."

Aidon sighed as he returned her hug, the dark coils of her hair soft against his skin as he rested his chin on her head. "Promise me one thing when you start sparring," he muttered.

"Anything."

Aidon drew back so he could give Josie a smirk. "Beat them all."

There.

A spark of light, small but noticeable, lit her irises as her lips twisted in a grin—a real grin.

It was enough to make relief swoop through Aidon, enough to make him forget, momentarily, the night from hells he'd just had, especially as Josie cocked her head, that subtle note of sarcasm and defiance he'd always associated with his sister weaving throughout her tone as she said, "I've beaten you enough that I'm thoroughly confident that won't be a problem."

Aidon barked a laugh and his smile remained, even as Josie inclined her head toward his desk. "Shall we write the contract now?" she asked. Another grin. "You can't tell me that sketch was going anywhere worth pursuing tonight."

She needs this.

"Fine," Aidon conceded with an overdramatic sigh. "Let's begin."

23

Aya knew stillness. She had trained her body and her mind to freeze in time, letting the world move around her while she waited, and waited, and waited until the perfect time to strike.

You should be prepared.

This stillness was different. It was forced on her, her muscles locking against her will, her mind emptying of everything except those four words the healer had just spoken to her with such gentleness.

You should be prepared.

Aya could barely make out the Anima standing in front of her, even though she was *still* speaking. Nor could she truly register Tova beside her. Everything had faded into a bright blur, as if the glaring white paint on the walls of the infirmary on the edge of town had blinded her.

You should be prepared.

"Aya?" Tova's voice was hesitant, her grip on Aya's arm tight.

He's in a coma, the healer had said. *We will do everything we can but…you should be prepared.*

As if she hadn't spent the last six months trying to be prepared and failing miserably.

As if anything could prepare her for *this*.

A laugh bubbled up from Aya's chest, the sound choked and harsh and so utterly wrong for the agony she was feeling. It was followed by another, then another, then another, until it became a chorus of hysterical, broken laughter that seized her lungs and tightened the pressure on her chest.

Aya bowed over, her arms crossing over her stomach, as if she could contain the way her muscles ached as she continued to descend further into hysteria.

Tova was saying something, but Aya couldn't hear her. Aya forced herself upright, blinking through the stinging in her eyes to see a look of horror on the healer's face.

Aya's laughter died.

Stillness returned.

You should be prepared.

And then Aya lunged.

She was screaming, vicious threats she couldn't even comprehend spilling from her lips as she grabbed the front of the healer's tunic. A vise grip locked around her waist, hauling her backward and ripping her fingers from the healer. Aya thrashed in the hold like a wild animal, her fingers grasping the air as she tried to reach the woman, tried to make her hurt, make her *bleed*.

You should be prepared.

"AYA!" Tova was yelling her name, her arms an unbreakable cage around Aya's waist as she tugged and tugged, half carrying her out of the building. The cool, fresh air was like a slap in the face, as was the way Tova jerked her around to face her, her hands gripping Aya's arms tight enough to hurt. "AYA!" Tova shook her roughly. "Stop!"

Aya panted, her throat searing with each breath as she looked past her friend at the door to the healing center. "He can't… She has to… There must…" The words were choked pleas that disappeared on every sharp inhale. Aya met Tova's gaze, watching as that sharp assessing look in her hazel eyes faded, only to be replaced by tears.

"I know," Tova muttered as she pulled Aya into a fierce hug. "I know."

24

WILL WAS WELL ACQUAINTED WITH DESPERATION. IT was what broke those he questioned, what caused even the most iron-willed to shatter beneath his affinity and beg for mercy. He knew its taste, its weight, its shape, and how it settled in the gut and scratched at the throat and made the heart beat so hard it might just crack one's chest.

Will was well acquainted with Desperation. But he hadn't spent much time with his own.

He could feel it now, though, warring for attention over Exhaustion as he stood in Gianna's chambers, his eyes fixed on one of the iron flowers that decorated the mirror of the vanity at which she currently sat.

"You searched the premises?" his queen asked as she dotted her cheeks with rouge. She'd dismissed her attendants as soon as he'd come in. It made Will wary.

"I did, Majesty," he said, meeting her gaze in the oval mirror. "Whoever did this covered their tracks incredibly well. I have two Royal Guards monitoring the property." He paused, his jaw shifting as he considered his words. "I imagine Aya will want to search the home as well, once she's able."

He wasn't sure when that would be.

It had been hours, and yet Aya's screams were fresh in his mind, as was the picture of her falling to her knees in her father's blood, that white healing light flaring uselessly from her hands into his chest.

It had killed him to send for Tova—to act like he didn't want to stay with Aya after he'd finally calmed her enough that they were able to get Pa's body to the closest infirmary. When he'd returned from seeking out the general and alerting the necessary people that an attack had occurred, Aya and Tova were gone, and a shaken healer was muttering about violence and rage.

He heard Tova had managed to get Aya to Suja for a calming tonic.

"And you were the one who found her?" Gianna's question cut through Will's thoughts.

"Yes," he replied steadily. "I saw her escaping through her window. I followed her to ensure her safety."

The lie fell easily enough from his lips, as did the exasperation that he knew Gianna could read on his face as he continued. "Aya rejects protection. I had much experience with her disdain for it in Trahir."

Gianna let out a noise of agreement. "Even so, she will need it now more than ever, what with her display at the Sanctification. Kahn and Lamihr will stay stationed at the entrance to the Quarter, and Aya will have a Dyminara escort from now on." She began to line her eyes with kohl before adding, "And Tyr, should he remain bonded to her."

"If he doesn't, it would be a great loss indeed," Will murmured, more to himself.

Gianna sighed heavily as she set the liner down, her hands falling into her lap. "I will not dispute that. Aya has faced enough. And her road ahead...it will not be easy."

Will's next words were carefully chosen. "You think the gods will test her in such a way, Majesty?" He was sure not to point to Gianna in his question, to lean instead into her beliefs.

He wondered if it should worry him, how easily manipulation came to him.

Again, Gianna's voice was heavy. "I believe the Divine test us all, William. And that they require greatness from those they call on." He didn't have time to parse through her words before she continued. "I pray her father will pull through."

This had been what he had truly come to her for. A chance to feel out her involvement. Gianna did nothing without having something to gain from it, and while he couldn't fathom what she would have to gain from ordering an attack on Aya's father, he would not rule it out.

A coma, the healer had informed him. *It is in Mora's hands now.*

Perhaps it was up to the goddess of fate. But getting answers? That was Will's proficiency, and if it was all he could give Aya for now, he would do what was necessary. So he felt no guilt as he lowered his shield and called his affinity up to sense his queen, searching for some indication of Gianna's intentions. It wasn't a perfect method outside of interrogation or forcing sensation, but sensing someone's state was typically enough to gather at least a hint.

"Do you have any theories, Majesty, on who would commit such a crime?"

Her full lips pursed in contemplation, a small divot appearing between her brows. "No," she replied, her voice hardening. "We are a nation of devotion to the Divine. To attack one related to a saint..."

"I had the same suspicions," Will murmured. "That he was attacked because of who Aya is. Which means whoever did this knows enough about her to be aware that Callias Veliri is her father."

Will focused his affinity, *sensing* rather than pushing, letting Gianna's emotions wash over him, but he felt nothing that indicated guilt. No heaviness other than sadness met his affinity as Gianna murmured, "Even without all she's faced, to lose both parents…" She took a steadying breath before meeting his gaze in the mirror. "Well, let's just say, the pain of it never leaves you."

Will had been too young to pay attention when the queen passed, and he hadn't had any particularly strong feelings about the former king's death. If anything, it had been an opportunity for him—for all of them—as Gianna formed her own Tría. But he did recall Gianna's grief, and how it had seemed to linger. Anyone could have seen she'd been a ghost of herself for months.

Perhaps the murmurs had also played a role. There had been whispers that she wasn't fit to rule. Too young, they'd said. Too naive, especially when she'd chosen three young Dyminara above those more seasoned to form her Tría.

She had certainly silenced those doubts over the years.

"May their Majesties rest eternally in the Beyond," Will replied, his head dipping once. Gianna smiled softly, her chin tilting as she considered his reflection. Silence settled between them, long enough that Will had to remind himself not to shift under the queen's gaze.

"I am not beyond admitting my own faults, Will," she finally said softly.

Will's attention perked at that, his brow furrowing in anticipation of what she was about to share.

Gianna hesitated for a moment, her tongue wetting her lower lip before she continued. "The threat of war has made me rash in some areas I ought not to be. I was too hasty in doubting your allegiance. I should not have questioned your loyalty while you were in Trahir. You have proved it time and time again. I apologize."

Will was careful to hold her gaze, to let her see the calculation she would expect. His affinity was still open to her, her human nature unable to detect it as he sensed that warm yet firm essence he'd long associated with Gianna. There was still no hint of a lie in what was emanating from her. No betrayal, which often felt like both heaviness and a twisted pleasure all at once.

Just a soft blanket of remorse.

Finally, he let his posture loosen, just enough for her to notice. "I understand why you did doubt, Your Majesty."

And gods, it was a risk, but he was tired of searching for answers only to come up empty. So he raked a hand through his hair, letting his hesitation show as he continued. "I was curious if your fears were aided by Tova."

Gianna pivoted on her bench to face him fully, a frown marring her golden brow. "What do you mean?"

"Nothing in particular," Will answered, his hands sliding into his pockets as he gave a blithe shrug. "I just know that Tova is not particularly fond of me. I wouldn't have been surprised if she'd confirmed your suspicions out of spite when you questioned her."

The words tasted vile and bitter as they left his lips, but...

A necessary evil. If it meant getting one godsdamned truth, one answer that might ease his mind, ease *Aya*'s mind, then he would use his fraught relationship with Tova to do it.

But Gianna merely shook her head, her hand waving dismissively. "She had nothing to share." She turned back to the vanity and reached for a diamond necklace before she stood and approached him. "Unfortunately, my suspicions were my own."

She handed the necklace to him and turned, lifting her long golden hair in a wordless command. "I let the threats we face overrule my better judgment, and then I punished you harshly in a way that I fear has cost us something in our relationship," she said softly.

Will reached around her, placing the necklace on her throat.

Dangerous territory. This was dangerous territory. Especially because his affinity, still sensing her, identified exactly what now rose in her:

The ache of longing.

The heat of desire.

"Our relationship stays ever strong," Will murmured as he worked the small clasp, his fingers brushing against the delicate skin at the nape of her neck. "I am devoted to you, Majesty."

She waited until he finished before turning back to him, her head tilting up to meet his gaze. "You are, aren't you?" she breathed.

"Yes."

Gianna's hands settled on his chest, her fingers toying with the button of his shirt. "You would do anything for me, would you not?"

Will stilled, his eyes darting across her face.

Forward—she had become so much more forward. Gone were the longing glances and subtle touches. This was outright desire, and she had only shown it this boldly once before, just after the Athatis attack.

Perhaps she had grown tired of their cat-and-mouse game.

Will was well acquainted with Desperation. But he hadn't spent much time with his own. Not enough to know that his didn't look like screams and begging and the spilling of secrets, but standing still and willing his breath to stay steady as his queen undid the first, and then the second button of his shirt, her hands warm against his bare skin as they slid through the opening in the fabric.

And it was Desperation who answered for him in a rough voice Will had only used to seduce at taverns when he longed for someone to help him feel worth more than a night. "Yes. I would do anything for you, Majesty."

Gianna's lips were close enough that her breath was a mere caress across his mouth. "Then put your hands on me."

Desperation was not enough to keep his heart from hammering or his mind from whirling as he tried to determine if this was some sort of test, because he could not tell, even with his affinity, which sensed only her desire, *he could not tell.*

Will swallowed as his hands found Gianna's waist.

Forgive me.

He wasn't sure who he was praying to. Pathos? All of the Divine?

Aya.

He needed an out—a believable one that would not undo this progress but would allow him to leave. To maintain the one sacred thing he had left in his life. He needed it now, because her lips were mere inches from his, her eyes fierce in a way he had never seen as she stared up at him.

"As much as I would be honored to continue this, Majesty, I have duties to attend to."

Her hands left his chest, her fingers gripping the fabric of his shirt and untucking it from his pants. "And if I were to change your duties?"

It was an impulse, the way Will's fingers dug into the soft curve of her hips to push her away, as natural as the muscle that clenched in his jaw. But Gianna didn't seem to take it as anything but reciprocated desire as her hand trailed to his belt buckle.

Enough.

He reached for her wrist just as a knock sounded at the door. He hardly had enough time to step back from the queen, his hands falling to his sides. But Gianna kept ahold of his belt, even as the attendant stepped into the room.

"Apologies, Your Majesty," the woman stammered, her face blushing at the image before her. "I didn't realize you were otherwise occupied."

"We were just finishing," Gianna said lightly, her fingers trailing the silver of his buckle before finally dropping from him. "Is it time for the dinner, Kenna?"

"Yes, Your Majesty," the attendant responded. Will could see her eyes fixed on his disheveled state, and he bit back a curse.

The rumors had always been there, but Gianna had never done *this*.

This is a good thing, Desperation whispered to him. *You*

are back on the inside. You have her attention again. And yet he couldn't quite muster any feelings of victory. Especially not as Gianna stepped around him, her back straightening into that posture of regality as she followed her attendant to her door and called back to him, "Assign someone to the search for whoever attacked Aya's father." She glanced over her shoulder, shooting him a coy smile. "As you said yourself, you have other duties to attend to. Resolve those quickly, would you? So we can discuss something *new* for you?"

Will waited until the door was shut and her footsteps had faded before he let his mask crack, his hands curling into fists as he fought the urge to punch a hole straight through the wall.

"Fucking hells," he gritted out as he slumped against the stone.

This news would be throughout the Dyminara and the Guard by midday tomorrow. And then it would stretch beyond—to the councillors, the lower merchants, all those who paid attention to the gossip of Gianna's court.

To Aya, too.

She knows the role I intended to play.

He couldn't tell if it was Desperation or his own voice whispering the assurance in his head. After all, this had been his plan, hadn't it? Restore his place in the court. Regain Gianna's confidence. Hold her attention and force out her answers and make sure he was never, ever a viable weapon to use against Aya again.

But how far would Desperation have him go? How far until he shattered this ruse with Gianna? Gianna, who had always been intent on the chase but now seemed tired of waiting.

"Fucking hells," Will cursed again, but this time his tone was soft and broken.

He looked down at his rumpled and untucked shirt, and Desperation went silent.

In its place, Self-Loathing began to make itself heard.

25

"Don't touch it." Aya's words were sharp, and they had Tova shooting her a look of a surprise from where she knelt by the puddle of blood in Pa's kitchen, a rag in her hand.

She'd need more than that flimsy thing. The blood was dry now, the spot a dark-crimson stain on the wooden floor.

"We should clean it, Aya." Tova used the same gentle tone she'd been speaking to her in since she'd dragged her from the healer yesterday. The only time her friend hadn't spoken to her like she was a wounded animal was when something in Aya had snapped yesterday. She'd yelled then. But the soft, wary tone had returned as soon as Suja had forced a calming tonic down Aya's throat.

The tonic hadn't taken the pain away but it had muted it slightly. The pain, the fury, the sadness, the fucking *raging* guilt that threatened to eat her alive.

I should have been there.

The tonic made it easier to quiet the thought. It helped her bury those sharp feelings, the ones that threatened to poke and prod until they burst from her the way her power once did, back when she had no control.

It helped her focus on what mattered: Finding whoever had done this to her father.

"Aya?" Aya blinked and refocused on her friend, that rag still hanging in Tova's hand.

"I'm not done looking for evidence," Aya muttered. She turned back to the counter, her fingers trailing across the worn surface. The towel that sat on the edge of the sink had been damp yesterday—as if Pa had just folded it.

"The Royal Guard will exhaust every avenue, Aya," Tova reasoned from behind her.

Aya nearly scoffed. The tonic had helped with that, too. It had kept her calm, her face blank, as she'd stood before Gianna and accepted her queen's deepest sympathies and promises to find the perpetrator.

But a suspicion had begun to form in the back of her mind as soon as the tonic had cleared away enough of her panic.

"Unless it was their doing," Aya muttered darkly, her gaze trailing the edge of the sink. She turned to find Tova leaning a hip against the kitchen table, her arms crossed and brow furrowed.

"You think *a Royal Guard* did this?" Her evident skepticism set Aya's teeth on edge. She'd sensed that same skepticism in Will's voice last night when he'd snuck into her room.

I used my affinity. I sensed no guilt, he'd said. *It's not a perfect method, but…Gianna is strategic, Aya. She never makes a move unless there's a direct return on her investment. What would be the point of this?*

Perhaps Aya's show of power had done more to intimidate her queen than Aya had intended. And what better way for Gianna to tighten the leash than to hurt yet another person Aya cared about?

Who would she even task with such a thing, Aya? Will had pressed.

"I don't know," she ground out to Tova, perhaps to the

memory of Will, too. She doubted Gianna would be so obvious as to use her own guards. But that didn't mean she'd eliminate the option. "That's why I need to keep looking—"

"Aya." Tova cut her off with a note of authority. It was the command of a general. She crossed the kitchen in three long strides, her hands grasping Aya's arms lightly. "I know you want to find out who did this," she said, her voice softening slightly. "I do too. But we spent hours here yesterday. And this morning. There is *nothing* here."

"We could have missed something—"

"No, we couldn't have. Especially not you. On my oath, you are a *spy*. If there was something here, you would've found it."

She was a spy. Or at least, she used to be. Ever since she'd looked down at her palm in that dungeon, Tova's screams echoing in her ears, and found her oath to the Dyminara gone, she hadn't been sure what she was. When she'd been in Trahir, she'd been there as a presumed saint, only to think she was something *other*—something filled with darkness. And she'd been so consumed by that fear, by that possibility, that she hadn't been able to trust her instincts.

She'd put herself in foolish situations, in desperate situations, as if her training hadn't even *mattered*. As if it had been wiped away as easily as her oath had been.

You should be prepared.

She'd been rash. She'd let her emotions control her.

You should be prepared.

She would not make that mistake now.

"Talk to me," Tova urged.

Will had said the same thing when she'd gone silent last night after his reflection on Gianna. *Talk to me, Aya.*

She'd tried to ignore the pain in his eyes when she'd turned away from him at the request, just as she tried to ignore Tova's now as she stepped out of her hold.

"I'm due to meet Hyacinth," Aya said as she made her

way toward the front door. She'd been excused from her first session at the Synastysi yesterday, but the High Priestess would not be kept waiting. Nor would Gianna.

"Aya," Tova urged.

"I'll be back here later if you want to—"

"Aya, *stop*." The vexation in Tova's tone had Aya pulling up short, a frown furrowing her brow as she turned to face her friend. Tova's cheeks were flushed, her eyes bright with emotion. "Just...stop. I know what you're doing."

Aya's eyes narrowed. "*What I'm doing*," she repeated slowly.

Tova waved an irritated hand through the air. "You're shutting me out. Just like you always do when you don't want to deal with something. You didn't even ask me to come with you to see your father yesterday. Instead, I find you with *Will*, of all people—"

"I told you," Aya cut in. "I came alone. I came across Will when I was looking for a healer." She felt no guilt at the lie. Not with the way Tova was glaring at her, her temper building.

"That's not my point!" Tova barked, her hands clenching by her sides.

"Then make it!"

An incredulous scoff burst from her friend. "You're fucking impossible sometimes. You know that?"

Gods, did she ever. But she couldn't bring herself to be agreeable, not now, not when she'd longed for home for fucking months only to return to enemies on all sides who inflicted nightmare after nightmare.

"Forget it," Tova snapped, her hand raking through her long hair with frustration. She threw the rag onto the kitchen table. "Go ahead. Shut out the *only* person you have left if that's what you want to do. End up alone." The taunt was delivered with a clip of Tova's shoulder as she stormed out the door.

Aya whirled to face her friend, her lips parted in anger.

How dare she? How fucking dare she?

But Tova was already at the gate, her stride quick in her fury. Aya's frustration bled out of her just as fast, her body sagging against the entryway to the kitchen as she watched Tova leave. A long breath escaped Aya's lungs, carrying the last of her anger with it and leaving a heaviness she was all too familiar with in its wake.

Tova wasn't the only person she had left—but she was one of the few. The reminder made Aya's insides twist.

She didn't know how to mend whatever was broken between them. The events of the last several months seemed too big, too overwhelming, to not continue to chafe at their bond. And then there was the matter of Will, and the conversation Tova refused to acknowledge either from anger or loyalty to Gianna. Aya wasn't sure which. And as much as Aya wanted to continue to blame her queen, and did...

Aya was the real reason Tova had been disgraced. She was the reason Tova had been questioned not once, but twice. Aya had created this chasm between them, and she worried she would only continue to widen it.

She swallowed as she turned back to the kitchen, her eyes fixed on that crimson mark on the floor.

Tova wasn't the only person she had left—but she was one of the few.

And gods, did that make her feel so fucking alone.

Aya found Liam, her Dyminara guard for the day, waiting at the edge of the long road that led to her father's. The Persi was leaning against one of the tall lantern posts, his arms crossed, body relaxed, but she didn't miss the way his eyes scanned the fields, as if a threat might be lingering in the tall grass that swayed in the spring breeze.

At least he'd given her a modicum of privacy.

Aya hadn't had it in her to fight Gianna on the new orders

for protection. She hadn't trained with Tyr yet, and with Aya's rash display of power and now her father's attack, Gianna had the perfect excuse to have a member of her elite guard following her at all times.

The leash Gianna was keeping around Aya's neck was tightening each day. Her queen was making sure of it. And perhaps if Aya had Tova's fire, or Will's impertinence, she would have challenged her. But instead, she'd merely nodded when she received the order, lost in the numbing sensation of the calming tonic.

Aya gave Liam a brief dip of her chin as she started toward town. Liam remained blessedly silent as he fell into step beside her, as if he could sense the tension rolling off her. Or perhaps he simply didn't care to talk. It didn't truly matter to her. She preferred silence.

Word of her father's assault had spread faster than uncontrolled Incend fire, leaving Aya dodging empty platitudes from several of the Dyminara when they crossed her path.

Well, those that dared speak to her, that is. Most simply stared, as if she were no more than a mythical creature from a childhood story. But those that did speak... Each empty condolence pricked her skin, leaving her raw and flinching whenever someone approached.

She didn't want their sympathy. She wanted revenge. She wanted the person who had done this to pay in blood, in pain. She wanted something, some action that could ease her fury, her *shame* that she had missed her chance to tell Pa the truth. To explain to him why she'd been this distant and cold *thing* for years. To apologize because she still didn't know for sure, and never would, if her power had been the catalyst for her mother's death.

Aya's steps slowed as she registered the side street she and Liam were passing. A gaggle of merchants openly gawked at her, their hands not enough to conceal their whispers about the saint, but Aya paid them no mind.

Instead, she frowned at the run-down alley, its dilapidated storefronts looking more fit for Rouline than the heart of Dunmeaden.

"Where are you going?" Liam called after her, a hint of annoyance in his voice as she stepped into the alley.

"Wait here," she ordered. "I just need a moment." Aya stopped before one of the storefronts, its windows filled to the brim with various odds and ends.

"We're already late," Liam called to her.

"A minute," Aya snapped back.

And then she ducked through the door.

26

HYACINTH DIDN'T SEEM BOTHERED BY AYA'S LATE ARRIVAL. Perhaps the High Priestess was simply relieved to see that Aya had shown up. Liam, on the other hand, had traded his silence for a string of curses as soon as he saw the miniature flowerpot that Aya slipped into her pocket.

"Really," he'd deadpanned. "That couldn't have waited?"

"No," Aya had replied curtly. She'd repot one of Pa's flowers after her studies and leave it at his bedside in the infirmary as an offering to Cero, the god of earth. Perhaps Pa's patron god would bestow their favor upon him or, at the very least, encourage Mora to work her own miracles.

"I am sorry to hear about your father," Hyacinth murmured as she led Aya to the study alcove where she'd met the priestesses two days prior.

Had it only been two days? It felt like a lifetime since she'd stood here. The chairs around the table were empty now, but the worn wooden surface was still full of manuscripts and leather-bound books. The pile had grown since she'd last seen it.

"Callias was a good man," Hyacinth continued.

Aya ground her teeth as she sat down. "He's not dead."

Hyacinth's eyes flared wide, her hand reaching for Aya's. "Of course. And I am praying fervently to Mora that she restores him to his full health." She hesitated for a moment, her teeth digging into her bottom lip. When she spoke again, there was a hesitance to her voice. "Her Majesty says you tried to heal him?"

Aya's fingers curled under the table. She had. She'd knelt in his blood, in the kitchen he so loved, that white healing light flaring in her palms as she tried desperately to bring him back to consciousness. It hadn't worked. She hadn't known what she was healing, and even when she did, it did not matter.

"Healers are not gods," Suja had reminded her when she'd given her the tonic for peace. "And neither are you."

Aya knew the healers had limitations to their powers. She'd seen enough death, had had enough of her own injuries, to prove it. They were particularly limited when it came to afflictions that impacted the mind. And yet she couldn't help the anger she'd felt in that moment, the anger that still simmered now.

She'd brought Will back from the brink of death. Why couldn't she do the same for her father now?

"Boundless though my power is rumored to be, there still appear to be limitations," Aya muttered.

"It is difficult to heal that which we cannot see. That is true," Hyacinth said thoughtfully.

The words had Aya's gaze snapping to the High Priestess. They reminded her of something she'd shared with Aidon during one of their training sessions. Something that had saved all their lives more than once.

It's the inside wounds I struggle with more.

Hyacinth smiled kindly at her, her palms splaying flat on the table. "Well, I won't take up any more of your time. I know you have much to do." And with those parting words, she pushed herself up from the table, leaving Aya to face the looming mess of books before her.

She shouldn't be here. She should be with Pa, in case he woke up when she was gone.

Her leg bounced beneath the table.

She wanted to act. To move. To do.

To sit here when there was so much at stake...

Aya closed her eyes, forcing air to fill her lungs.

The sooner you find answers, the sooner you can put an end to all of this.

Even if she didn't hear from the gods immediately, one of the manuscripts could shed light on the veil. Aya opened her eyes, her jaw set in determination, and tugged one of the leather-bound books toward her.

"You seem frustrated," Hyacinth's lilting voice drew Aya's gaze up from where it had been fixed on the floor, her eyes tracing the swirling pattern on the plush red rug between them. They sat across from each other in oversized leather armchairs. On the far side of the room was a bookcase, and across from it sat an ornate desk covered in parchments.

Aya tucked her feet beneath the arm of her chair as she curled further back into the worn seat. Hyacinth had wanted to know all Aya had uncovered today, pushing her for each and every detail she'd retained from what she'd read.

The manuscripts had been a waste of time.

She'd gone through sheaf after sheaf of translated text, her eyes blurring as she skimmed the pages for something, anything, that might prove worth pursuing.

She'd found nothing.

Even the diary she'd began to read—an original, as it was written in the Old Language—had left her wanting.

Aya's jaw shifted as she met Hyacinth's gaze. "As you've likely garnered from all I've shared, I've found nothing," she retorted. "Merely more recollections of Evie's power and greatness, and those were recounted even in the books in the Maraciana in Rinnia."

She didn't dare share that she'd also been looking for something—*anything*—that would help her understand the veil further.

Naturally, she hadn't found that either.

Hyacinth cocked her head. "Such accounts should not be dismissed. People considered her a leader, a trusted connection to the gods. They followed her even though her power could have been seen as a threat."

Aya picked at a piece of torn leather. "And yet, that does nothing to help me understand how to use *my* power to fulfill the prophecy, does it?"

She knew she shouldn't show such insolence—not to the highest member of the temple. But Aya's short fuse had worsened since arriving home, and the hours she'd wasted in the dark second floor of this godsforsaken place had been the final straw.

Hyacinth leaned forward, a curious look on her face. "You believe you will not be able to help, don't you? That the gods will leave you unprepared?"

Aya's gaze was steady. "I believe if the gods wanted another Evie, they should have looked elsewhere."

"Why is it you believe the worst in yourself?" Hyacinth's question was soft, gentle. It hollowed out something in Aya, wedging itself into the spaces she often kept locked tightly away.

She stared at the High Priestess, her lips pressed together in a thin line. Aya was used to letting silence grow until it pushed against her marks, forcing their mouths to move.

Hyacinth lasted longer than Aya expected. But she did eventually fold, a heavy sigh sending her sheer veil fluttering.

"Part of your training here, Aya, will be healing that which might keep you from connecting to the Nine Divine. We teach our priestesses how to purify their minds and hearts, so that they may be an open channel to hear the word of the gods. To go within themselves and face that which keeps them from being all the gods have called them to be."

Aya stayed stock-still, her muscles tensing as she fought off the urge to fidget. Hyacinth's training hardly sounded different from what she'd endured with the Vaguer in the desert of Trahir. Touching Evie's sword had almost killed her. And while perhaps Lorna was right, and Aya's unwavering belief in being dark had been why she'd had such visions in the desert—why her own fear had manifested that way—it wasn't as though she wanted to revisit such exploration of herself.

Especially with Hyacinth.

The High Priestess let out another sigh. "That's all for today. We'll try again tomorrow after you train with Galda."

Aya didn't bother to say goodbye as she turned her back and left.

27

Aya swept through the front doors of the Synastysi, tugging the hood of her cloak up so it concealed her face. She didn't care to see the stares again as she walked through town.

She didn't bother to wait for Liam to fall into step beside her. She was too focused on getting *out*, on putting as much distance between herself and this godsforsaken temple as she could.

She sensed Liam reaching for her, his fingers just brushing the sleeve of her cloak. She snatched his wrist and wrenched her arm back as she whirled to face him. "Do *not*—" She bit off her words as she met Will's bemused grin, his hands opening in a sign of innocence.

"Easy, love." And while the words were painted with humor, there was a sincerity to them—a low understanding and perhaps even a gentle warning as he cut a glance to the wall of guards beyond them, keeping curious townspeople at bay.

Aya let out a hard breath and released him. "I thought you were Liam."

Will cocked a brow. "Should I be jealous? You're typically only that feisty with me."

Gods above.

Aya narrowed her eyes at him.

"I relieved Liam of his saint-sitting duties," Will continued with a roguish grin that didn't quite meet his eyes. "You're with me this afternoon, and I have somewhere I need to go, so..." He gestured at the path ahead of them.

But Aya didn't move. She was too busy searching his face, trying to find some indication of what was causing the heaviness he was trying so desperately to mask.

"You'll like it, I promise," Will added, misreading her hesitation. Another moment passed, and he sighed as he straightened. "What?"

"What's wrong?"

A nudge to her lower back. "You won't *move*. That's what's wrong."

Aya bit back the urge to press him on it. He hadn't forced her to talk last night, or any night for that matter. She could give him the same space.

Will's grin turned soft and genuine as she relented. They made their way through the town, sticking mostly to back streets and winding alleys to avoid the stares that followed Aya. Even though his posture was loose and easy, Aya could sense the tension in Will as he monitored the few strangers passing by, their eyes tracking Aya despite her cloaked figure.

"I can protect myself, you know," she murmured.

Will cut her a glance. "I'm well aware. But that doesn't mean I fancy the idea of you having to fight someone who wants to off the saint."

"You're insufferable."

"Interesting," Will replied lightly. "That's not what you said the other night." He let out a grunt as her elbow met his gut.

"Tell me where you're taking me." He was leading her to the outskirts of the town and into the mountains.

"Not a chance now," he retorted, his hand subtly skimming the small of her back as they maneuvered around two tradesmen. "You'll know soon enough anyway." He dropped his hand immediately, but the warmth of the touch lingered as they trudged up the steep inclines of the streets until they eventually reached the forest. That easy peace filled the space between them as they trekked deeper into the woods, and Aya tugged off her hood and tilted her head back, taking in the towering pines that surrounded them. She could feel her muscles loosen and her shoulders drop the further they walked.

The forest had often been able to steady her. To help her breathe and her mind settle just for a moment. She felt Will's gaze on her, but she kept hers fixed to the trees as she said, "I hate when you call me that, you know."

From the corner of her eye, she saw him frown. "Call you what?"

"A saint."

"Ah." He slid his hands into his pockets, his head tilting back to take in the sky. "You know that's not..." His voice trailed off, his steps slowing to a stop as he turned to face her fully. "That's not what you are to me."

Aya swallowed.

Magnificent.

Strong.

Beautiful.

Divine.

She didn't feel any of those things right now. She mostly felt empty. And angry.

As if he could read her thoughts, Will pulled her to him, the warmth of him bleeding into her as he held her tightly.

Aya let herself sink into his hold, her head settling on his chest as she let out a long breath. And even though her muscles loosened further...

"I need to go back to the house," Aya murmured as she began to pull away. "I wasted enough time today. I should be looking for—"

"One afternoon," Will interjected softly, his arms tightening around her waist. He pressed his forehead against hers. "No threats. No duties. No wars. Give me one afternoon."

She didn't know how to give him what he wanted. Not when there were so many unanswered questions. But that heaviness she'd sensed in him earlier was even more evident now, painting tight lines across his face that he couldn't hide.

She pushed up on to her toes and pressed her lips against his, letting the steady beat of his heart against her palm anchor her.

For him, she could at least try.

"One afternoon," she echoed as she pulled away.

Aya had been too lost in her thoughts to pay much attention to where Will was leading her. So when they were suddenly before the Zeluus-forged wall that separated this part of the mountain from the lower region, Aya paused, her brow furrowed as she looked to Will.

"The Athatis compound?"

The sacred wolves who protected the Dyminara had over half the mountain to themselves, as well as the sprawling lands that led to the Pelion Gap. Aya and Will stood just outside the iron gate—the nearest point to the barn where the wolves rested. Aya could glimpse part of the wooden structure through the trees.

The hole, which had been ripped through the wall by the Diaforaté who had tampered with the wolves and released them on the Dawning festival, had been fixed since Aya and Will had been gone.

Will dragged a hand through his hair and shrugged. "I know Gianna pushed off your reunion with him to next week with all that unfolded with your father—and that seeing him isn't the same as fighting with him, as seeing if your bond stands in battle. But I just thought…you shouldn't have to wait to do at least that. See him, I mean. Make sure he at least recognizes you despite the new power in your veins. And… that you'd prefer to do that without an audience."

Aya's throat tightened.

She'd hardly had time to examine the fear that Gianna had planted—that she and Tyr were no longer bonded. It had been buried beneath her terror at the Sanctification, and then the agony and regret for her father. But it came roaring to the surface now, her mouth going dry as she wrestled with the possibility that this would be yet one more thing taken away from her.

Fighting with Tyr was one of the few times that Aya felt truly safe.

Truly *seen*.

She could always feel Tyr's steady awareness of where she was, even when he was on the advance, his teeth snapping at an oncoming threat. She could feel his loyalty, his love, in every step, every lunge, every vicious howl that should make the hair on her neck rise but instead settled that piece of her that always seemed to chafe against who she was and who she wished she could be.

Tyr had seen every piece of her.

Blood-splattered, vicious, cold, and even cruel when she needed to be.

He met her sharp edges with his own, and he never expected her to dull them.

It was what a bonded was: an equal. A reflection of your very soul.

To lose that, after she'd already lost so much…

End up alone.

Tova's taunt from this morning came roaring back, far more vicious than Aya remembered her friend sounding. Was that the fate that awaited her?

"Did I…did I make a mistake?" Will's voice was hesitant in a way he typically wasn't as it pulled her from her thoughts.

She turned to see him watching her carefully, his uncertainty clear on his face.

It broke something in her, seeing him like that. Fragile, uncertain.

Go ahead. Shut out the only person you have left if that's what you want to do. End up alone.

No. She wasn't alone. She *wasn't* alone.

"No." Aya cleared her throat. "No. You're right. I wouldn't want the first time I see him to be…" She let her voice trailed off, unable to even say the words aloud.

Will stepped in front of her, gripping her chin with his thumb and forefinger. "Tyr remains bonded to you. I'm sure of it. He refused to leave your side when he came to the night of the attack."

The corner of Aya's mouth lifted at the steady reassurance. She nodded, letting Will guide her through the gate and into the clearing that led toward the barn. She paused there, her hand falling from Will's grasp as the smell of old wood and hay came over her.

Some of the wolves were lounging in the sun, and they paid her no mind as she slowly approached the barn.

We are bonded. That is something not even the gods can break.

Yet her heart hammered anyway, her palms tingling as she neared the old structure.

A hair-raising howl ripped through the air. It brought Aya to a dead stop in the middle of the path, her breath catching in her lungs as she saw a flash of gray barreling down the long hallway in the barn.

"Tyr."

His name was a whisper on an exhale that she didn't even finish before the wolf was on her, his powerful paws hitting her chest and sending her flat on her back.

Aya hit the ground hard, her breath wrenched from her lungs.

She may very well have broken a rib.

She didn't care.

Because Tyr was whining, his wet nose brushing against her neck as he nuzzled her shoulder, trying to get as close to her as possible.

He knew her.

He still knew her.

Aya threw her arms around Tyr's neck, a broken sound escaping her as she dug her fingers into his fur. Some of that pressure inside her eased as tears spilled down her cheeks, her body trembling with relief, and perhaps even release, as she sat up and buried her head into his thick fur.

Tyr knocked her cheek with his maw, a relieved huff casting warm breath across her skin.

"I missed you, too," she whispered, holding him tighter.

They'd still need to train together. Who knew how Tyr would react upon *seeing* her power. But...this was enough, for now. This was all the proof Aya needed until she could formally test that their magic worked together, still. That weight in her chest that seemed to keep growing colder and deeper every moment she was home was finally easing slightly, a piece of tension falling away as Tyr's scent washed over her, and that was enough for her.

Tyr let her cling to him for several long moments, his powerful body relaxing against her. When she finally pulled away, she gazed into those brown eyes, rich like spring soil, and had to swallow another wave of emotion that threatened to pull her under as she saw nothing but steady devotion in her bonded's gaze.

The last time she'd seen him, he'd been desolate. Broken. After the Diaforaté that Lena had captured had persuaded him to attack the town, he was a shell of his usual wild wolf.

But now he looked just as he always had. Stubborn. Brutal. Cold in all aspects except for how he looked at her.

And Akeeta, she supposed.

As soon as the thought crossed her mind, a soft yelp drew

her attention to the barn, where the snow-white wolf stood in the threshold, her head held proudly.

Will let out a laugh, that quiet joy he often hid from the world lighting his face as he stepped forward. "I didn't forget you, Akeeta," he called to his bonded. "No tackles for me then?"

Akeeta tossed her head as he closed the distance between them, but Will just laughed again as he crouched down beside her, his fingers scratching under her jaw. She held that proud position for a moment longer, as if Will's own insolence ran in her veins, before succumbing to his affection. She nuzzled her head against his, her nose mussing his hair.

Something warmed in Aya as she observed him. She'd seen Will with Akeeta, but mostly in training or when an assignment called for the wolves' reinforcements. They weren't exactly discreet, and in the times when a mission didn't suit their massive frames, they took to prowling the mountains to secure the outer borders of their homeland.

Still, she'd never observed this softness before—not from Akeeta, who typically held herself with a sort of regality. Nor from Will.

His body was loose, his face tender as he stroked her fur. He was murmuring softly to her, something Aya couldn't make out across the stretch of path between them, but it made her lips quirk regardless, if only because she knew the words were fueled by a lightness that hadn't been there a moment ago.

He had done this for her. She knew that. But he had needed this, too.

Tyr nudged Aya's shoulder, jarring her from her reflection. She turned to find him staring at her, his head cocked and a mischievous look in his expressive eyes. He let out a gruff growl, a sound of mocking annoyance, and nudged her again.

Hypocrite, he seemed to say.

Aya narrowed her eyes playfully at him, her fingers scratching behind his ears.

"Shut up," she muttered.

28

I T HAD BEEN A GAMBLE, BRINGING AYA TO SEE TYR. BUT AFTER
that emptiness in her gaze last night, Will had needed to
do *something*. He thanked all nine of the Divine that it had
worked—that the heaviness that had seemed to physically
weigh her down had, while not disappearing, at least lightened slightly.

They sat in a meadow now, far away from prying eyes. Tyr
and Akeeta lounged several paces away, but Will didn't miss
the alert prick of their ears whenever they picked up a sound.
They would know well in advance if anyone approached.

Perhaps that was also why that thin line of Aya's lips had
softened, a contemplative look now gracing her features as
she lay against his chest, her petite form tucked between
his legs as he leaned against one of the thick pines reaching
toward the Beyond.

Her gaze stayed fixed on Tyr, who batted at Akeeta lazily,
vying for her attention with the ravens that cawed in the tree
above them.

Will eyed the birds, something warm settling in his chest.
Most saw the raven as a sign of death, especially with how
they followed the Athatis to consume their carrion. But

Will had always been drawn to them. There was something about the way they worked with the wolves—their symbiotic nature—that made him think of resilience, and strength, and second chances.

He ran his fingers up and down Aya's arm, trying to sink further into that brief moment of comfort, but his mind would not allow it.

One afternoon. Give her one afternoon of peace.

Gods, it was the least that Aya deserved. She hadn't said a word about what had happened in the Synastysi. She didn't need to. Will had read the tension all over her, and it was just now beginning to fade.

He couldn't ruin it. He shouldn't ruin it.

And yet he couldn't stop the words that were crawling up his throat, the half-truths and lies that warred with each other to see who would be first to spill from his lips.

"There's something I didn't share with you last night. About my visit with Gianna," he murmured.

And with five simple words, that peace, or perhaps the illusion of it, shattered.

Aya tensed as she sat up, her head whipping around as her eyes met his. "About my father's attack?" she asked sharply, the hue in her irises far closer to that icy blue than the soft color of the sky they'd emulated earlier.

"What? No." Will shook his head as he straightened. "I told you everything about that. Her sympathy seemed genuine."

"Sensations can be faked," Aya retorted, her own brow furrowing as her teeth dug into her bottom lip.

"They can. As I told you, sensing someone's state without…"

Torture.

The word died in his throat.

Will looked toward the wolves. "Let's just say it's not a perfect method for getting the truth," he finished. He tried not to think about how this could cause her to doubt *him*. To question him again about what had unfolded with Tova and whether or not he was being honest.

The wind blew a strand that had come loose from her braid across her cheek, and he couldn't help but reach for it, his fingers brushing her skin as he tucked it behind her ear. Some of the glint ebbed in her eyes then, and gods, he loathed that he'd be putting it back there in mere moments.

Will's hand dropped to his side. "The rumors about Gianna and me...they're going to get worse."

Aya cocked her head, that searching look still on her face as she waited for him to explain.

"She's forgiven me, it seems." Will inhaled, his hand raking through his hair.

"So you said the other day."

"Yes, but...it seems she's forgiven me...fully."

The cawing of the ravens was the only sound between them for a few long moments.

"Fully," Aya repeated.

Will swallowed, forcing the words to unstick themselves from his throat, which had gone dry. "She's become far more brazen about her desires than she ever has been before."

"How brazen?" The words were short, as if Aya had to bite off every syllable to keep from choking on it. But her anger did not keep him from holding her gaze.

"She was quite hands-on," Will forced out. "I don't doubt there will be news of my disheveled state. She unbuttoned my shirt and untucked it. When the attendant walked in, her hand was on my belt."

Aya swore, the sound a bitter hiss that left her lips as she turned her face away from him. Her hands curled into fists, her knuckles white as she looked toward Tyr, who had abandoned Akeeta to focus on his bonded. The wolf's ears were perked toward her, his head held at attention as he considered her. Gauging whether to intervene.

"Aya."

She wouldn't look at him.

"*Aya.*"

Another breath, two, before she met his gaze. Her jaw was tight, her eyes blazing with anger.

"Nothing happened," Will said steadily. "I would never... I would have stopped it before it got too far. I *was* stopping it when the attendant walked in. I don't even know if this isn't some wretched game," he continued. "It could merely be a test to see how far I'll go, how loyal I'll be. I don't know if she was toying with me or if—"

"Or if she intended to have you."

Will was on his knees before her before he could even register how he'd gotten there, or how her face had ended up in his hands. "*There is only one woman who will have me.*"

Aya's eyes were still that cold blue, but there was a fierceness in them that had his heart searing as she held his gaze. "And I have to refrain from questioning the Divine as to why she would even consider it lest I spoil the one beautiful thing they've granted me in the midst of these seven hells."

His chest was heaving. Desperation tasted different with Aya, he was realizing. It was sharp, and hot, and wild, and it made him willing to do anything, gods, anything, if it meant she wouldn't look at him like she currently was.

Like keep secrets. Tell lies.

Aya's lips shifted, her eyes scanning him, as if the words she parsed through in her head were written in his features.

"It is not you I am angry at," she finally murmured, a slight tremor of that rage in her voice. She pushed herself onto her knees, her hands grasping his wrists as if anchoring herself there. Her throat bobbed, her eyes fluttering shut for a mere moment as she took a steadying breath. "I know what getting back into Gianna's good graces entails. I know that you have a...reputation...to uphold. Or, at least, the illusion of one."

Will's stomach twisted, but Aya pressed on, her gaze softening slightly. "I trust you."

The words burned. Because she didn't really, did she? Not when she'd had to rely on her power to believe him just days ago. And though he'd asked her to read him—hells, though he understood why she'd needed to—it didn't change the lingering hurt that had lodged itself somewhere deep inside of him.

The lingering doubt.

You'll never be right for her.

Will glanced away, his gaze finding the ravens once more as he steadied himself. "We'll need to be more careful," he murmured.

Aya smirked, but the light of it didn't touch her eyes. "I'm not the one who dragged us up here."

The laugh that escaped him was unbidden, but welcome. "I'm serious."

"I know."

Aya frowned. She was holding something back, whether for his sake or her own, he wasn't sure.

"Tell me," Will ordered, his thumb stroking her cheek. But that stubborn hesitation stayed written on her face as she tried to pull her head from his hands. Will refused to let her go.

"Tell me," he repeated steadily.

He could handle it. At least that's what he told himself as he buried the aching that was already stirring inside of him.

Aya toyed with the necklace around her neck—her mother's—a new nervous habit she'd developed since she'd taken to wearing it after Lorna had given it to her in Trahir. Her voice was quiet as she finally conceded.

"Sometimes, out of all the things stacked against us, I'm afraid Gianna will be the one to ruin us."

Gone was that bitter anger, replaced by a soft vulnerability that he'd rarely seen in her. And dammit if that didn't make the aching inside him that much worse, because *he* had done this. He had put this doubt here. And even though he knew getting back into Gianna's trust was the right choice, the smart choice, it didn't change the way the consequences of it wrapped around him tighter and tighter, like the fitting of a noose.

"I promise you," Will muttered, his thumb tracing that familiar path on her cheek. "I *promise* you I won't let that happen."

"On your oath?" Aya rasped, her eyes wide as her hands found his chest.

Will swallowed.

"On my oath."

It tasted like a lie.

29

G ALDA KEPT A SMALL OFFICE IN THE TRAINING COMPLEX OF the Quarter. It was more of a closet, not that Aya would ever admit it to the trainer. Aya stood in its doorway now, one hip leaning against the frame, her arms crossed.

She'd been wary about this first meeting with the trainer. And yet she kept her face clear of any such emotion as she held the gaze of the small woman behind the desk.

Galda was dressed in her own fighting leathers, her boots propped up on her desk. Her white hair, curly and cropped close to her head, was even brighter than usual thanks to the sunlight that streamed through the window behind her. Aya hadn't noticed the other night, at the Sanctification, that the wrinkles in Galda's dark skin had deepened since Aya had left Tala—as if the stress of the trainer's job was getting to her.

But even with that, Galda looked completely at ease as she twirled a knife in her hand, her eyes fixed steadily on Aya.

They'd been staring at each other in silence for two minutes and twenty-three seconds, by Aya's internal count.

Galda traded twirling her knife for tapping the pointed end on the already scratched wood of her desk. "Private lessons again, hmm?" she finally muttered in that voice like gravel.

Aya felt the thrill of victory wash through her, a smirk begging to break through her stoicism. There was a time, years ago, when Aya would never have been able beat Galda at holding silence. Even now, overcoming the trainer at her own game was rare. Possible, but rare.

Yet the pleasure of winning their game was washed away by the reminder that Gianna was pushing Aya further away from the Dyminara with every order.

"So it would seem," Aya replied tersely. She couldn't help but wonder just how much Galda was involved in such decisions. But she didn't dare push that matter. Information, she'd long since learned, was sacred, and there was something far more pressing she wanted to discuss.

Galda surveyed her for a long moment, as if she could read every thought that flitted through Aya's mind.

"Ask me." Galda's command reverberated across the space.

Aya drew in a steady breath through her nose. "You knew about my power."

Aya had stood in the dark hallway of Will's family town house the night she'd forced him to jump from the Wall and listened as he pleaded with Galda to remove her from the Dyminara qualifications.

She's too dangerous.

And yet Galda had blamed Will and his shield.

But Galda wasn't a fool. She knew.

The question was…for how long?

After all, she was the one who had found Aya in the woods after she'd learned her mother had died. And Aya was willing to bet it was her raw power that had overcome Galda that day, not her persuasion affinity.

Galda scratched the knifepoint across the desk, her brows rising as she glanced at the line she'd made. "That's not a question," she remarked lightly.

Aya turned over the hundreds of questions that seemed to

flutter through her mind, plucking out the one she wanted to know most.

"Fine. Why didn't you tell Gianna?"

Galda would never have dismissed a potential threat, unless she thought there was one greater.

The trainer's eyes flicked up, but her expression was unreadable. Slowly, she lowered her feet to the ground, her boots hitting the floor with a muffled thud.

"That is an assumption."

Aya pushed herself off the doorframe. Galda was testing her. Aya just wasn't sure for what purpose. Control, if she had to guess. Galda had always been on her about her control.

Now Aya knew why.

She faced her trainer head-on. "You're avoiding the question."

"And you're being lazy with your questioning. Making assumptions is how you make mistakes. I've trained you better than this. Though perhaps I haven't. You would've caught the heretic king far sooner if I had. Should I blame myself?"

Aya's hands clenched into fists at her side. "My duties were to learn of my powers. Powers we weren't sure were gods-given. Forgive me, Galda, if I was mildly distracted."

"You don't get distracted," she growled.

It wasn't an observation. It was an order.

And yet...

"I'm not looking for a lesson," Aya muttered. She wasn't one for insubordination, especially not within the Dyminara. But she and Galda... Perhaps it was because the trainer had been a constant in her life since she was eight that Aya had always been able to speak her mind with Galda.

She wasn't a confidante, but she was someone Aya didn't shy away from, even when the woman put the fear of the gods in her.

"Fine," Galda retorted as she stood from her seat. "We can have this conversation when you are." Aya's jaw ached as she bit back a retort. She wanted to argue, wanted to force Galda to tell her the truth. But Galda fixed Aya with a level look as she passed her. "Let's go. I've promised Hyacinth our training won't interfere with her schedule, and you're due in the Synastysi this afternoon."

Aya swallowed the irritation that threatened to burst from her. The Synastysi was such a godsdamn waste of precious time. At least she would get to do something useful before going.

It was enough of an incentive that she followed Galda out without another word.

Aya had always been proud to be a Persi.

Like most Visya who joined the queen's forces or became a member of the Dyminara, that pride had driven her, in her younger years, to prove that her affinity wasn't to be trifled with.

It was typical for disagreements to break out between Visya about which affinity was most coveted between the Orders.

Despite the Sensainos and the Persis being united under the Espri, the competition was worst between the two. Aya had shattered the shields of her fair share of Sensainos, Will's included, just to be able to persuade them to do something foolish if only to prove a point: that Persis may not be able to control sensation, or *force* answers, but they were still the affinity to be reckoned with. They could still bring a Sensainos to their knees.

Yet as Aya found herself on *her* knees now, her bones aching as she slammed into the dirt of the training ring, she wondered if this was some sort of Divine reckoning for the years she'd spent driven by pride.

"Get up," Galda ordered, her Sensainos affinity unrelenting as it lashed into Aya's shield with undiluted agony. Sweat poured down Aya's back, her shield splintering as she dug her fingers into the ground. She could feel Galda's power starting to seep through the cracks, the hint of pain a mere taste of what awaited once her shield finally broke.

She reached down deep inside of herself as she staggered to her feet, trying to pour *more* of her very being into that inner barrier all Visya had to protect themselves from affinities.

Galda had given her explicit orders:

No retaliation.

No affinity use.

Just shielding.

But as that pain turned from physical to something *more*, something all-consuming that had tears building behind Aya's eyes, she ground her teeth, her frustration rising.

So easy, it would be so easy to send a lash of her own power at Galda, to get her on the defensive.

That was how Visya fought.

How the *Dyminara* fought.

They balanced their affinities with their shields. They used them *in tandem* to build off one another and fuel their fight.

But you're not training with the Dyminara, that small voice reminded her. *You don't belong there anymore.*

Aya let out a grunt as she tried to focus. She might be a member of the Dyminara in title only now, but still…

She should be *using* her power, should be ensuring she was growing as strong as possible, so she could prepare for what Gianna had in store for her, for what the *gods* had in store for her. This was more wasted time, more pointless training that would get her nowhere—

Aya's frustration peaked, and her shield shattered like glass.

She crumbled to the ground, a shout of pain wrenching itself from her throat as agony slammed into her, stealing her breath and pulling a choked, "Fuck," from her lungs.

Her bones felt like they were snapping, sending her body into a trembling frenzy as tears slipped down her cheeks, and even then, Galda did not stop.

Aya should have known. Galda wouldn't care if Aya were sent from the Divine themselves; the trainer would rather die than go easy on her. It was her duty, after all, to make sure Aya was prepared.

And this...this was a level of Galda's power that Aya had not been subjected to before.

Aya reached for the tattered remains of her shield, trying desperately to weave it back into place, but it was no use.

"Get. Up," Galda ordered, her affinity unrelenting.

Aya tried. Gods, did she try. But she was tired after another sleepless night, and angry, and she couldn't bury her frustration and reach that calm place that Galda had taught her to settle into in order to control her power.

"I yield," Aya ground out.

Galda's power ceased immediately, even as bitter disappointment twisted her features. She gave Aya the space of three ragged breaths before she started in on her.

"How many times have I told you that a tangled mind is a defenseless mind," she snapped. "Your thoughts, your emotions, they are the essence of you. You allow yours to make you weak!"

The mountain air burned in Aya's chest as she pushed herself off the ground. "I am not weak," she snarled through battered breath. "I could have used my power to—"

"I don't care what your power can do if you can't protect yourself." Galda cut her off, authority ringing in every syllable as she stalked toward Aya. "Your shield is stronger than this!"

Aya swallowed her bitter resentment at the truth in Galda's words. Her shield *was* stronger than this. At least it had been...before.

Gods, that was the marker for everything, wasn't it? Before?

When she'd been a better spy.

A better daughter.

A better Visya.

"Using my power is exactly how I will protect myself!" Aya seethed. "The prophecy says it is to rival Evie's—"

Galda was in her face now, and her thunderous expression was enough to bring Aya up short. "Your enemies will use every single weapon they have against you," she hissed. "You are naive if you think brawn is how you will defeat them. They will find your weakness and exploit it, and yours has *always* been your mind. Why do you think I spent godsdamn years teaching you *control*?"

The word was kindling to Aya's temper, fourteen years of lessons on how to bury the broken, messy parts of herself bearing down on her shoulders.

The trainer stared at her for a long moment before giving a bitter shake of her head. "A fucking waste of time, if this is all you have to show for it."

Aya's hands curled into fists as Galda's disapproval settled heavily in her gut. She could see the truth in her words as clearly as she could see the anger in Galda's gaze now. Anytime she had lost control, anytime her shield had slipped, it was because of what was happening inside of her.

Anger. Fear. Doubt. Sadness.

An affinity had always been fueled by the essence of a Visya, and Aya had long learned the essence of herself was turmoil.

That turmoil had only grown worse in Trahir; had only intensified after returning home.

Galda took a step back. "I want you working on reinforcing your shield daily," she ordered. Aya's jaw shifted as she bit back the argument bubbling in her throat. The exercise was practically remedial. She should be beyond this.

Some saint.

Galda glared at her, all too familiar with that look on her face, that glint of disagreement in her eye. "Something to say?" she growled, her tone just daring Aya to argue.

Control.

Control.

Control.

"No," Aya replied, her voice as level as she could manage with the fury burning inside of her.

Galda cocked a brow. "Good. You're finally learning."

30

WHEN I DREAMED OF BECOMING A SAJ OF THE
Maraciana, I can assure you this was not an exercise
I thought I'd gain so much experience in."

Aidon raised a brow at Natali from where he stood at the
far end of the dungeon cell, his arms folded across his chest,
back resting against the cold stone wall. He'd selected one of
the furthest cells for this meeting—one near where Aya and
Will had been held. And though he hoped to look at ease
to Natali, he was anything but. The wall was steadying him,
keeping his tremors at bay.

"No? Isn't this what you Saj of the Maraciana do? Study
the affinities?"

Natali gave a dismissive wave of their hand. "You know
what I meant."

Aidon sighed as he stood up straight. He shook out his
arms, facing the Saj head on. "Right. Well, let's thank the
gods that you do have this experience. I have a feeling we're
going to need it."

Natali snorted. "I didn't take you for one of the devout,
Your Majesty." There was enough sarcasm in their retort that

Aidon didn't bother to answer. He merely gestured to the space between them.

"Well? Are you going to instruct me?"

The Saj's lips shifted as they surveyed him, their face pinched in concentration. "Always so eager for action," they muttered, mostly to themselves. They began to pace a steady line, back and forth, their thumb smoothing across their chin. Aidon watched them, his weight shifting between his feet in anticipation. "After you left the Maraciana last week, I started reviewing my notes on the tonic."

"You've been studying it?" Aidon interjected, his brows raising in surprise. Natali cut him a glance.

"Of course. As you said, it is my duty as a Saj of the Maraciana to study power. And the tonic, while not affinity-borne, is a means of power. It has the ability to repress an affinity. To keep it hidden. Even to control the uncontrollable, for a time. But as we both know, there are ways of rendering the tonic ineffective." They shot him a knowing glance, and Aidon swallowed. He swore he could feel the vibrations of his knife ramming into Aya's chest just then, could hear the sickly squelch of her skin and tissue and blood as he cut through it.

"Make your point," Aidon ordered.

Natali shrugged. "Until we saw such a thing, we did not know that the tonic could be rendered ineffective in such a way. That inner power would work differently than what we present outwardly, enough so that it could override the tonic entirely."

Aidon frowned. "But Aya's power is supposedly limitless. Or at least close to it. It's completely different from Incend affinity." He wasn't naive to how affinities worked. He'd had to be knowledgeable to train the Visya in his forces. Aidon knew Visya affinity resided in an inner well, the depth of which was rumored to be determined by the gods.

Natali gave another shrug. "Perhaps. Or perhaps your

power is reacting in a similar fashion. Not limitless," they said, holding up their hand as Aidon went to argue. "But perhaps by burying it for so long, by masking it, your affinity has begun to work against the tonic in a similar fashion."

"And how will you prove this?"

"Have you taken the tonic today?" Natali asked with a cock of their head. Aidon nodded. "Excellent." They took a step back, leaving plenty of room between the two of them. "Call your flame forward."

Aidon just blinked at the Saj. He could feel his face burning, that discomfort itching in his very veins as he said, "I can't. I just told you I took the tonic this morning. Besides, I've never called it forward intentionally before." The Saj frowned, and Aidon looked away from them as he continued. "When I used it to save myself and Aya and Will from the attackers, it was instinct."

"You know how the affinities work," Natali argued curtly. "You spent years commanding Visya warriors in your uncle's armies, did you not?"

He had, but that was different. Knowing and doing weren't the same. But Natali, it seemed, would not be swayed. "Do not let your fear render you foolish, Your Majesty."

Aidon's gaze cut to them, his frustration beginning to build. "This is not fear. The tonic—"

"Yes, it is," Natali interrupted, their voice clipped. "Call your power forward."

"I can't—"

"Now!"

"How?"

Aidon felt frustration rip through him, his shout searing his throat as he flung his arms wide. Natali raised their brows, their gaze fixed on his right hand. "Like that."

Aidon followed their gaze, his throat growing dry as he took in the fire flickering in his palm. Gods, he hadn't even felt it. But now, he could feel his skin tingling as something in him stirred, no, not stirred, *flared* like the first embers of a roaring fire.

He looked back at the Saj, his breath heaving, but Natali was frowning in concentration, their gaze fixed on the Incend flame. "Good. Now call it back."

He...couldn't. It was as though he'd torn something open inside of him, and he couldn't get that flow of something to stop. Aidon dropped his hand, and the fire simply ebbed slightly, but flames flung from his hand as he tried to shake the fire off of him.

Fuck. Fuck fuck fuck.

A searing pain ripped through his hand, and Aidon flipped his palm, watching the skin blister before his eyes. Gods. It was burning him. His own flame was burning him.

"Godsdammit!" he seethed as he shook his palm again, his eyes stinging with the pain. Natali was in front of him in an instant, their hand a vise grip on his forearm, as if they hadn't a care in the world about the fire that nearly grazed their fingers.

"Cut it off," they ordered again, their amber eyes locked on his. "Like a sword to sinew."

It was just the visual he needed.

Aidon sliced that imaginary sword across his very chest, imagining that inner inferno flowing out of him cutting in half and falling deep within wherever the tonic smothered it.

The fire vanished.

Natali let out a heavy breath, their grip falling from his arm, and Aidon staggered backward, his back slamming into the stone wall. He felt light-headed, his limbs trembling. His legs buckled, but he managed to catch his footing before he fell.

"What the hells," he panted. He was vaguely aware of the sweat dripping from his temples, his shirt clinging to his damp chest. He cradled his hand to his chest, the skin raw and blistered and reeking of that particular smell of charred flesh.

Visya were supposed to have shields that could protect them from affinities.

Yet another thing he had never learned how to do.

"It's just as I thought," Natali muttered, their brow furrowed. Aidon waited for the Saj to expand on the topic, but their eyes were darting across the floor, as if they were reading a book he couldn't see.

"I don't suppose you'd care to elaborate?" Aidon hissed between clenched teeth. His breath was still sawing in and out of him, his chest heaving with the movement. Gods, this hurt. And not just in his hand, but everywhere. His body felt beaten and bruised, as if the affinity had pulled at the very essence of him when he wielded it.

Natali's gaze snapped back to him. "Prolonged use of the tonic has rendered it ineffective. I suspect you've built a sort of immunity to it. Your power can override it."

Aidon braced a trembling hand on the wall, forcing himself upright. "Then we increase the dose," he said through sharp breaths.

Natali pursed their lips, giving a contemplative hum. "We could," they conceded. "But I imagine you would face the same hurdles eventually."

He didn't give a damn about *eventually*. Hells, he wasn't even sure they'd make it to eventually if Kakos had their way. Aidon forced himself to breathe, inhaling deeply through his nose before letting out a long breath.

"What aren't you telling me, Natali?" Because the Saj was hiding something, of that he was sure. He could tell by the way Natali was still watching him, their brow furrowed in concentration as their eyes darted across his face.

They twined their arms behind their back, their head cocked as they considered him. "It's mere speculation. I cannot sense your power in the same way with the tonic in your system. But"—they inhaled deeply before continuing— "Visya are taught from a young age to control their power.

Those that don't know how to manage their well either become ill or die from improper power use." They began to pace, their eyes wide as they remained fixed on him. "You, of course, have avoided such effects through the tonic. But I believe that by suppressing your power, it's become unstable."

Aidon frowned. "Meaning?"

Natali sighed. "Meaning it very well might kill you."

Aidon blinked at the Saj, their words taking a moment to register in his mind. When they did, he gave a short laugh. "All the more reason to increase the dosage of the tonic then."

But Natali was shaking their head, a crease appearing between their silver brows. "I fear if you continue to take the tonic, this will only get worse."

Something heavy settled in Aidon's gut as he stared at the Saj. "You want me to *stop* taking it?"

How would he train? How would he fight when war arrived without his power making itself known?

"With practice, we could perhaps help you build your stamina around it. But if your power continues to grow unruly under the tonic, it may be too late by the time the tonic is rendered completely ineffective."

"So I risk death either way," Aidon remarked bitterly as he rubbed a hand across his jaw.

"We all risk death every day, Majesty. That's what mortality is."

Aidon couldn't stop the noise of agitation that burst from his lips. His sword hand curled at his side, as if desperate to snatch the weapon and start swinging.

"Trahir cannot afford more instability," he muttered. "If continuing to take the tonic is what allows me to *fight*—"

Natali's eyes narrowed into slits. "Joining your troops on the battlefield would be foolish," they snapped. "And you are not a fool, Majesty. Even with the tonic, you risk revealing your power in such a situation."

Aidon forced air through his nose, trying to steady the

pounding of his heart as he held the Saj's gaze. "You would ask the king to stand by while his people go to war?"

Deceiver. Usurper. Murderer.

Coward.

Natali's steps were quick as they crossed the cell. They poked his chest, their round face tight with frustration as they hissed, "I would ask the king to be smart in his decisions. Even with the tonic, there is no guarantee that you would not act once again on instinct and call it forward. Revealing that you have broken the one fundamental law of the Divine would be suicide. You think your people are wary of you now? You won't just be forced to relinquish your throne. You'll be murdered in the worst possible way!"

"It's suicide either way!" Aidon straightened, his tall figure towering over Natali. "I'd risk discovery by any overly curious Saj that crosses my path if I stop taking the tonic. And even if I do, aren't you saying there's no telling whether my power won't simply consume me anyway?"

"Yes, but—"

"So it's death now or death then!"

"It is *not*," they retorted. "You are choosing a guaranteed death over the possibility of one. If you train your magic, if you learn, there is a chance—"

"I do not have the luxury of taking such chances!" The words ripped from somewhere deep within him, his eyes burning as frustration and anger warred for his attention.

Duty. Commitment. Responsibility. That's what he'd always been taught—what had been drilled into his very soul since he was a child. He and Aya had been foolish to talk of making choices for themselves. Aidon would never have that luxury. Not really. Every choice, every decision, was for Trahir.

Always for Trahir.

He sucked in a steadying breath, his hand bracing on the wall beside him. "I will not ask my people to take part in a war I will not fight in," he said finally. "And I would rather

235

choose a guaranteed death later by continuing to take this tonic until the power consumes me entirely or I show my power on the battlefield, than risk one now and allow my people to fall further into turmoil with Kakos knocking at our door."

Natali's lips thinned in clear disagreement, but they remained silent. Aidon cocked his head, his brow furrowing as he stared at the Saj. "Why do you care? Why help me? Why hide Viviane? What's in this for you?"

Aidon knew what was driving him to put himself through these hells, but Natali? What did they have to gain? The Saj of the Maraciana weren't particularly known for their devotion to their kingdom. Aidon suspected they remained in Trahir all these years not out of any great loyalty, but because of the kingdom's deviation from the Old Customs of worshipping the gods and the libraries they had established.

It created a better environment for those Saj who wanted to study power specifically, than a place like Tala, which was far more devout.

Natali shifted on their feet. "I have devoted my life to studying the affinities. You and Viviane offer a particular challenge I haven't experienced in years."

Aidon's laugh of disbelief echoed across the small space. "So this is nothing but academic interest?"

He didn't believe it for a second, even as Natali gave a blithe shrug. "I think you have larger concerns than my motivations, Majesty."

"On the contrary. A general knows motivation is key to understanding strategy."

The Saj's brows rose. "And yet, you are not a general anymore. You might do well to remember that." They gave him a pointed look, their words burning Aidon as if he'd been subjected to his Incend fire once more.

He wasn't a general anymore. He knew that. And yet that was what he knew how to be.

A strategist. A fighter. A leader on the battlefield. So what the hells was he now?

Not a general.

Not a Visya either.

Not even a king—not truly. Not if he'd obeyed what the gods decreed.

You wouldn't even be king if you hadn't murdered your uncle.

He didn't regret it. But that didn't mean that in all his years of preparation—for all his lectures on and his best efforts toward how, one day, he would be king—Aidon had ever imagined it quite like this.

Deceiver. Usurper. Murderer.

"I may not be the general," he muttered finally, his hands fisting at his sides. "But I would rather hang than stand aside while I send my people to die."

Natali let out a steady breath. "Then let us be grateful war has yet to arrive." They gave him another piercing look, as if they could see straight to his core. "You are sure about this course of action?"

Aidon nodded. The throbbing in his hand returned, his blistered skin stealing his attention, as if now that he was certain about his next steps, the world around him came into sharper focus.

Natali sighed. "Double your tonic intake, then." They paused, their mouth quirking. "I would also take care to avoid any situations that might...provoke you," they added slowly.

A laugh rasped from Aidon, weak and hollow, as he leaned his head back against the wall. He was due to meet with the Merchant Council this very afternoon to introduce Ryker and Clyde. "My every day includes multiple moments of provocation, Natali."

Natali smiled, but the expression seemed stilted. "You'll want to think of a decent excuse for that hand, too."

Aidon grimaced. He'd need to head to the healers now if he was going to make it to his next appointment in time.

He stood, motioning toward the door. "Luckily I've become quite adept at lying," he muttered darkly.

Lies. Lies, lies, and more lies.

It seemed like all he had to his name as of late.

And as they stepped out of that dungeon cell, their eyes blinking rapidly to adjust to the light of the halls, he didn't miss that Natali didn't bother to disagree.

31

"I YIELD."

Josie dropped her blade from her competitor's throat, sucking in a ragged breath.

Fifth time today.

Not that Aleissande would care. Josie had a feeling the general was trying to exhaust her into quitting. Or maybe she was just trying to humiliate her.

Josie cut a glance to where the general stood at the edge of the outdoor training ring—a large circular structure with a raised platform in the middle used for sparring. Aleissande's lean arms were crossed, her feet braced apart. A pillar of golden stone, coated in the formfitting brown material of their fighting leathers.

Josie was annoyed that she couldn't help but notice how *perfectly* they hugged her lithe figure, as if they were fused to her very skin.

It wasn't enough to change that right now Aleissande looked...

Unmoving.

Unyielding.

Her blond hair was woven into a complicated plait, and

it had the effect of making the sharp angles of her face look even more severe. Her brow was stern as she met Josie's gaze, as if daring her to back down.

Josie merely twirled her sword in her hand.

"Garrons, you're next," Aleissande barked.

It helped, actually, to have Aleissande order her to train until she could barely move. It quieted the thoughts that haunted her in stillness. Like how she and Vi could hardly have a conversation unaccompanied by awkwardness. Or how Josie could barely stand to look at Vi without her heart breaking all over again.

Garrons stepped into the ring, his lumbering frame towering inches above Josie. She quickly flipped through that mental log she kept on the warriors she'd been studying for weeks now.

Garrons was strong, and deceptively fast. But her endurance was better. Or it was when she hadn't gone five steady rounds after a day's worth of exercise.

Still, outlasting him was her best strategy.

Josie quickly backed into defensive maneuvers as Garrons lunged toward her, letting him think he had an easy win.

Block, block, parry. Block, block, dodge, block.

Her sword arm trembled, her breath sawing in and out of her chest. She could feel Aleissande's gaze tracking her as Garrons forced her around the ring.

Block, block, dodge, bl—

The glinting of their swords caught the sunlight, and Josie's eyes burned against the brightness. The world tilted, and she let out a grunt as her back slammed into the ground. The sharp edge of a sword pressed against her neck, and in the blinding light of the sun, she saw Garrons smirking down at her.

Godsdammit. He'd maneuvered her right into the sunlight, using it to blind her.

"Yield, Josie," Aleissande commanded.

Josie panted, her eyes fixed on Garrons, searching for a weakness. He pressed the blade tighter to her skin.

"Yes, *Princess*. Yield," he muttered, just soft enough for only Josie to hear.

Josie gritted her teeth, but she dropped her sword, her palms facing the sky in surrender. "I yield," she muttered. Garrons grinned, and there was a stinging sensation across her neck as he removed the blade. Josie's hand clamped down on her skin, something wet coating her fingers.

The bastard had nicked her.

She stood and glared at his bulky form, graceful as he hopped off the platform, formulating all the ways she could kill him next round. If Aya were here, she'd say to hells with the rules of combat; she'd throw a knife in the asshole's back. But Josie didn't have Aya's quick temper, nor her blatant disregard for, well, everything.

Gods, she missed her friend terribly.

With Aidon so occupied with his new duties as king, she hardly had anyone to talk to who truly understood all they had been through. There was only so much she could tell her friends, and Viviane...

Viviane was healing from her own trauma.

But Josie still couldn't shake the nightmares—the echoing screams that drove her from sleep, her breaths reduced to shallow gasps as she asked herself again, how the hells had she missed it all?

Her uncle's affiliation with Kakos, Vi's affiliation with the Bellare.

Josie sucked in a steadying breath as Aleissande pushed herself off the fence.

"We're done for the day," the general said. "Josie, you're on polishing duty in the weaponry room," she ordered. Josie fought the urge to roll her eyes—it was the third time she'd been given this grunt work. It usually went to the lowest-ranking warriors, those who couldn't win a duel to save their lives.

But Josie was one of the best.

She's testing you, Aidon had said when Josie begrudgingly requested he demand she be allowed to train. It wasn't as though anyone *else* was turned away from the forces.

Not with war coming.

"Unless you have courtly duties to attend to, Princess. We wouldn't want to get in the way of your crown." Aleissande's eyes—such a pale blue, they were almost gray—were challenging as they fixed on Josie, who had yet to reply.

Something pulled taut between them—something that Josie had noticed the moment she joined the forces. But a wave of snickers rippled across the training ring, shattering it as quickly as it had come.

"No, General," Josie said evenly. "I'll report back when the polishing is done."

Aleissande shrugged. "No need." She gave them all a swift glance. "Dismissed."

Josie's body ached as she snatched her sword from the ground, her fellow warriors already swarming toward the exit. All except one: a scrawny man with sand-colored skin and wiry black hair.

Cole, he'd introduced himself as earlier in the week. He was new to the force as well, and awful—not that Josie would ever tell him as much. The man practically vibrated with nervous energy as it was. He was already fidgeting as he approached her, his fingers bouncing across the pommel of the sword that looked far too large to be sheathed at his narrow hip.

"I can help," he said as he fell into step beside her. "With the polishing."

Josie kept her eyes fixed on the training complex. "I'm fine, but thank you."

Cole was undeterred. "It should be me anyway. Everyone knows you're one of the best warriors we have. They're just picking on you because you're new. And, well, you." His words were rapid, and he sucked in a needed breath before continuing. "Aleissande does appear to be extra vicious lately." A side-glance at her. "Especially toward you. Why do you think she has it in for you? Do you two know each other or something?"

Josie repressed a sigh. Normally, she loved people who were talkative, and forthcoming, and full of energy. *She'd* been that way. Maybe she still was, under the layers of grief and betrayal and confusion that kept suffocating her.

Her eyes cut to Cole. He was jittery, the same way Aidon used to get when they were children and snuck into the palace kitchens to gorge themselves on desserts. And yet he was also at ease—or, at the very least, completely oblivious to Josie's reluctance to share space with him, let alone carry on an actual conversation.

"Hardly," she finally said as they entered the training complex. She'd known *of* Aleissande for years now. It was hard *not* to notice the woman. She was known to be an incredible warrior, and, well...

Josie could at least admit that Aleissande commanded attention, yet in the most subtle of ways. There was something that drew people to her—even if her personality left something (everything) to be desired.

Regardless, Josie hadn't been surprised when Aidon appointed her general of the forces. And though no one beyond her family knew it, it was Josie who had recommended Aleissande for the position as Aidon's Second once Josie had refused her brother's offer.

All of that aside, Josie couldn't scrounge up a single interaction she and Aleissande had had that would have caused *this* much contempt from the woman.

"Huh," Cole said. "Maybe she just doesn't like you." Josie whipped her head to Cole, an incredulous look on her face, but Cole just shrugged. "I like you."

"Why?" The word was out of her mouth before she could

stop it. Josie had plenty of friends, but none of them were in the force. And it wasn't like Josie brought her vibrant personality *here*. She mostly kept her head down and her mouth shut.

Cole blinked at her, and she could see the confusion written on his face. "Why do I like you? I don't know." Another shrug. "You seem kind enough."

Josie almost laughed. Kindness—he was looking for *kindness* in the Trahir Royal Army.

Gods.

Her lips twitched. "Okay, Cole, I'll make you a bargain. You help me with the polishing, and I'll help *you* with your fighting."

He grinned, his body nearly bouncing with excitement. "Great! But...why would you help me with my fighting?"

Her brows rose in amusement. "Because you're horrible."

His face turned thoughtful, as if he were reviewing his most recent fights—none of which he had won, Josie almost reminded him.

Finally, he nodded once. "Fair enough. You have yourself a bargain."

32

Aidon was something of an expert in combat. He had practically been through the seven hells and survived.

So it would truly be a shame if this meeting were the thing that finally killed him.

Yet as he stood before the Merchant Council, Clyde now occupying the seat of Lead Councillor, and Ryker, the smirking bastard, in Avis's chair, he wondered if it just might.

The appointment of councillors was simple, really. A mandate from the king, and a formal introduction to the Council. And yet, if the wary looks he was receiving were any indication, the Council had not warmed to him.

Or Ryker.

At least Clyde's appointment had gone over well enough.

A throat was cleared, drawing Aidon's attention to the man on Clyde's left.

"Be it not up to me to question your judgment, Majesty," his smooth voice began. Aidon had known Zarad for years—since before the man's brown skin had wrinkled and his dark curly hair had faded to gray. It was strange to be addressed as King by the man.

Would he ever get used to the moniker?

Would his people?

"But the position of councillor is one of esteem." Zarad turned his gaze to Ryker. "What qualifications do you have, boy?"

Ryker ran a finger along the top of the mahogany table, his black brows flicking toward his silken hair. "Enough to make me a man, for starters."

"It is important that those on the Council reflect the many different voices of Trahir," Aidon cut in. "Ryker will represent those outside the Upper Merchants."

"And the humans," Ryker drawled.

Aleissande, now seated in Peter's old seat, her posture stiff as a board, leaned forward, a frown painting her brow. "The humans have several voices on this Council. To suggest otherwise hints at bigotry toward the Visya who sit in this room."

Ryker merely shrugged. "Agree to disagree, General. We find ourselves on the brink of another war started by Visya at the expense of humans." Ryker looked to Aidon. "Am I wrong to assume that such matters will affect our trade? Our coffers? Our people?"

"It is not our war," another merchant barked from the far side of the table. "Let Tala fight their righteous battle on their own."

"It is very much our war, Lenora," Clyde said, his voice low with authority. "Least of all because it *will* impact trade whether it reaches our shores or not." Clyde gazed around the table. "When the Second Saint rallies the kingdoms to fight against the evil of Kakos, do you think the realm will give a damn about the rich foods and spices of Trahir?"

Aidon felt a rush of gratitude toward his friend, even as a rumble of dissent broke out around the table. Aidon kept his face impassive, letting the arguments unfold.

He'd expected this. Though his previous position hadn't required his attendance at Council meetings, Aidon wasn't ignorant of the way they worked. The councillors quarreled and bartered and preened until some resolution was reached.

It was merely a show, political posturing at its most extreme, and yet Aidon found his frustration rising as the echoes of argument between the councillors grew louder, creating a steady drumming in his ears that matched the headache building behind his eyes.

"Saint or not, it gives her no right to demand..."

"A drastic attempt to get our armies involved..."

"Both should be tried for espionage for their meddling..."

"No proof the late king was even..."

"Enough." Aidon's command sliced through the din. He didn't need to shout. His time leading the forces had taught him how precisely he could wield his voice to create order. The councillors stopped speaking, the abrupt silence nearly louder than their quarreling.

"I've heard *enough*." Aidon moved his gaze down the long rectangular table, staring at each merchant in turn. "Your outrage is duly noted," he told the councillors in a drawl he realized would have made Will proud, the arrogant bastard. The thought was tinged with affection.

This meeting *must* be driving him mad.

"Particularly, the focus of your rage," he continued, his fingers drumming steadily on the table. "More anger toward one who can save our realm than for a pawn of Kakos. Interesting."

"On the contrary, Your Highness," Zarad said. "We're horrified to learn of the king's betrayal."

Horrified...

Horrified like Aidon had been when he'd walked into that dungeon with Viviane chained between six guards to find his friends and sister there as well? Horrified like when he'd stood by and watched Viviane be turned into a Visya? Like when he had plunged that knife into Aya's chest, hoping she could save them all?

Deceiver.

Usurper.

Murderer.

"Believe me, Zarad," Aidon replied, his voice low. "You haven't known true horror." He lifted his chin as he addressed the rest of the table. "But that is exactly what awaited us, had my uncle's plans not been uncovered."

"He should have been tried for his crimes," another merchant spat out. "And the Tala girl—"

"Would have been *killed*," Aidon snapped, hands gripping the arms of his chair as his frustration began to build. "And that *woman* has a name. You should learn it, seeing as Aya will likely be the very one to save your neck, Kirkwood."

Breathe, Aidon. Don't lose control.

"Perhaps, Majesty, if we could see proof of her power," Zarad interjected. Aidon didn't bother to hide his sigh as he stood.

"I've seen proof enough—just as I have here. I understand your shock, Councillors. Truly, I do. But let me make myself perfectly clear: any advice I seek in such meetings is given out of respect for the positions you hold in this kingdom. I am not naive enough to think that without your support, our coffers—and our people—would not suffer." Aidon braced his hands on the table, heat rising in his veins. "But I am your king. And when Tala calls for aid, I do intend to answer. I recommend you sort through your allegiances before that day comes." He straightened, his hands steady as he fixed the sleeves of his jacket. "If not, you can expect to meet the same fate as those who partnered with my uncle."

He let himself look around the table once more—just enough to let his frustration fuel the authority ringing in the deep baritone of his voice as the threat fell from his lips.

"You will hang."

33

I HEAR YOUR SESSIONS IN THE SYNASTYSI HAVE BEEN CHALLENG-ing, Aya."

Gianna's question was as light as the clinking of her spoon as she stirred sugar into her tea, but it didn't stop Aya from tensing where she sat on her usual love seat in Gianna's chambers.

Challenging would be an understatement.

For the last week, Aya had done just as Gianna had commanded her. She had spent her days cloistered in the Synastysi, and every few mornings hidden away with Galda, and the sessions were so draining that even Aya's endlessly whirring mind couldn't keep her from sleep.

And yet she'd made little progress. The journals she perused told her nothing of note about Evie and provided no detail on how the First Saint had managed to call forth the veil. And Galda...

Well, Aya was surprised she even had a shield left after the rigor Galda had put her through. She'd improved, but the trainer was still dissatisfied, and still reluctant to use their time for more than reinforcing Aya's shield.

Shielding is what Visya learn first, Galda had snarled when

Aya had demanded to know why they were training in such a way. *Your power is something new. We must return to the basics.*

Aya was growing to loathe those sessions as much as her time in the temple.

"It is true the texts have yielded scant results, Majesty," Aya finally replied. "However, my studies in Trahir took several weeks. I am not discouraged by the lack of progress made in just one here."

Will sat beside Aya, his face cold and impassive, even though she could read the tension emanating from him. He'd hardly spared her a glance since they'd sat down.

An act, she reminded herself. It was a reminder she'd had to repeat several times over the last week as they kept their vow to stay away from each other in the name of being more discreet.

But with his frostiness not just here, but in the walk over with Tova, and with Tova sitting in the ornate armchair to Aya's right, the Tría united at last, it hardly felt like anything had changed since the last time the three of them had sat in the room together months ago.

Except it had.

Everything had changed.

Gianna made a contemplative noise, the pink of her lipstick staining the white rim of her teacup as she took a sip. Aya hadn't missed how much effort Gianna seemed to have put into her appearance this morning. Nor had she missed the way her gaze had lingered on Will, dragging down his body as if she could imagine every inch of him unclothed.

Aya's nails dug into her palms.

"And your sessions with Galda?" Gianna pressed.

"They are...instructive," Aya said carefully. "But I am worried about limiting my training to those sessions alone. With a new type of power, is it not unwise to fail to ensure the Dyminara are prepared for battle?" she murmured, cutting a glance to Tova.

She wanted to train. She *needed* to train. Truly train, not just shield as Galda tried to bring her to her knees. Aya was making sure to use her power in small ways, if only to lessen that pressure she could feel building under her skin. But…she needed to fight. And not just in preparation for war, but so she could release some of the frustration stewing in her.

There was only one group of warriors who could possibly provide such a challenge.

"I think it would be beneficial as well," Tova agreed, her chin propped on her fist. "In fact, I think she should train not just with the Dyminara, but with the general forces. If we are to truly prepare for war, we must know how to fight together," she explained. "All of us," she added as she looked to Gianna pointedly.

The queen's eyes darted between the two of them, her silence lingering. "You're due to test your bond with Tyr tomorrow, are you not?" she asked Aya.

Aya nodded.

Finally.

"Let's start there. If the Athatis does not have a negative reaction to you, then perhaps we can reconsider. For now, your priority is your studies in the Synastysi."

"With all due respect, Your Majesty, Aya's use to us will be on the battlefield, not in the temple," Tova interjected. "Limiting her ability to train with us—"

"Aya's usefulness to us is as a chosen of the Divine," Gianna interrupted, her voice still aggravatingly level as she set down her cup. "And the Divine don't whisper instructions in sparring rooms, Tova. They do it in the holiest of places."

Aya forced a steady inhale through her nose. She appreciated Tova's defense, even if it came through the lens of thinking as Tala's general. Yet…

Aya's usefulness.

She was no better than an object, that weapon she'd dreaded becoming when she was in Trahir. Passed along to

251

whoever could sharpen her that day, whoever could make sure she yielded the maximum results.

She didn't feel useful. She felt hollowed out. Distant. Untouchable, and not because she was a threat, but because she was *alone*.

Next to her, Will leaned back, his leg bumping hers as he crossed an ankle over his knee. It drew her from her thoughts, and though his face was still that cold, calculating mask, she couldn't help but feel as though it was exactly what he had intended.

"Aya learning how to right the greatest wrong, as the prophecy states, is all that matters," Gianna was saying to Tova with a note of finality that made it clear the discussion was over.

Tova nodded, her frustration evident, but she didn't push any further. Tova was an expert at toeing this line with Gianna, at pushing just far enough to make it clear the queen had chosen well in her selection of general, but not so far as to diminish the trust Gianna had in her.

"Speaking of which," Gianna continued, turning her attention to Aya. "You're due in the Synastysi soon, are you not?" It was a clear dismissal that was only made worse when Gianna said, "William, you and I will continue updates alone."

Tova shifted, readying to leave, likely for further training of the forces, but Aya stayed in her seat in her own show of subtle defiance. "Actually, Majesty, I have time to be briefed on the search for the supplier."

"No."

For a moment, Aya didn't register that the refusal came not from Gianna, but from Will. She frowned at him, her spine straightening. "Why the hells not?"

She didn't need to fake any of the frustration that coated her voice. Will's jaw was tight as he met her furious gaze, even as his voice slid into that drawl that used to make her skin crawl. "Because that's *my* assignment, Aya love. And Lena and I have no need of your assistance."

Tova snorted in annoyance, but Aya's anger was far more subtle. Her mouth snapped shut, her teeth grinding against each other as she held Will's stare.

Another door closed. Another person keeping her at arm's length.

"You may outrank me," Aya retorted softly, "but I am still the spymaster."

"This order is not his," Gianna intervened. "It is mine."

"You told me Lena would keep me apprised," Aya bit out, not bothering to hide her frustration from her queen. "I've heard *nothing*."

Gianna's eyes glinted in the sunlight that streamed through the windows. "I also told you, time and time again, that your priority is your work in the Synastysi. Your insistence on being involved in matters outside of it leads me to believe you're ignoring its importance. Is that why Hyacinth reports on your stubbornness?"

The room went silent.

Gianna had never spoken to Aya in that way—as if she were no better than a petulant child. Even Will seemed to stiffen beside her, that easy smirk vanishing from his face as his gaze found the floor.

Aya held Gianna's stare for a beat, then two, the silence growing heavier with apprehension the longer she did. But it didn't bother Aya. Galda had taught her how to weaponize the quiet.

But this was not some mark. This was her queen.

The warning came roaring to her mind just as the tension reached a breaking point. Aya averted her gaze, her chin tucking in as she stared at the floor. "Forgive me, Majesty," she muttered with the deference Gianna would expect. "Adjusting to my new role is taking…time."

She hoped the hesitation behind her words would appear as vulnerability, not anger. It seemed it did, because Gianna leaned toward her, her voice far softer as she said, "I cannot imagine, Aya, what you are facing. The only living one of your kind. It must feel so…isolating. I understand why you reach for the familiar."

The words *burned*.

Aya looked at Tova, their argument echoing in her mind. Aya cleared her throat. "Thank you, Majesty. If that's all, I should be getting to the Synastysi. As you said, it is the priority."

It was thanks to Aya's years of obedience that Gianna didn't seem to sense the resentment in the words. The queen nodded her agreement, and Aya could feel Will's eyes on her as she stood. She didn't return his gaze as she followed Tova out of the room.

Aya's stride was quick as she stormed from Gianna's room, but it didn't stop Tova from keeping up, nor did her friend refrain from making her own opinions heard.

"Fucking prick," Tova muttered as they reached the end of the long hall. "I swear, he's gotten worse since you two returned from Trahir."

Aya clamped her mouth shut, her gaze fixed resolutely ahead. Cleo was to accompany her today as her guard and would be waiting in the main hall. The sooner Aya could get to her, the sooner this conversation would end.

And it needed to end. Because with every step, Aya could feel her frustration building, until she couldn't sort through what part of it belonged to Gianna and what part belonged to Will.

He was freezing her out in his search for the supplier. Why? This had to be more than not trying to draw attention to themselves. It had to be.

"And Gianna just lets him be as arrogant as he pleases, as if she wasn't furious at him only months ago for his failures in Trahir," Tova was ranting, her hands fluttering through the air as if she could brush off the annoyance she felt with their queen. "I swear, his cock must be—"

"Stop."

Aya's command slipped out of its own accord, and while it was quiet, Tova ceased her talking immediately, a frown marring her face as she jerked her head to Aya. "What?"

There was a hint of affront in Tova's voice, but Aya didn't care. She just wanted it to stop.

"I don't want to think about Gianna and Will…" She couldn't even bring herself to say it. But she didn't have to, because Tova drew to a stop, her arms folding across her chest as her brows flicked toward her high ponytail.

"It's not like it's some new development. They've been fucking for years," she retorted.

"And it's been disgusting for years," Aya snapped, her frustration finally bursting forth as she whirled to face her friend. "So fucking leave it be."

Tova's eyes went wide, her lips parting in surprise at Aya's outburst. But just as quickly, a subtle smirk replaced the expression as Tova shook her head with a chuckle. "Of course. I should have realized."

Cool dread slipped down Aya's spine like ice, washing away the heat of her frustration immediately. Had she been so obvious? Had she gone too far? "I only meant—"

"He must have been insufferable about it in Trahir," Tova cut in, dismissing Aya's half-formed explanation with another wave of her hand. "Sorry, I didn't even think about how often you must have had to hear him bragging about it. Sometimes I forget you had to spend so much time with him."

Aya paused, half-formed excuses still lingering on her tongue. There was a flippancy in Tova's voice that chafed at Aya. Tova, whether she wanted to admit it or not, knew of Will's feelings for her. She didn't know of Aya's, but still.

"Lucky you," Aya finally replied softly.

It wasn't fair of her to say it. Tova hadn't meant any harm.

Seven hells, Tova had been in prison all that time. And yet Aya couldn't bear to take it back.

Tova's smirk vanished, hurt flitting across her face before she schooled her features into careful composure.

There it was—that awkwardness between them. That chasm that seemed to grow larger with every interaction. Aya might as well be the one hammering its walls, the way she continued to further this divide.

She swallowed as she caught Cleo's gaze across the main hall.

"I should go," Aya muttered.

Tova shifted her weight between her feet, her ponytail swinging with the anxious movement. "Right. Me too." She had already turned away from Aya and begun to cross the hall without her before she paused, her shoulders dropping slightly as she looked back at Aya. "I'll see you later?"

The uncertainty in the question cut like a knife.

"Of course," Aya rasped. And yet the uncertainty lingered, this time in her own response. "Of course," she said again.

She wasn't sure which of them she was trying to convince.

34

AYA WAS SURPRISED TO FIND HYACINTH WAITING FOR HER outside the doors of the temple, her crimson robes fluttering in the wind that was slowly becoming a gentle breeze the further they moved into spring.

The High Priestess's arms were twined behind her back, the placating smile on her lips visible beneath her sheer veil.

"I thought we'd try something different today," her soft voice called as Aya approached.

"Different?"

"Yes. As I mentioned when we first spoke of your training, there are several practices the priestesses take part in to open their minds to the gods. And given you seem...*reluctant* to accept what the gods have seen in you..."

Hyacinth buried her frustration beneath her sickly-sweet tone, but Aya knew it was there.

"I am not reluctant, Hyacinth. Your scrolls simply haven't provided any helpful insight."

Hyacinth frowned. "Or perhaps you simply cannot see yourself in them."

Aya didn't bother to dig into the meaning behind the High Priestess's words. "Where are we going?" she asked instead as

Hyacinth pushed past her, walking in the direction Aya and Cleo had just come. The High Priestess glanced over her shoulder, that unnerving smile still playing on her plump lips.

"Katadyré."

Aya drew up short.

"Katadyré," she repeated dryly. The prison sat on a small island, if it could even be considered that, just outside of the port basin. Death's Door, they called it.

"What business do the priestesses have there?" Aya asked with a frown. Katadyré held the worst sort. It was where prisoners were taken either to live out a life sentence or...die.

Execution Isle was its other unfavorable name.

"We listen," Hyacinth said with a shrug. "There is a small temple within the prison. We hear the prayers of the lost and provide counsel for those who might yet meet the Divine in death."

"And what does this have to do with me?"

Hyacinth let out a sigh as she turned to face Aya fully. "You are a beacon of hope for our people, Aya. A connection to the gods. In war, you will inspire even the most desperate. Consider this a lesson in doing so."

Aya hated that she could see the reason in it. Because who was more desperate than those at Death's Door?

"Come," Hyacinth said, her eyes darting between her and Cleo. "We can leave your guard at the docks."

Aya had only seen Katadyré from a distance. It usually fell on the Royal Guard to escort prisoners here, or the lower Dyminara if the convicted were truly dangerous enough. Aya had expected, as they'd taken a small rowboat to the rock-covered island, that the prison would resemble the dungeons of the palace. But as she stalked through the halls, all iron and rock and barnacles left there from the dense ocean air, she was surprised by how...light it was.

Sun streamed through barred windows that lined each floor, five stories in total that stretched toward a ceiling with skylights. Aya tilted her chin back as she looked up toward the glimpses of gray sky she could see through the old, dirty windows.

All that light…it should have made the prison feel warmer. But instead, it made Aya's skin prickle. It wasn't a blessing, or a mercy. It was further punishment for prisoners who could see so much life but would never again taste it.

"Effective, is it not?" Hyacinth murmured, her eyes darting to Aya as they walked down one of the prison hallways. Aya made a noncommittal sound.

It seemed more sadistic than necessary, and rather contrary to "giving hope," but she didn't feel like arguing the finer points of mercy with a priestess.

They reached the end of the long hallway, their escort of prison guards—all Visya—nodding to the sentinels at the large iron door that led to a small courtyard. Aya sucked in a deep breath of fresh air as they crossed the small space, a patch of rocks and dirt rather than anything else, the towering walls of the prison giving tantalizing glimpses of the world beyond through the small square windows that Aya could hardly fit her wrist through. She let the sounds of the sea calm her as they approached a smaller square building, its gray facade the same hue as the sky.

"At least one priestess visits the temple of Katadyré every day. Those who are new to the calling spend an entire month guiding the lost to reconciliation with the gods."

An initiation of sorts, Aya supposed. Every group had some sort of ritual that involved newcomers doing the least favorable tasks. The Dyminara's was far more violence-filled than this.

Hyacinth nodded at the guards to the temple, and they pushed open another iron door, revealing flickering firelight and darkness. Aya followed Hyacinth inside, her eyes taking a moment to adjust to the low light.

The room sloped downward, as if a smaller square were stacked inside the larger. Priestesses and guards lined the upper walkway, looking down to where several prisoners were scattered about—some at altars to the Divine, some on the floor, facedown, their bodies writhing in the dirt, and some standing in line all facing—

Crack.

A long brown whip snapped against a kneeling prisoner, his tattered gray robes marred with filth. The man jerked forward with the force of the impact, his body righting just in time for another blow.

He was shouting, his cries echoing across the silent space as the whip came down on him again. And again.

Aya curled her fists, her feet carrying her forward before she could even think. But Hyacinth's hand shot out, her grip surprisingly firm as she grabbed Aya's arm.

"He wants this," Hyacinth muttered.

"No one wants this," Aya spat out, ripping her arm from the priestess.

"Listen to his pleas," Hyacinth urged, nodding her head to where the man was still shouting, his arms stretching toward the ceiling.

For a moment, all Aya could hear were his cries of pain as the whip cracked against his skin once more. But she forced herself to stay, to hear, and that's when she could make out his words.

They were shouted prayers. Prayers for mercy, for forgiveness, for early punishment so that he might live in the Beyond and not the hells.

The man took two more blows before he collapsed, unable to continue.

And then the next person in line rushed forward, a woman of Aya's age, her face set with fear and determination as she knelt before the whip and started to shout her own desperate pleas to the gods.

Aya felt her stomach twist, her body going cold. The Conoscenza spoke of repentance, and even the punishment the Divine might bestow to salvage the lost before it was too late, but this...

This was wrong.

She turned to Hyacinth, her anger building as the sound of the whip cracked through the space again, but she didn't get a chance to voice her contempt. Because suddenly, the woman was not the only one shouting.

There was a prisoner on the ground, writhing in the dirt, pleading desperately to the gods to spare him from the seven hells. And then another, before the altar of Nikatos, patron to the Zeluus, keening as she pleaded for the god of war to bestow a punishment before his judgment came, so that she might earn his forgiveness. And then another, and another, until the temple was a chorus of distraught voices yelling to the gods, prostrating themselves on the ground, on the altars, before the whip, with a frenzy of desperation that Aya had never witnessed before.

Aya gasped as something latched on to her leg, yanking so hard that she nearly stumbled. She barely had time to see the prisoner holding on to her shin before he was ripped from her by two guards, but that didn't stop him from lunging toward her again and again, his hands reaching out in desperate supplication.

"Please! Please! Do not let me suffer for eternity! Please! Deikosi!" Aya took a step back, her heart hammering as she shook her head. "Please!" The man wailed, his voice cracking as he struggled against the guards. "Grant me pardon with the gods, Deikosi!"

I am not a god.

The words were lodged in her throat, stuck beneath the panic that shortened her breaths as she took another step back. She looked to Hyacinth, but the priestess merely watched her, her hands folded in front of her, that look of utter serenity so out of place in this example of the hells.

The man's plea had caught the attention of the other prisoners, and soon they were swarming toward them, the guards darting down the steps to act as a barrier as the condemned threw themselves at Aya, their dirt- and blood-covered hands reaching for her. There were so many of them, and their pleas were like daggers, carving out some piece of Aya that she didn't even know that she could give, didn't know if she *should* give. All that she knew was that it hurt, and it was wrong, and she couldn't stand here and face these people.

"You see, Aya?" Hyacinth murmured in her ear, her veil tickling Aya's cheek. She hadn't even seen the priestess step beside her. "You are not so dissimilar from the accounts of Evie. You give the people hope. You *can* speak to the gods. These people know it. You must merely *believe* they will answer you."

No, Aya thought as the guards wrestled with the prisoners while her and Hyacinth's escorts closed ranks around them. *We did not give them hope.*

We gave them a lie.

35

WILL STARED AT THE WHITE TOWN HOUSE, ONE IN A ROW of many that lined the Merchant Borough. There was nothing particularly unique about it: its flower boxes were perfectly kept, its white brick stainless, its windows grand, just like the others. And yet there was something about his childhood home that seemed dark. Uninviting.

Godsdamn him to the hells for being here. For seeking out the one man who could shatter Will's carefully crafted coldness without lifting a finger.

But Desperation was tightening its grip with each day that Will searched for the supplier and failed, each day he tried to find some connection to Gianna and came up empty.

Each day he kept his true whereabouts from Aya.

And though the extent of their time together in the last week had been mere passing glances and the brushing of hands in empty halls, Will knew Aya could tell something was grating on him.

It had been foolish of him to snap at her in that way today. Gods knew he would pay for it.

But his groveling would have to wait.

Will smoothed the lapels of his jacket and pushed through

the small iron gate, his steps swift as he jogged up the stairs and knocked on the front door. An attendant he didn't know opened it, her face young and shy as she stared up at him. Will opened his mouth to introduce himself, but the words died in his throat as his father's voice rang out from behind the girl.

"The wayward son returns."

It was a barbed greeting, bitterness masked in Gale's aristocratic drawl. The girl startled as she realized who stood before her; her steps hurried as she opened the door wider to allow Will inside.

"Master Castell," she stammered. "Welcome home."

"William is fine," he corrected with a nod. Most Dyminara informally shed their surnames, their unity within the elite force serving as a new sort of family, he supposed, but Will hadn't claimed his for far longer than that.

"Father," Will greeted as he stepped further into the foyer. His father stood on the grand staircase that curved up the wall, its marble steps gleaming in the bright sunlight flooding through the windows. Gale's three-piece suit fit him impeccably, the gold threads that decorated the black of his jacket and vest winking in the light. His merchant sigil sat over the pocket on his right breast and was integrated seamlessly into the jacket's design: four arrows of a compass embedded in a gold coin.

Gale's gaze raked over Will, his lips twisting with displeasure. "It appears being the queen's plaything doesn't buy you better grooming."

Will let the insult roll off him as he leaned against the polished oak banister. It wasn't anything he hadn't already heard in town this week. He'd been right—news had certainly spread about the state the attendant had found him and Gianna in.

"I was hoping we could discuss a sensitive matter," Will began. His eyes scanned the foyer, taking in the oil paintings that lined the walls. The attendant had already disappeared, but he knew better than to let the empty foyer lull him into a sense of security. Will had long since learned the only place his father didn't have ears was his office. He'd been given the beatings to prove it.

Gale let out a belabored sigh. "Fine. But I don't have long. I have an important meeting I cannot miss."

Will nodded as Gale walked down the stairs, following as his father strolled through the long hallway that led to the back of the house. Gale stopped at a closed door on the right, pulling a golden key from his pocket. Will tried to repress a smirk. Gale kept his office locked day and night. But it hadn't stopped Will from rifling through his things. The door had made him an expert at picking locks.

The door clicked open and Will stepped inside, his gaze roving the familiar space. It was large, with a table covered in maps of the realm, marked with various trade routes. There was a floor-to-ceiling window on the right that looked upon the town house's private courtyard, and a bookcase on the left that stretched the length of the office. Gale's desk was ornately carved, the hints of real gold set in the edges of the wood a bit ostentatious for Will's taste.

But Gale loved to flaunt his wealth, and he took any opportunity to do so.

"So," his father drawled as he settled in the large chair behind his desk. The wooden back was high, Gale's sigil fixed on the two corners that towered over his shoulders. "Are you here to arrest me?"

Will settled in one of the smaller chairs across from him. He leaned back, crossing his ankle atop his knee as he stared at his father. "Now why would I do that?"

He kept his tone light. Curious. Maybe a little mocking.

Gale just grinned, his hands clasping on the desk as he leaned forward. "Come now, William. Surely you know whispers have begun to spread among the merchants. No one's keen to talk too openly, lest they draw attention to themselves, but…the queen's Enforcer, ordering the arrests of dozens. Especially those tied to merchants who work in weaponry…"

Will fought against the way his jaw clenched. He should've fucking known Gianna would paint the orders for the arrests as his own. She wouldn't want to get her hands dirty. She never had, not when she had him to do it for her.

And if word had begun to spread about the arrests, it was only a matter of time until…

No.

Focus.

There was a vicious gleam in Gale's eye as he leaned even closer, his voice dropping conspiratorially. "Tell me…does she wait until your mouth is between her thighs before she gives you such orders?" Will's grip tightened convulsively on the arm of the chair, and Gale's smirk widened. "Does she taste so good that you don't bother to—"

"Enough," Will snarled as he shoved his chair back, his hands slamming on the surface of the desk. "That is enough."

Gale recoiled, but only just. As if for a brief moment, he'd remembered who he was truly dealing with; that Will's moniker of the Dark Prince wasn't just given; it was earned.

"As much as it would please me no end to drag you by your tongue to the prisons to rot for all eternity, I'm afraid you aren't a suspect. At least for this crime."

Gale straightened his jacket as he sat taller. "Then do tell why you're here."

"I want names of everyone you know who trades outside of the Merchant Council."

It was risky to come to his father—to involve yet another party in this mess. It was part of why he'd waited a week before coming here. He'd hoped he wouldn't have to resort to *this*, that the arrests would be enough for Will to get some answers. But he'd found nothing. And it only made him more suspicious of what, exactly, Gianna was searching for.

It would only be a matter of time until other secrets came to light.

And that, he couldn't afford.

Gale laughed. "You think I consort with such criminals?"

"I think"—Will seethed as he leaned further across the desk, his face just inches from Gale's—"that if it were to put more money in your pockets, there is not much you would not do." His anger was growing, setting his heart into a pounding rhythm as he stared his father down. "After all, we both know you keep secrets. Tell me, whose body did we burn, if not Mother's?"

Gale's face drained of color, his green eyes widening as the words registered with him. "What?" he breathed.

Will chuckled. "Oh yes. I know Lorna resides in Trahir. In that ramshackle stone cottage she calls a home. She approached me five years ago. Tell me, have you met her new choice of son? You'd loathe him; hardly has any manners."

Gale's mouth was moving, but no sound was coming from it.

Will straightened, his finger trailing across one of the lines of gold in the surface of the desk. "You see how eager our queen is for any information that could help defeat Kakos." He brushed dust off the pad of his finger, his lips pursed in thought. "I wonder… What do you think she would give for the return of a Saj whose lineage foretold the prophecy of the Second Saint?"

Will met his father's gaze, and Gale swallowed, hard.

"Or better yet," Will continued, his voice dropping low. "What do you think she would give for a Saj who had a vision that could change the course of the war entirely? And what punishment do you think Gianna might enact once she gets what she needs from that Saj?"

Whatever monster his father was, Will knew him to have a weak spot. And that was Will's mother.

"You wouldn't," Gale breathed.

Will had never seen his father afraid. He wished he could appreciate it more, but his own disgust was roiling in his stomach, pooling in a thick pit as he spat out, "You have no idea what I would and would not do to get what I want. But tell me, Father... What would *you* do to protect her secret?"

Will let Gale see exactly what he wanted to see: the queen's Enforcer—brutal and depraved. Made that way by the woman he supposedly pleasured whenever she called for him. No better than a dog on a leash.

Gale's lip curled in disgust. "I'll give you the names. But let's make one thing clear: from this moment on, you are no son of mine."

Will straightened his lapels, his jacket free from any sigil. Free.

"That's a title I haven't claimed in quite some time," he muttered.

Gale blinked at him, something shifting in his expression that Will couldn't place. He didn't stay around to figure it out.

"I'll look for your list tomorrow evening," he said as he made his way toward the door. "Send it with the attendant to Eden. I'll be at the bar."

No one would bat an eye at an attendant delivering a note in the fine establishment. The richest of the merchants were constantly hanging around Eden, bragging about their coin while their attendants fluttered in and out like silent birds, keeping their empires running while they dined on caviar and guzzled liquor.

"And if I do this, you'll keep it secret that she's alive?" Gale called after him, the note of genuine fear in his voice making Will's stomach turn. "Gianna would kill her as soon as she's done with her if she knew the truth."

Will held no warm feelings toward his parents; especially not since he had discovered Lorna was alive and well, and that

Gale had known. But still...to know his father truly feared him, to hear it in his voice...

It felt like another piece of Will dying, another part of himself he willingly destroyed so that maybe, he could do some good.

"Yes," he finally answered, his back still to his father. "If you do this, you have my word no one will learn she is alive."

It seemed there was not one single part of him Desperation would not demand he forfeit to save those he cared about. Because in another breath, Will was turning his head to meet his father's gaze, his voice dripping in that soft violence as he added, "But if you cross me, I promise you that by the time Gianna and I are through with her, Lorna will be begging for that death you faked for her."

It's for the good of the realm. You're doing this for the good of the realm.

He wasn't certain it would matter in the end.

36

SOMEONE WAS HOLDING AYA BACK, THEIR ARMS LIKE IRON around her waist, their hold so tight it stole the breath from her lungs. It didn't stop her from fighting with everything she had to break free, to reach Will, who lay bloody on the ground.

Not dead. Not dead. Not dead.

But there was his bone, jutting through his arm like one of the jagged mountain peaks that surrounded them, and there was his head, lolled to the side, his gray eyes vacant as they stared at her.

She had done this to him.

The realization bludgeoned into her, followed shortly by the recognition of the hold on her. It was the raven-haired healer, the one with cobalt eyes that always appeared in this nightmare.

I'm dreaming.

But the healer was saying something to her, muttering something in Aya's ear that she couldn't hear because she was still screaming, because she could *feel* that hold, could *smell* the blood and death that lingered in the air, could *sense* the way her power began to surge from somewhere deep within her, ready to obliterate everything in her path, because she had done this, she had done this, she had—

Aya lurched awake, her breath coming in a strangled gasp.

"Shit, did I wake you?"

It took her a moment to place the voice—to place where she even was. Her eyes darted around the room, her heart racing under the hand she held to her chest. She took in the black dresser. The desk, scattered with books. The crimson duvet she'd fallen asleep on top of.

Will's room. She was in Will's room.

Aya looked to where Will was watching her, one hand still on the handle of the closed door. He was dressed in a fine black suit, and exhaustion lined his features.

She glanced at the window to see the dark of night still painting the sky black. It had been just after midnight when she'd snuck in here. She'd told herself she was coming to rip into Will about his dismissal of her in Gianna's chambers but in truth…

She hadn't been able to sleep after visiting Katadyré today. And though they'd made a point of avoiding each other out of discretion, she'd needed him.

"What time is it?" she rasped as she pushed her hair out of her face.

"The bells just chimed one."

She must have dosed off shortly after beginning the book he'd had on his bedside table. Indeed, it lay open in her lap, the pirate ship on the cover so worn, it hardly stood out against its background.

"I'm sorry," he murmured as he walked toward his dresser, his fingers undoing the top buttons of his shirt. "I didn't know you were waiting for me."

Aya barely heard him over the pounding of her heart. She

swallowed, forcing her breath to ease as she laid her palms flat on the bedspread.

It had been months since she'd seen the healer in her dreams. Not since before she'd hallucinated that the woman was behind the veil during the Soul Trial with the Vaguer. The trip to Katadyré had clearly unearthed fears she had barely buried in Trahir. Fears of what her power could mean, of who it could hurt.

Who it had already hurt.

The thought faded along with the residual panic from her dream as she noticed Will hadn't moved from the dresser. He stood stock-still, one hand braced on the polished surface, his gaze fixed unseeingly on the drawers. His jacket lay discarded on the chair. She hadn't even noticed him shuck it off.

"What is it?" Aya asked as she stood. "What's happened?"

Because this…this was far more than guilt about their exchange in the queen's chambers. She could see it in the rigid lines of his body and the deep furrow of his brow.

For a moment, she wasn't sure he'd respond. He just kept staring at that chest of drawers, something dark and bitter emanating from him. But finally, Will straightened, his hand falling to his side as he turned to face her.

"I paid my father a visit today."

Will didn't speak of his father often, and when he did, it was with resentment that had surprised her even before she'd come to truly know him, before she learned he was different from the man who honored greed above all else.

Aya cocked her head. "Why?"

She couldn't imagine Will's visit to Gale had been a cordial meeting.

Will's jaw shifted, his movements tense as he undid another button on his shirt. He looked as though the fabric were choking him.

"I thought he had information that could help me with the supplier," Will replied gruffly. "I know it makes no sense that Gianna would send me after them if she had something to do with it, but I *know* she's involved."

Aya took a step closer, her brow furrowing as she scanned him. The comments about the supplier and Gianna should have irked her. It should have brought back that earlier indignation that had ebbed since Katadyré but had not vanished. It should have had her demanding answers and forcing him to truly *look* at her.

But she couldn't find a trace of her irritation now. Not as she noticed that Will's face had a hardness to it that she hadn't seen in some time. There was a thin sheen of sweat on his skin and a flush to his cheeks and a dull sort of focus in his eyes that spoke to a mixture of misery and alcohol.

"Did he? Have information that could help you?" Her prodding was gentle but steady, the type of questioning she might use against a skittish source.

Will rubbed the back of his neck, right below where his hair had curled from sweat. Wherever he had been after Gale's, it was somewhere humid. A tavern in the Rouline, most likely. They were the most crowded.

"I don't know. Probably not," Will muttered darkly. "It's not as though I expected much from him, but…" He shook his head bitterly before scrubbing a hand across his face. "I'm sorry," he repeated dully. "I would've come sooner if I had known you were here."

Aya shook her head. "You don't owe me an apology."

Will scoffed. "Don't I?"

She ignored him. "I didn't mean to intrude."

It hadn't occurred to her when she'd snuck in here that maybe he wouldn't want her waiting for him. That maybe, he didn't feel quite the same ache that distance seemed to bring her the longer they were apart. That maybe his rejection in Gianna's chambers had been genuine.

"Do you…do you want to talk about it?" Her question was quiet. Hesitant. And perhaps some pathetic, selfish attempt to get him to allay her fears and soothe her insecurity.

"You never intrude," he murmured. And though his avoidance of the question was an answer in its own way, and she had no ground to stand on when it came to shutting people out... Will was looking through her, and not in the piercing way that made her feel as though he could read her as easily as breathing.

"Will," she pressed, and his focus sharpened. Unease flooded her stomach the longer he stared at her. Because he still wasn't there, and it wasn't inebriation keeping him away, but something else, something she couldn't read, and gods, the distance between them in those few silent breaths felt wider than the Pelion Gap, and Aya wasn't sure how to close it.

She wrapped her arms around herself, her weight shifting between her feet as she glanced at the dark stone of the floor, its surface worn and scuffed from the years of his boots walking across it.

"Do you want me to leave?"

"No." The word was out of his mouth before she'd even finished the question, and the intensity in it had Aya frowning. Will raked a hand through his disheveled strands, his agitation manifesting in movement as he let out a hard breath. "No," he tried again, gentler. "I don't want you to leave."

But he wanted...something. She could tell by the way his hands clenched and unclenched at his sides, the corded muscles of his neck twitching, as though he was holding back his words.

Perhaps, for once, Will wasn't sure how to speak them.

Perhaps he didn't need to.

Aya hesitated only for an inhale before she stepped forward, her stride slow and measured as she closed the distance between them. Slowly, as if reaching for a startled animal, she raised her palm to his cheek. His skin was colder than she'd expected from the flush on his cheeks, as if that light sheen of sweat hadn't been caused by humidity, but a clammy cold Aya's own anxiety had made her no stranger to.

Will leaned into her touch, his eyes fluttering closed as he let out another long breath. This time his shoulders dropped slightly with it. Aya brought her other hand to his face, stepping even closer, so her chest brushed against his as she pulled his forehead down to hers.

They stood like that for several long moments, until Aya could feel the tension bleeding from his body. Finally, his hands settled on her hips.

"Does it make me a coward to want us to run away from it all?" His question was hardly a whisper, his breath brushing across her lips.

Aya trailed her thumb across his cheekbone, her voice hard as she said, "You are *not* a coward."

He opened his eyes, that blank look gone. Now, a violent storm of emotion swirled in those irises she could forever be lost in. "Then what am I?"

The question hung between them, his anger masking the vulnerability he laid before her.

Aya held his gaze, letting him see every emotion she couldn't put a name to but could feel swelling inside of her as she tightened her grip on his face.

"You're mine."

And then she kissed him, the press of her lips against his firm and searing as she willed him to feel the truth in her words.

Will's grip on her waist tightened instinctively, and he tugged her roughly in to him, matching her fervor as he slid his tongue through her parted lips. His groan at the first taste of her was hungry and desperate, and wrought with that edge of anger that sparked her own.

She would kill Gale. She would kill him for making Will feel like this, for making him question his worth...

She would kill him.

Aya grabbed the collar of Will's shirt, pulling him toward the bed. They stumbled over themselves, their hands quick as they tore off each other's clothes. Aya turned them, her hand meeting Will's chest as she shoved him backward onto the mattress. His brow rose, and Aya smirked as she crawled onto the bed, settling between his knees.

He was hard already, but it didn't stop her reaching for him, relishing in the hiss of pleasure that fell from his lips as she stroked him. She leaned down, her hair brushing his thighs, but Will caught her chin, his breath already heavy as he panted, "What are you doing?"

Aya arched a brow, a sly smile tugging on her lips. "Proving it," she murmured. She waited for his subtle nod. And then she put her mouth on him.

His hand tightened on her chin before dropping to the bed, his fingers grappling for the comforter as he tilted his hips up. Aya decided then and there to commit herself to her task with the same level of duty that she once showed her oath, her tongue swirling around him before she bobbed her head and sucked hard.

She'd seen Will in a lot of different states, but as he choked on another strangled moan, a string of curse words and praise mixing together in an unintelligible symphony of murmurs, she thought this might be her absolute favorite.

The duvet was twisted in his hand, his other tangling in her hair as he held the back of her head. He was trying to control himself, his teeth digging into his lip as he tilted his head back, his eyes still fixed on her face.

But Aya wanted him undone.

Entirely.

Her tongue trailed up his length, swirling around the head before her hand joined her mouth in its descent.

Will snapped his hips, his breath punching from his lungs as he let out a guttural "*Fuck.*" And then his fingers were tightening in her hair and his hand was on her arm and he was tugging her up and twisting them so she was beneath him.

"What's—"

"Please," was all he said.

"Yes." Aya's confirmation died on a gasp as he slid into her, his hand moving down her thigh and hooking her leg over his.

"Seven hells, Aya," he panted, the words half-formed as he slowly dragged out and thrust back in. "You're fucking perfect." His lips latched on to her neck as they found a rhythm, his breath hot on her skin as he tried to force his words from where they seemed stuck in his throat. "Need you."

His voice was dark and rasping in a way that heightened Aya's own pleasure. Her staccato breath hitched when his thumb found her clit, and Will lifted his head, his grin devastating as he coaxed those breathy, high-pitched sounds from her with every swipe of his thumb.

"Was s'posed to—*gods*—be—about you." Aya barely got the words out as his thrusts sped up, her body moving further up the bed with the force of them. Will wound an arm beneath her, holding her close.

"Us," was his only response, the word a mere breath against her ear. And that single word, full of more meaning than either of them had the ability to explain in this moment, shoved Aya over the edge.

Her fingers dug into his back as a moan left her, and she trembled and shook in Will's hold while he continued to move, drawing out every ounce of her pleasure. He followed her shortly after, his body stilling as a shudder ran through him, his eyes screwed shut, mouth open as he groaned.

His forearms gave out beneath him, and there was something uniquely satisfying about his full weight resting against her, his hair damp with sweat and tickling her neck as his head dropped into the space where her neck met her shoulder.

"Fucking hells," Will panted. He stayed like that for a moment longer before shifting to the side, his leg still tangled with hers as he threw an arm over her waist. "Remind me to seek you out for self-assurance more often," he muttered as he tugged her in to him.

Aya's fingers stilled where they'd been toying with the hair at the base of his skull, a breathy laugh bursting from her. Gods, the sound felt foreign after so much desolation.

"You're ridiculous," she admonished, but the words were interrupted by another gentle hiccup of laughter she couldn't suppress. Will turned his head, still half-buried in the pillow as he cracked an eye open and smiled at her.

And in that moment, their limbs tangled and bodies buzzing with the remnants of pleasure, there were no insecurities or fears. There was just Will, his heartbeat as grounding as an anchor as Aya let it lure her to sleep.

37

WILL HAD SEEN SEVERAL BEAUTIFUL SIGHTS IN HIS lifetime. Pathos had blessed him with a home in the Malas, the most magnificent mountain range in all the realm. He only needed to look out the window to see beauty, and that said nothing of the travels he'd gone on as a young man who was brought up to take over a merchant empire.

But no sight compared to Aya standing before his floor-length oval mirror, her bare body covered with nothing but his white dress shirt, her lips pressed in steady concentration as she pulled her hair, messy from their evening, into a ponytail.

Gods, it *hurt* to watch her. It was the most exquisite pain he had ever felt.

She caught his gaze in the mirror, a soft smile gracing her lips as she gave the leather strap in her hair a final tug. "What?"

"I told you once that I suspected you'd look better out of my clothes. I'm considering retracting that statement," he drawled as he lounged back against his headboard, his arm propped on his knee. He didn't miss the way Aya's eyes raked down his bare chest and torso, lingering where the duvet hung low on his waist. He raised a brow at her in the mirror, a smirk twisting his lips as a rare blush stole over her cheeks.

Aya fought off a smile as she turned to face him. "Unfortunately, my own clothes will have to suffice. It's nearly dawn."

The light-gray sky illuminating his window warned that she had better leave before their fellow occupants of the Quarter roused from sleep. Besides, she was due to test her bond with Tyr this morning. But he couldn't quite urge her to go, and it was a mixture of longing and resentment, not at her, but at himself, that followed such a thought.

He didn't deserve her comfort. Her presence. Just like he didn't deserve the reassurance she'd given him last night.

But Aya seemed equally hesitant, her weight shifting between her feet as she folded her arms across her chest.

"You're nervous," he remarked. He had long learned to read her moods, mercurial and hidden as they were. He loved puzzling her out, had spent years learning to read the blank expressions of the Queen's Eyes. "About Tyr."

"I'm fine," she murmured, her fingers toying with the end of her ponytail. Always fidgeting, always moving. It was what he'd noticed about her first, when he'd truly started studying her years ago. When all of the warriors stood still, Aya was always in motion.

Not in any obvious way. But in little subtle motions that seemed to draw no other's eyes but his. A tuck of her hair behind her ear. A tapping of a rhythm with her pointer finger on her thigh. A scratch against her cuticle on her thumb.

"He remains bonded to you, Aya. Again, I'm sure of it."

She let out a noncommittal sound. "Maybe proving such a thing will help me convince Gianna to let me train with the Dyminara," she muttered. She flashed him a small smile. "Then we could spend more time together."

"I haven't been at training."

The words fell from Will's mouth before he could

reconsider, before he could *think* about the snare this simple truth could lead him into.

Aya frowned. "You haven't been training?"

Fuck.

Will was well versed in secrets and lies. The more they grew, the more opportunities arose to completely shatter them.

"My search for the supplier hasn't been conducive to maintaining the Dyminara's schedule," he said as he smoothed his hands over the comforter. It wasn't a lie, not entirely, and yet the words tasted bitter in his mouth anyway.

Questions were building behind Aya's eyes. And though it was horrible of him to use Tyr of all things to turn her attention away from *this*, Will reached for his own inquiry without a second thought. "Is that why you came here last night? Because you were worried about testing your bond with Tyr today?"

"No," Aya said slowly, her gaze still narrowed as she watched him. "I went to Katadyré yesterday. With Hyacinth."

Will straightened, his fears of his own hidden truths forgotten. "What?"

Aya looked around the room, her fingers tugging at the hem of the shirt as she hesitated. "She was trying to prove a point. Trying to show me how people believe in me. That they are relying on me to…speak to the gods. *Hear* from the gods."

He remembered the way she'd paled at the Sanctification when the worshippers fell to their knees before her. The way she kept her hood tugged up in town, and her eyes averted.

"Aya…" he began.

Her lips quirked. "Or maybe I just wanted to yell at you for being an utter ass in Gianna's chambers." There was jest in her tone, but he didn't miss that the light of it wasn't in her eyes.

"I'm sorry." They weren't words he uttered often. In fact,

he was sure the most he'd ever said them was to her. He didn't expect that to change anytime soon. "For not realizing what was happening last night. And for Gianna's chambers. I know our arrangement isn't..." He swallowed, his fingers running through his hair as he grappled with his words. "It isn't easy for me either," he finished.

It seemed to be the only sliver of truth he could give her.

Aya's jaw shifted as she considered him for a moment. And then she was climbing onto the bed, her legs settling on either side of his as she locked her hands behind his neck. "Why are you shutting me out, then?"

The question was soft, vulnerable. It made something inside of him twist, the bitter taste of guilt flooding his mouth as he wrapped his arms around her.

"I'm not."

Aya fixed him with a look. "You've hardly said anything about your search for the supplier."

Will's stomach tightened. "There's nothing to say."

Her doubt clearly lingered, if the pinch in the corner of her mouth was any indication, so Will pressed on, "It's just... you know how fine a line I'm walking with Gianna already. I didn't... I don't want you entangled in it. You have enough. You're dealing with enough. Between your research and the Synastysi and training with Galda... Let me worry about the supplier, okay?"

Her blue eyes stayed locked on his, and not for the first time, he felt as though she could see straight through to his wicked core.

I'm sorry. I'm sorry. I'm sorry.

She looked as though she would argue. He didn't expect anything less. His diversion was paper-thin. But instead, Aya glanced out the window, her face falling at the lightening sky.

"I need to go," she murmured. He pressed a kiss to her throat, relishing in how her body melted into his as he did so.

"You do," he agreed as his mouth continued to traverse

her neck. Her skin was his favorite place to map. Aya huffed a laugh, even as her head tilted to give him better access. His hands slid under her shirt, his thumb sweeping across the arc of her hip bone.

"You have to let me go," she breathed. Will's mouth stilled just below her chin. He could feel the flutter of her pulse against his lips, faster than just moments before.

You should. Let her go. It would be what's best for her. It would be what she deserves.

Slowly, he released his hands from her hips, his head tilting back to take her in.

I'm sorry.

I'm sorry.

I'm sorry.

He wondered if that would ever be enough.

38

AYA STEPPED INTO A LARGE SQUARE PADDOCK THAT SAT behind the barn, Tyr at her side. She inhaled the cool, crisp mountain air, her eyes taking a moment to scan the horizon.

She loved this paddock. It gave an unobstructed view of the mountain range, the peaks and valleys of the Malas stretching as far as she could see.

Tyr nudged her hand with his head, and she glanced down at him, her fingers scratching the space between his ears. "You ready?"

His brown eyes were calm, steady.

It was confirmation enough.

Aya looked across the paddock to where Galda stood with Ophelle—one of the only Auqin in the Dyminara. Aya didn't know the woman well, besides knowing she could weaponize water better than anyone and had been in the force far longer than Aya had. Ophelle's assignments often took her away from Dunmeaden. But Aya had heard enough of her reputation within the Dyminara to know Galda had chosen one of the most ruthless of the Dyminara's assassins.

Excellent. Aya wouldn't need to hold back.

Ophelle and Galda strolled to the middle of the paddock, stopping a short distance away from Aya and Tyr. Ophelle's eyes were already darting across Aya and her bonded, assessing her challengers. Aya took her own inventory as Galda cleared her throat and said, "I trust I don't need to instruct you both on etiquette."

Ophelle shook her head, and Aya mirrored the motion. There were rules for challenges within the Dyminara. But this...this was no ordinary training. Galda only affirmed it when she continued, "Aya, as this is a test for Tyr, you will give Ophelle first attack. When you defend, I do not want to see you touch your persuasion. It's no challenge for Tyr if you pull your usual tricks."

Aya's gaze cut to the trainer. Giving first attack was risky, especially with a fighter she didn't know well. But she dipped her chin in acknowledgment. At least she'd get to use her power today.

Galda jerked her head toward the entrance Aya had come through, and Aya retreated, Tyr's steady steps lost on the whistle of the wind as it whipped through the space.

She turned back to face Ophelle, who had taken several strides backward as well, leaving a large open space between them. Galda stalked to the paddock fence, her eyes narrowed in concentration.

"Begin," she barked.

It was the only warning Aya had before a jet of water came soaring toward her. Aya twisted to the left as Tyr darted right, the water slicing the space between them.

Aya let out a dry chuckle, catching Tyr's gaze from the corner of her eye.

So that's how Ophelle wanted to play it?

Fine.

Aya stalked forward. She didn't need to look beside her to know that Tyr was right there, falling into the same hunting formation he used with the Athatis.

Ophelle, to her credit, didn't move a muscle. She flicked her wrist, then the other, again and again as she sent spears of water at them.

Again, they dodged them easily, too easily.

Aya and Tyr stalked closer.

"Defense, Aya," Galda growled from her spot on the rail. Aya could imagine her stance—arms crossed, face tight with tension—but she didn't dare take her eyes off Ophelle.

She could feel Tyr monitoring her, a low growl rumbling from his chest as he tracked them both.

This time it was ice that Ophelle sent at Aya, its sharpened end just missing her shoulder.

Tyr snapped his jaws, not at the Auqin, but at Aya, a snarl loosening from his maw, as if to demand Aya quit playing around.

It was the opening Ophelle was waiting for. She grinned, her arms swinging wide, two walls of water forming beneath each one. Before Aya could even blink, Ophelle thrust her hands forward, the walls of water growing into a towering, cresting wave that raced toward her.

She saw Tyr's head whip to her, but Aya slammed her hands together before wrenching them apart, a ball of fire stretching between her palms. She shoved her arms forward and out, meeting that swell of water with fire.

She hardly had time to see the wall diminish to mist before she hit the ground, hard.

Tyr's snarl was hot on her ear, and Aya rolled, her heart hammering in her chest.

Please. Please. Please.

She braced herself as she came to a stop, ready to see Tyr standing above her, teeth bared.

But there was nothing but gray sky above her.

She shoved herself off the ground, her fingers reaching for the knife sheathed at her side, but she paused, a grin tugging at her lips as she took in the sight before her.

Ophelle was retreating slowly, her palms raised in submission as Tyr stalked toward her. He let out a vicious snarl, his hackles raised, and the Auqin blanched.

"Call off your runt," she snapped to Aya.

Another snarl from Tyr.

Aya smirked. "He wants you to apologize."

"It was a godsdamn training exercise!"

"Not for the water—for the insult."

The glare Ophelle shot her was nothing short of murderous. Aya whistled once, and Tyr let out a sharp breath through his nose, his ears pricking. He shot Aya a look, more like a glare, before he stalked back to her side.

Galda pushed herself off the fence, her stride steady as she came toward them, but Aya didn't pay her any mind. She dropped to her knees before Tyr, her fingers tangling in the coarse fur around his neck as she pressed her head against his.

"I knew it," she breathed. Something was bubbling up in her chest, filling her with a comfortable warmth that had a smile fixed to her face as Tyr butted her chin with his nose, that exasperated look still swimming in his brown eyes.

Pride.

Aya pulled away, ruffling the top of Tyr's head before standing to face Galda. The trainer's arms were crossed, a muted sort of surprise set in her stern features.

"Well. I suppose that answers that." It was all she said before she jerked her chin at Ophelle. "You can go."

The annoyance hadn't left Ophelle's face, but she didn't argue with Galda. Aya wondered if Ophelle wasn't used to losing, especially as she stormed past Aya, her shoulder clipping Aya's roughly.

Faster than an asp, Aya had Ophelle's arm in her grip. She yanked the Auqin toward her. "For what it's worth," Aya gritted out, her voice a vicious murmur in Ophelle's ear. "This runt could rip out your fucking throat faster than you can conjure water."

She shoved Ophelle away from her, and Ophelle opened her mouth to retort, but Tyr growled again, his eyes narrowed as he took a single menacing step toward the assassin.

Ophelle swore under her breath as she turned on her heel and stormed out of the paddock.

Aya looked back at the trainer, and Galda shook her head in exasperation, her narrowed eyes darting between Aya and Tyr.

"You two deserve each other," Galda growled.

For once, Aya completely agreed with the trainer.

39

EDEN WAS RENOWNED AS THE FINEST DINING ESTABLISHMENT in all of Dunmeaden, with its sparkling stained-glass windows and dual fireplaces and golden-edged tables. But Will often found that the noise rivaled even the worst establishments in the Rouline.

Entertainment was entertainment, he supposed, and it didn't really matter whether it was found in the heart of the richest part of the city or in the bars and brothels that attracted a less polished patronage.

At least the barstools were better. He slid onto one of the plush velvet seats, lifting a finger to wave down the barkeep before scanning the restaurant. He'd picked a place toward the far end of the mahogany bar, giving him an open view of the tables scattered across the bar area as well as the main dining room. The place was alive, a steady chorus of negotiations, stories, and preening getting louder by the minute. A mop of blond hair caught his eye, drawing his attention to a table of merchants who were being seated for dinner.

Elias.

The young noble was a distant relative of the late king. The last time Will had seen the man, he'd been ogling Aya across the square at the Dawning festival. He'd never asked Aya about the details of her and Elias's relationship. Between the way Elias carried on, bragging about their dalliances, and Aya never once mentioning him in Trahir, Will could surmise enough.

Intimate, but not serious. He'd had enough of those himself.

He wondered what the noble thought now that he knew her to be a saint. Was he still sharing the most intimate of details about his previous relations with Aya?

The thought made Will's hand clench on the bar, and he forced his gaze away from the table before he was caught glaring.

He ordered a drink, the tense muscles in his shoulders easing at the first sting of the whiskey in his throat. His gaze swept the space again, his mouth tightening as he saw Lena in the corner with a member of the queen's forces. She was dressed for a night on the town, her silver dress high-necked and sleeveless, her coils free from the tight bun she kept while training. Her eyes flicked to his and she raised her glass in a mock toast, a smirk toying at her lips as she took a sip and turned back to her friend.

Gods, he was starting to hate her. She seemed to be everywhere as of late. Every time he turned around, there she was, smug and smirking. Her increased proximity to Gianna had turned her arrogant in a way that Will knew intimately, and perhaps it made him a hypocrite to loathe it, but he did regardless.

He sighed and turned back to the bar. His father's attendant should be here any moment. He'd get the list and then he'd leave, and he'd be free to spend the rest of his evening in peace.

"What's got you looking more dour than usual?"

Will paused, his drink still pressed to his lips as his eyes cut to Liam. The Persi slid onto the barstool next to him and ordered a drink of his own, his gaze expectant as he waited for Will to answer.

Will hissed as the whiskey burned his throat. "Your sister, for starters."

Liam glanced to where Lena was chatting happily with her friend. "Can't say I blame you. She's been annoying the fuck out of me, too."

Will arched a brow. "Aren't twins supposed to be inseparable? Built-in friendship and all that?"

Liam snorted. "What would you know about friendship?"

"Not much," Will confessed, taking another swig of his drink. And there was no one to blame for that but himself. Gianna may have made him feared, but the hatred? That was all Will.

"She's different. Has been for months." The musing was so quiet, Will nearly missed it.

"Who?"

A roll of Liam's eyes. "My sister. Ever since she's been given more responsibility, she's become insufferable."

Will made a noncommittal sound. He didn't exactly feel like investigating Lena's change with Liam. He had too much on his own mind to entrench himself in anyone else's.

"Power does strange things to people," Will murmured.

"That it does," Liam agreed.

"The documents you requested, Master William," a soft voice interrupted. Will glanced behind his shoulder to where his father's attendant stood.

"Thank you." He didn't bother to pass along a message in return to his father. He'd be damned if he ever showed that man a hint of gratitude.

The woman scurried off as soon as he took the envelope from her, and Liam let out a deep chuckle. "Gods, you do make them skittish, don't you?" Liam took a long sip of his drink, a smirk twisting his lips. "Do they run away from your bed like that too?"

"Hardly."

Liam just shook his head, that smirk widening into something like a grin. Teasing, but genuine. "How you have the time to find someone to warm your bed is beyond me. Who is she then?"

"Who is who?" Will drained his glass.

"The latest conquest."

Either Liam didn't believe the rumors that Will was bedding Gianna, or he wanted Will to confess to them. Neither option filled him with much pleasure. "Haven't you heard? I took a vow of celibacy."

Liam laughed again. "The day that's true is the day the gods return."

Will fought the urge to stiffen at the typical saying. That day might be sooner than they all knew, if Lorna was right about Gianna's desires.

He shot Liam a smirk as he stood from his stool. "Well, as entertaining as this has been, I'm off," he said dryly.

Liam wasn't fazed by his disdain. He merely shrugged, his voice light as he retorted, "Fine, keep it a secret. We'll all find out eventually. Your women love to suck and tell."

They did. Will was no better than a conquest. He wondered who was to blame for that.

"Do me a favor? Worry about your own cock," Will growled.

Liam rolled his eyes in exasperation, muttering something under his breath that sounded strongly like *irritable asshole*. But Will was already weaving through the patrons, the envelope tucked in his jacket pocket as he pushed through the door and stepped into the cool night air.

He didn't let his smooth stride falter until he stepped into an alley at the edge of the Merchant Borough. It was dark and quiet, and Will took a moment to lean back against the brick and let out a long breath.

"Fucking hells," he swore softly. He lifted his head off

the brick and tore the envelope open. He unfolded the two pieces of parchment, his eyes squinting as he walked directly beneath one of the torches. The light illuminated his father's messy scrawl, and he scanned the first list of names quickly, his frown deepening the further he read.

These names...they didn't match a single person in the prison.

If Gianna was searching for the supplier, why wouldn't she have arrested those who were *known* to operate outside of the law?

Will's murmur was as soft as the quiet he often sought in the dead of night. "What the hells are you looking for, Gianna?"

40

AIDON COULD FEEL A HEADACHE COMING ON. HE SAT IN THE high-backed chair behind his uncle's—no, *his*—ornate wooden desk, a stack of parchment scattered across the dark surface. Aidon's mother had been forgiving of him tarnishing most of the traditions Dominic had upheld, but refusing to use the king's office was one she would not stand for.

Aidon hated every bit of the circular space. The thick crimson curtains that rimmed the towering windows behind him. The bookcases that curved with the walls, the cracked leather spines of ancient ship manifests and trade accounts and history books filling the room with a musty smell.

Even the chair was uncomfortable, the delicate wooden designs carved out of the back digging against his spine as he shifted for the hundredth time that hour.

He hadn't been sparring, too worried to do anything that might provoke his affinity to break through the increased dosage of tonic. The lack of his normal routine and physical exertion had left him antsy and easily irritated. Even Josie had taken to tiptoeing around him, especially when she showed up at dinner in her fighting leathers, her face with that healthy glow that came along with a hard day of training.

Aidon pushed a piece of parchment aside, his fingers massaging his temple as he scanned the one beneath it. It was another trade ledger, this one detailing the weapons orders placed with Tala over the last six months.

Gods, he was surprised Will and the Tala Merchant Council had allowed such atrocious terms. The volume was hardly enough to warrant the ships it took to bring the weapons here. Had Dominic not thought to prepare his own people for the war he was willingly involving them in? Had he planned for them to die at Kakos's hand rather than join their cause?

Many would have chosen death, Aidon thought, rather than partner with the heretics. At least, that's what he would like to believe.

A commotion, loud enough to seep through the thick wooden door of the study, drew his attention away from his thoughts. It sounded like yelling, but he couldn't quite make out what the voices were saying.

Aidon was halfway out of his chair when the door slammed open.

"Banishment?" Ryker roared as he struggled against the guard who held him back.

Ah. So Avis's sentencing had been announced.

Aidon dropped back into his chair with a sigh, waving off the guard with a lazy flick of his hand. "Good afternoon, Councillor Drycari. By all means, come in. Sit down. Make yourself comfortable."

Ryker tugged on the lapels of his jacket, straightening the linen fabric as he shot the guard a glare. The guard remained unbothered as he stepped out the room and shut the door behind him.

"You cannot banish Avis," Ryker snarled as he strode toward the desk, his dark eyes glinting with rage.

Aidon cocked a brow as he settled against the stiff back of the chair. "Last I checked, sentencing threats to the Crown did fall within my purview. Has the role of King changed?"

Ryker's hands balled into fists. "The Bellare is no threat to the Crown."

"Oh, but they are. You saw to that, didn't you?"

Ryker slammed his palms on to the desk. "Avis has no knowledge of your power. Nor is he guilty of the crimes you've convicted him for, and you know it!"

But Aidon's people did *not*, and someone had to be punished for the crimes Dominic had framed the Bellare for.

So, Avis would spend the remainder of his life on a penal estate on the outskirts of Chamen. It was one of the only ways the remote kingdom was able to make any coin. The frozen tundra made for conditions that rivaled the seven hells, but...

It was better than death. At least, that's what Aidon told himself when the guilt began to stir in his stomach, when he lay awake at night and wondered how many innocents kings and queens had been condemned to a life of misery.

Not innocent, he would force himself to remember. *Avis is not innocent.*

Not entirely, anyway.

The Bellare may not have kidnapped Viviane, and they certainly hadn't murdered Avis's own daughter, but they were still responsible for attacks on the Visya in Rinnia. They'd vandalized businesses and intimidated citizens and, hells, almost murdered Aya and Will.

And Avis, as one of the most respected members of the rebel group, had been primed to take the fall.

Dominic had seen to that.

Aidon stood, forcing his guilt down as his palms braced on the desk. He leaned toward the young rebel before him. "Avis has threatened Visya citizens in my kingdom," he hissed. "Be grateful he doesn't hang with the other traitors."

Ryker's round jaw shifted as he straightened. "Banishment is worse than death."

"Then it will be a fitting message for your companions, will it not?" Aidon stood tall as well, adopting the low, commanding tone he'd wielded in the force. "I gave you a place on the Council, Ryker. I expect you to uphold your end of the bargain."

"What's that supposed to mean?"

"It means I know that the Bellare continue to grow their ranks. Leash your fucking dogs, or I'll have the City Guard do it for you."

Ryker had the nerve to look affronted. "That was not our bargain. Our bargain was that I control the Bellare's reaction to Avis's sentencing, a feat I doubt will be possible now that you've sentenced him to rot in Chamen."

Aidon cocked his head. "I suggest you find the means to make it possible."

The threat was evident in his words, but Ryker hardly seemed affected by it. He merely folded his arms, his black brows flicking toward his silken hair. "You forget the leverage I have, Majesty."

Aidon laughed as he settled back in his chair. "No, Ryker. You forget the leverage *I* have. The more bothersome you become, the more I think it might be worth you spreading falsities about me."

Ryker sneered. "And I'll be sure the realm knows those *falsities* came from Viviane."

"You overestimate my sister's loyalty to her partner. She may just be amenable to watching you and Vi hang together."

Ryker took a small step forward. "You wouldn't dare," the rebel hissed.

Aidon stayed in his relaxed position, his arms folding across his chest. The picture of ease. "Care to find out?"

Ryker's eyes darted across Aidon's face, as though he were searching for the lie somewhere in his features.

He would find nothing.

But Aidon…Aidon had found exactly what he had been looking for.

Ryker's throat bobbed as he took a step back, his shoulders

dropping infinitesimally. He would not risk Viviane's safety—and that confirmed Aidon's suspicions. There was some sort of kinship between the two, something deeper than mere friendship. Aidon wondered if Josie would know, or if he'd even have the nerve to ask.

"I will do what I can to control the Bellare's reaction to the sentencing," Ryker finally conceded, the words short and bitter, as if he spat out each one.

"See that you do," Aidon replied with a pointed look at the door.

Ryker gave him one last glare, his full lips twisting in disgust, before he turned his back on Aidon and stormed out of the study. Aidon let out another heavy sigh as the door slammed shut behind the rebel.

Seven hells, what he wouldn't give to be in the barracks right now. To be punching a sparring post or even one of the warriors he was evenly matched with.

Aidon glanced down at his hands. At least there was no sign of his affinity, despite the way he'd been fighting his anger. His palms were smooth save for the callouses from years of wielding a sword.

He wondered when those would vanish, too.

 41

FOR ONE NAIVE MOMENT, JOSIE WAS GRATEFUL FOR THE FLUSH to Viviane's cheeks as Josie stepped into her dormitory.

She'd expected to find Vi where she often found her when she stepped into her circular room in the Maraciana dormitories: at the window, staring off at the horizon as if she were hoping one day she'd reach it.

But today, Viviane was waiting for her. Her arms were crossed, color stealing across her cheeks as her gaze met Josie's.

Josie was so happy to see some hint of *life* in her that she nearly missed the way Vi's mouth was pressed into a firm line. Or how she practically seemed to be *vibrating* with rage.

"Viviane—"

"Do *not* come in here with excuses on your tongue," Vi hissed. "Banishment, Josie? Really? What crimes is Avis truly guilty of?"

"I have nothing to do with this," Josie replied steadily as she tried to step closer to her partner. But Viviane took a step back, a warning glare flitting across her face as she shook her head.

"That's bullshit."

It wasn't. There was a time when Aidon trusted Josie with such things. When she had been his confidante. But now, he came to her less and less. Josie had learned this news with everyone else, and she wasn't sure what she resented more: the sentencing, or that Aidon hadn't had the decency to tell her.

As if he didn't doubt, not for a single moment, that she would continue their family's lies—that she would continue to bludgeon this crumbling relationship for the sake of her duty and loyalty to her family.

To her Crown.

"You may dress up in those leathers," Viviane spat out, her nose scrunching as she looked Josie up and down, "but do not pretend you're more warrior than you are princess. You know exactly what goes on in that court."

The words were meant to hurt. Viviane wielded them precisely, knowing exactly which insecurity to push to get Josie to break. Josie had confided in her after all.

She was the only one Josie could confide in.

And maybe that's why it was anger, not sadness, that rose to meet Vi's taunt.

"The same way you pretend you're more victim than traitor?"

It made her sick the way a pulse of triumph raced through her as Vi's eyes went wide, her slender shoulders dropping as she took a step back.

"That's a fucked-up thing for you of all people to say to me," Viviane breathed. "Especially when it was your family who did this to me."

Guilt slammed into Josie, its impact as hard as any hit she'd taken during training.

Viviane placed a trembling hand on her chest, her eyes lined with tears as she shook her head. "I would rather have hanged than be subject to becoming this."

Josie took a tentative step forward. "You are Visya, Viviane," she murmured. "That is all."

She'd meant to reassure her, to let her know that though it had come through the worst circumstances, she was alive, and okay, and she *could* manage the affinity that now slumbered inside her, masked by the tonic that had saved Josie's brother.

But apparently, the words had only made things worse.

"I am not Visya! I am something entirely different—something created by dark magic," Viviane yelled through gritted teeth. She scrubbed a hand across her face, the red in her cheeks deepening. "I am an insult to the gods," she muttered. "Just like your brother."

Josie wasn't sure what it meant that *this* was the remark that cut her the deepest.

"Careful," she warned.

"Why?" Vi laughed. "You know it's true. Your brother is spitting on the very laws of the gods. And don't even try to spout your bullshit about what a wonderful king he'll make. Sentencing an innocent man to rot in Chamen proves your delusions wrong."

"Avis is not innocent," Josie snarled.

But Vi was already turning her back on her, her movements stiff as she walked toward the window seat. She gave a dismissive wave, not bothering to turn around. "Tell that to someone who cares."

42

Do you think Galda would take pity on me if I told her my headache was from a training injury?" Tova groaned, slouching in her chair.

Aya looked up from her porridge, her brows rising as she took in Tova's pathetic state.

Tova's eyes were bloodshot, bags of purple marring her pale skin beneath her lashes. Her hair, normally perfectly styled and shiny, hung limply around her shoulders.

"No," Aya said before taking another bite of her breakfast. Tova's eyes narrowed into a glare.

"Rude."

Aya shrugged. She doubted she looked much better. It had been another night of nightmares despite her successful training with Tyr, and her exhaustion was worsened by the nagging feeling that Will, who she hadn't seen since she'd snuck out of his room the morning before, was keeping something from her. The suspicion sat heavily in her gut, and after hours of tossing and turning, she had been desperate to distract herself from it. So she'd bathed and dressed and roused Tova for breakfast in the hopes that it might repair some of the damage done from their most recent argument.

And while Tova had groggily agreed, she had a feeling her friend was now regretting it, especially as she eyed the toast before her as if it were an enemy on the battlefield.

"Eat," Aya urged. "You'll feel better."

"I'll never feel better."

"You say that every time you're hungover."

"This time is different," Tova muttered as she ripped off the edge of her toast and popped it into her mouth.

Aya fought the way her lips twitched as Tova let out a pathetic groan. It wasn't rare for Tova to enjoy herself, but to be this utterly wrecked...

"Those Anima tested your capacity for fun, I see."

Tova let her head drop back, her hair flowing over the back of her chair as she stared at the arched ceiling. "Those Anima can fucking go to hells," she growled.

"Those Anima are sitting a table away, so I'd watch it if I were you," Aya shot back, nodding her head toward where a group of warriors sat at one of the three long rectangular tables that made up the dining hall. While the tables weren't technically divided by Order, some of the Dyminara preferred to sit that way—especially the Corpsoma.

Tova rolled her eyes. "Please. They give the saint a wide berth. They're intimidated by your holiness."

She gave Aya a roguish grin that Aya forced herself to mirror. It was true. No one sat within three chairs of them. Aya had made a habit of living on the outskirts of rooms. She was used to slipping into shadow and lurking behind those who relished the attention.

She was comfortable there.

But there was something about this particular distance that chafed at her. Perhaps because it was her own who avoided her.

Not your own. You're different now.

And Gianna was seeing to it that she stayed that way, wasn't she?

The porridge seemed to stick to Aya's throat on her next swallow. She let her spoon drop into her bowl and gently pushed it away from her. Tova's smile faded as her gaze darted from Aya to the bowl and back to Aya again.

"I didn't mean—"

"I know," Aya interrupted. "I'm just full."

Tova's jaw shifted as she considered whether to argue with her, but she pushed her own plate away instead. "Do you want to talk about it?"

"About what?"

Tova fixed her with a steady stare. "About why you were up at the crack of dawn. You look like shit."

"You have a way with words, you know that?"

"It's all the reading I do," Tova said with a dismissive wave of her hand. "Now spill."

Aya felt her shoulders slump as she dropped back in her chair. She desperately wanted to tell Tova the truth, and the fact she couldn't…it made her feel even worse. Aya missed the ease she'd once had with her friend. It was something she hadn't even known to appreciate until she found herself here, balancing half-truths and lies for the sake of their fragile friendship.

Aya sucked in a breath, her fingers toying with her spoon as she settled on something she could confide in Tova about. "I'm trying to find answers in the Synastysi. But what if I can't? What if war arrives, and we still don't know how the gods wish me to use this power to right the greatest wrong? What if we don't even know what the greatest wrong is?"

She hadn't missed the way Hyacinth's face had crumpled yesterday when she once again had nothing to report, even after their visit to Katadyré. Aya had struggled enough with the idea that the gods had chosen her, that she was somehow the one they thought could do this. The longer she went without hearing their guiding voices, without knowing what their instructions were, the more questions she had.

Questions unbefitting for a saint.

Questions like, why choose her only to abandon her when she needed them most?

And then there was the matter of the veil—a concept none of the texts seemed to want to delve into beyond the cursory explanations about how it was made up of godly power.

Enough godly power that to reopen it would *cost* them something.

"Well, we do know what it is," Tova murmured, drawing Aya's attention away from her thoughts. "The greatest wrong is the Decachiré. I mean, that's what Evie abolished in the first place, right? And it's what Kakos is trying to bring back. Corrupt, raw power that makes them more like gods than mortals."

And she said it so certainly, as if it were so *obvious*, that Aya's chest hollowed out even further. Aya looked up from where her gaze had been fixed on the rim of her glass bowl to find Tova giving her a contemplative look.

"You know what you need?" her friend said, her eyes brightening as an idea struck. Aya didn't bother to hide her groan.

"Not a night out."

"A night out!"

Aya shook her head, but she was unable to fight off a rare smile. "*That's* your solution to my fears of dooming our Eteryium? Drink and merriment?"

Tova shrugged. "I know you well enough to know anything I say to you when you're like this will go unheard. And we haven't had an evening together since you came home."

Aya opened her mouth to object, but Tova held up a hand, her eyes narrowing into a playful glare. "A *fun* evening," Tova corrected herself. Aya refrained from pointing out that their definitions of *fun* were drastically different.

She bit the inside of her cheek as she considered Tova's proposal. They could use this—this time together. Besides, there *was* something Aya needed in town anyway.

"Fine." She sighed as she downed the cup of water before her. "Are you sure you're up for it tonight?"

"Of course I am," Tova huffed. "Why wouldn't I be?"

Aya smirked. "Because you're still half-drunk from your *last* night of frivolity."

Time passed slowly and yet all at once inside the Synastysi. It was impossible for Aya to tell how long she had been sitting there due to the lack of windows on the lower floor, but she was willing to bet it had been hours, if the aching in her back was any indication.

She stretched her arms overhead and rolled her head from side to side, taking note of the torches that had grown dim. And yet no priestess had come to fetch her to discuss her findings with Hyacinth.

Tyr would be getting restless. He had accompanied her through town today, along with Liam. Both were required to wait outside with the temple's strict policy on weapons. Aya bit back a smirk as she remembered the look of apprehension on the priestess's face as she saw Tyr.

The Athatis made even the devout wary.

Aya sighed as she tugged another leather diary toward her. The pages were yellowing, the paper worn so thin, it was a blessing from the gods that it didn't tear as she flipped through the pages.

She paused when she saw Evie's name, her brow furrowing in concentration as she translated the scrawled entry. Again, it was hardly much of consequence—just a note that Evie had come to the diarist's camp.

Aya kept reading. It wasn't like she had anything else to do here.

She flipped through entry after entry that reflected on a worsening war, detailing battles, and loss, and hope, and regret. Evie appeared in mere flashes. A sentence here. A mention there. Until...

Aya stilled.

There.

This wasn't a mere mention, or a generalization about the benevolent saint. This was something *more*.

Detailed. Personal.

Aya flipped through the pages quickly, her eyes scanning the text. Evie's name appeared again and again and again, each mention becoming longer as the dates grew later. Aya felt a pulse of excitement rush through her as she settled back in her chair, drawing her knees up against the edge of the table. She rested the book on her thighs and began to read.

I witnessed her training. Evie fights with a precision that few can master, but I suppose it is to be expected of one who carries such power. I must admit, I expected her to be as sharp and cruel as the blade she keeps by her side—the one rumored to have been used in that horrific ritual that killed her parents. But she is no such thing. She is warm. Kind. She brought the camp hope today, even with news that the strongest of the Decachiré practitioners are pressing closer...

There's a sadness in her, left there by the atrocities inflicted on her parents. And yet she tells me she finds hope in the fact that in the very end, they chose love. Love for her saved them from the most severe evil, for only the gods are meant to be immortal. Yet she is utterly alone in her power. I do wonder how that weighs on her...

Took out an entire line without breaking a sweat, saving me and so

many others. And even so, she was the last to turn in tonight, the last to leave the tent of the injured, healing whoever she could. And when I urged her to turn in, she refused, instead taking those that did not make it and burning their bodies so that their souls might exist in the Beyond without delay. She did not lie that day when she motivated our troops before battle. "I have the power of the gods in me," she'd said. It is true.

Aya lifted her head, blinking away the bleariness from her eyes.

"*Y avai ti dynami a ton diag mesa mye*," the diarist recounted Evie saying.

I have the power of the gods in me.

Aya's teeth dug into the flesh of her cheek, her finger skimming the long-dried ink as she turned the words over in her mind.

All Visya had kernels of godlike power. Yet Evie's proclamation—and the writer's—spoke to *more*, to the fact that she was not limited the way the Visya were. It was obviously true. Everyone knew Evie's power was unparalleled.

And yet…Aya had never considered how bold it was of Evie to proclaim it during the War, even with the resistance having seen proof of Evie's abilities. After all, wasn't that exactly what the Decachiré practitioners had been trying to accomplish?

They'd wanted to destroy their wells so that they might have limitless power, like the gods. Like Evie's.

Didn't that mean Evie was the very thing the Visya had been fighting against? And yet…

People considered her a leader. Hyacinth's reflection came floating back to Aya now, and she turned the words over in her mind as she tapped an unknown rhythm on the diary.

Aya had studied the First Saint enough to know Evie had always been presented as a connection to the gods, not a threat to them. *When* had she gained the trust of those fighting to abolish the Decachiré? How?

Was it because she had been rescued by the Visya in the resistance after she'd interrupted her parents' attempt to become immortal? She *had* been raised for years alongside those who stood for good, after all. She'd had every chance to prove her innocence, to show them that though she had limitless power, she had not wanted it.

Aya rubbed at her temples, a headache settling somewhere behind her eyes.

If the Visya had known that unwanted power of Evie's could rip open the veil—that Evie would use it to do just that in a desperate attempt to call down the gods—would they have let her? Wouldn't they have worried that would make the gods vulnerable or might kill the one person who could change the tide of the war?

But she *couldn't* change the tide of the war. Not fully. That was why she went to the top of the Malas to tear the veil open, wasn't it?

Because they'd needed something *more* to eradicate the Decachiré.

Something like the gods.

Which would mean Evie's power wasn't truly limitless. If it had been, and the accounts of Evie's greatness were to be believed, then Evie would've killed every last Decachiré practitioner. Aya was sure of it.

So where were Evie's limits?

Where were Aya's?

Was there *any* way to truly stop the Decachiré? And if there wasn't, was Lorna right? Was the greatest wrong Evie opening the veil? Was it truly torn, and weak, and if it was…

Could Aya fix it?

Could she rebuild it in a way that protected the gods from Kakos, and the realm from the gods' wrath should the veil be opened once more?

"Aya."

Aya jolted, her leg banging into the table as she dropped her knees from the edge. She barely kept in the vicious swear threatening to burst from her lips.

"I am so sorry," the priestess said, her hand covering her chest. "I did not mean to startle you. Are you alright?"

Aya flipped the diary closed, her hand massaging her leg. "I'm fine. What is it?"

"Hyacinth is asking for you," the priestess explained, a concerned expression still on her face. Aya bit back a sigh as she stood.

Another day wasted, and all she had were more questions no one could answer.

43

I T WAS AN EASY THING TO AGREE TO TOVA'S EVENING OUT, even if Aya's motives weren't purely recreational. Not that Tova needed to know that. It was enough that Aya was here, enough to keep their friendship from straining further, at least for the evening.

Aya's only condition had been that they come *here*, where she was far less likely to be bothered. The devout hardly frequented such places.

But with the stench of booze and sweat and sex making her eyes water as she pushed her way to the bar, its rotted pine indicative of the general run-down nature of the establishment, she wondered if she should have picked the seediest tavern in the Rouline. It was worse even than the Squal, which was notorious for attracting the worst of Dunmeaden's patrons.

Less chance of being observed, Aya reminded herself, keeping the hood of her cloak pulled up as she ordered a drink. She wasn't quite able to ignore the prickle of guilt as she cut a glance to where her friend sat at a rickety card table in the far corner. Aya had lost every hand they'd played thus far to Tova and the two burly gentlemen Tova had charmed into losing all their money to her.

Tova could give even Aidon a run for his money. He'd beaten Aya thoroughly when they'd played in the palace in Rinnia. Then again, Aya was rubbish at cards, so that wasn't saying much about the prince—*king*—and his prowess.

She'd tracked down what information she could on both him and Josie, too worried as she was about Gianna's ever-present gaze to send a missive. It seemed Josie had joined the forces. She'd make an excellent warrior.

Gods, she missed her friends. She hadn't realized how much she would feel their absence, would long for the training sessions with Aidon in that small sparring room, or her walks with Josie down by the docks, laughing at some ridiculous story about the princess and her antics.

Aya nodded in thanks to the barkeep as he placed a tumbler of amber liquor before her, a large square of ice in the center. She took a sip, the sting of the whiskey strangely settling. The noise of the tavern was already giving her a headache, a raucous mix of shouts and laughter and arguments, all woven within the rush of the fiddler who stood on a stool in the middle of the floor.

But she needed the noise just as much as she needed the dense crowd.

Someone bumped into her, their shoulder clipping hers hard as they wedged themselves into a place at the bar.

"Apologies," the man said with a nod of his head. He was a few years older than Aya, with brown skin and wavy black hair that dusted his shoulders. Aya took a sip of her drink in lieu of a response.

The man faced the bar, signaling to the keep. The spot he'd chosen forced him to stay wedged against Aya, his shoulder pressed against hers, his body close enough that she could hear even his murmur beneath the noise of the crowd.

"Sorry I'm late. Got held up."

Eryx was nothing if not discreet. His years as a thief in Mathias's guild had taught him well—and had made him an invaluable asset when Aya turned him two years ago. He was a reliable source of information with his own network of trusted contacts.

Contacts that often frequented his lackluster shop in a run-down alley, its window filled with legally and illegally gained trinkets.

"Did your father enjoy the flowerpot?" Eryx muttered.

Aya rested her elbows on the bar, her gaze fixed on the liquor bottles that lined the shelf. "He's still not awake."

Eryx let out a noncommittal sound.

"Anything?" Aya muttered, her hood concealing her lips.

He'd sent word to her yesterday, asking for a place to meet. Aya had seized the opportunity when Tova mentioned a night out tonight.

Eryx shifted, his fingers tapping a steady beat on the bar's surface as he nodded his thanks to the keep for his drink. "No. The Royal Guard were all accounted for. They weren't behind the attack on your father."

Disappointing, but unsurprising. As Aya had suspected, it would be foolish for Gianna to use one of her own if she was behind the attack. Unless she'd wanted to send a clear message.

Aya took a sip of her whiskey, welcoming the burn to her throat. "And the others?"

The queen didn't limit her network to the Dyminara and the Royal Guard. Aya was part of ensuring that, and she'd made it a point to keep track of those Gianna favored.

"Also accounted for," Eryx muttered as he drank his ale. "Even those within our own ranks."

Aya's grip tightened around the glass tumbler, the cold of it biting into her hand. Eryx was reliable. He'd proven time and again that he'd lost his loyalty to Mathias's guild.

Not that he'd ever seemed particularly loyal to the crime lord.

Eryx was motivated by leverage, mostly. And Aya ensured he kept just enough to remain loyal to *her*.

Which meant his information was accurate. And she was back to being desperate for answers.

She downed her drink just as Tova appeared at her side. "You know, the whole point of coming out was to have *fun*," her friend chided. "I even agreed to come to this hellshole so you wouldn't be accosted." Her hazel eyes flicked to Eryx, but he was turned away from them, engrossed in a conversation with the woman on his other side. Tova's lips turned down. "And here I was hoping you'd at least be making a move."

Aya snorted. "Not my type."

Tova let out a dramatic sigh as she flagged down the barkeep. "There aren't any that are mine here either. Though I did see Nel earlier."

"Oh?"

"She's still not speaking to me."

Aya bit back a laugh. Nel had broken up with Tova after the Dawning festival two years ago, when Tova had accidentally spun her into a table of refreshments. It was Nel's loss, Aya had told Tova. Believed it, too. Anyone who couldn't handle Tova's passion for living didn't deserve her.

"The one playing billiards is handsome," Aya observed, jutting her chin toward the man polishing his cue.

"Then *you* go talk to him," Tova retorted. She ordered two shots of something that smelled sickeningly sweet, and Aya wrinkled her nose as Tova placed one before her. "*I* see no worthy candidates," Tova continued. "Though I suppose it's foolish to try to find love as war unfolds."

Aya raised a brow. "Isn't that the point of all those novels you read? Love above all, no matter the circumstances, et cetera, et cetera?"

"And here I thought you were of the opinion that they were nonsense."

"They *are* nonsense," Aya deadpanned. Tova let out a bright cackle of laughter, her head tilting back with the force of it. The sound provided far more warmth inside Aya than the whiskey had. It settled her for just a breath, providing a moment of peace amid so much uncertainty.

Tova had always been able to do that, though: give Aya stolen moments that felt like calm.

Tova held up her shot, urging Aya to do the same.

"Here's to me having better taste than you," she chided. "In men *and* books."

Aya's smile nearly flickered. But she shoved those raw emotions down and clicked her glass against Tova's, not bothering to hide her grimace as she downed the liquor.

"Better taste in men and books, maybe," Aya sputtered. "But certainly not in booze."

44

P AIN, WILL HAD LONG COME TO LEARN, WAS A PECULIAR THING. Sometimes it came in shades, the way the navy of twilight turned to black so gradually, he could hardly detect the difference until it was too late and the dark of the night was upon him. Sometimes it came in different colors entirely, each piercing of agony so unique, there was no way he could mistake them for each other, knowing the only thing they had in common was they both *hurt*.

Pain was varied, and depthless, and sometimes Will wondered if his years of getting intimately acquainted with it had made it a part of his very being, something he wasn't even aware was flowing inside of him.

Like the blood in his veins, felt only when it rushed like the waterfalls in the Malas.

He had been trying on hope as of late. But as he stared down at the man before him, he wondered if it weren't even more dangerous to feel too much of that particular sensation.

Perhaps that's how Desperation got its hold on people, how it sunk its claws in until it wrapped around one's soul like a poisonous vine, leaching the good out of it bit by bit.

Perhaps that's how Desperation had gotten its hold on *him*.

"I could do this all day, Porden," he drawled to the merchant sniveling on the ground.

He couldn't. Not with the way his own body was screaming in pain, his shield starting to wear thin the longer they continued. Pathos's own punishment rendered for Will's sins, he supposed.

But he wouldn't stop. Not now.

Because finally, *finally*…he was getting somewhere.

Two weeks of interrogations on Gianna's orders. Two weeks of disappearing into these godsforsaken dungeons to do the job he had made sure she gave him over three years ago.

Her Enforcer.

Her torturer.

Two weeks of dread and hope warring within him. Dread, because every day in here destroyed something precious inside of him. Hope, because he was desperate to know why Gianna was arresting lower merchants that he'd just learned, thanks to his father's list, were in good standing with the Council.

As if she *knew* they had something to do with the missing weapons supplier.

Gianna was in the middle of it all. He *knew* that. And if he could prove it, then perhaps he could *use* that to his advantage against his queen. Perhaps it was connected in some way to whatever Gianna's plans were for Aya.

Even if it wasn't, he could take the information and use it against her to demand answers.

If he could just *prove* it, then perhaps…

Perhaps Aya would forgive him.

For not knowing how to escape Gianna's commands. For continuing even though that list in his jacket pocket from his father was enough for him to know something wasn't right.

For lying to her about what he was doing each day, even if it destroyed him in the process.

Will was no stranger to keeping secrets from Aya. He'd done it for years—had buried his feelings and hidden his true motives. But this was different. Those secrets were kept from a woman who had loathed him, a woman he never imagined having a chance with.

But now...

Aya trusted him.

Does she? that insidious voice whispered in his mind. *It didn't seem that way when she used her affinity to make sure you weren't lying about Tova.*

He shoved the thought aside as Porden continued to whimper.

"I don't know anything," he gasped, just like every single prisoner Will had questioned in these last two weeks. The man curled in on himself, the iron of his shackles clanking as he trembled. He'd lasted far longer than the others.

Will had started with physical pain. The mimicking of a knife wound in his stomach. The sensation of the snapping of his arm. The lingering pain of skin peeling from his body. It was enough to make most break easily enough. Yet Porden hadn't given him what he'd wanted.

I don't know anything! I don't know anything! I don't know anything!

His screams had increased in volume the harder Will wielded his power, and yet...

The merchant was lying.

Porden, unlike the others Will had interrogated, was hiding something. Will could sense it, tucked deep within him. It felt like fear and determination, woven together into a wall not unlike a Visya's shield.

Desperation now lived in Will, as much a part of his being as his very breath. He didn't think he'd ever loathed anything more. But if interrogating these prisoners would get him closer to getting some godsforsaken answers—about the supplier and Gianna's involvement, or hells, even about why Gianna had arrested merchants that *weren't* trading outside of the Merchant Council, as if she suspected them to be involved with Kakos—then he would interrogate every last person in this godsdamn dungeon.

Even if his body was screaming at him to slow down.

Even if his soul was begging him to stop.

Will sighed, rolling up the sleeves of his white shirt to his elbows. "Perhaps another method would be more effective," he muttered.

"Please," Porden whimpered from where he lay on the ground. Tears streamed down his face as he met Will's gaze. "Please. I don't know why they arrested me. I have never had anything to do with Kakos. I am a loyal citizen of Tala. A man committed to the gods."

Will crouched down, careful to avoid the puddle of vomit in front of Porden's head as he braced his elbows on his knees. He kept his voice light but deadly as he said, "And yet, you're hiding something. I can feel it."

Porden blanched, his body trembling harder as his lips moved wordlessly.

Perhaps Will had been a fool to believe his life could change, that the happiness he'd found in Trahir, however complicated it was, would be lasting.

He let out a long breath at the confirmation as he stood.

"Please," Porden rasped. "Please—"

The merchant choked on his begging, a long, agonized scream tearing from his throat as he thrashed on the ground. Will clenched his teeth, keeping his eyes focused on Porden as he latched on to Porden's fear, his agony, and sharped it into brutal terror.

It felt like looking into death's eyes and realizing it planned to take its time, the way a lover might pay attention to those areas that made their partner moan, but instead of pleasure, it was painstaking attention to agony.

Will let his affinity flow, shoving his own pain away as the tendons in Porden's neck pressed against his skin with the strength of his screams.

Will was tired of being powerless, tired of having the air knocked out of him at every fucking turn. He couldn't catch his breath, couldn't stand still without something else crumbling around him, without some other tragedy threatening the few good things he'd managed to find in these hells they called their home.

And that exhaustion, that fury, fueled his power even more.

Hells. You are going to hells, that gleefully vicious voice in his mind whispered.

He didn't bother to tell it he already knew that.

"What are you hiding?" Will hollered, his command a mere rumble against Porden's screams.

Will could feel his shield straining, that godsforsaken issue he'd never been able to fix worsening the longer he pushed his power in this way. Porden's sensations were slipping through and making his muscles spasm, but he pushed on, his affinity crescendoing with Porden's shouts.

"THE FARMLANDS! SHE'S IN THE FARMLANDS!" The words ripped from Porden as if Will had reached into his throat and torn them out himself.

Will let his power drop immediately, his head swimming with the abruptness of it.

"Please don't hurt her," the merchant cried. "Please. I'll do anything. Don't hurt my girl. She's just a child. A child!"

Will frowned, his voice sharp as a blade as he snapped, "Your child?" He tried to remember anything about Porden's family, but his brain couldn't conjure up a single image, not with the agony radiating through him.

"I hid her," Porden blubbered. "In the farmlands. She's just fourteen, and she's not even part of the business! I only bring her to the docks to learn the business!"

Will crouched down before Porden, his fingers yanking the sweat-soaked strands of Porden's brown hair as he forced his head up to meet his gaze. "And she was in contact with the supplier?" Will bit out. "With Kakos?"

"No!" Porden gasped, his eyes wide. "She has nothing to do with that. Please, please, I told you, we don't know of any trades."

"Why hide her then?!" Will snarled, Porden's head jerking as Will tightened his grip. "What does Gianna want with her?"

"I don't know!" Porden wailed. "I just…I just didn't want them to take her. They're rounding up anyone connected to weapons suppliers, and I didn't, I didn't… She's just a girl! A young girl! Please! Please! I'll do anything! Don't take her! She won't survive you! She knows nothing! We know nothing!" Porden dissolved into racking sobs, and Will released his hold on the man, his head dropping to his arm like a stone as he wailed.

Will stood, his affinity reaching out as Porden's words were choked by hysterics.

We don't know… You'll kill her… A child… A child…

That wall he'd sensed in the merchant was gone, obliterated by pain and terror. All that remained was agony, and fear, and truth.

Porden was telling the truth.

Will could sense it as easily as he could breathe.

He had been hiding his family. Because Gianna was arresting people in droves, and Porden couldn't be sure the queen's wrath—*Will's* wrath—wouldn't extend to his young daughter whose only fault was being born to a father who worked with weapons.

Will took a step backward, his heart hammering in his chest. He was covered in sweat but was shivering, a cold deeper than ice settling in his veins as nausea roiled in his gut.

He could have killed him; he could have slaughtered a father trying to protect his daughter from…him.

Will's stomach twisted, bile burning in the back of his throat. The prison walls seemed to be closing in on him, threatening to crumble and bury him entirely.

Perhaps he should let them.

Because it had been two weeks of interrogations. Two weeks of telling himself he tortured for the good of his kingdom, in a desperate attempt to help the only woman he loved but continued to lie to day in and day out.

Two weeks of interrogations.

And the only thing he'd learned was every single one of those he had tortured was innocent.

45

A YA FOUND SOMETHING STEADYING ABOUT THE CLIMB TO the Quarter tonight. Perhaps it was because Liam walked several paces behind her, far enough that she had the illusion of being alone. With nothing but the gentle breeze rustling through the towering pines and the steady sound of her boots on the dirt path, she could almost pretend Liam wasn't there at all.

And then there was Tyr, of course.

Her bonded stayed close enough to her side that she occasionally let her fingers drag across his coarse fur, the darkness soothing her frayed nerves. It had been another agonizing day of early training with Galda followed by hours in the Synastysi.

The journal hadn't provided any answers to the questions it had unearthed.

Aya inhaled a deep breath as they stepped through the arch that divided the queen's grounds from the Quarter. There was no moon tonight, and while the stars were brilliant, Aya relished the darkness that surrounded her. Things had always seemed clearer to her on a moonless night.

Calmer.

As if the gods had bathed the world in peace, if only for a stretch of time.

She paused to take in the glittering windows of the Quarter, the flickering of flames from the torches inside making her home sparkle subtly against the night sky. Tyr nudged her palm with his snout, an impatient huff leaving his lips.

She shot him a look.

"Someone's eager to get to Akeeta," she remarked. Tyr butted her hip with his shoulder this time, hard enough that she stumbled sideways. "Sap," she muttered with a smile. "Fine, get out of here."

He left with one more affectionate bump of his head, his pace picking up as he made for the forest.

A soft smile tugged at Aya's lips as she made her way into the Quarter. It was a small thing, her bonded's love for Will's wolf, and it used to be a thorn in her side, but now, it warmed something in her. Bondeds were supposed to be a reflection of one's soul, and seeing their wolves drawn together in the same way she and Will were...

It felt as though the gods were affirming that their souls were the same. Destined to be mirrors, destined to be locked in each other's orbit.

Gods, she wanted to seek him out. She hadn't talked to him in days—had hardly exchanged a passing glance since their night together.

She was still contemplating sneaking into his room as she stepped into hers, a long breath escaping her lungs as she noticed a fire had been set in the grate. She closed the door and made it one step further into the room before she noticed the figure on the bed.

Aya reacted on instinct, her hand snatching her knife before her mind could catch up and realize who it was.

"Godsdammit, Will," Aya swore, her heart hammering as she dropped her blade. "You scared the hells out of me." She took a step back, her breath coming in shallow bursts as her head fell back against the heavy oak door. An incredulous laugh burst from her.

"Is this retribution for me sneaking into *your* room? I have to say, I imagined a more creative payback. Are you losing your—"

The words died in Aya's throat as she lifted her head and looked at Will—really looked at him.

He hadn't moved from the spot on her bed. His hands were clasped between his knees, his black fringe a mess across his forehead as he stared blankly at her.

Aya's stomach filled with dread at the devastation on his face.

She was across the room in an instant, her hands skimming his face, his shoulders, his arms, searching for some indication of what was causing him pain.

"What happened?" Her voice was sharp with fear. Because in all they had endured—torture, gods, near *death*—she'd never seen Will look like this.

He didn't answer. He didn't do anything but stare at her, as if the answer to some question was written in her features. Aya grasped his face, his skin like ice beneath her fingers.

"Will," she urged, her thumb stroking his cheek. "Will, talk to me."

His hand circled her wrist, his grip tight enough to hurt, as if she were the only thing keeping him anchored there. She could see the desperation racing through him, could *feel* it in the way his body was coiled tight, as if he were about to not just break, but shatter entirely.

"*Will.*"

"They were innocent," he rasped, his voice like gravel. A shudder racked through him, and his grip on her wrist tightened. "They were innocent."

Aya's gaze darted across his face, trying to find the meaning behind his words. "Who was innocent?"

But Will shook his head, devastation swirling in his eyes as he choked back a sob, his eyes bright with unshed tears. "I didn't mean… I didn't know… I still have to…"

And then he was shaking, his hand releasing her wrist, sharp breaths punching from his lungs as he buried his head in his hands. Aya crouched between his legs, her hands gripping his wrists. "Will…"

"They were innocent. They were innocent. They were innocent." It was all he was saying, the words ripping from him again and again. She pulled on his hands hard, forcing them away from his face.

Will raised his head, his cheeks wet with tears. There was something wild in his eyes, reminding her of the anguish she'd seen in that godsforsaken temple with Hyacinth, where the prayers of the truly broken shattered the silence as they pleaded with their gods for mercy.

"I didn't know," he rasped. And the words were so brittle, so broken, so full of pleading that it was pure instinct for Aya to climb on to the bed next to him and tug his head into her chest, her fingers tangling in the strands of his hair as she leaned her head on top of his and closed her eyes.

She wasn't entirely sure how to do it. She had never used her Sensainos affinity in this way. But she remembered the calm peace he'd wielded against her own panic that night on the ship. It was the same feeling he'd used to disarm her in training, the same feeling she'd felt in his arms while they danced at the Pysar festival. Aya reached for that feeling now, letting it fill her before extending it toward Will.

She met his shield, an invisible wall of iron he kept locked around him at all times.

"Let me in," she whispered. Will didn't yield at all. Aya opened her eyes. He was lost in his own misery, a mere shadow of himself staring back at her. She brushed her lips against his, his lips as cold as his skin, and her affinity mimicked the light caress against his shield.

326

"Let me in."

Will took a ragged breath and then another, his pulse hammering against where her fingers were clasped at the base of his neck.

Finally, he dropped his shield.

Agony slammed into Aya, the feeling so intense she felt it like a physical blow. She hadn't learned how to use this power without sensing another's state. She didn't care. She closed her eyes once more as she let his pain wash over her, imagining it was the rapids of the Loraine flowing around her and she was a rock—unyielding and steady.

Aya held on to that feeling of peace and let it wash over Will. The affinity brushed up against the cutting edges of his despair, smoothing the sharpness and filling the hollow spaces his pain had carved out of him. Will took another shuddering breath, his pulse still racing against her fingertips. Aya didn't dare try to slow it. Will could mimic Anima sensations without causing them, but she was worried she might accidentally slip into the affinity of the healer and death bringers, and his heart was not something she'd experiment with.

She leaned instead into that calm quietness his presence brought her, that sturdiness that she'd come to depend on, even longer than she'd once cared to admit.

And she stayed that way, pouring her affinity into him, until the agony washing over her lessened, and Will's muscles eased, and his breath settled, no longer choked by sobs.

46

AIDON HAD LONG LOVED THE MAIN THOROUGHFARE OF Rinnia at dusk. The crescent-moon beach, which stretched to his left as he ambled down the path, came alive at this time of day, as did the small restaurants that dotted this main stretch. Already, patrons were crowding into their small patios as music floated in from various buskers.

His people welcomed the end of each day with libations and bonfires on the beach, and it was a simple routine, really, but it never failed to lift his spirts, even now with a seething Josie beside him.

The walk down from the palace had been agonizing, the silence so tense he could feel it pressing against his skin like the heat that had settled in for the long summer season.

Josie was still angry.

Clearly.

She had had *several* words to say in regard to Avis's banishment and Aidon not telling her prior to it becoming public.

Josie had always been on the inside of court matters, but whether her frustration was at being left out, or because Viviane had previous ties to Avis in the Bellare and was likely angered by the sentencing, Aidon didn't know.

It had only gotten worse when Aleissande had walked in on them arguing and had some choice words about Josie weighing in on matters that she wasn't qualified to share an opinion on.

Aidon supposed Josie's mood today wasn't helped by Aleissande walking on his other side, her lips pressed into that usual expressionless line.

"It's your funeral," Clyde had said when Aidon presented his idea to his friend about forcing the women to spend time together with him as mediator. It was no good to Aidon if his Second hated his fucking *sister* and vice versa.

But in truth, Aidon was starting to think a funeral would have been more pleasant.

He cleared his throat and forced a smile to his face as he finally shattered the tense silence. "So, where are we thinking for a beverage?"

Josie just shrugged, so Aidon turned to Aleissande instead. She raised a blond brow at him. "I won't be partaking, Your Majesty. It's unwise for both of us to indulge simultaneously."

"Why, Aleissande?" Aidon asked, the exasperation evident in his tone.

The general straightened—impossibly so, given how stiffly she already held herself. She sucked in a breath, and Aidon suddenly realized he was about to receive a lecture in something like security, or the order of the court, or, gods forbid, propriety and how he was ruining that too as king.

"Forget I asked," he said before she could start. Beside him, Josie unconvincingly masked a snicker as a cough.

"Killjoy," his sister muttered. Aidon wasn't sure if the taunt was for him or for Aleissande, but his general's face flushed regardless.

"It's called professionalism," Aleissande retorted, her icy-blue glare fixed on the path ahead. "Something you've clearly failed to learn, despite your position—"

"That's enough, Aleissande," Aidon interjected before

Josie could unleash the hells that were surely building on her tongue. He rubbed the back of his neck and scanned the row of colorful awnings. Perhaps they should go somewhere more private. "We haven't been to our favorite spot in forever," he mused to Josie, smiling fondly. In fact, the last time he'd gone to the small tucked-away space had been with Aya. "Shall we share the honor of it with Aleissande?"

"This is foolish," Josie grumbled under her breath.

Aidon was almost inclined to agree. This *was* foolish, a horribly foolish idea fit for a naive boy, not a king. "Let's just g—"

"Excuse me, Majesty?" A soft voice cut him off. It took Aidon a moment to realize it belonged to a small child, a young girl who couldn't be more than five. She stood a few paces from him, her fingers twining together as she swayed shyly from side to side. Her mother stood a little way back, waving her on encouragingly.

Aidon beckoned the girl forward as he knelt. Aleissande—just as well, he supposed—instantly found someplace else to be, while Josie stood by, a smile finally breaking through on her face as the child approached.

"What's your name?" Aidon asked.

"Vera," she murmured.

"I'm Aidon."

Vera frowned. "I thought your name was Majesty."

Aidon chuckled as he caught Josie's gaze, his sister trying to hide her smile behind her fist. "Yes, well, my friends call me Aidon," he replied, his own grin wide. "And we should be friends, don't you think?"

Vera gave him a tentative smile. "I like new friends. I made one yesterday!"

"Really?"

"Yeah! She can do this too!" Vera held out her hands, her eyes and grin wide as flames flickered from her palms.

"*Vera!*" her mother gasped as she rushed forward, her hands outstretched for her daughter's arms. Aidon held up a hand.

"It's quite alright," he said, laughing. "Young Visya should be encouraged to explore their powers."

"I apologize, Majesty," the mother said anyway. "She hasn't quite learned control. Or when it's *appropriate to call her flame forward*," she scolded her daughter. And then, to Aidon, she gave a bashful shake of her head. "Hepha help me."

Aidon could feel Josie's eyes on him, but he kept his focus on Vera as he placed his hands on her shoulders. "I'm very glad to have met you, Vera."

This time, her smile was genuine. Bold. "Me too, Majesty—I mean, Aidon!"

Aidon gave her a gentle squeeze before pushing himself up. He hadn't even fully straightened when he registered a whistling sound so familiar, his body started to move before his mind truly knew what it meant.

But Aleissande was faster.

She slammed into him so hard, it knocked the breath from his lungs.

Later, Aidon would remember the difference between the two bodies. His general's, hard as rock as it shoved him to the ground to avoid the arrow that narrowly missed his head.

And Vera's, soft and warm as she took the brunt of his fall.

But in the moment, all Aidon could rely on were his instincts, and though they had been honed through years of training for moments just as this, and though they forced his body to twist, his arms wrapping around that small warm body in a desperate attempt to move her, his instincts were not enough to change the trajectory Aleissande had set.

The child's head hit the cobbles with a sickening crack.

"Stay down, Your Majesty," Aleissande barked in his ear over the screams that had erupted on the street. But he *couldn't*, because Vera's mother was yelling her name, and there was blood on his hands and the smell of death in his nose and a ringing silence coming from the child in place of the shouts of pain that should have been there.

Aidon shoved Aleissande off him and rolled to the side. Vera's eyes were open, staring blankly at the sky, her head cocked at an unnatural angle. He didn't need the heart-wrenching wail from her mother to know she was dead.

A hollow ringing filled his ears, his hands going numb as he forced himself to witness what he'd done. Vera's mother fell to her knees, her body draping over the child as she screamed and screamed, the sounds mixing with the melee around them. Aidon forced his mind to sharpen, burying the guilt and the anger and the sorrow as he rose to his feet, his sword in hand.

Later. He would mourn later, like all soldiers did.

Because right now, people were running and screaming, and the City Guard added to the chaos, and he could not help if he could not *think*.

Josie.

Aidon found her immediately. She was running toward the danger, her sword already drawn. Aidon grabbed the nearest guard roughly by the arm and shoved him toward his sister.

"Get her to safety," he ordered.

Josie whipped her gaze to him, fury written there. "You can't be seri—"

"*Now*," Aidon barked, not sparing her a second glance as the guard tugged her away, her shouts of refusal getting lost among the chaos surrounding them.

"We must get you to safety, Your Majesty," one of his guards yelled, but Aidon was already out of her grip, his eyes locked on where Aleissande was fighting off two men. Her sword found one's gut just as her knife slashed across the other's throat, his blood bursting forth like a fountain and coating her pale face in freckles of red.

Aidon didn't need to see their rose tattoos to know exactly who they were.

Or why they were here.

332

The Bellare wanted vengeance for one of their own.

That telltale whistling sounded again, but this time, Aidon was ready for it. He ducked out of the arrow's path, using one of the abandoned merchant carts as a shield as he scanned the rooftops.

They were clear, but in the light of the setting sun, he could make out a shift of shadow in the second-story window of a teal building several doors away. He watched as an arrow loosed from it, lodging itself in the head of one of the City Guards.

He was dead before his scream could fully leave his mouth.

Aidon dashed out from behind the cart, sprinting through fleeing citizens and fighting guards and trying his best not to count the bodies on the ground. Aleissande's eyes were bright with rage as he reached her side, her lips parting surely to order him to seek shelter, but Aidon snatched the knife from her hand and hurled it at the window before she could utter a single syllable.

The shadow paused, an eerie sort of stillness to it, before it disappeared from view.

"I want every single one of them arrested," Aidon ordered, his voice low and rough. "If they resist, kill them."

He didn't wait for her confirmation before he took off toward the building, stopping only to slit one of the rebels' throats before they could strangle the life out of the guard they had a hold of. Adrenaline sent Aidon's blood racing through his veins while anger, pure and undiluted anger, made his very skin *burn*.

Aidon threw open the door to the teal building and raced up the rickety wooden staircase, not bothering to mask his footsteps.

He wanted the rebel to hear Death coming.

The door to the second floor was locked, but Aidon threw his shoulder into it hard enough that it burst from the hinges as if it were no more than a toy barricade. He stepped into the room—a small studio apartment with a perfect view of the main thoroughfare and the beach beyond it.

And just below that window, his breaths coming in shallow pants, was a man with a knife lodged in his neck.

Aidon walked slowly toward the rebel, the tip of his sword dragging across the old wooden floor and leaving a thin scratch that would forever mark his path. He paused as he reached the man, his head cocked as he considered the way the rebel twitched on the floor. Blood seeped from the corners of his lips, his tongue flapping and fumbling as he tried to speak and only gargled.

I should let him choke on it.

The thought echoed somewhere in the recesses of Aidon's mind, some place he couldn't quite reach through his rage. It burned so fiercely he felt numb—detached. Like he was locked away in his own body, in his own mind, and couldn't break free.

Or perhaps he simply didn't want to.

Aidon held the man's gaze, his head still cocked in curious contemplation as he placed the tip of his sword on the man's chest.

Slowly, Aidon began to press his sword down.

Right into the rebel's fucking heart.

Silence rang heavy as he continued to press his sword into the man's chest, interrupted only by the thudding of the man's boots on the floor as he struggled weakly, and the heightened gurgling as his breaths came in terrified gasps.

But Aidon's inhales were steady as he pressed and pressed and pressed.

"Your Majesty."

He should have made it slower. He should have used the fire burning in his veins and set the man alight, and watched as it slowly devoured him the way the hells would surely devour the murderer's soul.

"Aidon."

Aidon blinked to see Aleissande beside him, her face covered with sweat and grime and blood. Her hand was unusually gentle as she laid it on his sword arm. "He is dead, Majesty," she murmured, that softness seeping into her tone as well.

Her hand moved to his wrist, and together, they pulled the sword from the rebel's chest. She didn't let go until Aidon's arm dropped to his side, and though rage still painted her irises a cold blue, there was also bitter understanding in his general's gaze as she dipped her chin and uttered the reassurance they both needed once more.

"He is dead."

47

AYA KNEW WILL WAS GONE BEFORE SHE EVEN OPENED HER eyes. His warmth, which had been wrapped fully around her, had been replaced by the soft cotton of her duvet, which crinkled as she shifted.

She scrubbed a hand roughly across her eyes before blinking them open, the soft light of dawn feeling harsh against the darkness of sleep. She wasn't sure when she'd dozed off. She remembered trying to move out of Will's hold to change into something more comfortable, but Will had merely pulled her closer, his breath deep and even, sleep having finally found him at some indeterminate time. She'd let him, her body too exhausted after another long day, but not before she whispered the words he'd once told her in the height of her own terror.

I see you.

Aya sat up in her bed, her reflection like a ghost in the mirror across from her. Those dark circles were back under her eyes, the purple marring her skin like bruises. But she didn't look half as destroyed as Will had when he'd broken down last night. The collar of her shirt was stiff from where his tears had dried, the skin at her collarbone red and irritated from where the stubble of his unshaven face had scratched as he sobbed.

They were innocent. They were innocent. They were innocent.

She could still hear his voice as he'd frantically repeated the words, and it made her chest ache, even now. Something had shattered him, digging through the layers of firm resolve that Will had built over the years until he was raw and broken, and Aya didn't know who to blame, or how to fix it, and she *hated* it.

She shucked off the covers and padded into her bathing chamber, not bothering to take a second glance in the mirror. She sat on the edge of her tub, the rush of hot water filling the iron basin blurring as she stared unseeingly at it.

Will was hiding something from her. She knew it as certainly as she knew the pitch and cadence of Tyr's howl. Whatever had broken him down like that last night had been building steadily, masked beneath arrogance and frustration and perhaps even lies, and that thought alone brought forth a stomach-tightening wave of dread as Aya tugged off her clothes and sank into the scalding water.

She relished the burn.

Aya stayed there until the red faded from her pruned skin, until the water ran as cold as the streams in the mountains.

Will was hiding something from her.

And perhaps she *was* rotten, and there was no redemption for her. Because as Aya pushed herself out of the bath, the rough fabric of her worn towel a welcome distraction from the roaring in her head, she made up her mind in mere moments.

And she didn't give it a second thought.

Making it through the upper halls of the Quarter without drawing suspicion was easy, especially with the bulk of the Dyminara out training or on assignment.

Picking the lock to Will's bedroom door was even easier.

She closed the door soundlessly behind her, that familiar silence falling over her as she stepped into his room.

It wasn't comfort; it was the focus of a mission.

It sharpened her gaze as she scanned the circular space, her eyes lingering on the untouched crimson duvet.

I see you.

She shut out the echoes of her own voice. Now was not the time for sentiment.

Aya went straight to the worn wooden desk, its surface still littered with books—more historical fiction, she noticed from her cursory glance. She worked through the three drawers easily, her fingers flicking through discarded quills and various odds and ends. She paused at the familiar sharp, jagged edge that indicated carved wood, her hand curling around a tiny figurine and pulling it from the drawer.

Aya's resolve wavered as she uncurled her fingers and gazed upon the small carving, no bigger than her palm. It was a small wooden mountain with snow etched into its peak—a reminder of home that she'd carved for Will after he admitted the mountains were what he missed most of Tala.

It was the only thing she'd carved with that block of wood and knife he'd given her. She hadn't even realized she was making it for him until she was almost done with the carving, and even then, she wasn't sure she'd give it to him. They'd only just established a steady peace, a friendship even.

But then one evening, he'd coerced her into begging off their affinity training in the hidden paddock and trading their usual fare in the palace for dinner in a small tucked-away restaurant in Old Town. The food had been delicious, and his company far less aggravating than she'd once found.

"Careful," she'd goaded him as he'd paid for both their meals. "You might give one the wrong impression."

Will had merely fixed her with a level stare, one brow arched in the cocky manner she'd long grown used to. "When I take you out, Aya love, it won't be on Gianna's coin."

She was too flustered to snap back at his arrogance, to correct the assumption that there would ever be a day she would allow such a thing. Or maybe, she knew even then that there would be. She had gone to dinner already, hadn't she?

She'd expected him to be insufferable about how he'd caught her off guard; she was fairly certain she'd blushed, and gods knew he'd never let her live anything down before. But Will was strangely quiet on the walk back, enough that when they'd parted ways at her bedroom door, she'd called after him and tossed the carving to him. He'd stared at it for several long moments, his expression entirely unreadable. But when he'd finally looked at her, it was with a softness she'd never seen on his face, his sputtered *thank-you* a soft rasp.

It was that expression that floated across her mind now as she stared and stared at that carving, her pulse ticking up in pace.

That expression, that softness, was no longer something unseen or unexpected. It was there every time he looked at her, every time he tucked her hair behind her ear or ran his thumb across her cheek or let his forehead fall against hers as they breathed each other in and found a moment of peace among the seven hells they were living in.

This is wrong.

She shouldn't be here, rifling through Will's things like he was someone she didn't trust. Like he hadn't knelt before Gianna and taken a whipping because of her—*for* her. Like he wasn't putting himself at risk every day to protect her, to help her unravel their queen's plans.

Aya dropped the carving back in the drawer.

This is wrong.

She'd already hurt him once, had already doubted him and proven it by using her power to read him. She shouldn't do this again. She should find Will and make him tell her what had happened, what had been happening to cause him to pull away from her.

She should demand he explain, and he would, because this was *Will*, and Aya did not believe there was anything he would truly deny her.

She should *show* him that she trusted him.

To share his burdens with her. To be open with her. To be *honest* when she asked him, point-blank, what was going on.

Aya shut the drawer and backed away from the desk. But she paused as she took in the jacket he'd tossed over the back of the chair. It was the same one he'd been wearing last night, and just as she'd noticed then, it was wrinkled and creased in a way that Will typically wasn't.

But in her focus on Will and her desperation to soothe him last night, she hadn't noticed the folded piece of parchment in the inside breast pocket. It peeked out at her now, swoops of black ink interrupting its tan surface.

Aya blamed the training that had been instilled in her for over ten years for the ease with which she pulled the parchment from the pocket and flicked it open, thoughts of guilt and wrongdoing evaporating from her mind as she scanned the paper.

Aya frowned.

It was a list of names.

She flipped the parchment over, hoping for some clue as to what exactly the names were for, but it was blank.

Had *this* been what Will had been seeking from his father? Possible connections to the weapons supplier to help him in the search Gianna had commanded he participate in?

Did he think Gale had connections to the missing person?

Aya looked up, her mind whirling as she stared at the wall above Will's desk.

They were innocent. They were innocent.

Dread, cold and unrelenting dread, settled on Aya's skin like a blanket of ice.

No. He wouldn't have hidden *this* from her. If Gianna had ordered him to…

No.

She would've known if he weren't out searching for people. If instead, he spent his days in the dungeons. He

340

wouldn't have kept that from her. She would have *heard* something.

They were innocent.

They were innocent.

The parchment crinkled as Aya's hand clenched into a fist. She knew exactly how to find the truth.

Aya dropped the paper on the desk, not bothering to hide the proof that she'd been there as she turned on her heel and left for the dungeons.

Aya shivered as she walked through the dank halls of the palace prison. There was a wrongness here she'd never recognized before. Perhaps it was because the last time she'd been in this dark place, she could hear the screams of her best friend echoing off the walls.

Now, she heard nothing but the echo of her footsteps and the distant drip of water. She was deep in the labyrinth of the dungeons, the cold biting her skin the further she pressed on. Dread hung heavy in her stomach, a gnawing feeling just behind her sternum forcing her onward.

She didn't even know what the hells she was *looking* for. Not really. But as she turned a corner, she came to a stop, a shiver that had nothing to do with the cold running down her spine.

It was utterly silent here. And not the usual quiet that followed dejected prisoners, but a complete, pressing silence that had the hair on Aya's neck rising, her hand reaching for the steadiness of her blade as she turned a slow circle.

"What the hells." Even her whisper felt muted, as if something was forcing her voice to quiet.

"What are you doing down here?"

Aya whirled, the silver of her knife flashing in the Incend light as she faced Lena. The Persi stood with her arms crossed and brows raised in subtle amusement as she glanced at Aya's knife. Ballor, a Caeli in the Dyminara, stood just steps behind her.

Aya bit back the same question that was burning in her lungs. Why the hells was Lena here?

Instead, Aya straightened, tucking her knife back in its sheath. "I'm looking for a prisoner," she lied smoothly, pulling a name from the list she'd found in Will's pocket. "Galen Hardeen."

Lena frowned. "No one here by that name."

They were innocent. They were innocent. They were innocent.

Aya took a single step forward. "You're sure about that, are you?" She'd intended to intimidate Lena or, at the very least, to push her until she could garner something from the Persi. But the woman merely smirked.

"I am. But by all means, have a look around." Lena swept an arm toward the long corridor of cells.

"Lena," Ballor murmured. "I need to do it now, or else—"

"No," Lena cut him off sharply. "Let's make it easier for Aya to find what she's looking for."

Aya opened her mouth, a bitter retort bubbling to the surface, but she didn't have a chance to voice it. Because suddenly, the air was shifting, *lightening*, and the change was so drastic that it took her a moment to realize the ringing in her ears wasn't the return of sound.

They were screams.

Aya didn't bother to wait for Lena before she moved. Because those screams...they struck something deep inside of her, some part she hadn't fully healed, and maybe never would. Aya lunged for the door in the middle of the hall, the screams growing louder and louder, and perhaps some of them weren't coming from that cell at all, but from the memories that kept Aya awake at night, the shouts of her best friend pleading for mercy as Aya tried desperately to get to her.

She reached the cell and wrenched the door open, her breath seizing in her lungs as she took in the sight before her.

Because there stood Will, his hands in his pockets as he stared at a kneeling figure on the ground, her screams tearing through the cell, through *Aya* as his affinity showed her no mercy.

Time seemed to slow as Will turned, his eyes wide as he realized who had walked into the cell.

They were innocent.

The woman's screams stopped, a wrenching sob tearing from her throat as she fell forward, her hands breaking her fall.

They were innocent.

Will's lips were moving, but Aya couldn't hear him as she took a step back, and then another.

He had kept this from her.

They had *all* kept this from her.

They were innocent.

Aya was out of the cell, her knees buckling as she went stumbling into the far wall. She couldn't get her feet beneath her, couldn't get her shaking legs to cooperate as she tried to stand, tried to *run*, tried to leave this place that only ever tore her open and left her to bleed dry.

"Aya!"

There was a hand on her arm and a voice in her ear and she was turning before she could even stop to *think*, slamming Will into the wall so hard that she heard a vicious *crack* as his head hit the stone.

"Aya, please," Will rasped. "I had *orders*—"

"Fuck your orders," Aya snarled. It wasn't fair, and later, when something wasn't cleaving her chest in half, she would realize that. But for now, she stared at Will, a horrible realization dawning on her. "You told Gianna to keep this from me, didn't you?"

Will's face crumbled.

It was confirmation enough, so much so that Aya barely heard his whispered *yes* above the roaring in her head.

343

And it was worse, so much worse, with the knowledge that he hadn't just kept this from her, but had partnered with Gianna to do it.

It shattered Aya so entirely that she couldn't help the broken noise that escaped her.

"Aya, please, let me explain."

"Do *not* say another fucking word," she ordered, unable to keep the tremor from her voice. Will's eyes, desperate, pleading, stayed locked on hers.

"Aya, please," he begged. "Just listen—"

She pressed him tighter to the wall. "You *lied* to me."

"I didn't lie," Will wheezed.

"Don't—"

"I *didn't* lie."

Aya ground her teeth, fighting the urge to scream. It was semantics, and she didn't fucking *care* because he hadn't *told* her about this, and he had asked Gianna, of all people, to help keep Aya in the dark, and that alone felt like the worst sort of betrayal.

Aya had been right. It wasn't the gods or Aya's power that would destroy them.

It was Gianna.

"You promised," she rasped. On his oath, he had sworn Gianna would not come between them. Aya angrily blinked away the tears in her eyes, but one slipped out anyway. Will tracked it as it slid down her cheek, his face crumpling as he whispered, "Please."

Aya forced herself to pull away, her fists clenched so tightly, she knew there'd be red crescent moons on her palms. Will wisely stayed against the wall, his palms flat against the stone.

"Please," he breathed again, his chest heaving. "Aya, please, *please* listen to me. They're not trading outside the Council. She *knows* something about why they might be connected to the Council. If I can find out how they're involved with her, I can—"

"Do *not* make excuses for your atrocities," Aya spat out. And again, it was unfair of her, so unfair of her after all she had done in the name of her queen. Of her *kingdom*. But she didn't care. She had to get out of here, she had to *leave* before she did something she would surely regret.

"Do not follow me," Aya hissed. "If you do, I won't hesitate to slice a blade through your fucking throat."

PART THREE

Consolation in Death

48

AYA HAD NEVER BEEN ONE FOR TEARS.

It's okay to cry, mi couera, her mother used to say when she'd find Aya clenching her fists, her muscles tense as she forced those feelings down. *It is not weak.*

She hadn't known how to explain it, not at the young age of seven or eight. She hadn't known what words to use to describe how she felt so much—*too* much—and was learning it was easier to not feel at all.

And then her mother had died, and Galda had taught her the importance of *control*, and Aya had known for sure then that burying it all was better. That succumbing to tears was succumbing to a brokenness she would not recover from. And so she forced her fractured pieces to stay together, to hold even as they were battered and beaten time and time again.

She supposed it was what she was doing now, her body slick with sweat and eyes burning as she ran through the winding paths of the forest, the incline getting sharper the further up the mountain she pressed.

She'd returned to her room after storming out of the dungeons, but only to change into her fighting leathers.

Hyacinth could give her a godsdamn day outside of the Synastysi. It was the least of what Aya deserved.

But Aya hadn't been sure where to go, where to release some of the agony threatening to explode from her. Will might check the training complex for her. Or the Athatis compound.

So she'd snuck off and found herself lost in the thick of the forest, her body aching as she continued up the mountain, her breaths getting sharper the thinner the air became. And even though she'd been pushing herself for the better part of an hour, it had done nothing to cool the fury that was pulsing through her.

Perhaps that was for the best.

Because beneath that anger that came so easily to her was crushing despair, its hollowness just barely masked by the sharp edges of anger that kept it stifled.

He'd lied for weeks about what he'd been doing. He'd lied, and she'd been too consumed with her own grief, her own orders, her own suspicions to press him about the loose explanations he'd been giving her when she asked him about his days, or why he seemed to close in on himself more and more.

It had all been right there, as clear as day.

Gods, she hated him. But she hated herself more. She'd *known* he was keeping something from her, but she'd been too afraid to push, too worried to break them, especially after she'd hurt him when they'd first come home.

What did it fucking matter now?

He'd partnered with Gianna. He'd kept her in the dark, and he'd used the worst person to help make sure she stayed there.

Sweat dripped down Aya's back, a strangled noise coming from her throat as a vision of that woman on her knees rose in her head. She accelerated into a sprint.

Her body was truly protesting now, her muscles spasming as she continued up the steep incline. She didn't care.

He had kept this from her, just like those letters in Trahir. What else was he hiding?

What other lies had she allowed?

Had he faked his sensations the day she visited him in the healing quarter? Using a Sensainos affinity wasn't an immaculate way to get the truth. Will had admitted that himself. Had he ever really talked to Tova? Had he truly tried to spare her from torture that day in the dungeon?

Aya slowed to a stop as the trees parted, giving a magnificent view of the valley beneath the mountain ridge. Her hands braced on her knees as she sucked in a sharp breath. And then another. Another.

He wouldn't lie about that. He wouldn't…

Would he?

You don't know what he would do. You didn't think he'd keep secrets from you with Gianna, did you?

Aya righted herself, something in her chest cracking as her thoughts continued to spiral. She'd thought she could trust him, thought they had chosen each other, and yes, it had been in the midst of hells raining down on them, but they'd made that oath because they…because *she*…

Aya didn't bother to throw up a shield of air as she tilted her head back and screamed. The sound ripped from her lungs, ricocheting off the rocks and echoing across the vale that stretched far below her.

Broken, she felt utterly broken, and alone, and though she had wondered if she might not survive all that was coming for her, she'd never thought that Will would be the source of her pain. Not like this.

It's okay to cry, mi couera. *It is not weak.*

But loving people is, Aya thought bitterly as tears streamed down her cheeks, the wind whipping her hair around her face.

Loving people had only ever caused her pain.

351

The wind was bitter this high in the Mala range, no matter the season. It ripped Aya's hair from its braid as she stood on the edge of a small cluster of homes. Few lived this high in the mountains anymore. The remote communities had mostly migrated south, those who wanted to avoid the bustle of Dunmeaden heading into the more temperate farmlands or the basin villages that stretched toward the Midlands.

Aya followed the dirt path around a bend, rocks shifting beneath her feet.

She stopped, her brow furrowing as she took in the scene before her. This wasn't a mere cluster of homes. It was an entire village, built between the sharp granite of the Malas.

What is this?

She didn't realize she'd said the question aloud until a voice came from beside her.

"My home."

Aya jerked, her head whipping to the side.

No. Gods, no.

The raven-haired healer smiled.

I'm dreaming. I'm dreaming. I can wake up.

"You could," the healer mused, tucking a strand of silken hair behind her ear. "It's your head we're in. I'm only here because you called me."

Called her?

"I didn't—"

"But while you're here, you might as well join us." The healer was already walking, beckoning Aya to follow.

"Join who?" Curiosity drove Aya slowly forward, and she fell into step with the healer as she walked further into the heart of that village, the blurred details solidifying on the edges of Aya's mind as they went. She hadn't ventured this deep into the Malas before. Even her Dyminara training hadn't brought her this high.

"You'll see," the healer chimed, a coy smile twisting her thin lips.

They walked further on, a low hum spreading toward them. It seemed to live on the air, crackling toward them like Aya's power once crackled across the Artist Market.

Aya paused, a frown flicking across her brow as she registered the healer's attire. She wasn't wearing the typical tunic Aya was used to seeing in Dunmeaden. Instead, she was dressed in fighting leathers not unlike Aya's.

"I thought you were a healer," Aya murmured.

The healer looked at her thoughtfully. "I am many things."

The humming grew louder, and despite her feet being planted, Aya was still moving, the world around her warping to mist and dust as she and the healer traveled down the path.

Aya's heart began to race, her awareness prickling as the hair at the nape of her neck rose. This wasn't like the other dreams she'd had—the ones where the healer tugged her away from Will's dead body after the Wall. Those were memories turned nightmare as Aya played out her worst fears, the outcomes they'd so narrowly avoided.

This was something she didn't recognize. Something that tugged on the edges of her consciousness and made her feel out of control as the scene moved faster and faster around her, as *Aya* moved faster and faster even as she stood still, and, gods, she wanted it to *stop*.

As if she commanded it, the world around her halted, the dust and dirt clearing from the air. Aya's arms flew out to brace herself, her knees bending as she lurched to a halt.

Slowly, she straightened and turned in a dazed circle. There had to be hundreds of people surrounding them, seated along carved stone benches that descended into a pit. And at the heart of that pit stood Aya and the healer. Their arrival had caused some sort of upheaval, but Aya couldn't make out what the people were shouting.

Were they expected to fight? Had she stumbled upon one of the fighting rings the Zeluus favored so much?

No. Those were in the heart of the Rouline.

This was something else. Something *frenzied*.

The healer raised her arms and the noise quieted, reverting back to that steady hum. Still, there was a restless energy here as people shifted on their feet, waiting for...something.

The healer met her gaze, her cobalt eyes twinkling with knowing. She kept her arms raised, her gaze locked on Aya as she shouted, "*Y avai ti dynami a ton diag mesa mye!*"

I have the power of the gods in me.

49

ALEISSANDE HAD INSISTED A HEALER LOOK OVER AIDON once they returned to the palace—or perhaps *demanded* was a better word. Because even when he'd refused and summoned the Captain of the City Guard and his mother to his office, Aleissande had appeared moments later with an Anima healer in tow.

The healer moved wordlessly around him now, unbothered by how he ignored her and addressed the Captain of the Guard instead.

"How many dead?"

"Four of ours. Eight of theirs."

Five of ours, Aidon thought. He swore he could feel Vera's blood on his skin, but as he looked down at his hands, they were clean. When had he cleaned them? He couldn't remember.

"And the rest?" Aidon bit out.

"Arrested, Your Majesty. Once our guardsmen got there, they were outnumbered. They went down quickly, especially once their sharpshooter was taken out. You have a good eye, sir."

Aidon's gaze darted to Aleissande, who stood cloaked in

the shadow of the bookcase. She was monitoring him closely, her face still splattered in blood, utterly unreadable.

"You're shaking, Majesty." The healer's soft voice had Aidon shoving himself from his place perched on the edge of the desk, his arm ripping away from her hand, the touch of which he hadn't even felt, much like the tremors that had him stuffing his hands in his pockets.

"I'm fine."

"Is he injured?" his mother pressed, her eyes widening as she moved toward the healer.

"*I said I'm fine.*"

Zuri pulled up short at his tone, a heavy silence following in its wake. Aidon pinched the bridge of his nose as he took a steadying breath.

Don't lose control. You cannot lose control.

He let his hand fall as he fixed the Captain of the Guard with a hard look. "Bring me Ryker Drycari," he commanded. "I want him imprisoned here tonight."

They nodded and bowed once before leaving the room.

To the healer, Aidon said, "My sister is in her room. Please attend to her."

The door was hardly closed before his mother rounded on him, a fury in her face that Aidon was sure was reflected in his own. After all, it was Zuri who had taught him to fight, who had trained Josie in the dead of night when Dominic refused to let his niece explore her prowess with a sword.

"He promised he would keep them in line," she said. "That was the trade he made you, was it not? A position that scum doesn't deserve for his word that he would control these traitors when Avis was duly punished?"

"I do not need a reminder of the deal I struck," Aidon replied, his voice level despite the rage growing in him. He shoved it down, bottling it up until he could release it.

Soon.

But his mother's anger would be heard, and it would be

heard now. "He is responsible for the murders of four of our people!"

"*I* am responsible for the deaths of our people, as I am king!" Aidon shouted. Aleissande shifted from her place against the bookcase, just enough to remind him of her presence, but he couldn't stop. "I am fully aware of the consequences of my choices, Mother. And there are *thirteen* lives that now hang on my conscience."

His voice trembled as the truth—no, not the truth, not really—left his lips. There were more.

The four that hung at the gallows. The unknown number that would die in a war he would agree to participate in.

And yet it was the thought of Vera, the young Visya who had just discovered her affinity, who was so eager to show him, so *proud* to call forward her flames… It was the thought of Vera that had his throat tightening and his hands shaking, and he wasn't sure if it was fury or grief or both that had him staggering back into the desk.

"Aidon," Zuri breathed, her hand outstretched toward him.

"Don't," he said from behind the hand that he scrubbed over his face. Because as much as he wanted his mother's comfort, as much as he craved sinking into her reassuring hold like the fragile boy he currently felt he was, he could not.

Not now.

His mother paused, her hand still outstretched toward him. Slowly, she lowered it to her side, her eyes softening in understanding. She dipped her chin once. "What do you need, Son?"

Revenge.

Aidon swallowed the word. He had given the man with the bow the death he had been due. Now was not the time to get lost in such sentiments. He needed to strategize, not fight. Some battles were won by one's brawn, it was true. But wars…those were won by one's brain.

So he took a deep, steadying breath, letting it cool the flames of his fury as he straightened. "I need the City Guard looking for anyone in the Bellare who may have escaped the attack. I want absolute certainty that all assailants are either dead or awaiting trial in our dungeons."

Zuri nodded. "Then it will be done." She turned toward the door, but she paused, hesitation written in the rigidity of her shoulders. And then she was before him, her soft, warm hand cupping his cheek.

"Weakness is not found in grief or rage," she murmured. "It is found in the unfeeling."

She patted his face gently before she left.

Aidon counted the ticking of the clock as silence settled between him and Aleissande.

Twenty ticks. Thirty. Sixty.

At one hundred and ten, he finally spoke, his eyes still fixed on the door his mother had walked out of. "Surely you have opinions."

A rustle from his left as she shifted. "I always have opinions, Majesty. I simply know the correct time to share them."

Aidon raised a brow as he finally looked at his Second. "Aleissande. Was that a *joke*?"

Her face pinched at the word, as if the mere suggestion of her *ever* resorting to humor was offensive. "It was the truth, Majesty," she replied tersely.

An exasperated breath escaped him, as if a laugh had tried to make itself known but failed because such expressions couldn't possibly come from him now, not when his body still ached, not when he could still hear the crack of a child's head against the pavement.

"Aidon." He met Aleissande's stoic gaze. She opened her mouth once, twice, before she finally found her words. "Her death lies with me."

That aching was back in his throat, his lungs searing as he forced himself to swallow, to breathe.

358

She was wrong. Vera's last breaths had been taken in his hold as he desperately tried to spare her.

"I thought you knew when to share an opinion," he said flatly. It was wrong of him to be bitter to Aleissande, who was nothing but loyal to him.

A strong soldier. A smart Second.

Perhaps even a burgeoning friend.

But Aleissande was not fragile. It was one of the reasons he had chosen her as his Second after all. His bitterness was nothing more than an irritant as she shook her head, her gaze hardening into insistence.

"It is not an opinion, but a fact, Majesty."

There would be no winning this battle—and truly, did it matter? Vera was dead. And while the man who had loosened the arrow that led to her tragic loss had met his fate, there was one more person Aidon could hold responsible.

"I'll need you in the dungeons tonight," he muttered, his jaw shifting as he glanced at the clock.

Aidon could still feel that visceral rage simmering inside of him, and he had no doubt it would make itself known the minute he laid eyes on Ryker. But he could not afford to react as he did earlier in the apartment.

And Aleissande knew that.

He looked to his Second, noting the grim understanding on her face. Wordlessly, she held out his crown. It must have fallen off when she'd tackled him. He hadn't even realized he didn't have it, hadn't spent a moment wondering where it might be.

Aidon took the crown from Aleissande, that rage growing as he marked what now marred the bottom of the silver, visible even in the low torchlight.

Dried blood.

Vera's blood.

Aidon didn't bother to clean it as he placed the crown on his head.

The dungeons, like the other parts of the palace in Rinnia, were grand. But while Aidon's home was bright and open and complete with fixtures of gold that reflected the wealth of Trahir, the labyrinth of cells that sat beneath the palace were ornate in a different way.

A darker way.

Much like his gilded city, the dungeons had been constructed to make sure no one could claim there to be a lack—in this case, of darkness, of stone, of dreariness.

It was a place that always felt cold to Aidon, despite the heat and humidity that made the rot from the cells permeate throughout the halls. He never had been able to fight the way his nose scrunched when the smell first hit him, no matter how many times he'd walked these halls.

Just as he couldn't fight it now.

But even the stench of misery and filth could not distract him from the steady anger that drove him toward Ryker's cell. Aleissande's steps were steady behind him, a solid weight at his back as he wrenched the door open.

He didn't bother to see if Aleissande had closed it before he had Ryker in his hands, the rebel's linen shirt twisting in his grip as he slammed him back against the stone wall.

"We had a deal." Aidon's voice was dangerously quiet— quiet enough that he heard the soft *click* of the door as Aleissande finally made it inside.

"I tried," Ryker rasped. It took Aidon a moment to register the boy wasn't fighting him. In fact, his body was limp against the wall, his hands hanging uselessly at his sides. In the flicker of Incend flame set high in bowls on the prison wall, Aidon could just make out the bruises on Ryker's face. His tawny skin was dotted with purple, one eye puffy and black. There was a cut on his mouth, blood dried on its edges, and his top lip was swollen.

Aidon pressed him tighter against the wall. "You didn't

try hard enough," he bit out. Ryker had clearly been beaten, but he wasn't dead.

Not like Vera, who had done nothing more than approach an imposter of a king.

"Tell me," Aidon hissed between clenched teeth. "Was the arrow meant for me, or for the Visya girl showing me her affinity? Was it my sin or hers that led to her death?"

He already knew the answer. This wasn't about Visya, or him holding the crown against the wishes of the gods.

This was about Avis.

This was about losing control, becoming a pawn.

His mother had been right.

Letting Ryker walk free that day had been a mistake. And now Aidon was paying for it in blood.

"I swear," Ryker rasped again, terror choking his words, as if he could read Aidon's thoughts. "I *swear* I tried to stop them. I was going to come warn you, but by the time I came to..."

So they'd beaten him unconscious.

Distantly, Aidon felt a pang of sympathy for him. And yet it was smothered by the memory of Vera's head cocked to the side, her neck swelling in the mere seconds he gave himself to witness her loss.

"What good are you to me if you cannot control the Bellare?" Aidon growled. "What use are you to me if you cannot uphold the one simple task I gave you in exchange for your fucking life?"

Gods, Aidon was so utterly furious he thought it might shatter him. He tightened his grip on Ryker's shirt, hoping his clenched fists would contain his trembling. But his fury was like wildfire, and it raced through his veins until his very skin felt hot with it.

Ryker's eyes went wide, his gaze darting to where Aidon clenched his shirt, but then Aleissande's hand was on Aidon's shoulder and she was firmly pulling him away from the rebel.

361

Scorch marks marred the white linen of Ryker's shirt.

"Leave him," Aleissande murmured. "Let him rot in here."

And then she was tugging Aidon out of the cell, her grip around his bicep tight enough to hurt. But it wasn't the hallway she dragged him down. It was to another cell, an empty one, where they could not be overheard as she closed the door and faced him, that stoicism finally shattered by shock as she looked at him and breathed, "My gods. You're Visya."

50

AYA SUPPOSED SHE SHOULDN'T BE SURPRISED SOMEONE finally tracked her down. She'd missed two days of training with Hyacinth: one after she'd found Will in the dungeons, and one after she'd awoken from that godsforsaken dream in which she'd seen…

No.

She shut down the thought immediately as Tova dropped into the chair next to her. For a moment, they simply sat there, their gazes fixed on the steady rise and fall of Pa's chest.

"You can't do this shit," Tova finally muttered, shattering the silence. "Hyacinth was in a rage last night when you skipped training again."

"I needed a break."

Tova's hazel eyes cut to Aya. "Then *ask* for one. On my oath, Aya, you're lucky Will covered for you. He said Galda had need of you. What if Hyacinth had gone to Gianna? Or to Galda? They could have sent the Royal Guard searching for you."

Aya kept her face blank, even as something inside her twisted at the mere mention of his name. Will hadn't known where she was, but he knew enough to protect her from the queen's wrath.

He'd lied for her, and she couldn't even muster a sliver of gratitude for it.

"Why tell him and not me?" Tova pressed, her voice soft and gentle.

Aya didn't bother tearing her gaze away from Pa, even though she could feel Tova's stare boring into her. "He was the first person I saw," she answered flatly.

Silence reigned once more, but this time, the heaviness of it didn't seem to touch Aya. Perhaps she simply couldn't hold anymore.

"Aya," Tova murmured.

Aya didn't respond.

Tova's hand fell on her shoulder. "*Hey.*" Aya's head felt heavy as she turned to meet Tova's concerned gaze. "You've been through…so much. And the weight of it all, of what Gianna, the *realm*, is expecting of you…I know this is a lot."

She didn't, though. Not really. No one did. No one except…

"Have you ever come across a description of Evie?"

Tova frowned at the change of subject. "No," she answered slowly. "Isn't that the whole deal with her? There's no account of what she looked like? Isn't that why temples depict her as a burst of light?"

Each statement was a question, but a rhetorical one at that. It was no secret the saint wasn't depicted in the Conoscenza. Aya hadn't found it to be jarring—the book of the gods focused less on appearance than power. And yet…

"Don't you find that strange? The gods have physical depictions. Why not the First Saint?"

Tova shrugged. "I don't know. Maybe because she's not a god?"

Aya chewed over the suggestion. That could be, but something still felt off about it all. As if the answer were lying right there beyond her grasp, cloaked in a fog she couldn't see through.

"What does it matter?" Tova asked, that confused frown still tugging her brows together.

Aya bit the inside of her cheek.

It was just a dream. Not real. Just a dream.

But what if it wasn't?

What if the gods had sent Evie to her to finally fill in the gaps she'd been missing? To finally give her answers?

Something in her longed to unburden herself, to share this nagging feeling with *someone*. And Tova's gaze, while still imprinted with that confused frown, was open. Welcoming. And Aya wanted, so much, to not feel so damn alone that she found the words spilling from her mouth of their own accord.

"I think I've been dreaming of Evie."

Tova blinked at her.

"Okay…" The word was drawn out into two long syllables. "That would make sense. You've been studying her."

Aya shook her head. "No, I mean…I think she's been visiting me in my dreams. For years." It took her a moment to find the words to explain, to speak about the recurring nightmares she had of the time she shoved Will off the Wall, and the way the healer had always appeared in the worst of them. Tova's frown returned, deepening with each recounting.

"And she appeared to me in Rinnia, and…" Aya inhaled sharply, her body going still.

"What is it?"

"The desert," Aya breathed. "She appeared in the desert."

This time, it wasn't confusion in Tova's gaze. It was concern.

"Aya," she started softly, as if speaking to a scared child. "You don't mean she *actually* appeared to you. She died over five hundred years ago. She's not a god, and even the Divine don't…*appear* in the mortal realm." There was an uncomfortable beat of silence in which it took Aya a moment to realize it wasn't a question. Not until Tova added, "Do you?"

There was enough skepticism in her tone that Aya knew better than to answer. She couldn't even find it in herself to say anything anyway, not with the way that aching loneliness filled her as Tova continued to look at her as if there was something broken in her.

Perhaps there was.

Tova grabbed Aya's hands, her legs bumping Aya's as she turned to face her fully. "Listen to me. You have been through...terrible things. Truly awful. And you haven't even been able to catch a breath."

Tova cut a glance to Pa, as if he were evidence enough.

"Those apparitions in the desert were supposed to be your worst fears, weren't they?"

Aya nodded, and Tova squeezed her hands. "I'm sure that's what your mind is doing now. It's unearthing all the things that you keep buried, and it's toying with you, Aya."

Aya had spent the better part of yesterday telling herself just that. She'd wandered through the mountains with Tyr, hoping to find some evidence of what she'd seen in her dreams. Yet hearing the words echoed back now...

A gnawing feeling Aya couldn't name churned in her stomach as she forced her objections down.

Burying those, too.

"You're right," she rasped, slowly removing her hands from Tova's grip as she turned back to her father. But Tova wasn't keen to let it go that easily.

"Is that why you were hiding yesterday?"

"I wasn't hiding," Aya replied tightly. "I told you. I needed a break."

Tova's stare lingered, that familiar, full silence building between them. But this time, Aya couldn't find it in herself to bridge it.

"It's time to go," Tova finally murmured. "Hyacinth will be waiting."

It was foolish that the words triggered a sting of betrayal. And yet they did.

"We wouldn't want that," Aya intoned.

Tova didn't bother to reply as she pushed herself out of her chair and left the room.

Aya had already come to loathe Hyacinth's office, but today it was worse.

"Your heart is heavy," Hyacinth remarked, her voice unusually solemn. "The weight you carry, the road you walk...it is a lonely one."

Aya couldn't help the incredulous scoff that burst from her lips. Hyacinth had no fucking idea. She shot the High Priestess a withering glare. "And I suppose you'll tell me that until I surrender to it, the gods will not speak to me," she quipped sarcastically.

Hyacinth blinked. "I would advise you of the opposite. The Divine did not deem our realm free from despair or disappointment, but they also have given us hope. Evie was proof of that hope. *You* are proof of—"

"Evie," Aya gritted out as she cut Hyacinth off, "is proof of nothing but failure. She opened the veil, and it *killed* her. Her godlike power? The very thing she boasted of? It led to her *death*."

Aya couldn't explain the sudden resentment she held for the saint, except that it felt like she, too, had abandoned Aya.

"Evie's sacrifice led to the salvation of thousands of people," Hyacinth responded levelly. "I would not call that a failure."

Aya's hands curled into fists as her frustration rose. But it *was*. It *was*, because the Decachiré had returned. Evie had died, and for what?

For me to take her place on the sacrificial altar.

"Don't you see, Aya?" Hyacinth breathed, shifting forward, not in anger, but in subtle excitement. "*You* are hope. Because *you* have been given the opportunity to do what Evie did not—abolish darkness for good."

367

"And yet nothing, *nothing* I've studied has prepared me for that, has it?" Aya bit out. "All of those journals, all this *time* spent here, and the gods haven't answered the *one* question I need. I cannot abolish darkness if I don't know *how*!"

Hyacinth sighed. "I do not pretend to know the inner thoughts of the Divine, Aya. But I know they will guide you when the time is right."

The words were meant to be reassurance, hope in and of themselves. But they merely spiraled Aya further, until her fingers tingled no matter how tightly she kept her fists clenched. She felt disconnected from her body, from the very room—as if she were watching her conversation with Hyacinth from far, far away.

Without instruction from the gods, there were few ways Aya knew of accomplishing such a feat of which Hyacinth spoke.

She could kill every last one of the Decachiré practitioners, but the realm had already learned that hadn't worked when the gods banished them to hells in the War and still darkness had returned.

There was no way to eradicate darkness fully, unless…

Unless I kill everyone.

Or she tore open the veil and let the gods do it for her.

51

"Y OU'VE HARDLY EATEN, MY DEAR."
Josie's head jerked up from where she'd been staring at her plate, pointlessly pushing berries from side to side. Her father was watching her, his graying brow furrowed in concern. Josie blinked. She hadn't even registered Enzo's presence.

"How long have you been here?" she asked, resting her chin in her hand as she moved her fork around her plate once more.

"Long enough to know something is bothering you." He laid down the parchment in his hand, the bold lettering at the top detailing the terror that had struck the town. Josie scrunched her nose at it.

"Anything accurate in there?" she asked dryly. The gossips in town *loved* to print falsehoods. It was nearly impossible to unearth the truth if it didn't come from the court or Council itself.

Although she supposed that wasn't true either. It wasn't like Dominic's court had been honest. And they all knew the Council had their own agenda.

Enzo chuckled, the deep sound seeping into Josie's tired

body and warming her heart slightly. "Well, your brother is reported very much alive, so I suppose they got one detail right."

Josie huffed a tired laugh. "And the Bellare?"

Enzo tapped a finger on the table, his green eyes warm and steady on her. "I think the time for understanding the Bellare and their desires has passed. Don't you agree?"

Ah. This wasn't about the paper; this was about Viviane.

"I haven't seen Viviane since Avis was sentenced," Josie retorted, her irritation flaring. That love was coming to a bitter end, and she had known it for weeks. Maybe even from the moment Dominic unveiled Vi's treason.

It didn't make it hurt any less.

"I punish myself enough for not seeing what was right in front of me," Josie muttered as she slumped back in her chair. "I don't need your reminders. Or Aidon's."

Her father held up his hands in a gesture of innocence. "I did not mean to, what is the saying, rub spice in the wound?"

"Salt," Josie corrected with a shake of her head. "But I assume spice would have a similar result."

Enzo grinned. "Ah yes, how foolish of me."

Her father knew exactly what he was doing. Josie never believed that a worldly man such as he, who had led the Merchant Council of the most prosperous kingdom in Eteryium for years, didn't know the simplest of things. She and Aidon often tried to catch him in the joke. They never had.

"What is this about Aidon?" Enzo pressed gently.

Josie let her fork clatter onto her plate. "He won't take me seriously."

"He asked you to be his Second. What could be more serious than that?"

Josie *knew* that. But ever since she'd refused him and joined the forces instead, something had changed between them.

No. It was before that. It was the moment my fist collided with his face when I thought him guilty of working with Dominic.

"He ordered the City Guard to bring me to safety

during the attack," Josie tried to explain, her hand motioning toward the city, which was just coming to life under the early morning sun.

Enzo only looked confused. "You are his sister. Of course he wanted you safe. Not to mention you are the princess of Trahir—"

"*That* is exactly the problem," Josie interjected. "I am the princess of Trahir. But I am also a warrior. And I am good, Father. Great, even. But the longer he treats me like some damsel who cannot manage to hold a sword—"

Enzo let out an amused laugh. "You have beaten your brother to a pulp enough times that he brags about your prowess. Loudly, if I remember the several incidents with your uncle that became arguments *I* had to intervene in."

The joy of the memory faded as soon as Enzo realized who he was speaking of, as if the memory of his twin brother was removed, if only slightly, from the traitor of a king he had become.

Her father's throat bobbed, a look of sadness Josie hadn't realized was now a familiar feature on his face settling over him once more. It made him look older, smaller.

Josie inhaled deeply through her nose as she pushed her plate out of the way and clasped her hands on the table. "I feel like he doesn't trust me anymore," she admitted quietly.

Enzo sat back in his chair, that grief still staining his eyes. "Perhaps that's because you don't trust yourself."

Just as he didn't trust himself, not anymore. Josie had been perhaps the only one to truly understand why her father had stepped down from the Merchant Council. Where Aidon saw abandonment, she had only seen herself. Enzo was lost. He wasn't like Zuri, who threw herself into her work to distract from her pain. He felt his fully, and now it seemed grief had paralyzed him.

"You could go back," she said quietly, ducking her head so her father was forced to meet her gaze.

Enzo didn't need to ask where. "I do not wish to."

Josie cocked her head in curiosity. "Then what is it you wish to do?"

Her father's smile was sad. "I don't know," he admitted. "I never gave much thought to it. I never knew I would need to." He turned his gaze to the sea, stretching endlessly toward the horizon. And as he murmured another truth, it was one Josie knew as intimately as the three words that had become their family's maxim of sorts.

Duty. Responsibility. Loyalty.

They were the only things that could drive her father to admit with quiet regret, "I only ever thought of my brother."

Breakfast had done nothing to soothe her whirling mind, and Josie fully intended to work out some of her emotions in the training complex before she was due in town for her patrol.

After the attack, Aleissande had assigned various members of the force to patrol with the City Guard, if only to calm any lingering fear in their people. Josie had been surprised she'd been chosen, but then she and Cole had been assigned to the quiet residential area next to Old Town. Absolutely *no one* spent their time there during business hours, and she was back to ruminating over Aidon's dismissal of her aid during the attack.

"At least you're alive," Cole had said after one of her particularly long diatribes the other day. She'd shot him an incredulous look, ready to ream him for his insensitivity, but he was looking at her with that innocent expression that reminded Josie that Cole was simply being, well, Cole.

Josie let out a long breath as she stepped into the small sparring room at the back of the complex where she and Aidon had once dueled regularly and paused, something twisting in her chest as she looked around the space.

She hadn't been to this particular room in ages.

Someone had removed the sparring post—perhaps because Aleissande preferred them to practice in large settings, or maybe it simply needed replacing after all these years. Still, it made Josie sad to see it gone, enough so that she walked to the far wall, where their tally of fights was carved.

She ran her finger down the grooves, each a tiny tick made by their swords, except for a small gouge just below their tally that one of them must have made during a particularly intense duel. Or maybe it was Aya. Josie had forgotten Aidon trained with her here.

She let out another long breath as she thought of her friend. What would Aya say if she were still in Trahir? Josie closed her eyes and tried to picture Aya sitting on the edge of her bed, her hair in a messy plait.

Have you discussed your frustrations with Aidon?

She could hear the question in Aya's voice. The irony of Aya, real or not, telling *her* to talk out her feelings wasn't lost on Josie, and the thought had the corner of her mouth lifting until she heard a throat clear from the doorway.

"Are you meditating, or sleeping on your feet?" Aleissande asked.

Josie kept her eyes closed for another moment, enjoying a last breath of peace before she turned to face the general. Aleissande was dressed in her brown fighting leathers, her blond hair pulled back in its customary tight bun.

She stood with her feet braced apart—a fighting stance—but her arms were crossed and her expression calm as she met Josie's gaze.

"I came to train," Josie answered before motioning to the empty space where the sparring post once stood. "But the sparring post is gone."

A small crease formed between Aleissande's brows. "That it is." Her eyes flicked to the carvings on the wall, then the far bench, before landing on Josie once more. "I haven't seen you since the attack."

"I've been in training and on patrol," Josie shot back, bristling at the insinuation. Aleissande just shook her head.

"If you'd let me finish," Aleissande continued dryly, "then I would have been able to say that I have been busy and have not had a moment to tell you that I saw what you did that day."

Josie's lips pressed together, her argument already building in her throat. She hadn't wanted to leave the scene of the attack. She'd *tried* to stay, but there was nothing she could have done short of turning her sword on their own Guard.

"Your sword was in your hand before I'd even gotten the king to the ground," Aleissande said, cutting through Josie's flurry of thoughts. "They lost eight of their members in that fight. Two of them died by your blade before His Majesty even registered where you'd gone."

"Yes," Josie murmured. It wasn't a question, but she felt the confirmation was needed, because Aleissande was staring at her in a way the general never had before. That coldness was still there. But beneath it was a subtle *something* that had the air filling between them, thick and heavy.

Aleissande blinked once. Narrowed her eyes.

"Why did you join the force?"

The question had Josie cocking her head in confusion.

"I'm a skilled fighter," she finally retorted, her arms folding across her chest as she leaned a hip against the wall.

Aleissande rolled her eyes, the corner of her full lips twitching up, fighting off a smirk. "I'm skilled at seducing women, and yet you don't see me working in one of the brothels. Skill is not enough."

Surprise had Josie straightening as she stared at the general, her mouth moving wordlessly as her mind fired off several entirely unhelpful thoughts all at once.

Aleissande was...flirting? Or perhaps she was being completely serious, but she was talking to Josie about sex of all things, and this was so at odds from the stoic, strict general Josie usually saw that she wasn't quite sure what to do with it.

374

And now…

Well, now Josie was *picturing* Aleissande having sex, and she wasn't as disgusted as she should be, given Aleissande had made her disdain for Josie crystal clear and Josie returned it on principle.

"Are you…?" Josie shook her head and cleared her throat. "Are you saying you're skilled but not skilled enough to work in the brothels?"

"I'm saying," Aleissande deadpanned, "we can be good, even great, at some things, but it is not enough to warrant us making a career out of it."

Josie tried to unpick the general's meaning—tried to understand if she was saying Josie didn't belong here or simply wanted confirmation as to why she did—but her mind was tripping over itself, because she was *still* picturing Aleissande having sex, and now it was *great* sex, and fucking hells, Josie's face was heating.

"What?" Josie breathed, and she wasn't entirely sure she'd said the word aloud until Aleissande gave an irritated jerk of her head.

"Forget it," the general muttered. She was halfway through the door before she called back, "Work on your footwork."

Josie stared at the place where Aleissande had just been, her voice lodged in her throat for several moments after the woman was gone. When Josie finally managed to swallow and speak, she could only rasp one thing: "What the fuck was that?"

52

THE NOISE OF THE TAVERN WAS A CACOPHONY OF LAUGHTER and taunts and music, but it swirled around Will in a muted way as he sat at the bar, his fingers slowly spinning his glass, the amber liquid rippling inside. He'd lost track of time, but if the warmth of his whiskey was any indication, he'd been here for hours.

And yet the idea of moving, of getting off this stool and going...

Where? Where could he possibly go? There was not a single place that could offer him relief from the godsdamn agony that was shredding his insides, not even this shithole of a tavern where drink and dance and debauchery promised to make one forget.

Will pushed his glass away with an aggravated breath and ran a hand through his hair in frustration.

Five days. He hadn't spoken to Aya in five days. He'd tried, of course. Had knocked on her door, had even crossed paths with her in the Quarter. But it was as if he didn't exist.

No, it was worse than that.

It was if he existed as he did before. Before she'd let him

in, before she'd given him hope that maybe someone could see all parts of him and love him anyway.

Not just someone—her. The one person he'd ever wanted but hadn't dared hope for until suddenly, hope was the only thing keeping his head above water in Trahir.

"Are you ill?" Gianna's question had come with a concerned furrow of her brow and a soft hand on his cheek when he'd arrived in her chambers the day after Aya had found him in the dungeons.

Not ill, he'd thought to himself. *Destroyed.*

What did it matter if Gianna had been involved with the supplier?

What did anything fucking matter?

It didn't. Because when he'd told Gianna of the innocence of those in the dungeons, lying through his teeth as he said he'd finished questioning them all, she'd nodded grimly and wondered if it was time to call Lena off the search as well.

No more arrests. No more torturing.

He'd done it at all for fucking nothing.

And he wasn't sure Aya would forgive him.

Not for the torture—he was sure that Aya could see through that if he could just explain. But for keeping this from her, for asking *Gianna* to do the same.

Will had once believed that the sliver of hope he'd felt when he started to think perhaps Aya could feel something toward him could kill him. But now he knew he'd been wrong. It was worse, far worse, to get what you hoped for. To be given the one thing you've ever wanted, only to have the gods rip it away.

Not the gods. You did this on your own.

And yet, it was the worst sort of punishment. And it was no more than he deserved.

He'd just wanted...

He'd wanted.

To keep seeing that light in her eyes when she looked at

him. To keep thinking he could be some semblance of a man who deserved her. To keep...

Her.

He'd wanted to keep her, and perhaps he'd always known he couldn't. That's what this all boiled down to, wasn't it? What his choice had been to achieve?

He could tell himself over and over it was for the good of her and the kingdom, that the ends justified the means. But really, he'd wanted to keep the one thing he'd ever dared to want, even though he knew, he *knew* there was no way the Divine should allow him to do it.

He'd let himself get carried away—let himself think he could. Because he loved her. Gods above, he loved her more than he'd ever loved anything, ever *would* love anything.

He loved her.

And it was killing him.

53

A YA COULD TASTE BLOOD. IT COATED HER TONGUE WITH ITS metallic bitterness, turning her saliva bright red as she spat on the ground.

"Again."

The command came from a voice like gravel, the bark of it cold and sharp and unforgiving against the ringing in Aya's ears.

Aya peered up from where she knelt on the ground, her fingers digging into the dirt beneath her, as if gripping the earth would keep it from spinning. Sweat coated her body, sticking the strands of hair that had come loose from her braid to her face.

Yield.

Yield.

Yield.

She wouldn't.

Gianna had given Aya another bread crumb, as if she knew the hurt she was suffering. Aya was finally allowed to train with the Dyminara.

And while she loathed to be grateful to Gianna for anything, Aya had seized every single moment to train with her fellow warriors like a woman starving.

Perhaps that's why she forced herself to stand now, despite her trembling limbs, and face Cleo.

The Sensainos was before her in an instant, and Aya barely had time to raise her fists before Cleo was throwing another punch, and Aya was ducking, still under strict orders from Galda to focus on shielding instead of pushing her affinity forward.

Her shield had gotten better. Much better. She'd proven it in the few times she'd been able to spar with the Dyminara in the last week. But today, it didn't matter. It didn't matter that Aya was strong, or that she'd been shielding since she was a child, or that she was one of the best fighters of the Dyminara. She was exhausted, and there was only so much distraction from her pain that training could provide, and the next thing she knew, Cleo was in front of her, her uppercut sending Aya's head snapping back.

When she blinked, she was on the ground, a heaviness making everything muted and blurred. Galda and Tova were standing over her, her friend thrusting a finger into the trainer's chest as she yelled something Aya couldn't yet make out.

"She's not trying," she heard Galda spit out. "Cleo didn't even need her Sensainos affinity to best her." The anger in the trainer's stare became clear as Aya's vision sharpened. "What have I told you about managing your mind? About controlling your emotions? About *focusing*?"

Aya sat up, her head swimming with the movement.

She was *trying* to keep her head clear, but...

This past week had been hells, and there was only so much burying she could do. The last few nights, she'd taken to roaming the streets under the cloak of night, cornering unsuspecting connections to the Royal Guard in dark alleyways and questioning them until she could *smell* the fear in their sweat, in the hopes of finding her father's attacker.

No one knew a thing.

But she'd thought if she could keep moving, keep *going*,

then perhaps that suffocating grief and fear she was barely keeping at bay wouldn't pull her under.

Apparently, she was wrong.

"She's been going for hours," Tova bit out.

Galda waved a dismissive hand. "This has nothing to do with her physical endurance." She glared at Aya as Tova helped her up. "A tangled mind is a defenseless mind," the trainer all but snarled. "How many times have I told you that?"

"Back off," Tova warned.

Galda ignored her as she stepped into Aya's space, her brown eyes fierce. "You will face far worse, should Kakos get their hands on you," her trainer snapped. "You do not have the privilege of weakness."

Weakness.

The word tore through the careful hold Aya kept on her temper.

She ripped her arm out of Tova's grip, something like satisfaction flashing across Galda's face—as if she'd been waiting for Aya to lose control, to finally snap. Aya's jaw clenched, her hands curling into tight fists as she turned her back on the trainer before she did something truly foolish, like raise them.

She'd made that mistake before. It had landed her before Suja faster than Tyr could run.

"We're not done for the day," Galda barked as Aya stormed toward the door.

"I am."

She would regret this. She knew, even before she hit the hallways of the training complex with impressive pace, that she would regret this.

But right now, she didn't fucking care.

It didn't take long for Tova to catch up to her.

"She's out of line," her friend muttered as she fell into step beside her. "Don't worry about it."

"I'm not."

"You've been at it for hours. You need a break. Galda shouldn't have—"

"I'm fine, Tova."

"But honestly, this training schedule isn't—"

"I said I'm fine, Tova!" Aya stopped walking, the words cracking between them like a whip. Tova paused beside her, her face unmoved. Because Tova...Tova knew her. Every sharp edge, every brittle, cold piece of her, Tova knew.

Or she had.

Aya took a steadying breath, her fingers pinching the space between her brow. "I'm sorry. I—"

"It's fine," Tova cut her off. Her round jaw shifted as she looked Aya over, as if she were biting back her words. "I'm needed at the armory. I'll catch up with you later." Her hand was light as it brushed Aya's arm. "Take a break."

They both knew she wouldn't.

Tova left, and it wasn't until her friend was strolling past his lounging figure that Aya noticed Will leaning against the wall. He was frowning, his gray eyes dark as they swept over her.

"It's rare that Tova and I agree," he started, pushing himself off the wall. "But you look like shit."

It was true, Aya already knew it. But Will...

Will looked as though death had been stalking him through the week.

His sun-kissed skin had a sickly pallor to it, and there were dark circles beneath his eyes that spoke of little sleep.

Aya didn't bother to respond as she shouldered past him, but Will caught her arm, his hand warm through her sweat-drenched leathers. She tried to pull away, but his grip only tightened.

"Let. Go." Her command came through gritted teeth, but Will shook his head.

"Not until you and I have a conversation. You owe me that."

"I owe you *nothing*," Aya spat out. "And I have places to be."

"You're not due at the Synastysi today," Will remarked, as if he had nothing better to do than memorize her schedule.

"Have you forgotten my father was attacked?"

Will didn't take the bait. "There's nothing in that house you haven't already seen." And though she would have hated him more if he coated his words in pity, the matter-of-factness in his voice only pushed her rage further.

"You don't know that."

"I do. You turned that house over weeks ago, and I knew *then* there was nothing you hadn't already found. You're using this as an excuse to avoid me, because you'd rather—"

"Don't you dare," Aya snarled, wrenching her arm out of his grasp. "Just because you'd be all too happy to let your father die doesn't mean I should share in your callousness and abandon my own."

The words escaped her before her mind even registered she'd said them. She should have been horrified, but she was too angry, too fucking hurt, to care that she'd hit him, and hit him hard.

Will just looked at her for a moment, his face unreadable. And then he shook his head, a dark chuckle rumbling through him. "I'd almost forgotten what it's like to be on the receiving end of your viciousness, Aya love."

She took a step toward him, her mouth open to curse him to the ends of the realm, but he had her arm again, and he dragged her into one of the training rooms, slamming the door behind them.

Aya wrenched herself free once more as she whirled to face him. "What the hells are you doing?"

"You want to fight?" His tone was deceptively light as he took off his jacket, tossing it onto the old wooden table at the far end of the room. His hair brushed his brow as he rolled up his sleeves. "Fine. Let's fight."

For a moment, Aya simply stared at him. He couldn't be serious. He couldn't actually think they should spar *now*.

"You clearly aren't getting it all out in your training," he drawled, and while arrogance seeped into his tone, his eyes were still dull as he gave her an easy shrug. "So come on, then. Let it out on me."

"No." The word was cold and final, but Will didn't move from his spot in the training room, his body blocking her path the door.

"No?" A small pulse of his power lashed into her shield. Not enough to hurt, but just present enough to sting. "We could talk instead, but I know how much you *love* to share your feelings."

Another pulse of power.

"Fuck you," Aya spat out. "You don't get to throw that in my face. Not with the secrets you've kept from me."

"One," he said solemnly. "One secret, and I regret it more than anything. And trust me, I have plenty to regret."

She didn't care. She didn't *want* to care. Because gods, it hurt too much to do so.

"I am not going to fight you."

Another pulse of power, stronger this time. Aya stepped back, but he sent another. Another. He was goading her, and he wasn't even bothering to hide it.

"Stop," Aya hissed.

"Would you rather talk, then?" Another pulse of power followed the taunt, and Aya gritted her teeth. "I have plenty to say, and I imagine you do as well. I'll even let you go first."

And while the words were coated in a mocking tone, there was something else in them too. Something he'd been trying to keep away from her, trying to hide these last weeks behind a loose and easy posture and smooth drawl. But she'd seen it. In his jaw. His brow. His eyes.

She just hadn't known what it meant.

Will sent another pulse at her. This time, she was ready for his affinity. Her shield deflected it easily.

"You're being childish," Aya growled.

Will shrugged. "Maybe so." His eyes glittered, the dull look in them fading as something like mischief took its place, edged with a tinge of that darkness neither of them could fully rid themselves of. "So play with me."

It was the only warning he gave before he unleashed himself on her, his power spearing for her shield, searching for a hairline crack, the smallest weakness that it could edge itself into.

Aya blocked each assault, her anger growing. He had hurt her, had broken her trust, and if he didn't stop pressing her now, she could hurt *him*—hurt him badly enough that this wouldn't be some game, but something far worse, far darker than either of them could survive.

She could break him.

Break *them*.

But Will refused to back down. His power kept coming, and he stalked closer to her, a predator fixed on its prey. He picked up two swords off the weapons rack on the wall between them.

"Come on, Aya," he said softly. Gently. The words a lover's caress. He tossed her a sword. "Fight with me."

Those three words shattered her.

Gone was that flimsy grip she kept on her emotions. Will's words, a recounting of the whispers he'd muttered against her skin in the Trahir dungeons, plunged her straight into the depths of her despair.

But it was not the hollow pit she had been expecting.

It was something churning and vile and violent. A bitter storm of rage and sadness and bitterness that threatened to swallow her whole if she did not get it *out*.

The clang of their swords meeting was deafening in the silence of the training room, and it brought Aya's awareness back to Will. She hadn't even noticed she'd lunged for him, but now their swords were locked, and his eyes were bright as he stared at her through the space they crossed.

"Good," Will breathed. And then he was on her again, his sword moving as fast as his affinity as he parried with her.

She reinforced her shield, gritting her teeth as Will's power came at her again and again. Her arms trembled with the force of their blows, the vibrations shooting pain down her tired muscles.

Yield.

Yield.

Yield.

No. Because it wasn't enough. It wasn't enough to feel the ache in her arms, or the sweat dripping down her back.

It wasn't *enough*, because she could still feel that brokenness, that hurt that had tears stinging her eyes as she looked at Will and could think only of the sting of his betrayal.

She couldn't take it. She couldn't *take* it.

Aya's power crackled just beneath her skin, begging for release. The pressure was building, her feelings so intense she thought she might burst.

No.

She would not use it—not like this. She would not give in, she would *not*—

Will hooked a foot around her ankle, sending Aya careening to the ground. She landed hard, her sword flying from her hand, the breath knocked out of her lungs.

Still, his power didn't let up. It slipped through her shield, sending a pulse of hot agony through her. It was as if he'd doubled her despair, had taken his own and poured it into her, and *gods* it hurt, it hurt, it hurt.

Aya let out a scream of frustration, extending a hand in his direction. A gust of wind hit him square in the chest, and Will staggered back, the burn of his affinity disappearing as Aya leaped to her feet.

"Good," he panted.

More.

Relief was right there, just beneath the surface. She could feel it pressing against her veins, stretching her skin across her bones.

Aya summoned wind, letting it curl around her, lifting the tendrils of her hair and sending the dirt on the training room floor swirling around them. The walls of the training room seemed to groan under the wind she sent gusting around the room, forming a hollow funnel around her in the center.

The wind was howling, or perhaps it was her own mind, her own *throat*, screaming with the pain and fear she'd been battling not just from their fight, but for weeks, or maybe for her whole godsdamn life. She wasn't even sure anymore.

The wind continued to swirl and Aya closed her eyes, relishing the relief that came with the release of such power. It flowed from her effortlessly now, as if she didn't even have to try to let out more, more, *more.*

She couldn't remember who she was or why she was standing here or what she'd been feeling before this blessed release. All she knew was the never-ending flow of power that spilled out of her like a broken dam, held back for too long. Far too long.

She should have released it ages ago—released it so those who dared to threaten her knew exactly who they were dealing with.

If only they knew how threatened they *should be.*

If only they could see that I could destroy them in a single breath.

Something slammed into her, jerking her head backward as pain shot through her arms. Aya opened her eyes to see a figure before her, their hands gripping her biceps, but her mind couldn't place their face. They were a mere blur against the power surging through her, through the room, through the *world.*

Her power buffeted them back, sending them staggering,

but they were before her again in an instant, that vise grip circling her arms once again. They shook her, and her teeth clattered together with the force of it. The pain cleared her mind slightly, and she could make out gray eyes and black hair.

Will.

She wasn't sure if she spoke his name or thought it. Her throat seared either way.

They had been sparring. They had been sparring, and she'd...

No.

She tried to release her power—to stop that wind—but it was too strong, that well inside her too raging.

The storm kept coming, inside of her and out. She was no more than a vessel for some undeniable force that needed *out*, and she couldn't turn it off, not even as Will shook her again, his lips moving rapidly.

This...this had never happened before. In Trahir, her power had devoured her. But now, it was as though she'd broken a tap, and the flow was endless. Her tongue turned metallic with the taste of her own fear as she remained rooted to the spot, lost in the bevy of power that flowed out of her.

Aya swore she could feel the ground beneath her feet trembling.

Will.

Her voice was urgent inside her own mind.

He needed to leave. He was too close to her, too close to the destruction she was surely about to wield as her power surged inside of her.

She must have found a way to articulate the command, because Will tugged her closer, his voice rough as he snarled, "Like hells."

But Aya could feel her power peaking as the wind raged around them, as loud as the Ventaleh.

"Please," she begged him, her teeth gritted against the rising force that wanted to burst from her. She tried to find that connection to it, that thread that kept her in control of her well, but it was lost within the maelstrom of power inside of her.

Because she didn't want this. She didn't want to hurt him.

Will's hands moved to her face, his grip still tight. "I'm not leaving." His eyes darted across her face, his breath coming in uneven pants. "Let it out, Aya."

A broken sound wrenched itself from her chest.

It hurt now, that relief that she had thought she'd find in this release. It pressed against every inch of her, and she was certain her body could not contain it.

Will pressed his forehead against hers, his gaze fierce. "Let it out."

She did.

Aya screamed as hoarfrost burst from her, its white sheen exploding across the training room. She let out another dry sob as she threw every ounce of herself into controlling the power as it left her, shaping it around them, forcing it to curve around where they stood, anchored together.

Always seemingly anchored together.

The stone wall across from her fissured as the frost spread like roots from a tree, the ice cracking and popping. The window burst as the ice hit it, but Will didn't move. He kept his eyes fixed on her, soft words of assurance falling from him as he held her face, keeping her focused on him.

"I've got you."

Aya felt her body go slack as the flow of her power finally ceased. She staggered forward, but Will was ready. He wrapped an arm around her waist, catching her as her head hit his chest. She could feel the rapid pounding of his heart against her ear.

"I've got you," he whispered once more.

Aya let her eyes fall shut, her body trembling as she tried to find her bearings. Her legs felt weak, her body coated in a fresh layer of sweat, her hair plastered to her cheeks and neck. Her breath came in uneven pants, and nausea had her stomach roiling. A side effect from letting her power overtake her in such a way. From not managing the flow of it, from ripping it from herself too quickly.

"Are you hurt?" The question was sharp with worry, but Aya couldn't find the words to reassure him. She was still reeling herself back in, still picking up the scattered pieces of herself that were strewn about the training room floor. "Aya," Will urged, pushing her back slightly so he could see her face. "Are you hurt?"

"No," she managed, the words thick, her tongue like sandpaper. She forced herself to swallow.

Will took a shuddering breath and pressed his lips to her forehead. His kiss was firm, and desperate, and tinged with lingering fear. He pulled away and looked over her again, as if he didn't believe her.

She wasn't hurt...but he...he...

"I could have killed you," she rasped. The trembling had spread to her entire body now, terror choking her voice as she dug her fingers into his arms. She shoved him away from her. "I could have *killed* you."

He had put himself in danger. Had goaded her until she had exploded, until she'd forgotten who she was and what mattered to her, and then he'd *stayed*, as if she wasn't about to destroy the *best* thing the gods had ever given her.

She was gasping for air again, her whole chest heaving as sobs raked through her. "You can't... You can't..."

"Can't what, Aya?"

"You can't keep acting like this doesn't matter! Like *we* don't matter!"

Will's eyes flashed as he took an angry step forward. "This," he hissed, pointing between the two of them, "is the *only* thing that matters! Why do you think I hid what I was ordered to do from you?"

"You expect me to just accept that?"

"No!" Will hollered. "I expect you to accept the truth that I have always known—that I am a *horrible* choice for you!" There was something wild in his eyes now, something devastating about the pain that he didn't bother to hide from his voice. He dragged a trembling hand through his hair, his fingers gripping the strands tight. "I should have told you," he rasped, his chest rising and falling rapidly. "I should have told you the moment I learned that she had gathered those people and waited for my return to question them. I should have told you she served them to me on a fucking platter, like some sick welcome-home gift."

Something cold ran through Aya at his words, but Will wasn't done.

"I should have told you, and there are not enough apologies in the world to fix that I didn't. But when you…when you looked at me with that disgust, when you thought I'd lied about Tova…" Will shook his head. "You didn't trust me then. And I know I was the one who told you to use your power to read me, but I just…"

Will swallowed his words, his eyes bright with unshed tears. "I told myself to wait until after the Sanctification. But then your father was attacked, and you looked at me with that lifeless expression that I would *murder* for if it meant it wouldn't mar your face again, and I couldn't be another thing causing you pain. I thought if I could find the supplier, or if I could prove that Gianna was somehow tied to all of this, then I'd be able to explain myself to you. But I was lying to myself. Is that what you want to hear? I was lying to myself, I was making fucking *excuses* because I wanted…"

His voice trailed off, his breath heavy as he stared at her. Aya's heart hammered in her chest as she held his gaze. Will's throat bobbed, his fingers flexing at his sides. "You cannot blame me for wanting to delay the inevitable," he finally rasped.

Tears spilled down his cheeks, and Aya took a step forward,

her body moving before her mind could even decide if she wanted to. Her hand reached for him, her fingers brushing his jaw as—

"What the hells."

Aya tore her hand away from Will, her body going cold as she whipped her head toward the back of the training room.

There, in the broken window, stood Tova, a look of the deepest betrayal on her face.

As if she had heard everything.

"Tova," Aya breathed. But Tova just shook her head.

"If you two are quite finished, Gianna needs us." There was something else beneath Tova's anger—a graveness that rose to the surface as her friend said, "There's been an attack."

54

ALEISSANDE WAS NERVOUS. OR PERHAPS UNCOMFORTABLE was a better word to describe the pinched expression on her face. Aidon sat back in his rickety wooden chair, the legs creaking as if they might snap under his weight.

He and Peter used to take bets on which one of them would be the first to finally break it. They had spent many an early evening in this beachfront tavern, unwinding after Council meetings, or training, or whatever else their duties had required of them.

Remembering his friend was complex. Aidon loathed him for his betrayal, and yet he missed the times he was ignorant of Peter's true loyalties.

He took a sip of his sparkling wine, the crisp apple notes soothing in the early evening heat. "If you are going to be so displeased, Aleissande, we might as well have stayed in the palace," he finally drawled, raising a brow as his Second scanned the room once more.

They sat in a far corner, far enough from the door that Aleissande could monitor the crowd, but close enough to the open arches that led to the sidewalk seating that they had multiple ways to exit should they need them.

"It's important the people see you out after the attack," Aleissande murmured. "It shows them all is normal."

"All *isn't* normal." Aidon frowned. He let his gaze travel to the spot on the main thoroughfare that had been washed of a young child's blood. He had chosen this restaurant not for the memories of his friend, and not to soothe the fears of his people, but to address his own grief. To face it head on, to stare at it until his ears stopped ringing and his body stopped feeling the sickly sensation of blood on his skin.

He turned to find Aleissande watching him, her eyes narrowed in an expression that seemed to be fixed on her face ever since she'd dragged him into that cell and whispered those damning words.

You're Visya.

He'd nodded, and she'd simply stared at him for a breath before she turned on her heel and left.

She hadn't mentioned the incident since.

"We need to discuss Ryker's release," she said pointedly.

"Is *that* the most pressing thing we have to discuss?"

Her grip tightened on her water glass. "Yes."

Aidon leaned back in his chair as he took a long sip of his drink. "You cannot put off this conversation forever, Aleissande."

"There is no conversation to be had, Majesty, other than what to do with the scum we're housing in our dungeons. I think it's best if we—"

"Speaking of the dungeons," Aidon cut in airily. "You haven't—"

"*Aidon.*" His name was no better than a bitter curse as it left her mouth.

Aidon pouted. "I thought you called me that when you were being my friend."

Aleissande's eyes flashed. "I am not your friend," she asserted as she leaned forward, her gaze darting around to see if they'd attracted attention.

Aidon tried to keep his hurt look playful, but he couldn't deny the comment stung.

"I am not your friend," Aleissande repeated, her voice kinder now. "I am your Second. It is my job to serve and protect you. Which is why I am telling you, *there is no conversation to be had.*"

She looked at him pointedly, as if willing him to understand...what?

That she didn't *care*?

"It doesn't bother you?" Aidon asked incredulously.

"What bothers me is there is a councillor in our dungeons who is a member of the Bellare that you have some sort of arrangement with," Aleissande murmured, shooting another furtive glance around. "And I want to know why."

Aidon considered his Second for a long moment. He had chosen Aleissande for a reason when Josie had declined him. She was tough, and smart, and loyal. But he hadn't realized *how* loyal.

"He knows," Aidon finally confessed.

"How?"

Again, Aidon took his time before responding. How much could he tell Aleissande?

A burst of laughter sounded from his left, and he let his gaze follow it, landing on a table of friends who were joking and lounging in their chairs, enjoying an evening after a long day of work. Aidon downed the rest of his drink and stood.

"Where are you going?" Aleissande pressed.

"The palace," Aidon muttered, motioning for her to get up. "If we're going to have this conversation, we can't do it here." He eyed her water glass skeptically before adding, "And we'll both need a drink."

"The answer is easy."

Aidon let out a very unkingly snort at Aleissande's

comment. They'd been sitting on one of the palace terraces for over an hour, a bottle of wine, now with only a pour left, sitting on the small iron table between them. Aleissande had remained silent as Aidon told her everything—from Dominic's betrayal to Viviane's treason, to Ryker's black-mail and his threat to bring Vi down with him should Aidon retaliate.

Aleissande's face was flushed, her cheeks red, and he couldn't tell if it was in anger at what he'd told her, or the several glasses of wine she'd poured to fortify herself as his tale progressed. Either way, the light of the setting sun only made it worse.

"Easy," Aidon finally scoffed, taking a sip of his own wine. Still instead of sparkling this time, but crisp and cool regard-less. "By all means, do tell what the *easy* solution is."

He went to add that if it involved murdering Viviane, he wouldn't hear of it, but Aleissande had already started speak-ing. "Either Ryker becomes a spy for us, and he tells us who the other person he told is...or we kill him."

Aidon wasn't sure he didn't want to kill him either way. But a spy could be useful—if they could ever trust him.

"And if he doesn't comply and his source spreads the news?"

"Then we use Viviane to send a message of what happens when people speak lies about our king," Aleissande said darkly, her brow furrowed as she gazed at the setting sun. It painted the sky in deep oranges and pinks, streaks of red interrupting the beauty of it.

Aidon thought they looked like blood.

"I'm not killing Viviane," he muttered. He could feel Aleissande's glare, just as he could feel the frustration emanat-ing from her as he kept his eyes on the boats that dotted the horizon.

"And why the hells would you spare her life?"

Aidon drained his glass. "Because she has power that

could be useful to us. Because she is an *example* that could be useful to us—one that shows us what happens when the saint's power is given to humans."

Aleissande scoffed. "You don't honestly think the saint would sully the laws of the gods by creating more Visya, do you?"

No. He didn't. But Aidon had to think of all possible scenarios. Or maybe that was just the flimsy excuse he held on to now, the desperate attempt to keep his hands clean from one more murder. To keep his *soul* clean from yet another stain.

Either way, he wasn't sure Aleissande should be making comments about sullying the laws of the gods while talking to *him* of all people.

"Viviane is—was—Josie's partner," he muttered finally.

He'd left *that* out of his story.

There was a beat of silence before his Second responded. "So?"

Seven hells.

"Have a heart for once, Aleissande," he sniped, cutting her a look.

"You did not ask me to be your Second because of my sentimentality," she shot back. "And if your sister were loyal, she would want her partner hanging from the gallows."

Aidon turned his head to her fully, his movements slow as he set his glass down on the table. "You have no idea the depths Josie has gone to out of loyalty to me," he retorted. "So you be careful when you speak about my sister with that tone."

Aleissande's jaw tightened. "She does not need your coddling."

"Nor does she need your disparagement," he bit out. Her mouth opened, as if a rebuttal was primed on her tongue, but she stopped herself and sat back against her chair, her back as stiff as the iron that made up their seats.

Silence fell between them, interrupted only by the sound

of the crashing of the waves against the cliffs. The king and his Second stayed like that, watching the ocean, before Aidon finally broke the silence.

"Still think the answer is easy?" he drawled, ready for a change of subject.

Aleissande barked a laugh. "I do. So you don't want to use Viviane as leverage. That's fine. We'll use the Bellare."

Aidon cocked his head. "What?"

She shrugged. "If Ryker doesn't want to become our mole, then we won't just kill him. We'll kill them all."

That was, perhaps, the first time Aidon had realized how truly terrifying Aleissande could be. But in the end, she was right. Because three days later, she had secured a name from Ryker. A day after that, she had arrested the rebel and used her own Sensainos affinity to wrench the truth from him. He was indeed the person Ryker had told. The rebel was dead the next morning, and Ryker, with an understanding that he would report on the Bellare's activity weekly to Aleissande, was free.

They had their mole.

And she had made it look easy.

55

T HEY SAID THE BLOOD TURNED THE WATERS OF THE ANATH
so crimson, it looked black. That the wood of the ships
in the port of Sitya was stained with streaks of red, as if bodies
had slid down them slowly as they bled out.

Perhaps they had.

"How many dead?" Gianna's question was sharp enough
to pierce through the fog in Aya's mind. She blinked, the
room coming into focus. They were in Gianna's formal
meeting chambers, seated around the long mahogany table
where they'd sat after the Athatis attack—just hours before
everything unraveled nearly four months ago.

"It's impossible to know," Lena said heavily. She was
standing, her sculpted arms folded across her chest. "But from
what I could garner...at least one thousand."

Aya's stomach clenched.

One thousand. That had to be nearly all of Sitya and the
Midland forces Queen Nyra had ordered to guard the port city.

"Fucking hells," Will swore, his fist thudding to the table.
He tore his eyes away from the polished surface of the table
he'd been staring at since he'd sat down. "How did we not
have intel on this? We could have sent troops to assist!"

Lena's gaze narrowed. "No one thought this was possible. No one was prepared for Kakos to have forces to accomplish *this*. Besides, our best sources in the Midlands went dark weeks ago. Thanks be to Saudra, I even have news to share after the attack."

That wasn't surprising though, Aya thought bitterly. News of death and destruction passed easily. Especially in times of war.

Kakos would have made sure of it.

"We need information." Aya's voice was like gravel. "We can't win a war without it," she continued, clearing her throat. "We need to know Kakos's next move. We need to know *how* they had the ability to do something on this scale."

Clearly, Dominic's support of Kakos had made a difference. And clearly, the missing weapons supplier had traded with them before.

"Attacking Sitya is a strategic decision," Tova mused, her brow narrowed. She was careful to keep her gaze averted from Aya, her fists clenched tightly on the wooden table. "They could've marched inland, but instead, they took the port, just as Queen Nyra feared. They have more ships now. And ammunition."

"Which means," Will filled in, with a weariness that Aya was sure only she could detect, "they got exactly what they were missing."

"Yes." Tova gritted out her agreement, the malice in her voice like a knife. It went unnoticed by their gathering, however, thanks to the general tension rippling through the room. "With ships, they could go anywhere," Tova finished, her gaze fixed on the queen.

"If their strategy is to continue to build their fleet, then they'd head to Milsaio next," Aya muttered. The kingdom was made up of a string of four islands. It sat between the continent and Trahir, surrounded by nothing but endless stretches of sea.

"We should send some of our forces to aid them, then," Tova said, her response still directed toward Gianna.

"It's not enough for us to go on guesswork," Aya interjected. Her friend finally met her gaze, her hazel eyes glinting with anger. But Aya could do nothing to fix that—not now. She turned to where Gianna sat at the head of the table, her heart-shaped lips pressed into a thin line. "We need real intel. Let me help."

"No," Gianna answered immediately. "You have responsibilities here."

Aya's teeth ground together. "With all due respect, my responsibilities will not matter if we continue to operate on hypotheticals alone."

She didn't need the cut of Will's gaze to know her frustration was uncharacteristically close to the surface. But the thought of sitting in a temple while people were dying, while Kakos grew stronger...

Gianna leaned forward, her brown eyes flashing. "And information will not matter if our saint is not prepared once war arrives here."

There was a note of finality in her voice that had Aya swallowing any retort. She forced herself to relax back against her chair, giving her queen a shallow nod as Gianna continued. "Tova, I want a roster detailing the unit we can send to Milsaio immediately to shore up their defenses. I will send word to King Sarhash. Lena, I want you doing everything you can to make contact with our marks in the Midlands."

And with that, the queen let out a sigh as she stood, the rest of them following suit. "I want regular updates," she commanded, her gaze falling once more on Aya. "From all of you."

There was a moment of stillness as Gianna left the room, no more than a pause between an inhale and an exhale. But then

Tova shoved her chair out of the way, the wooden legs scraping against the stone floor, and stormed out of the door, and everything flew into motion.

Aya looked to Will to find him watching her.

They needed to finish their conversation. There was still so much she wanted, no, *needed* to say to him, but...

He jerked his chin toward the door.

She hesitated for a breath, long enough to try to untangle the look in his eyes.

"Go," he said quietly.

So she did.

Aya was out the door in an instant, not bothering to keep a steady pace as she tore down the hall after her friend.

"Tova!"

Tova didn't bother to turn around as she crossed through the entrance hall, her long stride quick. She shoved open the door, each rough movement marked with anger.

Foolish. Aya and Will had been *foolish* to have that discussion in the training room where anyone could have overheard them. Aya tore across the entrance hall and shouldered the door open, the fresh air sharp in her lungs as she followed Tova toward the forest.

She closed the distance between them, her hand reaching for Tova's elbow.

"Tova—"

"Don't," Tova ordered, ripping her arm out of Aya's hold. Her cheeks were flushed, her breath coming in uneven pants as she glared at Aya. "Don't even bother with whatever fucking lie you've prepared on your way over here. You've told me enough of them to last us both a lifetime."

Aya shook her head, her hands raised in supplication. "Please, listen to me."

"Were you even going to tell me?" Tova snapped, stepping forward. "Or were you going to keep lying until everyone found out you're fucking Gianna's leftovers?"

Anger pulsed down Aya's spine as she let her hands fall. She might be the cold one of the two of them, the bitter one. But Tova could still spew fire.

"Don't," Aya murmured. "Please."

Tova laughed, the sound harsh and so unlike the bright cackle Aya was used to hearing from her friend. "What's wrong, Aya? Ashamed of where's he been? I wouldn't want to be connected to the queen's whore either."

Aya forced a breath through her nose, forced herself to feel and *release* that anger, her clenched fists splaying flat by her sides. "I didn't want him to be another weapon to be used against me. Like you. Like Pa." She stepped forward, her gaze fixed on her friend. "*Everyone* I care about ends up in harm's way."

Tova's jaw shifted, and Aya swore fire sparked in her irises as she snarled, "And your precious lover has done his fair share of harming, hasn't he? Or did you forget that he was the fucking reason I was tortured?"

And though her voice was low, a mere growl, Aya could hear the blistering rage in it.

"If you want to blame someone for that, blame me," Aya urged. "I'm as much at fault as Will is."

"Clearly," Tova spat out, and she might as well have hit Aya with the way the word rocked her. But that anger sparked in her again, and this time, Aya let a little of it seep into her tone.

"Where's your shared fury for our queen, Tova? She was the one who ordered you tortured not once, but twice, wasn't she?"

The words were eerily close to the ones Will had snarled at her in Trahir, before she had known the truth about Gianna. But Tova just glared at her.

"Last I checked, she wasn't the one lying to me," Tova retorted. "I guess I shouldn't be surprised, though. After all, I spent years thinking the sea was responsible for your mother's death."

This time, the words did hit like a blow.

Aya stepped back, the air punching from her lungs as she stared at her friend. The one person in the world who had *always* felt like home.

How did we get here? How did we get here?

She didn't have a chance to ask. Because Tova was storming away again, her long stride brisk as she stomped through the thick woods. And this time, Aya didn't follow.

56

S OMEONE WAS POUNDING ON HIS DOOR. Will cracked open an eye, his neck stiff from the way he'd fallen asleep slumped against his headboard, his head still cocked toward the door.

Waiting for her.

He sat up fully, his hands scrubbing his face as that heaviness settled in his gut. He'd hoped Aya would come to him after chasing after Tova. That they would finish whatever they'd started in the training room.

Hadn't he learned by now how foolish hope was?

The knocking paused for a breath before beginning again. This time, it was hard enough to rattle his door.

"I'm fucking coming!" Will shouted, enough bite in his tone that the knocking ceased at once. It was quiet for a moment before Liam's baritone came from the other side, full of that aggravating steadiness.

"Take your sweet time, won't you?"

Will swore under his breath as he shoved himself off the bed, his back twinging as he stalked to the door and wrenched it open. "What do you want?"

Liam lifted a brow as he scanned his creased appearance. "Rough night?"

Will just stared at Liam before moving to close the door, but Liam blocked it, all signs of humor vanishing from his face. "Gianna wants to see us."

Fucking hells, she was relentless.

"Fine," Will uttered. "Give me ten minutes."

Liam frowned as he scanned Will's appearance. "Only ten?"

He swore as Will slammed the door, his hand snatching back just in time to avoid being caught between it and the doorjamb. "Asshole!"

Will pinched the bridge of his nose and forced a long, steadying breath into his lungs. His skin felt too tight, his pulse too fast, and while he knew it was because Aya hadn't come and he was fighting against the agony of what that might mean, there was something else that had him unsettled. Something he couldn't name.

That feeling only grew when, seven minutes later, he met Liam in the hallway, his fingers sweeping his hair back from his forehead.

"Any idea what she wants?" Will asked as they began the trek to the palace.

"No," Liam confessed. "Perhaps she has new assignments given what happened in Sitya."

Silence reigned for the remainder of their walk to Gianna's quarters, but Will's feeling of foreboding grew with every step. It had his gaze sweeping the halls, his awareness pricking as he searched for some sign of a threat. Yet nothing was out of place—not the guards who stood sentinel at Gianna's doors, not even Gianna herself, who was seated in her usual seat across the glass table in her sitting room.

Yet inexplicably, the hair on the back of Will's neck rose as he knelt with Liam, his fist covering his heart, which twisted something vicious as his fingers brushed against the scar of his oath to Aya.

"Thank you for coming so quickly," Gianna said by way of greeting. Will stood, his brow furrowed as he approached the queen.

"Of course, Majesty. What do you need?"

There was a heaviness in Gianna's expression as she considered him, her head tilting to the side.

"I need you in Milsaio," Gianna murmured finally. "You'll leave with the unit today."

A cool ripple of shock worked down Will's spine. He barely remembered to hold on to a sliver of decorum as he traded his *What?* for, "Pardon?"

Gianna inhaled deeply, as if steeling herself. "If Kakos does attack Milsaio, I want their forces heavily damaged. Given the bulk of our army will remain here until Aya is ready to act, I need a trusted member of the Dyminara to lead those who go to the islands."

Will's jaw shifted. The argument was logical enough, but King Sarhash's forces were competent. While Will agreed sending a contingent of troops as reinforcements was a wise decision, to send *him*…

"Majesty, if Kakos does indeed come here, I would be of better use to you protecting Dunmeaden and its citizens," he stated firmly.

"This is not a request. It is an order." Gianna's gaze cut to Liam. "Will you assist the Enforcer in readying to leave and escort him to the docks once we're finished?"

It was a command and a dismissal, and it had Liam glancing at Will before nodding and exiting the room. Will waited for the door to shut fully before he spoke.

"Majesty," he began as Gianna stood, forcing the desperation from his voice and replacing it with dutiful concern. "This is unwise. Your protection—the *saint's* protection—are of the utmost importance. You need me here."

Gianna's steps were slow as she approached him, her hand soft as she laid it against his cheek. Desperation had him

407

leaning into that touch, his stomach churning as he stilled, waiting to do whatever was necessary to *stay*.

"Do you know what I'll miss most when you are gone?" Gianna's question was a brush of air against his lips. She stroked her thumb across his cheek, her lips grazing the other as she moved her mouth to his ear.

Will shut his eyes. He could feel Gianna's lips trailing against the shell of his ear, her breath warm as she whispered, "I'll miss watching you whore yourself to me, as if you don't drop to your knees for her."

Will went rigid.

No.

Gods, no.

Gianna chuckled, her nails digging into his skin as she tilted her head back to look him in the eye. "I must admit, I was hurt when Tova told me you loved another. I realized this must mean your pursuits had always been insincere. Is that true?"

Will didn't dare answer as dread and fury mixed in the rush of his blood. Tova had told her. Tova had *told* her, and she had lied, and Gianna had manipulated him for *weeks*.

Gianna sighed. "It was amusing to see how far you would go to convince me otherwise once you returned. Tell me, had my attendant not come in that day, would you have let me take your cock in hand?"

Will felt sick.

Her nails dug deeper into the skin of his face and neck, enough that he bit back a hiss of pain as her other hand latched on to his belt and tugged him in to her. "You want to stay, William? How badly?" Her gardenia scent, sickeningly sweet, flooded his senses as she leaned in, her lips a hairsbreadth away from his own, a look of hunger and hatred mixing in her eyes. "Would you get on your knees for *me* if I allow it?"

Will slid his hands to her wrists, his grip firm as he wrenched her hands away from him.

"Why punish me now?" he rasped. "Was the whipping not enough?"

Gianna raised a brow. "Punish? Who says this is punishment?" Each word was delivered with an edge of laughter that had Will tightening his grip on her wrists. But it did nothing to intimidate his queen. "I knew of your feelings, but Aya's…" Gianna tsked in disappointment. "She cannot afford any distractions."

Fury pounded through Will as he realized Tova hadn't just betrayed them once… She'd done it twice. Once in the prison and, gods, again just yesterday, after she'd seen them in the training room.

"Kill me then," Will growled.

"When you're so useful to me? What a waste that would be."

He could feel her muscles clench as he squeezed tighter. Easy. It would be so, so easy to snap her delicate bones. To kill her with a few steady pulses of his power. He could do it without a change in his heart rate. Without a second thought. Without a modicum of guilt. He could be exactly what she made him to be.

Someone to be feared.

Someone to be hated.

I see you.

Aya's voice was a whisper in his mind, a reassurance she thought he hadn't heard that night he'd been utterly broken. Destroyed, because of the queen before him.

I see you.

He wouldn't make it out of this palace if he killed her. But at least Gianna would be in the seven hells where she belonged. And Aya…

I see you.

Will released Gianna's wrists and stepped out of her reach, his heart hammering in his chest. Aya would be left to weather this storm alone. Because even without Gianna, Kakos was still coming for them. For *her*.

I see you.

Will swallowed as Aya's voice echoed in the back of his mind. A reminder that he was more than what Gianna had molded him to be. His soul did not belong to her. His *fate* did not belong to her.

Not anymore.

He turned his back on his queen and made his way to the door, that same prickle of awareness creeping down his spine as she watched him go.

"You don't deserve her, William," she called as he reached the door. He paused, his hand on the handle as he looked back at her. There was a small smile on her face, like a predator toying with its prey.

"Neither do you."

57

HYACINTH WAS FAVORING ONE OF AYA'S WEAPONS: SILENCE. The High Priestess had greeted Aya at the front of the Synastysi, saying nothing more than they'd begin in her office today. Once they'd gotten situated in their normal seats, Hyacinth had folded her hands in her lap and simply waited. And while silence typically didn't bother Aya, today it chafed. She was already raw, and worn, and *exhausted*. She'd barely slept last night, even though her explosion of power and fight with Tova had drained her of her energy entirely.

Aya hadn't even been able to bring herself to get under her covers. Instead, she'd lain on top of her bed and stared at her ceiling for hours, Tova's vicious words tangling in her mind with the other memories that haunted her.

Memories she thought she'd buried in Trahir.

It was as though the fury that often fueled her had drained out of her when she'd released her power in the training room, and all that was left was an aching emptiness that made her mind murky and her muscles ache. She felt so utterly alone—so utterly isolated, and vulnerable, and terrified that every decision she made might put someone else in danger, might put the *realm* in danger.

"I'm so godsdamn tired," Aya rasped.

She hadn't meant to say the words aloud. But they slipped from her anyway, her eyes burning as she stared at the rug. "When does it fucking end?"

Because on her oath, if she wasn't sick of the waiting.

Waiting for Pa to wake up. Waiting to untangle what Gianna's intentions were. Waiting for the gods, who never spared her a fucking whisper, to instruct her on how to fulfill the prophecy. Waiting to find *some* information on the veil that could be useful, should Gianna truly want to call down the gods.

Waiting for her mind to stop playing tricks on her.

Evie hadn't visited her dreams again. Tova had been right. Her mind was using her fears against her. And Aya felt foolish for hoping it had been anything more.

Hyacinth's robes rustled as she shifted, before her soft voice said, "Aya. Look at me."

Aya turned her head, her body aching with the small movement from the little sleep, the constant training, the agony she'd been trying and failing to bury.

Hyacinth leaned forward, her hands braced on her knees as she observed Aya from beneath her sheer veil. "Evie's road was one of isolation and darkness, too. And yet she did not allow it to consume her. You *must* rise above it."

It had been a lesson Aya had to learn from her time in the desert with the Vaguer. And yet for all she'd learned in Trahir, she still wasn't able to manage these feelings—to let her guilt and anger and fear flow through her instead of consume her.

"How?" she asked, her voice cracking. She dug her fingers into the arm of the couch, the leather scratching beneath her nails.

"We release it to the Divine, and we trust in their ways." Hyacinth tilted her head, her veil fluttering with the movement. "They would not have chosen you if you were not able to do this, Aya."

"Then why haven't they *helped*?" Aya couldn't keep the bitterness from her voice, frustration mixing with her pain.

Hyacinth made a contemplative sound. "Perhaps they have, and you simply can't see it through your anger. The gods do not always speak so directly."

"Pardon me, High Priestess." Aya turned her head to where Liam stood, one hand on the door, a troubled look marring his face. "I have to speak to Aya." His eyes fixed on her, his mouth tightening into a thin line as he added, "Now."

Aya was out of her chair before Hyacinth even acknowledged Liam's request, dread pooling in her stomach. Distantly, she registered the High Priestess's agreement, but it didn't matter—not with that look on Liam's face. She waited until he closed the door, his hand gripping her arm tightly and tugging her toward the staircase, before she muttered, "What happened?"

"It's Will," Liam responded in a low tone. "Gianna is sending him to Milsaio."

58

THERE WAS SOMETHING EXCRUCIATING ABOUT WATCHING Cole fight. Perhaps because it reminded Josie of a hunter cornering a helpless animal.

One that was particularly sweet, if not a bit aloof.

"Watch her footwork!" Josie barked from the side of the sparring ring. They were indoors today, in the main sparring room, the shade offering little relief from the heat. But at least they didn't have the sun to worry about.

Josie stood several paces from the nearest warrior, her arms braced on the thick ropes that surrounded the training platform. Despite the distance she kept from her comrades at arms, things within the forces had gotten slightly better for Josie.

Or at least, they hadn't gotten worse.

Most of the warriors tolerated her, if only because they were starting to understand what would happen if they didn't. It wasn't the king they had to worry about. It was her. She'd sent more than one of them to the healers since joining this lot, and she'd continue to do it if it meant solidifying her place in these ranks.

And yet, the others who were also on combat training

were still purposeful in their avoidance of her. Especially with Garrons in the room.

He stood a few paces before a small cluster of warriors, his thick arms folded as he watched the fight. He looked more like a crime lord with his cronies than he did a loyal member of the Royal Army.

Arrogant asshat.

Josie turned her focus back to Cole, wincing as he took another blow from Verena to his side.

Then another. Another.

Seven hells. This wasn't a fight, it was godsdamn target practice.

"Slip left; cross," Josie murmured under her breath. She'd made Cole practice the combination at least a hundred times in the last week alone. He could pack a mean punch with his left hand, but only if he had a chance to *use* it.

Cole twitched as the fighter came at him again, his head jerking as if he were about to do exactly as Josie had taught him, but he wasn't quick enough. There was a *crack* as Verena's punch landed on his jaw, his wiry hair flopping as his head snapped backward.

The warriors lining the ropes let out a collective groan, but Josie didn't miss the snickers and taunts that followed from those surrounding Garrons. Even Verena smirked. She made a show of flipping her red braid over her shoulder before brushing her knuckles on her leathers, as if to wipe off the blood Cole's lip had left on her skin.

Josie gripped the rope tighter.

Yield, dammit. Yield, and let me have a shot at her.

But Josie's stubbornness seemed to be rubbing off on her friend, because Cole did no such thing. Instead, he spat a glob of blood on the ground before raising his fists once more. His muscles were trembling, not from fear, but from fatigue, but he didn't seem to give a damn as he jabbed, his body lunging with the movement.

Verena dodged him easily, her foot slipping beneath Cole's and sending him stumbling.

His arms pinwheeled, a grunt bursting from him as he slammed into the ropes.

Another round of laughter rippled from the far side of the ring. Josie tore her gaze away from Cole to glare at Garrons. "Next person who opens their godsdamn mouth can fight me," she snarled.

"Careful, Princess," he drawled. "Wouldn't want to bend your crown."

"If it's from shoving it up your ass, Garrons, I'll save it as a keepsake," Josie replied sweetly.

"Had enough?" Verena taunted Cole, her grin sharp and vicious.

Cole ran the back of his hand across his mouth, wiping away the blood and sweat. "I could go another round," he answered easily, as if he were chatting about the weather and not agreeing to getting beaten to a bloody pulp.

Josie repressed a groan. This friendship would be the death of her, she was sure of it.

"Gods, put him down already," Garrons lamented, his proud voice carrying across the ring. "Or better yet..." He grabbed the ropes and hoisted himself into the ring in one smooth leap. "Let me do it."

That's it.

Josie reached for the sword sheathed at her side, but a hand grabbed her bicep, the grip warm as it halted her movements. "Get out of the ring, Garrons." Aleissande's command was flat, bored. She didn't even bother to look at Josie as she released her arm, her stride purposeful as she walked to the ring and ducked under the ropes.

Josie frowned. She hadn't noticed the general enter the room. Usually, the energy shifted whenever Aleissande was present. It grew tight and tense, like something deadly had walked in, and no one particularly wanted to draw its attention.

If something happened in Josie's stomach in those moments, some low, swooping motion she had long since ignored, well…that was her own business.

That tense feeling settled over the space now as Aleissande gave a jerk of her head, wordlessly dismissing Cole and Verena from the platform. The warriors all seemed to straighten, their attention focusing solely on the general as a heavy silence fell over the room.

Aleissande was outfitted in her fighting leathers, and Josie found herself admiring the general more openly than she had before. Her lips, full and pink, were pursed as she surveyed the warriors, the curves of her hips evident as her hands rested there. Once again, Josie was flooded with those distracting images that had haunted her since her talk with Aleissande in the sparring room.

Only now, they were getting worse. Because it wasn't some random stranger that was running their hands over the dip of Aleissande's waist, it was Josie, and *what the fuck was wrong with her?*

"Sitya has been attacked by Kakos," Aleissande said in that curt way of hers.

The fantasy in Josie's mind vanished instantly.

A murmur rippled amongst the warriors, but it died as soon as the general lifted her hand. "While one attack does not warrant war, it would be unwise for us to be unprepared. As such, by order of the king, we will be forming a Visya guard to defend the kingdom and lead the front lines should Trahir be dragged into the conflict."

Another ripple of mutters, this time painted with disbelief. And…anger?

Josie scanned the gathered warriors, noting the frowns marring several faces. Her own brow had furrowed, she realized, and she smoothed her expression, locking her rising frustration away.

What the hells was Aidon playing at?

"I want to make it clear that in no way is this to say you are lesser warriors," Aleissande was saying. Garrons made a sound not unlike a snort, which he quickly covered with a cough. Josie couldn't help agreeing with his sentiment.

Aleissande had already increased their separate trainings from the Visya from two a week to three. This would only further the divide in the forces.

And the kingdom, Josie realized.

Though Aidon hadn't spoken further of his concerns about Visya and human relations in Trahir, no one was naive to the tension that was growing in the kingdom, its epicenter emanating from Rinnia. Did he not realize that he was pouring kerosene onto a fire that was already burning—*had* been burning before the threat of Kakos was ever truly imminent?

"S'not a bad idea," Cole said from where he'd appeared at Josie's side. Josie blinked. She'd been lost in her thoughts and must have missed Aleissande's dismal. The warriors were shuffling about, and the general was nowhere to be found.

Cole sported a gruesome black eye, and that wasn't even the worst of it. Already, there was a blue mark stretching the length of his jaw, which had swollen on one side. His lips, bloody and puffed, made his next words muffled. "They'll give us a better chance at winning."

"This is not a game of cards," Josie snapped.

Cole's eyes widened—or at least one did—and the sight was so pathetic that Josie immediately found herself shaking her head, her hand landing lightly on his arm. "I'm sorry," she murmured.

But Cole was watching her, his gaze darting across her face as a small V formed between his brows. "You *don't* think it's a good idea?" The question was hesitant, and loaded, and as much as Josie yearned for the type of openness she'd once had with her friends, there was no way in the seven hells she could oppose Aidon *here*.

Not with so many listening ears.

Besides, how well did she even know Cole?

She'd thought she knew Viviane better than anyone and look what happened.

"I think my brother knows exactly what he's doing," Josie responded carefully. "Now come on." She gave a gentle tug on Cole's arm, guiding him toward the door. "Let's see a healer about that jaw."

59

THE DOCKS OF DUNMEADEN WERE CROWDED WITH THE usual tourists and tradesmen, but Will marked an additional frenzy as the warriors made their way to the ship, the lower members of the Royal Army lugging spears and shields and armor.

He stood in an alleyway, leaning against the brick wall of an old tavern as he watched the progress. Next to him, Akeeta sat stoically, her eyes fixed on the ship.

There were a few Visya who had been assigned to the unit, but most were human, their crimson uniforms marked with silver thread rather than white.

Will was the only Dyminara who would be making the voyage.

"Go to the docks," Liam had ordered as soon as Will stepped out of Gianna's chambers. "Delay if you have to. I'll get her."

Will had only stared at him blankly before Liam gave a small shrug. "You deserve to say goodbye."

Someone must have sent for Akeeta, because she'd arrived moments ago, her head held high, as if honored to be selected for such a mission. Will was grateful that she would be with him, at least. It had been a long while since they'd traveled together. It wasn't rare for the Dyminara to travel without their wolves, especially when either discretion or diplomacy was needed or when Dunmeaden was shoring up its defenses, but that didn't stop the ache that settled in an Athatis when their bonded warrior was far away, especially as time progressed. Who knew how long Will would be gone this time?

He swallowed against the tightening in his throat as he watched the warriors, his pulse still racing from his exchange with Gianna.

She could have killed me. Why didn't she kill me?

The question went unanswered no matter how many times it echoed in his head. He should have been relieved. But to be a weapon against Aya instead…

It hadn't mattered. Their whole fucking plan hadn't mattered, and there was one person to thank for the misery that was about to be inflicted on both of them, and she was approaching him now.

"What are you doing down here?" Tova's voice was sharp as she stalked down the alley.

Akeeta growled, and Will gave the general a long, cold look, not bothering to move from his place on the wall. "As if you don't know," he replied darkly, his gaze moving back to the ship. "Go, Akeeta. I'll be along in a minute."

His wolf huffed but obeyed, her steps slow and steady as she made her way toward the docks.

"She's sending you to Milsaio?" Tova frowned.

She could have killed me. Why didn't she kill me?

Will straightened, fury pounding through him as he turned to face Tova fully. "Are you truly surprised? Or is this another act?" he snapped with enough venom that Tova reeled back. "I must say, Tova, it's difficult to fool me, but I suppose with our history I can believe the lengths to which you went to do so. But to betray your best friend?"

"What the hells are you talking about?"

"How much did you tell her? Was it simply my feelings for Aya, or was it that I suspected Gianna had ulterior motives?"

But he already knew—he knew because Gianna had had him whipped, had suspected him of treason, and she had *known* this whole fucking time how he felt about Aya, and those offenses could only have been bestowed on him by one person.

Tova's eyes widened, even as anger darkened her gaze. "What the fuck are you *talking* about? I didn't even know about you and Aya until yesterday."

"Another brilliant lie." The words were punches of breath between gritted teeth. "Tell me, how quickly did you run back to Gianna when you confirmed Aya returned my sentiments?"

"I don't know what you're—"

"*Enough*," Will snarled. "You're lucky I don't kill you."

Because that fury was still there, and so was his power, nudging against his skin as if to remind him that he could destroy so easily if he wanted to. Tova's eyes flashed, fire wreathing her hands at the threat. Will ignored it as he took a step toward her.

"What changed between the prison and now?"

Perhaps he could've understood her doubt of him had he not felt her resolve in the cell that day. Had he not looked her in the eye as she realized what he had always known—that Gianna was dangerous.

"Gods, at least have some sense of self-preservation. Who do you think planted those papers on you?" Will spat out. "Who do you think *used* you to manipulate your best friend?"

Tova shook her head. "You've lost your mind," she said with an incredulous laugh. "Accusing our queen of working with—"

"I stood there in that fucking cell with you and begged you to help me! I told you I loved her!" The words were ragged, and gods, to have to have this conversation with Tova instead of Aya might actually kill him faster than war ever could.

Tova shook her head again, her fire spiraling up her arms as her anger ratcheted higher. "You told me NOTHING!" she shot back. "You came into that godsforsaken cell and you tortured me knowing I was innocent."

"You knew I had no choice! When Cleo arrived, our plan to fake your questioning went to utter shit, and you *knew* that. Godsdammit, Tova, you *knew* that!" There were a thousand curses he wanted to hurl at her, and his jaw clenched as he bit back each and every one.

But Tova stilled, her flames vanishing as her lips parted. She cocked her head, something like confusion flitting across her face. "Cleo wasn't there."

A dark, incredulous chuckle rasped from Will. She couldn't be serious. She couldn't go *this* far to deny what had happened. What was the point now that he knew?

"Gods above, Tova," he muttered, tugging a hand through his hair in frustration.

But Tova was still staring at him, her brow furrowed as her eyes darted across his face. "Cleo wasn't there," she said again.

There was something urgent in her voice, some note he couldn't quite latch on to because he was too busy thinking about how he could fetch Cleo *right now* and prove the Sensainos had been in the room, and what type of fucking fool did Tova take him for—

Will paused, his fingers still tangled in his strands as he looked at her.

Truly looked at her.

Her skin, usually flushed pink, had paled slightly as her hands clenched and unclenched at her sides. Her chest rose and fell in shallow movements, and while typically her gaze was sharp and steady, there was a faraway look in her eyes now, even as she focused on him—as if she were looking at him and through him all at once.

"Tova..." Will muttered.

She didn't appear to hear him. It didn't matter. Because a realization was clicking into place inside Will's mind, and it left an overwhelming sensation of dread as a devastating truth took hold.

"You don't remember," he breathed. The words tasted like bile on his tongue, bitter understanding sinking in further. "You actually don't remember."

Tova wasn't lying.

She didn't *remember*.

Will's stomach churned, his mind racing as it tried to wrestle this new information into place. He'd heard of such things before—people's minds erasing entire events when the trauma of them was too great. But Tova's mind hadn't removed the details completely.

She recalled him torturing her, hells, she recalled Gianna's entire plan to keep her imprisoned for Aya's benefit, but she didn't remember Will coming to her, *begging* her for help.

Horror settled heavily over him as he stared at her.

"What did she do to you?" Will breathed.

Tova went stock-still, her eyes blinking rapidly. She stayed that way for the span of a breath, until someone from the docks shouted her name. It broke whatever spell had befallen her, and her eyes focused, her agitation clearing instantly.

"You're despicable," she rasped.

"Tova," Will urged. They needed to talk about this. He needed to understand. "Wait."

But she was already gone.

Will wasn't sure how long he stood in that alley, staring at where Tova had been. His mind had gone blank, his lungs tightening as he stared and stared.

From the docks, a shout rang out, echoing down the lines of soldiers readying to board the ship. It shook Will from his dread enough for him to register that it was nearly time to go.

And Aya wasn't here.

Delay, Liam had said. But perhaps he shouldn't. Perhaps Aya had made up her mind about him. Perhaps that was for the best.

After all, there was a reason Tova had been tortured. A reason something so horrible had happened to her that her mind had twisted on itself, creating lies as truths to bring her a sliver of peace.

He was responsible for this. Will had asked Tova to put herself between the queen and Aya. He had asked Tova to lie for him. He had asked Tova to trust him, and he had left her there with no escape and no hope he would return.

He had as good as asked Tova to die for her friend.

And perhaps she would have, had Gianna not broken her.

Gods, how could he have been so foolish? So naive?

How could he have missed this?

Will could not blame Aya for deciding to stay away from him, for deciding he was too damaged, too *dangerous* to love. It was what he'd wanted to hide from her all along.

Another chorus of shouts echoed from the ship's bay.

Three seconds. He would give himself three seconds to feel the pain he was trying desperately to bury, and then he would go. Will's throat tightened, his pulse thudding in his throat as he closed his eyes and let it wash over him.

One.

Two.

Three.

He forced himself to swallow, his hand scrubbing down his face as he took a deep breath and straightened. He was two strides toward the alley entrance when he saw her.

Aya stood at the mouth of the alleyway, the sun lighting her from behind, like a shadow wreathed in sunlight.

Will froze, his heart hammering enough to hurt—or perhaps it was the beauty of her that threatened to bring him to his knees under the rush of emotion that went through him.

425

Aya drew closer to him, and he noticed her hair had come loose from its braid, wild strands framing red-stained cheeks. She was breathing heavily, as if she'd run all the way from the Synastysi. She stopped just before him, and his pulse impossibly accelerated, as if desperate to be locked in her own rhythm and cadence.

Gods, there was so much to say to her, but his throat wasn't working, the words trapped somewhere beneath his guilt and sorrow and regret as his lips parted uselessly.

But then Aya was moving again, and suddenly she was in his arms, her body warm and firm and so fucking *right*, her hold tighter than it had ever been as her head settled into that spot that was made for her. And he couldn't breathe, couldn't speak with the way relief and regret warred within him.

"I'm sorry," he forced out, his voice a mere whisper into her hair. "I'm so fucking sorry."

It didn't scratch the surface of what he needed to tell her, but they were the only words he could manage, and he repeated them like a desperate prayer for redemption.

Shouts echoed from the docks a third time.

Will peered over Aya's head to see the line of warriors starting to move toward the gangway, but Aya's arms stayed locked firmly around his middle, even as she peered up at him.

"Gianna knows, doesn't she?" she murmured, her jaw tight and fury blazing in the blue of her irises.

It wasn't a question, but he nodded anyway.

"I'll kill Tova for this," Aya breathed. "I can't believe she went to Gianna after seeing us." Her eyes were wet with unshed tears. Will took her face in his hands, his eyes memorizing every detail.

He had so much to tell her—gods, he had so much to tell her. And he would. He would share all of it when he returned. But if there could only be time for one thing she had to know, it was this.

426

"I don't think it was just when she found us the other day, Aya. Something isn't right with Tova," he muttered urgently. "I thought she was being stubborn—purposefully aloof— whenever we talked about what happened in the dungeons. But she doesn't remember. At all."

Aya's face paled as she stared at him for a long moment. "How do you know that?" she asked finally.

"Because when I told her Cleo was there, she didn't remember. But ask Cleo. She'll tell you she was there. I promise you…every bit of what I told you about what happened in the prison with Tova is true."

Aya's hands slid up his forearms, her fingers curling around his wrists. "I know," she whispered.

Will fought against the way those words—that subtle confession of trust—threatened to undo him entirely. He didn't deserve that trust. Not with the secret he had kept from her, and not with what he had asked of the only person she loved aside from her father.

"Whatever Gianna did to her in those dungeons, I cannot blame Tova for confessing the truth. Not when it was terrible enough for her mind to…" He couldn't finish the statement, and not just because something was shattering behind Aya's eyes.

"I should never have asked that of her." His voice cracked with the confession, and he blinked away the burning in his eyes as his thumb stroked Aya's cheek.

He knew she could feel the way his hands trembled despite the way he still held her face. Aya shook her head, subtle defiance written in her face. "This is not your fault."

The words were tight with anger, and he opened his mouth to make her promise not to seek retribution, at least until he returned, but someone was calling his name.

His throat bobbed, his grip tightening on her face as he pressed his forehead against hers. "I have to go."

"Wait," Aya breathed, an edge of desperation in her tone.

She pulled back from him slightly, and for once, he could read every single emotion on her tearstained face.

Sadness. Fear. Love.

They warred for domination in her eyes, and it was love that won out as she rasped, "Will, I—"

He captured her lips with his before she could finish, another desperate moment echoing in his mind as he kissed her. She had stopped him from saying those words once. Had made him wait, and gods if he hadn't waited too long. And yet he couldn't bring himself to hear them now.

Not here. Not like this.

But he could show her in his own way. His hand tangled in the back of her hair as he deepened the kiss, and Aya, his beautiful, stubborn Aya, matched every stroke of his tongue with one of her own, until the heat between them was enough to light this godsforsaken kingdom on fire.

His name rang out from the ship once more, and Will reluctantly pulled away.

"Tell me when I get back," he rasped. Another brush of his lips against hers—to sustain him. "You know how I love motivation."

A choked sound left her lips, half sob, half laugh, and Will brushed a tear off her cheek before stepping away from her. He stepped past her, unable to linger in her presence. If he did, he would never get on that ship.

"Will."

He paused, steeling himself as he glanced back at her. Her cheeks were stained with tears but her eyes were dry, her mouth set in a resolute line as she sucked in a breath. "Come back."

It wasn't a plea.

It was a demand.

He lowered his shield, his affinity brushing against hers until she let him in. And he let her feel every ounce of truth, every ounce of love, in his words as he said, "I promise."

60

WHEN THEY WERE CHILDREN, THERE WAS HARDLY A place Aidon went that Josie didn't follow. *Thick as thieves and as exasperating as the Espri*, their mother used to say, before she'd roll her eyes, muttering something about *that Order and their "mind" magic*.

And while Josie knew the exasperation often came because she and her brother tended to band together against authority—*especially* when that authority denied them dessert—it also was earned in part by their boisterous arguments, which could be heard an entire wing away.

Aidon and Josie were both stubborn, and proud, and loyal, perhaps to a fault. When they cut each other, they cut deeply. And when they mended, they mended firm.

But as Josie stood outside of Dominic's, no, *Aidon's* office, her heart hammering in her chest, she couldn't help but wonder if those seams that bound them together, the ones that had always seemed able to fray but never truly break, had finally torn.

Maybe, after everything they'd been through, with Aya, with Viviane, with Dominic, with the Bellare, the damage was too great to return to any semblance of normalcy. Perhaps there would always be this gaping hole between them, unable to be filled despite their best efforts.

She rapped on the door, waiting for Aidon's muffled "*Enter*," before stepping into the office. Her brother was behind the ornate wooden desk, his posture hunched as he traced a finger over what looked like a map. Josie glanced around the circular room, marking the long bookshelves that rimmed the walls. Their mother had insisted that Aidon keep the king's office—especially given his reluctance to use the throne room. And yet it surprised Josie, taking it in now, that Aidon hadn't changed any of the furnishings. Even the curtains, which framed the towering windows behind the desk, remained. The sun streamed through those windows, casting long shadows across the office. They loomed like the ghosts of memories Josie couldn't erase.

"Josie." Aidon's voice cut through the haze of her thoughts, drawing her gaze back to him. "What is it?"

She slowly approached the desk, taking in the lines of exhaustion on Aidon's face. His jaw was dotted with stubble, his white shirt rumpled in a way that Aidon typically wasn't.

"When was the last time you slept?" she asked.

"Last night," Aidon muttered as his gaze returned to the map. "But I haven't had a truly restful night of sleep in quite a while."

Had she seen him that little since the Bellare attack in town that she hadn't noticed how worn out he looked? Had this space between them grown that great?

She had avoided him because she'd wanted to avoid another argument. But frustration simmered in Josie's veins now, frustration and nostalgia for the times when they could speak openly, not as king and princess, but as brother and sister.

As friends.

It created a bitter cocktail that sharpened her voice subtly as she said, "Aleissande says we're to have a Visya force within the armies."

Aidon hummed a noise of affirmation, his jaw shifting as he traced a line from Sitya to Dunmeaden. "What of it?" he muttered distractedly.

"*What of it?*" Josie asked. "Do you forget the Bellare's actions so easily, Brother? The Bellare fear the Visya are growing too powerful. You want to give them *more* power? Appointing a Visya force is only going to increase the divide between them and the humans." Aidon's gaze snapped to her, surprise flickering across his features at her tone.

"I am well aware of the Bellare's actions," he replied slowly, subtle anger seeping into his voice. "Creating this force has nothing to do with them. Sitya was ransacked, and—"

"It has *everything* to do with them!" Josie interjected. "They rioted simply because of Avis's sentencing. What do you think they will do when they learn their king has promoted only Visya in the military? What type of threat do you think they will make of that? Humans are no match for Visya power, and the Bellare will *use* that to paint the Visya as a further threat!"

Aidon cocked his head, his brown eyes narrowing. "You have quite an interest in the Bellare, Josie. Is this Viviane's influence, or your own?"

"How dare you," Josie growled, her hands slamming onto the surface of the desk as she leaned toward her brother. "My interest is and always has been in this kingdom. In *your* kingdom. I have chosen you time and time again. It is you who refuses to see that. Do not make this something it isn't."

"That's rich," Aidon snapped. "Because I was about to ask if this is truly about politics or if you're simply angry that you're ineligible for such a unit."

Aidon's words *hurt*. Josie stepped back from the desk, her hands falling to her sides as anger, hot and bitter, rushed through her.

How fucking dare he belittle her?

How dare he treat her in the same way Dominic once did?

Not good enough. You're never good enough.

"You want to talk to me about ineligibility?" Josie laughed, the sound harsh. "How hypocritical."

A muscle in Aidon's jaw jumped, his palms splaying flat on the desk as he stared at her. A tense silence settled between them, so brittle, a single breath could have shattered it.

"Leave," he ordered finally, his voice low. "Leave, before I do something I regret."

But Josie was too angry, too hurt, to heed his command. "Maybe Viviane was right," she snarled. "Maybe you *aren't* fit to be king."

The words were hateful, and a godsdamn lie, but Josie spat them out anyway.

Aidon's eyes glinted with rage as he shouted, "*Viviane* is lucky she isn't hanging from the godsdamn gallows! Perhaps she should!"

Josie was across the desk in an instant. She slammed Aidon against the windows so hard that the glass rattled, her arm barred across his chest.

"You may be king, but do not forget, *Brother*, that you are also my kin. I won't hesitate to meet your threats with my own," she vowed. "Do *not* threaten her again."

She expected Aidon to retaliate. Or at the very least, to shove her off him. But Aidon's muscles loosened instead, his body slumping against the windows as he let out a heavy breath.

He didn't even see her as a worthy opponent. Not anymore.

"Fight back," she ordered as she slammed him against the windows again. "Fight *back*!"

"I can't," Aidon replied, misery dragging his voice down low. Josie sucked in a breath, ready to curse him to the seven hells, but she paused as she took in the sadness in his eyes.

The resignation.

It wasn't like him to give in so easily. But there was that

exhaustion, drawing bags under his usually warm gaze as he said, "I've lost control of my affinity."

Of all the things Josie expected him to say, *that* had not been one of them. "What?"

Aidon sucked in a long, tired breath. "I left the coronation party and went to our sparring room. My affinity came forward even with the tonic. Natali suspects it's because I've been suppressing it all these years."

Josie frowned at her brother, her arm loosening its press against him slightly. "You burned the sparring post," she said, the realization washing over her like cool water. Aidon's throat bobbed as he swallowed.

"I've increased my dosage of the tonic, but I don't want to risk it. Not with you."

And while his brotherly protection should have warmed her, Josie's mind was too busy racing to catch up to more secrets she hadn't known. How could he not tell her about this? It had been *weeks* since his coronation.

He'd mentioned that he'd left early—that night she came to his room. But she never thought to press him on it.

"Why did you leave the coronation party?"

She was trying to understand, trying to tread lightly so she could rebuild the bridge they'd unknowingly left to burn between them.

Aidon looked down, as if he couldn't bear to hold her gaze. "She lied."

"What?"

"She lied," he repeated. There was something like pity in his gaze. "When Viviane told us that she hadn't shared my secret with anyone. She lied."

It took Josie a moment to truly understand what Aidon was saying. To weave together the words, which had a muted quality to them against the ringing that had started in her ears, and make them a sentence that actually meant something.

And once she did…

Josie stumbled away from Aidon, the back of her legs slamming into that godforsaken wooden desk that was becoming a marker of betrayal. The ringing in her ears grew louder with every shallow breath she took until eventually it was a dull roar that nearly masked her ability to hear her own guttural, "No."

She couldn't believe it. She wouldn't. Not after all they had been through. She wouldn't believe that Vi had lied to her, had betrayed her *again*, and that Josie was once more in the dark, alone and naive.

"It's how Ryker Drycari became a councillor," Aidon continued. "He blackmailed me at the coronation party. Viviane told him about my power, and he threatened to spread the word if I didn't give him Avis's seat. He had insurance, too. He'd told one other person who was prepared to share the news if Ryker didn't return from the party."

Each word was heavy, as if merely forming the syllables was an effort of extreme strength and will. Aidon ran a hand down his face, his fingers trembling slightly.

Slowly, Josie sat on the edge of the desk, her movements jerky.

"I'm sorry," Aidon rasped as his hand dropped to his side. "I'm so sorry, Josie."

Josie shook her head, her lips moving wordlessly as she tried to find something to say that could adequately convey the cleaving in her chest. "I can't... How could you keep this from me?"

Aidon pushed away from the glass, his face anguished as he took a step closer to her. "I didn't want to add to your pain." He swallowed. "You had to witness something truly horrible happen to your partner. And I *let* it happen. *I* caused you *this*," her brother said, motioning toward her, as if he could see some indication of the hurt lingering on her skin.

Josie frowned. "And so you lie to me?" She shook her

head. "You let her go free, just to spare my feelings? Even knowing she cannot be trusted?"

"I hadn't...I hadn't figured out what to do yet. But I knew I couldn't charge her with the crime. The cost would be her life."

"But you could live with me wasting *mine* with someone who would take everything from you." Josie couldn't keep the accusation from her voice as she held Aidon's gaze.

Yes, he'd wanted to protect her. But in doing so, he'd kept her in the dark, *again*. And perhaps *this* was what had broken their bond. Perhaps it had happened before Aidon turned his sword rightfully on Dominic, before Viviane was ever given Visya power.

Perhaps it happened the moment her brother started to suspect Dominic and didn't *tell* her.

Because that secret had almost cost them everything.

And here he was, keeping more.

Aidon's eyes were pleading as he held her gaze. "I couldn't do it again, Josie. I couldn't be responsible for destroying you."

Josie rubbed a hand against her chest, as if she could ease the ache that was building there.

She had spent weeks training alongside some of the best warriors of the realm. She had taken punches and kicks and even the occasional slice of a blade, and none of it came close to the pain she was feeling in this moment.

Josie pushed herself up from the desk. "I am not glass," she muttered. "It is not up to you to decide what breaks me." Aidon simply stared at her as she turned to walk around the desk, her gaze fixed on the door. "Banish her," Josie ordered, not bothering to look back at him.

"Josie—"

"*Banish her.*"

"You know I can't do that. Not with the power that she has."

"Then lock her up for all I care." She reached the door,

her hand on the brass handle, then paused, looking back over her shoulder. "I know you want to be different, Aidon. To be sure that nothing can make anyone say that there are any similarities between you and our uncle." Josie glanced around the untouched office before meeting his gaze again. "And so I'll remind you...Dominic kept secrets, too."

She didn't bother to wait for his reply as she stepped out of the office, the door closing with a heavy click behind her.

61

AYA'S CHILDHOOD BEDROOM WAS MORE OF A HOMAGE TO her mother than it was to her. The walls were the same yellow as the living room, her small wooden dresser painted a pale blue.

Aya had hated it as a teenager—the bright and cheery decor. But she hadn't had the heart to change it when it so purely reflected the joy that was Eliza. She hadn't even removed the colorful patchwork quilt that lay atop her bed.

The bed Tova now sat on, her face dull as she stared at the wall.

It had taken Aya three days to work up the nerve to face her friend. Three days to sort through her misplaced anger and deserved guilt. Three days of flipping through that godsforsaken diary in the Synastysi and losing herself in training as she turned Will's words over and over.

Whatever Gianna did to her in those dungeons, I cannot blame Tova for confessing the truth. Not when it was terrible enough for her mind to...

Aya had filled in the gaps in Will's sentences with the worst possible imagined scenarios, ones that drove her from her bed at night and had her clutching the porcelain of her toilet as she emptied her already empty stomach.

Now she shifted in the doorway. Tova didn't acknowledge her presence, but Aya knew her friend had recognized her footsteps as soon as she entered the house.

"I went by your family's home to find you," Aya muttered from her spot in the doorway. "Caleigh looks more and more like your mother every year." Tova's younger sister had their mother's honey-blond hair and green eyes. She had grown another foot since Aya had last seen her, and it wasn't nearly as jarring as the guarded look Caleigh had given her when she saw Aya on her doorstep, Liam and Tyr standing in the distance.

Liam had scarcely left her side since she'd emerged from the alley three days ago. She wasn't sure how he'd managed to secure himself as her regular Dyminara guard, but she didn't particularly care. While typically the constant presence of another would chafe at her, Aya couldn't help but appreciate Liam's silent but steady nature.

"She said you hardly come by anymore," Aya remarked, her arms folding across her chest as she leaned against the doorframe.

Tova picked at a thread on Aya's quilt, her gaze avoiding Aya's as she muttered, "This always felt more like home, anyway."

It was a statement that would once have filled Aya with a steadying warmth, but now it only reminded her of how much they had grown apart. Because Tova was right. This *had* been a second home for Tova of sorts. Not because Tova held any sort of resentment for her own family, but because they'd spent most of their time here as children and teenagers, away from the shining love of Tova's parents that served as a reminder of what Aya had lost.

It didn't fully explain why Tova was avoiding them now, but Aya didn't need to hear the reasoning. She already knew it. Tova's family would have been subjected to the same shame that was brought upon her when she was held responsible for the crimes she didn't commit. And though her image had been restored...

Aya knew what it was to let shame drive her away from those she loved most.

Tova finally dragged her gaze to Aya. Her eyes, usually a bright hazel, were a muddy brown. "Whatever her reasons for sending Will away, it had nothing to do with me, if that's what you've come to accuse me of."

Her voice was flat. Hollow. And it was enough that Aya pushed herself off the doorframe and took a seat next to her on the bed. "I didn't come to accuse you of anything," Aya replied quietly. Her hands gripped the edge of her mattress, her torso leaning forward as if she could hold back the tidal wave of emotions that threatened to drown her.

She didn't know where to begin. She had sought out Tova without a plan, her mind circling over all Will had said as shame and sorrow and guilt pooled in her gut with every step that brought her closer to her friend's family home. There was so much to sort through. Tova not remembering... Tova catching them in the training room the other day... Gianna waiting until Aya's feelings were confirmed to send Will away.

She wasn't entirely sure Tova wasn't lying about not running to Gianna a few days ago. She wasn't entirely sure it mattered.

She doesn't remember. At all.

Will's words were haunting and all-consuming, the repercussions of such a truth so great that it momentarily drove the agony of his departure from her.

And yet even so, she didn't know where to begin. How to apologize, how to ask what the hells had happened, how to sort through events Tova didn't remember, and honestly, thanks to the gods she didn't if they were horrible enough for her mind to do this to her.

Some traumas did not need to be relived. Aya knew that better than anyone.

But it seemed Tova had chosen a topic for them, because it was her voice that broke the silence, heavy and dull with exhaustion. "I don't understand how you could be with someone like him."

Aya's throat bobbed as she stared unseeingly at the doorway. "I know you don't."

At least that, Aya finally understood. The conversation Tova couldn't remember had made her trust Will. Without it, he was merely a monster.

She waited for Tova to continue, but an empty silence was all that was left in the wake of their confessions. They were broken—utterly broken. And while she could blame Gianna for it, and would, when she could muster up the fury to seek retribution, right now Aya couldn't escape the guilt that tightened her throat.

She had broken them first, and it didn't start with leaving Tova in those dungeons, but in the secret she had kept for the lifetime of their friendship:

The secret of her power, and what she had been afraid it meant.

"Do you believe him?" Tova finally asked in that same dead voice. Aya met her probing gaze. "Do you believe what he said about the dungeons? About Gianna framing me? About her using me?"

Aya fought against the burning in her eyes. "Yes," she rasped.

Tova's round jaw shifted, as if she were biting back anger, or disbelief, or some other bitter emotion she did not want Aya to see. "You realize those accusations could be seen as treason, don't you?"

"Yes."

Tova shook her head bitterly as she turned away from Aya to stare at the wall once more.

"Do you love him?" The question was spat from between clenched teeth.

"Yes."

Tova let her chin drop, her own hands digging into the edge of the mattress. She was quiet for a long moment before she nodded and stood. Her gaze was a quick glance. "I won't tell Gianna your suspicions."

"Tova..." Aya was reaching for her, but again, that distance was too great. Tova took a step back, toward the doorway.

Her chin quivered, her lips pressing together as she tried to fight off her emotions. "I need time," she murmured, her voice tight as tears lined her eyes. "I just...I need time."

Aya sniffed, forcing herself to swallow her objections, her *begging*, as she nodded. "Okay," she agreed. She could give Tova this. At the very least, she could give Tova this.

Tova dipped her chin, a goodbye of sorts as she stalked out of the room. There was a finality to it that made the crushing weight on Aya's chest only worsen as the sound of the front door slamming shut echoed through the house.

She hadn't known why she'd sought Tova out; hadn't known what to expect of their conversation. But it hadn't been *this*. It hadn't been a confirmation that they were strangers to each other now, the distance between them so great, it was insurmountable.

Aya hung her head and finally let her tears fall.

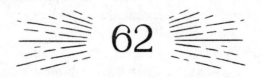

62

AYA SUPPOSED SHE SHOULDN'T BE SURPRISED THAT WHEN she finally fell asleep it wouldn't come with peace.

She heard his screams first—sharp and bitter, as if he were furious they'd escaped his mouth in the first place. She felt the rough stone of the Wall next. It bit against her hands as she gripped it tightly, his name ripping from her throat as she stared down that long fall.

No. Not like this.

She didn't want to see him like this.

But there he was, lying at the base of the wall, sharp bone punched through the skin of his arm, blood pooling beneath him so quickly, she was scared he might drown in it.

He shouldn't have survived.

It took her a moment to realize the words had been spoken aloud—but not by her.

Aya whirled to where the healer stood next to her, her face grave as she peered down at Will.

"He shouldn't have survived." The healer said it again, her cobalt eyes latching on to Aya. "The gods are merciful, are they not?"

"Don't," Aya growled as she took a step back from the

Wall. The healer—Evie?—only ever appeared in this dream when the outcome changed, when Will died, and Aya could do nothing to stop it.

She didn't want to see that; she *couldn't* see that. Not when he was on his way to the islands that might be the target of Kakos's next attack.

The woman simply cocked her head. "It's your dream, Aya. You are in control."

A lie—Aya had never been able to control this dream before. Will's screams grew louder, and Aya shut her eyes as if she could block them out entirely. At once, the air around them fell silent. Slowly, Aya opened her eyes to see the healer smiling at her.

"What do you want from me?" Aya asked. The woman laughed, the sound bright and full of joy and so out of place for the nature of this nightmare.

"This is about what *you* want from *me*," the healer said, one of her dark brows arching. "After all, it is you who summoned me."

"Summoned?"

The healer laughed as she leaned back against the wall, her arms folding over her chest. "You still have not accepted it, have you?"

"Accepted what?" Aya pressed, not bothering to hide the curtness in her tone.

The woman wasn't bothered. In fact, she inspected her nails, her voice light as she said, "Who I am. Who you are."

"Who are you then?" Aya bit out.

But she knew. There was that settling in her stomach that marked certainty, and even though it *could not* be possible, Aya knew even before the healer said the words, a small smile painted on her lips.

"Y avai ti dynami a ton diag mesa mye."
I have the power of the gods in me.

"Evie." Her name escaped from Aya's lips on an exhale.

443

The healer—saint—spread her arms and gave a polite bow. Aya took a step back as she shook her head. "This isn't possible. I'm dreaming."

"You are. But have you not been waiting to commune with the gods?" There was a flash of amusement in the woman's eyes as she held Aya's gaze. "Why not a saint?"

Aya's heart was racing, her hands tingling as she slid them into her pockets. "How...how is this possible? I tried to dream of you again, but you didn't appear. How did I summon you now?"

Evie shrugged. "I do not pretend to know how the gods work. It seems that somehow you and I share a connection that strengthens the further down this road you progress."

Aya frowned at the words. She hadn't made any particular progress as of late, unless Evie was counting destroying every relationship in her life. But perhaps that *did* count for something. Because Aya was alone, just as Evie was.

"Why are you here?" Aya asked.

Again, Evie shrugged. "I suppose I am to guide you."

"You know what I'm supposed to do?" The question was breathless as hope, vicious hope, rose in Aya so quickly, it tightened her throat until she almost choked on her words.

Evie's face softened, and suddenly, she looked so much younger than Aya had ever seen her look before in these dreams. "I am afraid my knowledge of the prophecy is quite limited. I was gone when the Divine proclaimed it."

And just like that, the hope vanished, leaving Aya empty and hollow. "Do you not commune with the gods?"

Evie's eyes sparkled, the blue in them pure and deep, like the waters of the Anath Sea. "The Divine do not look kindly on sharing secrets of the Beyond with mortals."

Aya's jaw clenched. "You're not mortal anymore, are you?" The statement came out with more bite than she intended, but Evie didn't seem bothered by her frustration.

444

"I am not. But I am not with the gods. That is not the way of the Beyond."

Aya tugged a hand through her hair, her breath leaving her in a sharp exhale. "How are you supposed to guide me if you don't know anything?"

"We are to learn from our history, Aya," Evie said gently. "There are only two of us to ever exist. Surely, I have something to offer."

Gods, the way she spoke…it reminded Aya of Natali and their riddles. Natali hadn't known how to fulfill the prophecy. The only one who even had a guess was Lorna, and that…

Aya stilled as the thought washed over her, something raw and aching stirring in her chest.

We've always believed that when the prophecy speaks of the greatest wrong, it speaks of the Decachiré. But what if the greatest wrong isn't the Decachiré? What if it's that Evie opened the veil in the first place?

Aya blinked at the saint, her head cocking in contemplation. "The veil," she muttered. "You can help me understand the veil."

Evie's face twisted in confusion. "The veil?"

"I summoned it in the desert. I saw you through it. Do you know how?"

There was a wariness to Evie as she eyed Aya. "The veil is…all around us. Unseen, impenetrable—or at least, so the gods had intended when they made it from their own power. There is a…likeness to it and our affinity. It is why I was able to summon it. And open it. It is a feat very few could accomplish."

Aya's breath caught as hope rushed through her, the sensation so severe that it almost choked her. "If you opened it, then I can close it!" she exclaimed. "That must be what the gods want from me!"

Because a cracked veil, a torn veil, made their realm vulnerable. If Aya could repair it, if she could make it *stronger*, then perhaps she could stop Kakos, could stop *anyone*, from ever calling down the gods again.

But Evie only seemed to grow warier. "I... The gods mended the veil after I opened it. Aya, the veil is not some *thing* to be trifled with. It *killed* me."

"But...a Seer had a vision of it torn," Aya explained desperately.

Evie shook her head. "There is no tear. That vision could be sometime in the future. After all, *your* arrival was predicted hundreds of years ago," the saint said, her tone gentle.

Aya opened her mouth to argue, but a realization had her snapping it shut, the hope draining out of her all at once.

If it was sometime in the future, did that mean Aya would be the one to tear it?

Evie was staring at her again, but this time her eyes had sharpened. "What are you trying to do?"

"I think my queen wishes for me to open the veil once more, so that the gods might obliterate the Decachiré for good." The words should have felt heavy, but there was something so damn relieving about being able to share this with someone else after carrying the burden alone for so long.

Not alone, she reminded herself. Will had held it too. But he was gone, and Aya was struggling with the weight of it all.

Evie's face had paled, and suddenly, she was before Aya, her hands gripping Aya's arms with surprising strength. "You cannot let that happen," Evie choked. "That would be catastrophic to the realm. The gods will not give it a second chance!"

There was true terror on her face, and it had Aya's heart ratcheting up, her mouth going dry as she shook her head. "I won't."

"Promise me," Evie demanded, shaking Aya slightly. "Promise me you will do everything in your power to stop her."

"I will," Aya stammered. "I promise. I don't even know how to call the veil forward."

"And yet you've done it before," Evie pressed.

Aya frowned, her breath rushing from her lungs. She had. But that had been different. She hadn't *meant* to.

Evie opened her mouth to say more, but suddenly the scene around them shifted, and Aya was before Will, who was screaming and thrashing on the ground.

She had almost forgotten this was a dream. A nightmare.

She looked around for Evie, only to find her standing by her shoulder, a forlorn look on her face as she cocked her head and took in Will's writhing form.

A sad smile pulled on Evie's lips. "There was a reason, you know, that the Decachiré practitioners saw love as the barrier to true power." She gave a heavy sigh as she shook her head, strands of raven-colored hair fluttering in the breeze. "It weakens us all."

Will's screams increased an octave, his veins bulging with the force of it.

Wake up.

Wake up.

Wake up.

Aya did.

63

Y OU'RE HESITATING!" GALDA'S FEEDBACK, MORE SNARL
than instruction, came a moment after Aya had dodged
Liam's blade. "If Aya were *paying attention*, she would have
read that move far earlier, Liam!"

Aya bit the inside of her cheek, her eyes narrowed as she
and Liam prowled around each other. The sounds of clashing
swords filled the dawn air, a call and response of sort to the
twittering of birds as several of their fellow Dyminara got
an early training session in before starting their duties. Aya
had been up for hours, thanks to the dream she was trying
to shove from her mind, especially as she narrowly dodged
Liam's blows, haunting every breath she took. At least she had
a day off from the Synastysi. She wasn't sure she would have
been able to face Hyacinth today.

Liam pushed his affinity hard enough for Aya to feel it
pressing against her shield, his persuasion looking for some
sort of weakness as he advanced on her with his sword.

He was hoping to persuade her into a maneuver that
would cost her the duel, especially as Galda had once again
given Aya orders to shield only.

"Focus, Aya!" Galda barked as Aya nearly missed her next block. "You're as sloppy as a drunk."

Liam smirked at her, sweat dripping down his face as he twirled his sword once, but it was his sister, who was watching from the side of their small circle, who said, "And to think, you didn't even have the queen's whore to keep you up all night, Aya."

Aya clenched her jaw so hard, she thought her teeth might snap. She'd expected news of her and Will to travel throughout the ranks. They weren't exactly discreet in the alley the other day. But it didn't stop her from shooting a look at Tova, who was dueling just beside her.

Tova ignored the comment entirely.

"Fuck off, Lena," Liam muttered as he lunged for Aya. Aya let out a hard breath as their blades collided, her arms shaking with the force of Liam's blow. She tried to breathe, tried to ignore the way her power writhed within her, begging for release.

It was like trying to hold water in her hand.

She felt uncoordinated, her power like a too-full well of water that splashed and overflowed, despite the way she'd found some release in sparring with Will.

Aya's temper flared as Liam pushed his affinity harder against her and unleashed a vicious offense. She parried, letting out a frustrated grunt as their swords locked.

Perhaps this was what Gianna had intended: for her saint to become weak and afraid, torn down until she was desperate enough to do her bidding.

Perhaps Galda was in on it, too. Why else would she refuse Aya her own power?

Liam came at her with another devastating blow, and Aya...

Aya snapped.

She freed her left hand from the pommel of her blade, risking Liam's sharp edge coming closer to her face as the

Persi took advantage of her weaker hold. But he wasn't fast enough for the quick, horizontal slicing motion of her hand, and the way the earth cracked with it.

Liam's eyes went wide as the ground crumbled at his feet, his legs buckling as he scrambled to catch his footing.

Aya wouldn't let him.

She was on him an instant, her teeth bared as she brought her sword against his again and again, forcing him backward toward the next duelers. With every slice of her sword, she opened up more earth underneath him, the Visya behind him scattering as Liam continued to scramble uselessly backwards.

"I yield," he finally ground out, but Aya hardly heard him over the rush through her veins, that blessed release that came from channeling her power into something *good*, something productive, something *worthy* of what the gods had blessed her with.

She wasn't a pawn or a puppet.

She was a godsdamn saint.

The ground continued to cave in around Liam, and Aya used her momentum to lunge for him. He fell to one knee, his teeth bared as he just barely blocked her sword.

"Godsdammit, I said I yield!"

Someone grabbed Aya's sword arm and wrenched it away from Liam.

Galda. The trainer's face was a breath away from Aya's, her dark eyes bright with anger as she snatched the sword from Aya's side and tossed it on the ground. "Where's your godsdamn control?" she spat out.

The reprimand was like a slap in the face.

Because *this* was what she had been taught—control, always control, until it had forced her to bury anything that might threaten it.

Every *feeling*, every aching, dark part of her, shoved further and further until she was hollowed out and cold.

Where had that control gotten her?

Fucking nowhere.

Aya took a step back, but Galda stepped with her, her index finger pointing viciously at her. "I don't give a shit if you're *divine*," she snarled, as if the word itself was a curse. "I gave you an order to shield only. And not only did you disobey me, but you ignored your fellow warrior's request to yield. When you fight with the Dyminara, you fight with honor, or you don't fight at all." Aya could feel her face burning as she held Galda's gaze, if only to avoid the curious looks from those fighting nearest to her and Liam.

Galda shook her head, a whispered curse leaving her lips as she stepped away from Aya. The trainer kicked Aya's sword, sending it sliding across the ground back to her. "You're done for the day."

Aya was halfway to grabbing her sword before the words registered.

"*What?*"

It wasn't the first time a warrior had been dismissed from training—hells, it wasn't even the first time Aya had been dismissed—but for this? It wasn't as though she was the first person to go too far, to get so caught up in the blessed release of a fight that they went too hard. How many times had Aya been on the receiving end of such behavior?

But Galda didn't respond. Aya turned to find Tova watching the exchange, her brow furrowed as her gaze darted between Aya and the trainer. Tova held Aya's gaze for a long moment before turning back to her dueling partner.

Aya snatched her sword from the ground, her gazed fixed unseeingly ahead of her as she stormed away from the training complex.

Tyr was lying in the grass a few paces away. He had been sleeping on the floor of her room ever since Akeeta left. Aya couldn't bring herself to send him back to the compound.

Perhaps she needed his steadiness, too.

He lifted his head now, his ears perking as she walked toward him, but then his gaze shifted behind her.

Aya glanced back to see Liam jogging after her. "Lena was out of order," he said as he caught up to her.

"I don't care about what she says," Aya retorted, her voice cold. She looked at Tyr and jerked her chin toward the forest. If she wasn't going to train with the Dyminara, she should at least get her exercise in with Tyr.

Perhaps it would soothe some of the fire that was still burning in her veins, or at the very least, wash out the tension that had crept into her after last night's dream.

"Why are you following me?" Aya muttered as Liam fell into step beside her.

"You need a Dyminara escort, remember?"

The steady comfort of his presence evaporated immediately. She changed her mind. He was bothersome.

Aya set her jaw, her focus on the trail ahead as she started into the forest. She'd drop her sword at the Athatis compound and take to the higher elevations. Maybe Liam would change his mind once the air got thinner.

They walked in silence for a long while, but Aya's mind was spinning. It was as if she was a young girl again, and the quiet was chafing against her skin.

"How did you know?" She didn't need to clarify what she was alluding to.

Liam sighed, reaching for one of the knives sheathed on his thigh. He twirled it lazily between his fingers.

"I didn't. Not for sure. But…" His voice trailed off, his brow furrowing as he tilted his head back and looked at the sky peeking through the pines. "He asked after you. After his whipping. Which was odd because Will never seemed to truly care for anyone but himself." Aya opened her mouth to argue, but Liam's grin, a slash of white, gave her pause. "You can't deny it, Aya. The man is a selfish bastard. Or at least that's the mask he wears for the world to see."

Aya swallowed her retorts. Liam had a point. Will had carefully crafted his image, enough that sometimes he even seemed to believe it himself.

For a long moment, there was nothing but their footsteps and the cawing of the ravens from high in the trees. Their haunting cries always served as a marker that the Athatis compound was near. That, or that a wolf had hunted and they were simply waiting for their meal of carrion.

"I tried to listen through the door when Gianna was speaking to him that morning," Liam finally confessed quietly. "I couldn't hear what she was saying. But when Will came out looking as white as Akeeta, I hazarded another guess—one that you all but confirmed when you took off toward the docks."

Aya's jaw shifted. "And now word has spread, naturally."

"I haven't heard any talk," Liam remarked slowly. "I don't know how Lena knew, but it wasn't by me."

What did it even fucking matter?

Gianna had won. After all they had done to ensure she would not have another weapon to use against Aya, after all they had done to try to get the information they needed...

They had failed. Again.

Aya welcomed the bitter anger that stirred inside her. It was a lovely distraction from the agonizing ache of sadness. She latched on to the heat of it, dragging it forward and letting it clear her mind.

Liam cut her a look, as if he could sense the shift in her. "What's going on, Aya? Gianna isn't one to play the scorned lover. She's too proud, too powerful. What have you two gotten into?"

Aya remained silent, but it seemed, after four days, Liam was pretending to be patient. He grabbed her arm and forced her to stop. "Let go of me," she ordered.

"Let me help you," he pressed, his voice dropping low. "Something is going on. And if it concerns the queen... Lena

453

is close to her now, Aya. Too close. If there's a chance my sister is mixed up in whatever it is, I want to help." The flash of protectiveness in his eyes reminded Aya so much of Aidon's love for Josie, of how he would kill if it meant keeping his beloved sister safe.

But Aya didn't have it in her to reassure Liam about the changes that had come once Lena had taken on more responsibility when Aya had left.

Aya's responsibility.

"Power does strange things to people," she replied, ripping her arm from Liam's grasp.

"That's what your boyfriend said," Liam growled. "But I know my sister. This isn't her."

Aya couldn't help the bitter huff of laughter that escaped her. "Even those closest to us surprise us, Liam."

The words fell from her lips so effortlessly that she thought they were her own. And yet a memory came floating back to her, the echo of the same sentiment in an aristocratic drawl she loathed.

Those words weren't hers at all.

They were Mathias Denier's.

The King of the Crooks had said that to her at the Sanctification. She could see the way he'd looked off into the distance, the statement so casual and light she hadn't given it a second thought, hadn't wondered why Mathias would think of the two of them as anything but distant acquaintances who used each other to accomplish their own goals.

He to continue a life of crime, and she to deflect unwanted attention away from the crown.

And yet he'd uttered that same sentence to her, had said it as he stared off at...

Aya stopped walking.

The drink table.

He had been staring off at the drink table. The same drink table she had been too much of a coward to approach, because her father had been there, and she couldn't stand to face him, even then.

"My gods," Aya breathed.

She had been so focused on Gianna, so *sure* the queen had something to do with this that she hadn't even considered...

"What is it?" Liam was frowning at her, his head cocked in concern as he tried to read the expression on her face.

But Aya was too busy putting the pieces together to bother to respond.

Seven hells, the answer had been in front of her all along. It had been staring her right in the face, had practically been confessed before the crime ever took place.

She knew exactly who had attacked her father.

And she knew exactly how to prove it.

64

AYA SAT ON THE FLOOR OF HER BEDROOM IN THE QUARTER, absently stroking Tyr's fur as she let the steady *tick* of the clock on her wall count every second of her patience. She'd quickly collected herself under Liam's watchful eye after the realization dawned on her, but she knew better than to expect him to buy her excuses.

She'd shown her shock, had reacted too visibly, enough that Liam knew her murmured *nothing* when he once again asked her what was wrong was nothing more than a lie. But he'd let it go when he realized she wasn't going to confide in him—about where her mind had been, or about Will either.

He had, however, stayed with her throughout her training with Tyr. She didn't have to force the aggravation that seeped out of her whenever she turned and saw him a few paces behind her. Finally, she'd given up and come back to the Quarter, Tyr beside her.

She'd bathed and tried to settle herself by getting lost in one of Will's books she'd stolen off his nightstand. It was dreadfully boring, but at least it passed the time.

That had been hours ago.

Still, Aya waited.

She sat on her floor, syncing her own breath to Tyr's steady inhale and exhale, and waited until his ears pricked, his head lifting from where it rested on her rug as he heard something she couldn't.

The town bells.

She glanced at the clock.

Two a.m.—just as she'd suspected.

Aya stood, her legs aching from being crossed for so long. She picked up the knives she'd laid out on her bed, sheathing them over her fighting leathers at her waist and thigh. From her dresser, she grabbed her black cloak and scarf, which she draped around her neck. She tugged up her hood, but paused before securing her scarf around her mouth and nose.

Tyr had gotten up, his long nails digging into her rug as he stretched out his front legs.

"You can't come," she muttered. Tyr let out a defiant breath, but she would not be swayed. "Discretion is important tonight. You cannot come." She pretended not to see the concern in Tyr's eyes at her sharp yet soft tone. But Tyr knew her—he knew every broken, wicked piece of her. There was no doubt in her mind that he sensed exactly what she intended to do without him.

Aya secured her scarf, cloaking her face in darkness.

She strode to her window and nudged it open. A quick glance at the path told her what she already suspected: it was empty. "I'll be back," she murmured to her bonded, not bothering to look behind her.

And with that, she flung herself out the window and disappeared into the night.

Back when Aya was younger, in the early days of her training with Galda, she used to recite verses of the Conoscenza silently to help herself stand still.

Quiet your mind, Galda would order while teaching her

how to go undetected in even the most obvious of places. *I can see your restless thoughts.*

Aya didn't know how to explain then that her thoughts left her mind and ran through her blood, sending it rushing and roaring behind her ears, and pounding in her pulse, and strangling her breath until she swore she would faint.

The stiller she had to be, the worse it would become.

She could not escape her fears in the quiet.

She supposed at some point, she had learned to become them instead. Because as she stood in the dilapidated alleyway outside one of the brothels of the Rouline, Aya did not need verses to quiet her mind or hold her body so still that not even the courtesan five paces away could detect her presence.

Perhaps that was because she was too focused on her task of sucking off the man who had tugged her outside and dropped his pants before she could even sink to her knees.

Either way, Mora had aligned the fates tonight.

Aya knew it as soon as the man let out a low groan, his body jerking as he came, and the woman, rather than continuing their evening, stood and wiped her mouth with the back of her hand before sauntering back through the side door from which they had come.

The man rested his head against the brick wall, his breaths coming in uneven pants as he let out a satisfied sigh. Aya waited until he pushed off the wall and turned toward the door, his hand reaching for his lowered breeches, before she moved.

She was behind him in an instant, one knife at his throat, the other at his dick.

"I always knew you were cheap, Eryx, but to not even pay for the full experience?" she cooed in his ear. Eryx stiffened, his hand frozen on the waistband of his breeches, which were still around his knees. "I hope you at least tipped the poor girl for having to pretend to enjoy your cock. Gods know, what with your trinket store and *other* doings, you have enough coin for at least that."

"What do you want?" Eryx hissed from between clenched teeth, his voice wavering slightly.

"Revenge," Aya murmured, her voice a soft lover's caress as her lips brushed his ear. Eryx whimpered as she pressed the sharp edge of her blade harder against his cock, enough to just break the sensitive skin. "But I'll settle for answers if you behave. *Real* answers, not the bullshit you fed me in the tavern that night."

She watched as a bead of sweat dripped down his temple.

"Here's what's going to happen. You're going to pull up your pants and come with me. You're not going to make a sound. You're not going to run. You're not going to do anything but follow me. If you do that, I'll consider letting you keep all of your appendages."

Eryx trembled beneath her knife, but he gave a subtle dip of his chin, as much as he could with her blade stop pressed against his throat. "Where are we going?" he asked, his voice quivering with fear.

Aya stepped in front of him, keeping her blade pressed tight to his throat as she let her other fall to her side. She cocked her head, letting him see the glint of hatred, of *rage*, in her eyes.

"Somewhere they can't hear you scream."

Aya's steps were heavy as she trudged back to the Quarter, the four chimes of the bells ringing at her back as she started the climb into the mountains. She tilted her head from side to side, stretching out the tension in her neck as the echoes of Eryx's pleas floated through her tired mind.

You promised.

She had gotten exactly what she had come for: confirmation.

Yet knowing did nothing to douse the fire of her rage. No, only true revenge would do that. And perhaps, even then, she would still feel the bitter sting of this betrayal.

She hadn't known about the debts. About the Rouline. About the gambling halls.

You promised.

Aya grunted as she scaled the wall to her bedroom, her muscles aching with the movement. She tumbled through her window, but she didn't let herself rest, not even as Tyr let out a concerned whine at her appearance.

She merely shucked off her scarf and walked out of her room, her steps silent as she made her way down the hall to the other end of the second floor.

You promised.

She raised a bloody hand and knocked softly on the worn wooden door of the far bedroom. It was mere moments before a click sounded and the door opened to reveal a half-awake Liam, the nearly extinguished torchlight in the hall illuminating the scars that marked the bare brown skin of his chest.

"Aya?" Liam muttered as he scrubbed a hand over his face. He blinked hard, his lips parting as his sleep-marred gaze focused on her. "Fucking hells," he breathed, his eyes tracing her blood-splattered face and fighting leathers. A muscle in his jaw jumped as he took in her blood-soaked hands. "What happened?" he asked sharply.

You promised.

Eryx had shouted the words over and over as she opted to use her knife instead of her affinity. She *had* promised— and she had stuck to that promise. He had retained all of his appendages. But that didn't stop her from slicing her knife into other vulnerable parts of him; it didn't stop her from wrenching the truth from him and then continuing to cut him open anyway, just so she could release a bit of that rage that threatened to obliterate the careful hold she kept on the pieces of herself.

"I need your help," Aya murmured.

She *had* promised.

Eryx had kept his appendages.

He had even kept his worthless fucking life.

"I need to kill Mathias Denier."

65

WILL HAD ALWAYS FOUND LIFE AT SEA TO BE TEDIOUS. He thanked the gods he wasn't born a Caeli, who often spent their lives like Aya's mother, Eliza, manipulating the winds for the ships of trade. There were four on his ship now who took turns doing it.

"Not much for me to do though," one had admitted to him. "The currents are in our favor, even for this time of year. We'll make fast time." Will wasn't exactly sure when that conversation had happened. It was sometime within the last ten days, but he was losing time the longer he was greeted with the same endless blue of the Anath Sea. He hadn't been sleeping well, especially so the further south they traveled. The heat had settled in days ago, like a warm, suffocating blanket he couldn't rid himself of. It made the paper-thin sheets, already uncomfortable, stick to his skin as he tossed and turned on the stiff mattress.

And while he'd traveled enough to expect the heavy warmth that was typical of the region, Will still loathed it. It set him on edge, until he couldn't tell if his racing heart was from the inescapable heat or some sense of foreboding he couldn't quite explain.

Perhaps he was simply bitter that *this* trip, while far shorter than his and Aya's three-week journey, didn't include the distractions he'd become particularly fond of the last time he was crossing the sea. When he'd finally succumbed to sleep's call last night, he'd dreamt of one such activity and had woken up with a raging hard-on that he'd had to tend to himself.

At least today they'd be arriving in Milsaio. He'd seen the fourth and third islands, the two furthest to the north, through his small porthole this morning.

Will had visited King Sarhash a few times over the last several years, and he was looking forward to the luxuries of his palace on the second island. The man was a gracious host, and a warm bath and a comfortable bed would be welcome after the last week.

Even though he'd much rather be home with Aya.

He didn't need a soft bed or warm water or the cool, crisp breeze of the mountains then to feel settled. To feel *joy*. He was certain he could be in the bowels of the seven hells with her and still feel at peace.

Will let out an aggravated sigh as he dropped the book he was attempting to read in his lap. The hammock where he lay swung gently with the movement of the ship, and he'd hoped either that or the book—nonfiction, which he despised, but was all that the first mate had—would lull him to sleep.

No such luck.

He wondered what Aya was doing now; what *Gianna* had done after he had left, now that she knew the truth about the two of them and the suspicions he had held.

Still hold, he reminded himself as he gazed at the horizon. Not that he had been able to prove anything. Gods, what a fucking waste his plan had been. Gianna had manipulated him at every step, and it *burned* to think how great a fool he had been.

You know what I'll miss most? Watching you whore yourself to me knowing you drop to your knees for her.

Fucking hells.

Another aggravated noise punched from Will's lungs as he rolled out of the hammock. He went to reach for his sword, which was leaning against the wall beside him, resigned to working out his frustration by sparring on the main deck until they arrived, but he paused, a strange scent catching on the sea breeze.

Will frowned and turned toward the helm of the ship.

It smelled like…smoke.

He jogged up the steps, his eyes searing in the sudden brightness as he hit the main deck. There were people clustered at the helm, and Will pushed through the soldiers there until he reached the railing, Akeeta at his side.

"My gods," he breathed.

He could see King Sarhash's palace in the distance. He would know the towering structure, designed specifically to be seen from afar by those who approached, anywhere. Four great towers, brilliantly white and topped with gold, twisting spires that seemed to pierce the Beyond, framed a towering curved palace that looked like an oval sliced in half and placed precariously on a mountain.

It was the marker of the king of the Anath Sea.

And it was burning.

Those beautiful towers were alight with flames—flames that leaped into the air like grotesque shooting stars. And on the island itself…not one, not two, but four columns of black smoke billowed into the air, coating the salt smell of the sea breeze with thick sulfur.

Will had seen Aya become a human torch. He'd witnessed the towering bonfires on the beaches of Rinnia, had felt the heat bask across his skin the closer he got.

But he had never seen fire like this.

Milsaio was burning.

Which meant they were too late.

Kakos had arrived.

The main deck was a maelstrom of rushing warriors assembling their gear as Will shouted out instructions. "The first twenty-five are with me! The second, approach from the north!"

He fastened his armor over his fighting leathers, his helmet at his feet as he surveyed the islands once more. There was a line of ships to the south—Midland ships, stolen during the massacre that had brought him here. Gods, there were at least ten by Will's count. Where were Sarhash's? His warriors were skilled at sea, their naval combat second to none. Had they already been destroyed? Surely the first island must have seen Kakos approach. Had the ostracized kingdom taken that island first? Or had they come straight for the capital, knowing that the burning palace would send a message to those at sea who might see it on the horizon?

Will grabbed two of the Caeli rushing past him. "Go straight to the third island and send a call for aid to Tala and Trahir."

He suspected Sarhash had already sent the warning to his own people, but...

"Then ensure the remaining two islands are ready for attack. Recruit all who can fight."

The Caeli nodded before sprinting to the smallest skiff. The messenger boats that ferried between the kingdoms were even smaller. With a Caeli on board...

They could make it to Dunmeaden and Rinnia far faster than anyone else.

But would it be fast enough?

Will picked up his helmet, his nose stinging with the growing smell of smoke as he shoved the doubt down, but his mind, flipping through battle strategies, brought it roaring back. He only had three Auqin with him. Between their water affinity and the remaining two Caeli, it would not be enough to help Sarhash's army smother those flames.

Just as fifty soldiers would not be enough to change the tide of this attack.

Aid will come. We need only delay until it arrives.

He gripped the thought and tugged, planting it firmly in his mind as he let the adrenaline of the impending fight become razor-sharp in his blood.

He would not fail here.

He *could* not fail here.

He had someone to return home to. Someone who was waiting for him, counting on him.

Will jumped into the skiff with his unit, one hand gripping Akeeta's scruff and the other gripping the edge tightly to maintain their balance as the boat dropped quickly into the sea.

"Oars in," he commanded the soldiers. They would not row. Not with the Caeli and Auqin at his back, who were already manipulating the wind and water to send them rushing toward the fight.

Will tugged on his helmet and willed his breathing to remain steady and calm. But his pulse was racing, racing as fast as they were across the waves. What would greet them once they reached the beach? What horrors had Kakos accomplished in their time there, alone and undisturbed?

The flames grew larger, the closer they got to the island, but that wasn't what had Will's stomach churning, dread weighing him down more than the heavy armor he wore. No, it was the screams that they could now hear. The screams of the dying, so shrill that they couldn't be warriors, but had to be citizens.

Families.

Fathers and sons and wives and daughters being slaughtered in droves.

Aid will come. Aid will *come.*

Will didn't pray often, but he sent up a silent prayer now to Pathos, to Mora, to whichever god deigned to hear his plea as he and his troops headed toward the heart of the fire.

# 66

DEATH HAD A PARTICULAR SCENT. WHETHER CAUSED BY sickness or violence or accident, the reek was the same. It invaded the senses and took up residence, until it was the only thing one could smell. Will had been smelling death for three days.

"Where is your king?" he had barked at the first commanding officer he'd found when he and his unit stormed the beach. The woman had pointed wordlessly at the burning palace.

The palace that was *still* somehow burning, as if the Incend flames that had been set to it were not Incend flames at all, but something far, far worse.

He supposed they were.

Because Kakos had come, with human soldiers and Visya warriors and Diaforaté—those who had managed to corrupt their affinity and create raw power. Will had seen his fair share of horrors over his lifetime. Hells, he had inflicted enough of them himself. But he had known no horror like facing a Diaforaté.

Their power, unpredictable and unstable, had no rhyme or reason. There was no possible way to anticipate which nightmare they might evoke, or how strong it would be, or which corrupted affinity they would wield next. Facing one was like facing nine ordinary Visya.

Perhaps that was why, slowly but surely, the capital was falling.

Will wiped dirt and grime from his face, retrieving the knife he'd buried in the temple of one of Kakos's human warriors. Another was sprinting toward him, but Akeeta was there, her teeth digging into the exposed part of his leg. The man screamed and fell to his knees. Will sent a pulse of power, nothing but pure pain and *death*, and the man's heart stopped, his eyes blown wide in terror. He slumped over with a sickening thud.

Will shoved his own pain down, his shield frayed at the edges from such prolonged use of his affinity and the intense sensations around him. Akeeta met his gaze between the slit in his helmet, her white maw stained red with blood.

Aid will come. Aid will come.

Screams erupted from behind Will, and he whirled on the spot, looking for the threat. He saw a woman standing before a storefront, a sword she had clearly never spent a day learning how to wield dangling uselessly in her hand as she screamed and screamed, her eyes fixed on the palace.

Will followed her gaze as the screams seemed to ripple outward through the town center as more and more people realized what they were looking at.

A man had climbed the iron gate that rimmed the palace, visible from streets away. He was thrusting something onto one of the pikes, something round and gray but also glinting in the sunlight.

"Fucking hells," Will breathed.

It was a head.

The queen's head.

Leanora was staring unseeingly at her capital, her mouth still open in a scream of terror. And the glinting was her silver crown, which the man had put atop her head.

Will stared for just a moment longer, long enough to see an arrow loose through the air and lodge itself in the man's neck, killing him before the fall ever did.

And then Will was staring at the ground, his body hunched over as he hurled.

He found himself in a makeshift war tent that night, a heavy silence hanging in the space. Kiara, the commander he'd met on the beach, was staring blankly at a map. Her black skin was ashen in the low firelight, her eyes dull.

"It's time to relinquish the capital," she finally murmured, breaking the silence. A third of their forces had retreated north the day before Will arrived, readying the next two islands after the first fell. They'd taken as many citizens from the capital as they could, but...

Not enough.

They hadn't taken enough.

"And what of the remaining citizens here?" Will asked, rubbing a hand down his dirt-streaked face. Kiara fixed him with a grim look.

"We are not one island, Enforcer. We will *all* be slaughtered if we remain here. We have lost this fight. The terrain on the third island is more rugged. We will have the advantage there."

Will bit back a bitter curse. Had he known, he would have sent the other half of his unit there. They hadn't made it to the capital city yet and he didn't want to think about what that meant for the souls he'd sent to the northern end of the second island. He only hoped their delay was because they were traversing the mountainous terrain. He wasn't certain how long it would take to reach the other side of the island—or where they had even come in.

Kiara dragged a finger across the map between them and indicated the northernmost point on the western side of the island. "We need to get to the northern port. We have reserve ships there we can take to the third island. It's a three-day journey if we leave at first light."

"And what of the king?" one of the warriors to Will's left asked.

Kiara's throat bobbed, even as her hands fisted at her sides. "The king knows the benefit of a strategic maneuver, and he is relying on us to preserve our *kingdom*. We leave tomorrow," she said curtly.

She could call this whatever she wanted, but Will knew exactly what it was:

A retreat, because the first island had already fallen, and so had the capital. A delay, because his call for aid would not be heeded in time to save them here.

A desperate attempt, because none of them wanted to die on this godsforsaken island.

He wouldn't argue with it, though. Especially because he was sure Kiara had come to the same conclusion he had as soon as he saw Leanora's head on the pike.

There was no reason to fight for the palace.

King Sarhash was likely dead.

 **67**

THE WAILS OF DEATH FOLLOWED WILL FOR THREE DAYS AS he journeyed north with the Milsaion troops and the remainder of his unit. Seven souls—he'd already lost seven souls, and that said nothing of the second unit he'd sent to the approach from the north.

The further they trudged across the mountainous terrain, the heat unbearable now that they were far from the ocean breeze, the more he came to terms with the fact that they were probably all dead.

And that the aid he had desperately begged for would not come.

Or would be too late.

I will not die here.

It was a steady refrain that kept his feet moving forward, over dust and rock and dirt and sand.

I will not die here.

He had promised Aya he would return and he would not break that promise, not for anything in this godsforsaken realm. He *had* to return, because he had to tell her, at least once, that he loved her, that he would always love her, and that if the gods had truly decided their realm was lost, then he would find her in whatever came next.

And so he would not die here.

Yet as he sat in their makeshift camp on that third night, he couldn't help but wonder if the Divine had made up their minds completely. Because when the scout Kiara had sent to scope out the northern port returned pale-faced and breathless, Will knew their hope was waning before the scout even uttered those condemning words:

"Kakos is at the port."

"How many?" Kiara's question was sharp, her face set in grim determination.

"Equal to our numbers, easily."

"So we're outnumbered," one of the warriors piped up from her place at the fire. "Those Diaforaté with their hells-given power might as well count as double."

More, Will thought grimly as a murmur of agreement rippled around the fire. But he kept his face void of any doubt as he said, "If we strike in the middle of the night, we catch them unaware."

"Our forces need rest," Kiara argued.

"They'll get plenty of it when they're dead," Will shot back. "Which we all will be the longer we delay. The unit at the northern port could send a call for aid and have help here in hours with the ships they've stolen from your main port. Better that we do not give them the chance."

Kiara's jaw shifted as she considered his words, but their two options were clear: take a chance and risk death tonight, or meet it with certainty tomorrow.

"Prepare to advance!" Kiara shouted into the camp.

Will looked to where Akeeta lay beside him, her eyes set with that same grim determination he'd just seen on Kiara. "One more fight," he murmured to his bonded, his fingers running through the soft fur on the top of her head. "One more fight, and then we rest."

She sighed as she pushed herself into a seated position, her snout nudging his chin, as if to agree with him.

One more fight, and then they would rest.

68

AYA THREW HERSELF INTO PLANNING THE SAME WAY SHE once threw herself into her training for the Dyminara: relentlessly. Ruthlessly.

It was all-consuming, enough that it pushed the haunting conversation she'd had with Evie in her dream far from her mind. During her moments in the Synastysi, or in training, her sole focus was on making Mathias pay. She wasn't studying journal entries. She was reviewing what she'd garnered the night before of Mathias's nightly movements and planning which route she would take that evening as she followed him once more. She wasn't sparring with a fellow Dyminara. She was perfecting her form and mulling over which combination of her affinities would be best to debilitate anyone who got in her way when her plan finally fell into place.

She had to be careful. Strategic. Now was not the time for that leash she kept on her temper to snap. Mathias had not become the King of Dunmeaden's Underbelly by being an easy target. She would have one chance to avenge her father.

And so she leaned into that patience that Galda had drilled into her at an early age.

And while she wasn't going to risk her chance by rushing,

going to Liam *had* been a risk. But Aya wasn't foolish enough to try to take down the crime lord on her own.

"We should go to the Royal Guard," Liam had argued after tugging her into his room that morning. "They're tasked with the protection of this city from ordinary threats."

"No."

She hadn't explained her refusal, and, praise Saudra, Liam hadn't questioned it, nor had he asked why she'd sought *him* of all people to help her. She wasn't entirely sure either, other than the realization that she had no one else.

No one she could trust, anyway.

And so for nine days, they spied, and schemed, and argued, and eventually came up with something that even Liam, in all his caution, couldn't pick apart.

"You're sure tonight is the night?" Liam's question was a soft murmur as he took a sip of his water, his eyes fixed on the men sitting two tables away. They were two of Mathias's lackeys, and if Aya's information was correct, they'd be escorting their boss to the brothel tonight.

The brothel that Eryx had conveniently discovered was planning on cutting their payments to Mathias's guild.

A lie, but a necessary one Aya had forced him to plant.

She took a bite of her rice, the grains feeling coarse on her tongue. They'd been in the small restaurant—casual, for the Merchant Borough—for at least an hour, but she'd barely made a dent in her plate.

"If Eryx is to be believed, yes. He'll be going to the brothel tonight."

Liam cocked a brow. "Is he? What's stopping him from seeking retribution?" He glanced at her hands, as if he could still see the blood. Aya took a long drink from her own cup, letting the cold water soothe her nerves.

"It turns out his visit to the brothel wasn't a professional one," Aya replied. "It was personal." Eryx had confessed to his relationship with the girl under great duress—and it was

475

exactly what Aya needed to ensure he didn't betray them. Because if he did, and Aya survived… Well, she'd made him another promise that detailed exactly how slowly his beloved would die.

Liam's stare was long and too heavy for Aya's liking. "Don't tell me you've changed your mind," she remarked.

"No."

"Then what is it?"

The Persi frowned. "I'm wondering if such behavior is fit for a saint."

Perhaps, had it been a few weeks earlier, the statement would have stung. But Aya was tired of waiting, and if she'd learned anything about Evie, aside from the fact that she was utterly useless to Aya in her sleep, it was that the First Saint had *acted*. She had wiped battlefields clean. Had become enough of a threat that the Decachiré practitioners had feared her.

Perhaps it was time Aya started inspiring some fear of her own.

"Don't forget to get there early," she ordered as she finished off her glass of water, ignoring Liam's question entirely. "If the madam takes too long to persuade to let us do what we need to, we'll miss our chance at intercepting him."

The two men at the far table were paying their bill, and Aya wanted to ensure they didn't make any detours on their way back to the town house that was just one of Mathias's lairs—or between now and when the meeting was scheduled tonight.

Liam would take care of the unsuspecting madam—and be waiting when Mathias, and Aya, arrived.

"Aya," he murmured. "You're sure you want to do this?"

It was the same question he'd asked her for the last five days.

"Undoubtedly," she replied, her gaze following the men as they left the restaurant. She cut Liam a look. "Don't be late."

Aya lay in the crevice of the two adjoining roofs across from the town house the two men had entered an hour ago. Her black fighting leathers, which she'd changed into behind the complex, blended seamlessly into the black of the roof, aided by the dark that was creeping in the further they pushed past sunset.

It was nearly time, and so far, the goddess of fate had been kind to her. There was no unusual activity from the house across the street, and thanks to the bright Incend light and the endless nights she'd spent staking out this very home, she'd identified a shadow moving inside that she knew to be Mathias.

She let the subtle sounds of Dunmeaden coming to life at night soothe her as she continued to monitor the home, her thoughts drifting slowly to Will. She had expected Gianna to confront her—or at the very least, goad her into confirming what the queen already knew. But Aya had hardly seen her since Will left thirteen days ago.

Her silence was far more unnerving.

Aya shifted slightly, her body aching from lying on the hard surface for so long. But the bells had just rung ten, which meant any moment now, Mathias and his cronies would be making their way to the brothel. Eyrx had set the meeting early enough that they could slip away into the crowds once it was done, but late enough that any noise Aya couldn't mask with her Caeli affinity would be drowned out by the grunts and moans of the patrons visiting the establishment.

"Come on," Aya breathed. She was getting antsy the longer past ten she lay there. Had Liam persuaded the madam to cooperate? Was he waiting in her lavish office?

Suddenly, movement on the street caught Aya's eye. She leaned further over the edge of the roof, craning to see through the dark. Someone was definitely there, and they were heading toward the town house.

"Godsdammit," Aya swore as it stepped under the light of one of the posts.

It wasn't a person. It was a wolf, its coat as black as night. Aster—Tova's bonded. And by the looks of it, she'd caught the scent of something.

Her.

Aya cursed herself for leaving her clothes behind the pile of abandoned boxes and crates at the back of the building. She pushed herself up from her place on the roof, crawling slowly toward the fire escape she'd climbed. She was down it in mere seconds, her boots hitting the ground with a quiet thud.

It was enough to bring Aster down the side street—but she wasn't alone. Because just as the Athatis spotted her, her ears perking in friendly recognition, Tova appeared behind her, her brow furrowed as she snapped, "Where the hells have you been?"

"You can't be here right now," Aya urged.

"I've been looking for you for hours," Tova continued as if Aya hadn't even spoken. "I couldn't find you anywhere. What are you doing out here?"

"Wait, you sent your fucking wolf after me?" Aster looked affronted by Aya's condemnation, but Aya ignored her. "I don't need to keep you apprised of my whereabouts."

Tova cocked her head, anger glinting in her gaze. "Would you have preferred I sent the Guard?"

Aya hadn't realized how close they'd gotten to each other in their argument until she was tilting her head to meet Tova's glare with one of her own, her fists curling at her sides. Gods, she could punch her.

"You cannot be here right now." The words were spat through gritted teeth.

But Tova didn't budge. "Why not?"

"Godsdammit, Tova!" Aya cut a look at the street. Mathias would be leaving any moment, and if he saw Aster, their whole plan was ruined. She ground her teeth as she looked back at her. "Send Aster away," she muttered hurriedly. Tova blinked, and Aya let out another low curse. "Send her away and I'll tell you what's going on."

Tova only hesitated a moment more before nodding to Aster, "Go."

The wolf took off into the night. Tova folded her arms and looked at Aya expectantly.

"Mathias is the one who attacked my father."

Tova's mouth parted in surprise, some of the color draining from her face. "How do you know?"

Aya shook her head. "I don't have time to fill you in on the specifics," she grumbled as she pushed past Tova. She glanced around the corner, into the street, a wave of relief washing through her as she saw the shadows were still in the town-house window.

They hadn't left yet. And hopefully they hadn't seen Aster either.

Tova grabbed her arm and tugged her back, stepping in front of her to block Aya in. "Make time."

Aya inhaled deeply. She had long appreciated Tova's stubbornness, but that was before it had been turned on her to such a degree. If Tova ruined this for her...

"He had gambling debts. I have a source on the inside who confirmed it," she gritted out, peering past Tova to the door. Tova followed her gaze, her eyes narrowing as she looked from the house to Aya and back again.

"If you already know, then why are you..." Tova's voice trailed off as it dawned on her. The color leached from her face further. "You're going to kill him," she said softly.

The door across the street clicked open. Aya tugged up her scarf, but Tova shifted, continuing to block her in.

"Get out of my way, Tova."

"Have you lost your mind?" Tova seethed. "If this goes wrong, he will murder you, saint or not. And he'll do it slowly."

Something died in Aya as her hand shifted to the knife at

her hip, her gaze steady on her longest—and only—friend. She had never thought she would find herself here, standing opposite Tova, her fingers brushing the handle of her knife, her meaning clear.

But as much as it destroyed Aya, she would do it. If Tova did not move, Aya would make her.

Tova's eyes tracked to the knife, then back to Aya's. There was a flash of hurt, but Tova buried it almost instantly behind bitter resignation.

"I'm coming with you," she murmured.

Aya went to argue, but there wasn't time. Mathias and his men were heading away from them down the street, and she couldn't let them get too far ahead.

She gave Tova a long, hard look. "Stay hidden," she ordered.

The brothel was conveniently situated on the main drag of the Rouline, facing the docks. Aya had chosen the location purposefully, knowing the heavy crowds making their way to the gambling halls and brothels and bars would offer further cover should she and Liam—and now Tova—need it. She and Tova kept to the back streets for now, using the connecting alleys to check their pace against Mathias and his men.

She could see Tova's jaw shifting as she bit back her questions. But she remained silent until they reached the back of the brothel, which looked more like a two-story home set among the more polished buildings in this particular stretch of the Rouline.

"So what's our plan?" Tova asked.

Aya raised a brow. "Our?"

Tova looked offended.

Aya glanced up at the second story, marking the window Liam should have unlocked for her. "When's the last time you were here?" she muttered.

"Maybe a month ago? You know this is the only establishment worthy of anyone's coin."

"So it won't be unusual when you use the front door," Aya remarked as she scanned Tova's attire, thanking the gods for her friend's preference for overdressing. She wasn't as dolled up as she might be on a typical night out, but one might believe she had ducked in unexpectedly.

Tova frowned in contemplation, but Aya pressed on. "Guard the front door. If Mathias or his men try to leave, stop them."

"Where will you be?" Tova asked as Aya began to scale the wall. Aya didn't respond, and by the time she reached the window, Tova had gone.

Aya let out a silent breath as the window clicked open. She was inside in the next moment, her boots landing silently on the carpeted floor of the empty bedroom. She scrunched her nose at the overpowering smell of flowers, placed bountifully throughout the establishment and coated with perfume to mask the smell of sex, but she didn't break her stride as she moved toward the door to the hallway.

Everything tonight depended on timing. If Mathias was too late to the meeting, Aya risked being seen by one of the courtesans and their clients as she made her way down to the first floor. And if she hadn't gotten through the window fast enough…

She would be too late. Liam was an excellent fighter, but she wasn't sure he could take Mathias and two of his men.

Aya crept down the staircase, keeping to the shadows that darkened the wall. The sitting room was full of patrons and courtesans milling about, and between their chatter and the music and the servers passing around wine or something stronger for those who needed it, Aya was able to slip into the hallway on the other side of the wall undetected.

And there, just a few strides ahead of her, were Mathias and his men, being led to the back office by the madam, who was unaccompanied.

481

Liam had been successful in his persuasion, then.

Take the meeting. Do not call for help. When you get to the office, let the men in first, ignore the Dyminara behind them, and close the door. Lock it. Do not come back to your office tonight.

Aya's victory tasted like vicious vengeance.

The madam laid a hand on the ornate iron door handle. She took her time unlocking her office, her face calm as she tugged the door open and motioned for the men to step inside. Mathias went first. Then his first crony. Then the second.

And then Aya was inside, not bothering to see if the persuasion held as she lunged for the man to the right. Her hand muffled his shout as she dragged the blade across his throat. His body hit the floor as the door behind her closed and locked.

She heard the other man's gurgle of death, Liam's grim face appearing from the shadows, his knife dripping with blood.

Mathias whirled, a knife already in his hand, his other reaching for Aya. He grabbed her leathers, tugging her toward him, and Aya ducked as he brought his knife down toward her chest. She slammed her elbow into his arm as she flipped her knife in her other hand, cracking the butt of the handle against his face.

Mathias let out a groan, his grip on her leathers instantly releasing as he stumbled backward, clutching his broken nose. Liam didn't give him a spare moment. The Persi grabbed Mathias's arms, twisting them behind his back and locking them into place as Aya twirled her knife again.

And though the crime lord struggled, he was no match for Liam's strength. Aya stepped over one of his fallen men just as the puddle of his blood reached her boots. She stalked toward Mathias slowly, stopping just in front of him. She grabbed a fistful of his silver hair, her grip tight as she wrenched his head back and placed her blade at his throat.

"You've been found guilty of attacking an innocent of Dunmeaden," Aya growled.

Mathias grinned through his panting breath, blood still streaming from his nose. "Don't I get a trial?"

Aya tightened her grip on his hair, tilting his head further back as she hissed, "The gods will judge your soul, Mathias."

Mathias merely chuckled, the sound dark and dangerous as it vibrated against the arm she had pressed against his chest. "My my, this *is* unbecoming of our savior." His teeth were coated in blood as he grinned again. "You may have everyone else fooled, Aya, but I know your true nature."

"Keep talking, Mathias," Aya cooed softly. "Let's see which idiocy you murmur is your last."

Inexplicably, the crime lord laughed again. Aya felt Liam's eyes on her, but she kept her focus on Mathias and that glint in his eye. She pressed the blade tighter to his skin. "You think I won't do it?" she asked, the handle of her knife biting into her hand as she gripped it harder. "I found my father in a pool of his own blood," she seethed, relishing in the thin line of red that blossomed beneath her blade. "He may never wake up, thanks to you."

Mathias tried to lift his chin to escape her blade, but she twisted his hair tighter in her fingers, making his eyes water. "Regrettable, truly," he panted, wincing against her hold. "But I only asked them to send a message, my dear. Not kill him."

"Then perhaps you should have been more specific," Aya snarled. "I'm sure someone will deign to let your people know that you paid for such carelessness with your life."

Mathias struggled to look down, straining to hold her gaze as she tilted his head back further. "You don't want to kill me," he rasped, that glint still in his eyes.

Even in death, the man was as oily as a snake. Insufferably so.

"Give me one good reason," Aya challenged.

Mathias's grin was something out of a nightmare. "Because I have your supplier."

Silence, tense and deadly, followed his words. Aya's hand shook as she kept that blade against his throat. "You're lying."

"I swear it on my life. And you know exactly how much I value my own life."

"Aya..." Liam's grumbled warning went ignored as she yanked Mathias's head back further.

"You're fucking lying!"

Mathias chuckled. "Are you willing to bet everything on that, Aya dear? I *love* a gamble, but even I must say, these odds are a stretch, are they not?"

He was lying. He *had* to be lying. There was no indication that the crime lord or his circle was involved in the illegal trades with Kakos. They had looked into it—she, Tova and Will had *all* looked into it before she left for Trahir.

"You just want to save your miserable life," Aya snarled.

Mathias blinked, the grin fading from his face. "I do," he replied earnestly. "So why would I lie to you?"

"*Aya*," Liam urged again, but Aya was still fixated on Mathias, her mind racing as she turned his logic over and over.

I could force him to tell the truth.

The idea came unbidden and she seized it, not questioning whether it was right or wrong or if the gods would approve of such use of the power they had given her.

She pushed her persuasion affinity forward until it wrapped around whatever essence was in humans, and she *tugged* and *forced* until she knew she could rip the truth from his lips as brutally as if she'd used a knife.

"Do you have the supplier?" Aya growled.

"Yes." The word was a hiss, and it was followed with a dribble of blood from Mathias's mouth.

"Enough!" Liam snarled as he jerked Mathias backward, out of Aya's grip. It was enough to snap Aya's power back into herself. "If this is true, we need him alive," Liam reminded her, his eyes tight in warning.

It's true, she wanted to say. But she swallowed the confession and instead locked her jaw and looked at Mathias. "Bring the supplier to us."

That dark chuckle was back, and it brushed against her spine in the worst way. "You think I would bring him here? You think I went through all of this to parade him through town?"

Aya bit back a curse. "The warehouse then. You know the one."

Mathias considered her for a moment before he conceded. "Consider it done."

69

W HAT THE HELLS HAPPENED?" TOVA MUTTERED AS AYA came storming through the reception room of the brothel, Mathias at her heels.

"Good evening, General," Mathias drawled. "If you'll excuse us…"

Tova stepped in front of them, her jaw tight, but Aya jerked her chin to the side. "It's alright, Tova." Her friend inhaled, readying her argument, but Aya continued, "I'll explain outside."

Reluctantly, Tova stepped aside, but she didn't go far. She fell into step behind Mathias, her arms crossing when they came to a halt on the street.

"Three quarters of an hour, Mathias. If you're not in the warehouse with him by then, Liam and I start killing your people. You saw exactly what we are capable of with your men inside."

"Such *violence*." Mathias clucked. He placed a hand under her chin, tilting her head up so he could inspect her face. "I still think sainthood is wasted on you, Aya dear."

"The clock is ticking," Aya snarled as she ripped her face from his grip. The crime lord winked before he turned on his heel, taking up a happy whistling song as he strolled off into the night. Tova stared at Aya expectantly, and Aya nodded toward an empty ship's bay. The street was still crowded with those seeking entertainment for the evening. It would not do to cause a scene right here.

Aya waited until she and Tova were seated on the dock, their legs dangling over the water, before she spoke, her voice low.

"He says he has the supplier."

Tova stared, her lack of response heavy with bitter disbelief. "You can't be serious," she finally scoffed when she realized Aya wasn't going to expand upon her explanation. "You think Mathias has the very supplier we've been combing Dunmeaden for?"

"Would you rather I kill him and risk us never knowing? This could be the missing piece to everything."

"If he does have the supplier, we should be alerting the rest of the Dyminara, or the guard, or *something*," Tova argued.

But Aya shook her head. "Will suspected that Gianna was involved in the trade somehow. If I can question the supplier—"

"Oh, *Will* suspected." Tova cut her off with a bitter laugh. "How I could I argue with that, then? I swear I don't even *know* you anymore."

Aya let out a long, hard breath.

Tova didn't understand—of course she didn't. Aya needed to be patient, needed to find a way to undo this damage. And yet she couldn't help the question that slipped from her lips. "Why are you here?"

Her voice was as quiet as the water brushing against the wood of the docks. She could feel Tova's gaze on her, could see her moon-white hair from her peripheral vision, but she kept staring ahead, too much of a coward to meet her gaze.

"How could you ask me that?" Tova's question was equally soft, not with hesitation, but with hurt. "You are family. That…that fucking cretin attacked my *family*. Where the hells else would I be?"

Aya swallowed the lump in her throat. "I wasn't sure you still felt that way."

"On my oath, Aya. I said I needed time. This…this *thing* you have with Will," Tova's fingers fluttered as she reached for a term she wouldn't say. "It hurts me. *You* hurt me. And I can see the appeal, okay? But I'm never going to be okay with it. He *tortured* me, Aya. And the fact that you believe him, *trust* him over me—"

"It's not like that," Aya rasped. But it *was* in a way, wasn't it? She had made excuses for why her friend was lying, but she had still chalked it up to a lie.

Because she had never imagined an alternative. And now that she knew there could be another explanation, a horrific explanation, she hated that she had doubted her friend.

"Then what is it like?" Tova pressed, her hand falling on top of Aya's. "Please, explain it to me. Help me understand."

She couldn't. She didn't know how.

Control. The word echoed in Aya's mind as her emotions threatened to obliterate her. She was burying too much—she was trying to *contain* too much.

Gods, how she longed for the days when all she'd felt was that coldness. Perhaps it was rotting her, but it had to be better than *this*.

Evie had been right. Love did weaken them.

"Aya," Tova urged, squeezing her hand. "Talk to me." Tova's voice cracked with the request, and it was enough to have Aya meeting her gaze.

She swallowed the lump in her throat. But there were footsteps on the dock, and suddenly Liam was towering over them, his face lined with exhaustion. "It's time," he murmured.

"Did you clean up the blood?" Liam's question was a soft exhale as they approached the abandoned warehouse on the outskirts of the Rouline.

"It'll blend in with the rest of the stains," Aya muttered. It wasn't as though she was the first to use the warehouse in such a way. It was the Dyminara's unofficial questioning location of sorts. At least for those they hadn't decided to take to the dungeons yet.

Besides, Liam wasn't one to lecture. He'd done his fair share in the name of his oath.

"How much time does he have left?" Aya asked as they stepped into the warehouse. The space was dark save for the moonlight that streamed in between the rafters from the hole in the ceiling. It illuminated the iron chair that sat in the center of the room—a grotesque throne, of sorts.

"Ten minutes," Liam answered, his mouth set in a grim line.

Tova, who had remained unusually silent on their walk to the warehouse, set about lighting the torches in rusted sconces on the walls. It brought the other features of the room to light:

The cement floor, with all its stains, Eryx's the freshest and most evident of all. His blood had dried, looking like a makeshift burgundy rug upon which the chair sat. The wooden walls were still cracked and moldy from years of neglect, the windows broken. But it didn't matter—no one frequented this part of town. The Dyminara had made sure of it.

Tova folded her arms and leaned back against one of the decrepit walls, her face set in a mask of concentration. She looked every bit the general she was as she said, "I assume you will take the lead?" The question was directed at Aya—no malice, no judgment, just strategy. Aya dipped her chin just as a knock sounded on the warehouse door.

Liam cracked it open. From her place in the center of the room, Aya could see Mathias's smirking face. "As promised," he drawled.

Liam opened the door fully, and Mathias and another man stepped inside. He was old, his skin weathered and hair white. And yet for someone who had supposedly been in hiding for the last several months, he certainly looked well kept. His hair was neatly combed and parted, his clothes modest but well pressed.

Mathias took care of his fugitives, it would seem.

The man took a single look at Aya and froze, his eyes lighting in recognition as he took in her fighting leathers. "You're delivering me to the queen," he said to Mathias, a tremor in his voice.

"That remains to be seen," Tova growled from her place against the wall. Aya cut her a look before motioning for the man to sit.

But he stayed frozen to the spot, his eyes wide in terror. "She'll kill me," he stammered. "She'll kill me!"

"I take it death doesn't appeal to you," Aya remarked, her persuasion reaching for the man. He was human—gods, this would be easy. Like her interaction with Mathias, she didn't feel a lick of guilt as she closed her affinity around him like a vise.

She tugged on that will to live as she ordered, "Sit. Let's talk."

The man walked forward steadily, his face blanched of all color. But he did sit, and Aya sent up a silent thank-you to Saudra that she didn't have to push her affinity any harder.

"What's your name?"

"Charles. Charles Bozzelli." Charles's voice shook so hard that Aya didn't think as she reached for her Sensainos affinity, cloaking the man in a blanket of calm. His shoulders loosened, his body slouching slightly in his chair.

"How did you get entangled with Kakos?"

Charles leaned forward in his chair, his eyes wide. "I didn't. I swear it to the gods, I didn't."

"And yet you were going to supply the two tradesmen from Trahir with weapons for the Southern Kingdom, were you not?"

Charles shook his head vehemently. "I met the two tradesmen in one of the gambling halls. I knew from their accents they were from Trahir, but I had no idea..." His voice trailed off, his throat bobbing as sweat beaded on his brow. Aya pushed her Sensainos affinity harder, and the man let out a long breath.

"We built up a friendship of sorts. Got to talking about ways we could make more coin. I had done a few deals outside the Council, but Mathias always covered my tracks. They weren't large enough to warrant attention, anyway."

Aya frowned. She believed he wasn't a major supplier. He would have been on their radar if he were. Then again, there were plenty of people who specialized in several areas of trade.

"Why would Mathias protect you?" she questioned.

Charles glanced at Mathias. "I gave him a cut of my business."

Aya looked to the crime lord, who gave a small shrug. "Passive income," he said with a serpentine smile.

Aya swallowed her retort. "Go on," she encouraged the man.

"One night, we were drunk, see, and they got loose-lipped about a plan they were brewing. Said Kakos would pay big money to get their hands on weapons. Would have me set for life." He wiped the sweat from his brow, his leg bouncing anxiously as he continued. "Now I wanted to deepen my pockets, sure. And I won't lie to you—not having to work the welding anymore sounded like a blessing from the gods. But I'm no heretic. So I went to the queen."

From the corner of her eye, Aya saw Tova take a step forward. Aya held out a hand to stay her, her gaze remaining fixed on the man's face, even as she went inward, into that well of power. It was pushing versus pulling—the difference between manipulating a sensation and opening herself to it. She let the man's emotions rush into her, sensing his fear, but also his desperation, his will to survive.

"What did Gianna say?" Aya asked.

"She thanked me for my commitment to keeping our realm safe," the man explained, his eyes wide and earnest. "She told me to set another meeting. An ambush on the tradesmen, you see. She said she would keep me safe, and that while the tradesmen would think they were meeting with an interested supplier, really they'd meet the Dyminara. She put me up in a hotel and set a Royal Guard there to guard me."

Aya's body went cold.

"Ronan," she breathed.

He had been assigned to the attack with her, but had never showed. He was found dead in a hotel room days later.

The man nodded. "A few days before the meeting, someone showed up at the hotel. She said the queen needed me moved, but Ronan wasn't having it. He had received no such orders. Something was just...off about it all. They got into an argument about it, and she...she killed him." The man took a quivering breath. "I knew then that the queen never intended on keeping me alive. Whoever she had sent wasn't relocating me. She was tying up a loose end. So I ran as fast as I could and I went straight to Mathias. Offered him every penny I had to hide me."

"Why stay in Dunmeaden?" Liam asked.

Charles shrugged. "I knew she was looking for me. Besides, I had nowhere else to go."

Aya shook her head slowly. "That's why Gianna wanted to find you so badly. Because you knew that she had knowledge of Dominic's betrayal. And instead of outing him to the realm, she used his tradesmen to try to publicly manipulate him into joining the war."

Liam swore softly from behind her, but it was Tova who said, "This can't be true. Why would she send you there knowing Dominic had sided with Kakos?"

But Aya could *feel* it. Every word the man was uttering, unbelievable as it was, was true. "Perhaps she didn't know how far in he was," Aya murmured. "Maybe she thought we could turn him."

"This is foolish," Tova argued, but Aya met her ferocity with her own as she snapped back, "I can *feel* his truth. And it explains exactly how those papers ended up planted on you, doesn't it? Gianna had them. For fuck's sakes, she *had* them!"

Will had been right. Gianna had been at the heart of it all. Aya clenched her teeth as she turned back to Charles and asked, "Did you get a look at the woman who came to your hotel that day? Can you describe her to us?"

Charles nodded. "I don't remember her name, but I see her face easily enough in my nightmares. She was average height, with brown skin," he explained. "A square jaw, brown eyes, black hair in a tight bun."

Aya dragged her gaze to Liam, the silence in the room pressing against her skin. His face had gone slack, his lips parted in shock, or perhaps horror, as he rasped the name they were all thinking, but didn't want to say.

"Lena."

Aya forced down her dread, even as it clawed at her throat. "Lena was in the dungeons the day I found Will. She knew about the questionings. She's been *leading* the search," Aya said, her gaze still fixed on Liam.

That was how Lena had known about her and Will. It wasn't Tova confirming it to Gianna. Lena had been involved all along.

Gods, she could even have overheard Will ranting on about finding how Gianna was connected to it all when he was trying to get Aya to *listen.*

Tova's face paled as she looked between Aya and Liam. "If a member of the Dyminara is involved in this…who the hells can we trust?"

No one, Aya thought bitterly.

They could trust no one.

70

I AM GOING TO DIE HERE.

The thought came as Will ducked behind a blown-apart piece of the sea wall, his body aching as fire rippled above his head. He had no way to track how long they'd been fighting to get to the ships save for the sun's position in the sky.

It had been fully dark when they'd charged the port. Now, all he could see was the blinding light of the sun high in the deceivingly clear blue sky.

It would be a beautiful day if it weren't for the blood and the death.

Will took a second to steady his breath, which came in uneven pants, his hand trembling as he pressed it to his leg. He'd gotten burned by one of the Diaforaté. He didn't know when. But the skin on his thigh was red, and bloody, and raw, and pain ripped through him so intensely that his head swam for a moment before he blinked it away.

He looked down the wall to see Akeeta, her white fur coated with dirt and blood, approaching him. Even his bonded looked weary, defeated.

The wall at his back shuddered as the Diaforaté he'd

dodged slammed a gust of wind into it, crumbling the rock just beside him.

I am going to die here.

Perhaps Akeeta could read his mind. Because she stilled in her approach, only for a second, before she started running, her blue eyes narrowing in concentration.

She was over the wall before Will could murmur a single command.

"No," Will croaked. Akeeta was too tired, too spent, to continue on like this.

He shoved himself up, a groan of pain punching from his lungs as he gritted his teeth against it and threw himself around the wall. The Diaforaté, his flesh rotting on the side of his face, lifted a hand toward Will's wolf. Visya affinity was supposedly useless against the Athatis, who were imbued with their own sort of magic, but Will had learned through Aya that raw power did not abide by the laws of the gods. He threw a knife as hard as he could, catching the man in his chest. It was enough that he stumbled back, arm still outstretched as Akeeta ripped into his neck. Will barely had a moment to ensure Akeeta was unharmed before he was turning to send a pulse of his affinity toward another Kakos fighter—a normal Visya, it seemed—who was locked in a duel with one of the Milsaion troops.

Will gritted his teeth against the pain he inflicted—the pain he felt—as he shattered her shield and sent the woman to her knees. The Milsaion warrior brought his sword down in a vicious arc, and the woman's head rolled.

Another round of shouts rippled across the fighting, Kiara's voice rising above it all. "They've brought reinforcements!"

Will's breath was shallow now, more of a rasp than anything else as he looked at the sea. Another ship was approaching from the opposite side of the island, and it had Will's gut twisting as hopelessness settled over him.

He couldn't outfight a new wave of soldiers. His shield

was in tatters, his affinity waning, especially with his injuries; calling his power forward felt like scraping against his insides, dredging up what little magic was left.

I am going to die here.

But they had gained ground, had gotten closer to the dock. He needed to hold on. He needed to hold on, just for one more fight…

"To the sixth ship!" The general's cry somehow rose above the din of the dying. Will's head felt like a weight as he lifted it and scanned the docks, his breath rushing from his lungs as he caught sight of the warships docked there, their flags flying high.

The first three were on fire.

Kakos was destroying their last chance of escape—was sacrificing their troops to hold them off while a small group was killing their last hope, while they waited for their fellow heretics to arrive and finish the Milsaions off for good.

Will watched as those warriors leaped from the third ship and started moving toward the fourth. He whistled to Akeeta as he broke into a sprint, his sword slashing into anyone he could reach as he fought his way toward the docks.

Toward the sixth ship's bay.

He did not want to die here.

His boots hit the boards, his lungs aching as he put on another burst of speed. The scene was utter bedlam, the chaos so intense he could hardly make out friend or foe as he reached the ship. Some of the Milsaion warriors were already hacking at the ropes, desperate to free their final chance at retreat from its ties.

Will turned to help pull Kiara over the edge of the ship, his eyes catching a flash of white down in the melee.

"Akeeta," he breathed.

She had followed him, but not to join him. No, Akeeta was still on the attack, ripping into warriors left and right as she helped clear a path for the remaining Milsaion soldiers who lagged behind.

"Akeeta!" Her name ripped from his throat, but she did not heed his desperate command.

She continued to fight, to forge ahead, to help those that would otherwise die.

Will gripped the edge of the ship, but Kiara's hold on his arm was a vise grip. "Don't!" the general snarled. "There's nothing you can do for her!"

Will ripped himself from her grasp as he vaulted over the edge of the ship anyway, his boots slamming into the planks of the docks so hard, it rattled his head.

And then he was moving, his sword and his affinity lashing into everything it could touch, everything that stood in his way as he ruthlessly fought toward where he could see those flashes of white fur. The air was thick with blood and screams, and he didn't care, he didn't *care*, because Akeeta was still fighting, she was still fighting *one more fight*, and he would not abandon her.

He reached his bonded, his hand finding the scruff of her neck just as a Diaforaté stepped toward her and the line of soldiers she was leading to safety.

The woman's pale flesh looked melted, her eyes the darkest black. She extended a hand toward Will. He could *see* her power—all light and chaos. It raised strands of her blond hair as her magic swirled around her.

"Get down!"

The shout came from one of the Caeli who had accompanied Will from Tala. She shoved past him and reached toward the Diaforaté.

Will's body reacted before his mind could. He threw himself on top of Akeeta, forcing his bonded to the ground as a deafening crack sounded.

Something hit him, hard enough that he could feel it pelting his armor, but still he stayed on top of Akeeta. There were screams again, but Will couldn't tell who they were coming from or what they were for as he stood, his hand still anchored in Akeeta's coat, ready to drag her to the ship.

He scrubbed a hand across his helmet, his vision a blur of red and beige and black. His hand came away warm and wet, chunks of something sticking to the blood there. He looked to Akeeta, noticing it on her fur as well.

"Her power devoured her," a voice beside him stammered. "Her...her power devoured her."

Will gazed at where the Diaforaté had been. There was nothing to prove her existence except chunks of flesh.

Will pushed up his helmet as he vomited, his eye catching the gore splattered across the breastplate of his armor.

More flesh, more blood, and a scrap of maroon fabric. A piece of the uniform of the Talan forces.

The Diaforaté had lost herself entirely to that raw, chaotic power. It had devoured its host.

And it had taken the Caeli with her.

I am going to die here.

The thought echoed dully in Will's mind as he saw the sixth ship pull away from the port.

I am going to die here.

Someone had a hold of him, and they were forcing him to his knees, their arm tight around his throat, stealing what little air he had left from his lungs. They ripped off his helmet, their arm tightening as they found the flesh of his neck.

Will locked eyes with Akeeta, watching as she snarled and fought against the grip of a Kakos warrior.

He and his bonded locked eyes, a high-pitched, broken whimper leaving Akeeta as she realized what Will already knew.

They were going to die here.

71

Y OU KNOW WHAT I CAN'T FIGURE OUT?" AYA'S QUESTION was a soft murmur against the early sounds of dawn breaking across the mountains.

"Plenty, I'm sure," Mathias drawled from beside her. They were standing outside the warehouse, waiting for Liam to finish persuading Charles to adhere to a strict set of rules that would ensure he'd keep their names out of his mouth.

Aya ignored Mathias's barb, welcoming the cool breeze of the early morning on her face. "You've hidden him for this long. Why come forward now?"

Mathias adjusted the collar of his jacket, a dark chuckle rumbling from his chest. "Are you surprised I value my own life above others?" He gave Aya a knowing look. "Don't tell me you thought I had become a patriot, Aya dear. It simply benefited me to hide him. This morning, it did not."

"And if I had summoned the Guard? The Dyminara? Gianna? You would face treason for this, Mathias."

Mathias's breath clouded in front of him as he let out a sigh. "I think we both know you've shed your collar. I wonder…" He raised a silver brow as he smirked at her. "Does Gianna know she's lost control of her best weapon?"

Aya took a small step toward the crime lord. "Are you threatening me, Mathias?"

His eyes flashed, even as that sinister smile twisted his lips. "Are *you*?"

The door behind Aya slid open, revealing Tova and Liam. "He's ready," Liam muttered to Mathias. "Remember, Mathias, any mention of us being here, any claim that we have anything to do with this at all, and we won't hesitate to find him and kill him, *and* you."

Mathias gave a small bow. "I expect nothing less."

"Let's go," Liam growled, shoving past Aya and Mathias as he started down the path that would lead them back to the Quarter.

"We should be bringing Charles with us," Tova argued as she and Aya caught up to him. "Letting him disappear again is foolish."

"It's not as though we don't have someone who can get us in touch with him," Liam remarked bitterly.

"And yet we're going to just take his word?" Tova spat back. "Despite the fact that it's utterly preposterous?"

Aya closed her eyes and took a steadying breath as she tuned out their bickering. She needed time—and some fucking *quiet*—so she could process what Charles had shared. So she could *think*.

Because this...

This revelation could change *everything*. If Charles was telling the truth—*He is; I felt it,* Aya reminded herself—then that meant...

Gianna had known Dominic was siding with Kakos all along. She had known, and she had done nothing but send Aya and Will into the heart of the lion's den, either to change his mind or to force his hand. But why? If she knew there was no supplier, then she knew Kakos wasn't getting weapons from them.

Unless...unless she knew Kakos already had them.

Gianna must have known that war was imminent. Why

else would she take such a risk in sending Aya to the one man who could deliver her into the hands of the heretics?

Or had she sent them there for another reason? Had she known Dominic would show his true allegiance in the end, and they would be forced to kill him?

Aya's mind whirled as she tried to sort through each and every angle, each and every possibility. As she tried to *think* the way Gianna thought.

Gods, she wished Will was here. He knew the queen's manipulation like no other. There had to be a piece of this she wasn't seeing, that she wasn't *grasping*—

"Aya?"

It took her a moment to realize Tova was calling her name and that they'd reached the Quarter. She opened her mouth to tell them she needed time, but a lone figure emerging from the Quarter stopped her.

It was Lena, and she was headed in their direction.

"Say nothing about this morning," Aya muttered, cutting them both a glance. Her eyes lingered on Liam until he dipped his chin subtly. Aya let her posture loosen, her arms folding across her chest as they met Lena in the middle of the field. Aya was all too aware of how conspicuous they looked— she and Liam in fighting leathers, and Tova in ordinary garb. But she'd quickly prepared a story of early morning trainings and late-night outings for her friend, the three of them just happening to cross paths on the way back to the Quarter, but she didn't get a chance to use it.

Lena didn't even bother to ask where they'd been, or why they were out at this hour. In fact, she didn't even seem to notice their attire as she said, "The queen needs us."

Aya's eyes narrowed as she registered the dull shock in Lena's voice. "What is it, Lena?" she pressed, her pulse inexplicably leaping into her throat. "What's happened?"

Something like pity darkened Lena's irises as she held Aya's gaze. "Milsaio has fallen."

The gods had a saying for death.

Il sy parigatin sto li mortera, ati li Diavni se promani li Péla.

There is consolation in death, for the Divine shepherd you to the Beyond.

It was meant to be a reassurance that even in death, those we love are cared for. That even in death, those we love have a home.

That even in death, there was peace in such consolation.

It was a lie.

Aya knew it as soon as the words left Gianna's mouth, each reaching her ears in a muffled, disconnected way.

Kakos. Milsaio. Fallen. Dead.

It was enough for her to put the pieces together just before her own shattered completely.

Milsaio had fallen to Kakos, and there were no survivors.

The gods had lied.

There is no peace, no consolation, in this death.

"How do you know?" The question came from Tova, and Aya suspected she was asking on Aya's account, her hand a steadying presence on Aya's arm.

"We received a message from the fourth island. The Talan unit...they're dead," Gianna replied, her tone thick with a sadness that she didn't deserve to feel. And for that alone, Aya wanted to kill her. Not swiftly, but agonizingly slowly, so that she felt a tenth—no, a hundredth—of the pain that Aya felt as she bowed over, her hands grasping her stomach as if somehow that would keep the agony inside.

As if somehow, she could contain the power that wanted to rip through her, rip through the *world* now that he no longer existed in it.

Will was dead.

And Aya knew, without a doubt, that she would not survive it.

Gianna was still talking, her voice a distant rumble responding to some question of Liam's that Aya didn't bother to hear. She mentioned something about the placement of their armies, something about preparing for the inevitable arrival of Kakos, but all Aya could hear was a rushing in her ears as she squeezed her arms tighter around her midsection.

"I know this is hard for you," Gianna murmured, her remark slicing through the din in Aya's head. "He was a good soldier. A good man."

"*Don't.*" The word ripped from the depths of Aya's agony as she peered up at the queen. "Do not talk about him as if you know anything about him."

Aya could kill her. She could kill her right here and be done with it. Be done with *her*.

But Tova's hand tightened on her arm, as if she could hear Aya's thoughts.

Aya shook it off as she stood. She had to get out of this godsforsaken room—this room that she, Tova, and Will had frequented as Gianna's Tría.

He would never sit next to her on that gaudy love seat again. Would never brush against her subtly in a move that had once annoyed her no end but had settled her of late, because it meant he was with her, and she was not alone in this.

Tova was calling her name, but Aya was already out of Gianna's chambers, her stride breaking into a run as she hit the hallway. She wasn't sure where she was going, but she couldn't spend another moment in this godsforsaken palace. She was out of the castle before she could form another coherent thought, her breath punching through her lungs as she ran, and ran, and ran, her feet carrying her deep into the forest.

She slowed to a stop, her hands bracing on her knees as she choked back sobs. But she couldn't escape the heavy agony that was sinking further and further into her very soul, or the stirring of power that demanded a release as she wrestled against the feeling threatening to overwhelm her.

She could not control this, could not *bury* this.

Aya was a saint, and while it supposedly meant salvation for the realm, it was little more than a death sentence to those who dared to care about her. And nothing—no training, no spying, no pleading to the fucking gods—was enough to change it, nor could it ease the constant ache that knowing this truth brought her.

Her mother.

Aidon.

Josie.

Viviane.

Pa.

Tova.

And now Will.

Aya's power *burned* in her veins. Or maybe it was her anger, or her agony, or some other torture the gods had devised for their *saint*. The word was a snarl within her own mind as her anger latched on to yet another target, because yes, Gianna was responsible for sending Will away, and yes, Aya would deliver retribution slowly and excruciatingly, but the gods…

The gods had only made her life a living hells.

Hadn't she given enough? Hadn't she *lost* enough? How could they take him from her? The one piece of happiness she had carved out for herself. The one person she had dared to let see all of her and who hadn't run.

"How could you take him?" The words were half scream, half sob as she clutched at her chest. She swore her heart was cleaving in two, the pain of it so great it nearly brought her to her knees as tears dripped down her cheeks, her breath coming in shallow pants.

She hadn't wanted this power. She hadn't wanted to be their saint. And yet she was trying. She was *trying* to ensure destruction didn't come to their realm, and for what?

For them to continue to torture her? To withhold answers and break her down until she had nothing left?

What did it matter then?

She might as well let the realm burn.

Aya stood, her lungs searing as she let out a scream, her arms flinging wide as a rush, a burst of *something*, exploded from her very core, detonating outward. It was strong enough to decimate the trees surrounding her, to make the very mountain on which she stood tremble, as if her rage and heartbreak had embedded itself in the rock.

Not wind. Not light.

Something *more*.

Aya took a shuddering breath, her eyes blurry with tears that she blinked away as she let her hands fall. Ash coated her tongue, a taste she didn't realize was familiar until it dredged up the memory of twelve years prior—the last time she'd screamed over a death that she hadn't caused, but might as well have.

Aya turned in a circle, taking in the small round clearing that hadn't been here before—the clearing that she'd *made*, the only evidence of the cluster of trees that had once surrounded her the pine needles that littered the ground.

She had destroyed every last one.

72

WILL'S FINAL THOUGHT WASN'T OF DEATH, OR WHAT awaited him once darkness embraced him fully. It was of Aya—her piercing blue eyes, which softened when she smiled; her low voice, which took on a rasp in the first few moments of the morning; the jut of her chin when she prepared to argue.

His power tried to rally as that arm tightened across his throat further, but he had nothing left. And so he let his eyes close, his mind conjuring up the one thing he would want to see if he had a choice in what his final moments in this realm looked like.

Gods, seeing her was like a breath of fresh air, so good, so *right*, it burned.

It took Will a moment to realize he *was* breathing, his body falling forward as the arm released its hold on him. He sucked in a desperate breath, his vision spotty, and then another, his lungs clenching and unclenching as someone grabbed beneath his shoulder plate and hauled him to his feet.

"Bet you never dreamt of being *this* glad to see my handsome face." Aidon's quip was delivered with that dazzling smile, even as he wiped his sword, coated with blood, on the warrior who had been suffocating Will to death.

Another dead body lay beside his—Akeeta's attacker. She was shaking out her body, a vicious howl ripping from her as she rejoined the fight.

With one hand still helping Will to stand, Aidon flung his sword out, spearing an approaching Kakos soldier in the chest. "This makes us even, yes?" he asked lightly as he yanked the sword from the man.

All around them, battle cries ringing out like prayers of hope, of *victory*, were Trahirian soldiers.

Visya Trahirian soldiers. Anima and Caeli and Terra and Auqin and gods above, they were rallying behind the abandoned Milsaion troops, the abandoned Talan troops, or what remained of them.

Aidon had answered his call.

"I could kiss you," Will gasped.

Aidon's mouth twitched. "We'll discuss the specifics of *that* with Aya. Assuming we don't all die. On your right."

Will's head swam, but he managed to steady himself enough to lift his sword. It locked with his attacker's, but Will twisted, bringing his elbow against the soldier's helmet hard enough that he stumbled. One swipe of Will's sword against his unprotected neck had the soldier falling, his body jerking as he suffocated on his own blood.

"The third island," Will croaked. "We need to get to the third island…"

Aidon nodded as he grabbed Will's arm again, hauling him forward. "Josie's manning the skiffs."

It took Will a moment to realize what Aidon had just said. Josie was here, too? He tried to find her in the chaos, but between the fighting and Aidon's barked orders to retreat, Will could hardly think straight.

He stumbled, and Aidon tightened his grip. "Come on, don't you want to mimic suffocation again?" Aidon chided as he fought off another attacker. Will tried to lift his sword, but his arm had gone numb. "If I recall, it was oddly accurate."

"Can't," Will choked out. "Used it all."

Aidon let out a noise of frustration as he fought off another attacker. Another. And still, he dragged Will forward.

They were lagging behind, the boats in the distance already mostly full. Will finally caught sight of Josie, her sword glinting in the sunlight as she fought side by side with the other Trahirian warriors who were protecting the skiffs. Akeeta stood beside her, her coat so coated in blood and grime that he could barely see a spot of white.

"Go," Will ordered Aidon. Trahir needed its king. "I'll catch up."

"Shut up," Aidon spat out. They were forty paces away.

Thirty.

Twenty.

Will wasn't sure how his legs were still moving.

Perhaps they weren't.

"You can't die here," Aidon grunted as he heaved Will past the Trahirian soldiers holding the line. Will vaguely registered the water splashing against his leathers, the sting of the salt making the burn on his leg sear with pain. "You *cannot* die here," Aidon repeated as he hauled Will over the edge of one of the skiffs. "As king, I fucking forbid it."

The next thing Will knew, he was in the boat. Aidon was beside him, and Will was trying to lift his head but couldn't.

"Akeeta," he managed to say.

"She's here." It was Josie's voice. Her face flickered in and out of focus as she leaned over him. He swore she said something else, but the words were lost to the wind. His tongue fumbled through the words he searched for to ask her to repeat herself, and Josie frowned. Her mouth moved again in another mix of syllables he couldn't untangle as his body sank further into the wood.

Her hand was on his shoulder, her voice increasing in

volume as she called out for someone behind her. A healer? Was someone injured?

Will's head lolled to the side, his eyes fixed on the clear blue of the sky.

Like Aya's eyes.

It really would have been a beautiful day if it weren't for the blood and the death.

It was Will's final thought as darkness dragged him under.

73

CREATING THE CLEARING SHOULD HAVE DONE SOMETHING TO her. Physically. Mentally. Hells, even emotionally. Aya wasn't sure where a burst of power—of combined affinities like that—fell in Lorna's warning about staying anchored in the light versus being dragged into the dark.

She wasn't sure she particularly cared anymore. It was agonizing to think that at one point, that was all that had consumed her. Guilt. Anger. Fear. Aya wasn't sure she'd ever fully rid herself of those feelings, but Will...Will had awakened others in her.

Joy.

Contentment.

Vulnerability.

Love.

Tell me when I get back.

She would never get that chance now. And gods, she wanted to be angry still. But she couldn't feel anything but aching sadness. She didn't even realize tears were coursing down her cheeks until one hit her palm, which was resting on her knee as she sat cross-legged on the forest floor.

How long had she even been here?

She glanced up, trying to track the position of the sun, but it was lost to the west, its rays blocked by the pines.

Hours, then.

Aya pushed herself off the ground, her body aching from spending so long in her seated position. She dusted her hands on her pants and gave the clearing one last, long look, before she stepped into the thick of the forest. She paused, the echoes of the ravens' caws overwhelming as she tried to work out where she was. She couldn't think, could barely *breathe*, not with the grief that had wrung her completely dry.

How was she to find her way back?

A twig snapped somewhere to her left, and Aya whirled to face the intruder, her hand reaching for her knife. It was another moment before a gray head emerged.

Tyr. Come to take her home.

His steps were slow. Hesitant. It made Aya wonder how long he'd been here, how long he'd watched his bonded grieve.

Just as *she* would have to watch him grieve, because eventually, Tyr would realize Akeeta was not coming home. Ever.

And that thought alone had a fresh wave of grief drowning Aya. She dropped to her knees before her bonded, her arms flinging around his neck as she buried her head in his fur, a round of fresh sobs shaking her violently.

And even though Tyr couldn't possibly know yet what had unfolded in Milsaio—couldn't possibly know what had become of his beloved Akeeta—Aya swore in that moment that he *did*.

Because Tyr—her fierce, irascible, unmovable Tyr—leaned his head back and let out a heart-wrenching, broken howl, as if he, too, were crying.

Aya's steps were heavy as she trudged up the stairs in the

Quarter. She went to Will's room instinctively, not bothering to shed her boots or fighting leathers as she collapsed on the top of his bed. The duvet still smelled like him, and she closed her eyes tightly and tried to summon the deep rumble of his voice in her mind, and the way it had soothed her when he read to her at night on the ship back from Trahir.

Tyr lay down on the floor next to the bed, but he was jumping up in the next moment, a low growl loosing from him at the sound of someone at Will's door.

Aya didn't move.

Let them find her here. What did it matter?

And while she couldn't muster the energy to lift her head, that didn't stop the flicker of surprise that coursed through her as Liam stepped into the room. His face was grim as he closed the door behind him and stalked to the bed. He hesitated only a moment, his gaze fixed cautiously on Tyr, before he sat down, the foot of the mattress dipping as he did so.

"I went to your room first," he said by way of explanation. He still wasn't looking at Aya, but his attention was solely on her as she remained unmoving, her hands tucked beneath Will's pillow. His throat bobbed, his hands clasping in his lap as he shifted uncomfortably. "Do you...? Is there anything you need?"

He finally turned his gaze to her, and there was an earnestness in Liam's eyes that filled the tiniest part of Aya's hollow heart.

She'd never had many friends. None, really, save for Tova, and then Josie and Aidon.

And Will.

It had always been enough for her. It had always been beneficial for her to keep her circle small, to limit the number of people she had to worry about, to decide whether or not she could show her full self to them.

To limit the number of people she was scared to lose.

But as Aya shook her head, a broken *no* falling from her,

Liam merely nodded, his gaze finding the door again as he sat there in silence.

As he stayed.

She didn't know when they had become friends. She wasn't even sure if he would use the word himself to describe whatever alliance had formed between them. But she could admit to herself at least that she was glad he didn't leave, even as Aya's eyes grew heavy, the events of the day weighing her down until sleep, despite the early evening hour and the grief that had her head pounding, seemed inevitable.

She'd nearly found that blessed escape when the door swung open, revealing a wide-eyed, shallow-breathed Tova. Liam was straightening, his *what the hells* halfway out of his mouth before Tova said, "She lied."

Aya blinked, her eyes aching from the onslaught of tears throughout the day. But it was Liam who said, "What the hells are you talking about?"

"Gianna," Tova croaked. She was shaking, Aya realized, as she took a few steps toward the bed. "It wasn't news that the islands had fallen. It was a call for aid."

Liam was standing now, a deep frown creasing his brow. "How do you know that?"

Tova's gaze cut to Aya for the briefest of moments. "I broke into her chambers." The confession was enough to have Aya sitting up, something twisting in her throat as Tova looked to her again. "He called for aid."

Aya stood, a wounded noise escaping her as her hand rested against the base of her throat—as if it could help her find the words she desperately needed. It couldn't be true. Gianna could not have ignored her own warriors' call for aid.

Why would she do that? Why let them die?

But there wasn't time to contemplate it—not now—not when Tova was still trembling, her hazel eyes wide as she took a step toward Aya.

"He sent the plea four days ago," her friend said, her voice cracking, as if she too realized what that meant.

Aya was already checking her knives, and tightening her hair where it was tied at the back of her head, and scanning Will's room to see if there were any weapons at all that could help.

"Aya," Liam murmured. "It could be too late."

"I don't care," she retorted, stalking to the corner of the room where a spare sword lay. She moved to Will's dresser, where she knew he kept another sheath.

"What are you going to do, sail to Milsaio on your own?" Liam pressed.

"No," Aya replied as she found the spare sheath. She fastened it around herself, securing the sword down her spine. "I'm calling in a favor."

"I've quite had my fill of you." Mathias's drawl was exasperated as two of his men dragged Aya into the small sitting room of his town house.

"Luckily for you, I'm leaving," Aya bit back as she ripped her arms from their hold, shooting them a glare before focusing fully on the crime lord.

He cocked a brow, his posture loose as he propped his ankle on his knee. A king on his high-backed, cushioned throne. "I wasn't aware saints had such freedoms."

She didn't. But there was no force in this realm that would stop her from going to Milsaio. Not if there was a chance Will was still alive. She took a step toward Mathias, all too aware of how his guards tracked her every movement.

"I need fighters. Milsaio is under attack, and if we do not send aid, they will fall to Kakos, and we will be next."

Mathias ran a finger down the tufted arm of his chair, his face bemused as he held Aya's gaze. "Milsaio will fall, or your beloved *Enforcer*?"

Aya's throat bobbed, and Mathias tracked the movement. But she let him see that vulnerability, let him have this weapon to use against her whenever it would benefit him most, because she *needed* his help, and she would do what she must to get it.

"What you said earlier," Aya remarked, her voice soft. "You were lying."

"You'll have to elaborate, dear, I lie for a living."

Aya took another step, the guards shifting with her at her back. "You didn't hide the supplier just because it benefited you. You hid him because you knew he was proof that Gianna is not what she says she is."

Mathias simply stared at her, his angular jaw shifting as he considered her words. "Do you have a point?" he asked finally.

"Only that perhaps we are aligned in our goals." It was the most she would allow herself to give him. Will, and a vague confirmation of her allegiances. A vague notion of her doubts about the queen they both found themselves defying.

"Let's say I do give you these fighters," Mathias mused as he straightened the lapel of his navy jacket. "What do I get in return?"

Anything. The word almost escaped Aya's lips, but she managed to force a breath into her lungs, stifling the flames of her desperation for another moment as she made her voice cold. "I thought you valued your life, Mathias. What do you think will become of it when Kakos arrives?"

Mathias's chuckle was low and smooth. "I appreciate the attempt, Aya, but let's agree to be honest with one another, shall we? This isn't about stopping Kakos, is it?"

Stay anchored in the light, Lorna had told her. But what had the light ever done for her? Where had burying these parts of herself gotten her?

Perhaps control wasn't found in hiding.

Perhaps it was found in facing one's self head on.

"I had really wanted to do this the civil way," Aya lamented.

The guards at her back moved for her, but Aya raised a hand. They inhaled sharp gasps, the *thud* of them falling to their knees reverberating through the floor. "You give me fighters, Mathias, and I won't kill you and every single person in this godsdamn house."

Mathias's eyes were wide as he straightened in his chair. "What are you doing to them?" he asked darkly.

"Mimicking the sensation of suffocation," Aya replied, her voice soft against the sounds of their choking. It was eerie how effortless it was to switch from her Sensainos affinity to her Anima affinity—to go from mimicking to *causing*, the men making desperate noises as they clawed at their throats.

"It's strange how similar the sensations are, is it not?" Aya mused to the guards. "Fake, then real, then fake, then real…" She switched back and forth between the two affinities as she said it, as easily as if she were flipping one of her blades between her fingers.

"That's impossible," Mathias breathed as he stood. "An Anima has to touch one to use their affinity."

It should be impossible. But something in Aya had cracked in the woods, and for once, she was all too content to let her power flow.

Aya's smile was cold. Vicious.

"I'm not an Anima, Mathias. I'm a fucking saint."

74

I T TOOK MATHIAS AN HOUR TO ASSEMBLE A TEAM OF FIGHTERS for Aya. Visya, human, she didn't particularly care. As long as they could wield a sword, that's all she needed. And the Caeli—she wanted as many Caeli as possible to help accelerate their journey.

And Mathias had delivered.

Twenty fighters—Visya and human alike, readied a small vessel at the far end of the docks of the Rouline, packing it with empty crates under the guise of loading a shipment, lest someone be watching who would report back to Gianna. It wasn't nearly enough to form a true unit, but…it was something. And Aya was in no place to demand more. She didn't have the time.

She stood in the shadows of a towering ship in the next bay, cloaked in black and anxious to leave. "This could be a fool's errand," Liam muttered from his place beside her. He was frowning at the vessel, his lips set in a firm line of disapproval. "At least take Tyr."

"No," Aya argued. "I don't know what I'm heading into."

"Once Gianna realizes you're gone—"

"Perhaps then she'll send reinforcements." Aya cut him

off. "I'm going, Liam. There's nothing you can say that will stop me."

Tova shifted on her other side. Her friend had been unusually quiet since she'd burst into Will's room with the revelation that Gianna had left her own warriors to die.

Tova's warriors. They might fight for their queen, but their leader was their general.

"Ready when you are," one of the Caeli muttered as she approached the trio in the shadows. Liam let out a long breath as he turned to face Aya.

"I won't be able to cover for you," he muttered. Another attempt to make her stay, she supposed.

"I don't expect you to," Aya replied. "Nor do I expect you to act on what we learned until we all return." She shot him a level look, her meaning clear. "Don't be a hero."

Liam snorted at her irony. "Don't die," he shot back before cutting a glance at Tova. "I'll give you two a minute."

Aya waited until Liam reached the main dock before she turned to Tova. "I mean it," Aya said quietly. "Don't confront Gianna on your own. Hells, don't even confront Lena. Until we know how deep this goes—"

"I'm coming with you."

Aya paused, unsure if she had heard Tova correctly. But Tova's gaze was fierce with determination, her chin set in that stubborn way of hers.

"Tova …"

"These are *my* troops. She left *my* troops to die," Tova pressed, her voice trembling with anger. "If there is any chance they are alive, then I have to go. If there is any chance we defeat Kakos, or at least damage them, I have to go. It is my duty."

She ground her teeth and forced out, "I should have listened to you. I should have listened to you both." Aya shook her head, but Tova continued, her face flushing red. "She did something to me. And whatever it was, it made me her puppet." An angry tear slipped down Tova's cheek, and she brushed it away roughly with the back of her hand. "But she doesn't control me anymore." Tova sucked in a shaky breath as if to steady herself. "I am with you. If you go, I go. That is my choice."

A choice she deserved more than anyone, especially when so many had been taken from her.

"You're right," Aya agreed softly. "It's your choice."

Tova sniffled, the corner of her lips lifting slightly as she nodded once and motioned to the readied vessel. "Let's go then."

PART FOUR

Deceiver.
Usurper.
Murderer.

75

Three days prior

IT WAS THE MOST AT HOME AIDON HAD FELT IN WEEKS—BACK aching, hands braced on the table, brow narrowed as he scanned the map. A crumpled piece of parchment sat beside it, the words so hastily scrawled that it had taken him several moments to make out what it said.

Milsaio under attack. Tala unit calls for aid.

Aidon had sat in his room, the parchment gripped tightly in his fist, as he tried to come to terms with the fact that war was here. War was here, and he was not ready. His people were not ready.

But that was the thing about conflict, Aidon had learned. It didn't wait to be welcomed graciously. It tore into the most fragile of places and made its presence known, often as brutally as possible.

So he had sent for Aleissande and gathered his mother and sister, and the four of them had been locked in this makeshift war room for the better part of an hour.

His mother stood beside him now, her white gown a bright spot in the gloomy room—one of the few in the palace with no windows. She was unusually quiet as she stared at the far wall, her gaze distant and her lips pressed into a firm, straight line. Across from him, Aleissande stood with her arms folded across her chest, her brow pinched as her eyes darted across the map, as if she were reading some text only she could see. Beside her, Josie paced, so lost in thought she hardly reacted when Aleissande straightened and said, "We don't have enough information to get involved."

Aidon let out a frustrated breath, his hands curling around the edge of the table. "We know Kakos managed to decimate Sitya. That type of large-scale attack requires some sort of weaponry. And now that they have Sitya's ships too..."

He let his explanation hang. Everyone in this room knew what it meant. Kakos had force behind them, enough that Sitya had been so damaged that the reports from the attack were scattered and lacking. But it didn't take a genius of war to know that with more weapons at their disposal now, Milsaio was in grave danger.

"Is the saint even there?" his mother murmured, her hazy gaze blinking into focus as she looked at Aidon.

"I don't know," Aidon confessed, his brow furrowing as he scanned the map again.

"Surely Tala wrote back to their own as well," Aleissande interjected. "Why not let them handle it? If her power is what you say it is, she should be able to help, should she not?"

"As should we," Josie muttered darkly, her features twisted into a look of disgust as she paused her pacing. Aya was her friend—*their* friend. To suggest she fight this battle alone...

"Majesty," Aleissande drawled, ignoring Josie completely. "Might I suggest that we limit this conversation to the three of us." She looked pointedly between Aidon and Zuri.

Josie's eyes flashed in anger. "You can't be serious."

"You don't have the authority to be involved in such matters," Aleissande ground out, her gaze still fixed on Aidon.

"I am a member of the royal family—"

"And a member of the forces I command," Aleissande interjected, her voice cracking through the room like a whip as she turned to face Josie. "Do you see any other lower-ranking soldiers in this room?"

Zuri stiffened beside Aidon, but he placed a gentle hand on her elbow to stay her.

"She stays, Aleissande," Aidon said.

Aleissande shot him a look. "Her opinions are colored by her friendship with the Second Saint—"

"And you can say mine are colored by the fact she was to be my betrothed," Aidon growled. "Josie is not the only one with personal feelings toward her."

Aidon might even argue his were far more complex. While he did not love her in such a way anymore, it didn't change the softness he held for Aya. She was his friend, too. And at one point, he had wanted her to be more. He could admit that now—now that he'd separated his feelings from his orders.

He didn't regret his choice in the end, but it did not mean he did not care for her.

"Josie stays," Aidon ordered again, all too aware of the three sets of eyes that were fixed on him. He straightened, taking one last look at the map before making up his mind.

"I know Tala well enough to know that if they are calling for help, the situation is dire. Milsaio is the only thing standing between us and Kakos, and I gave Tala my word that when they called on us, we would respond." He looked to Aleissande. "We send the Visya unit. And we leave today."

Aleissande frowned. "We?"

"I will not ask my people to fight in a war that I do not join."

"No." The objection came from Aleissande and Josie simultaneously. It was perhaps the first and only time they had ever agreed on anything.

Aidon raised a brow as his mother said, "I am inclined to agree. You are needed here, especially if war is truly progressing. Our people will need direction, and hope, and..."

"And you will lead our people well in my stead," he finished for her.

Zuri blinked at him. "Aidon…"

"It is not unusual for the King's Advisor to be regent in a monarch's absence," Aidon pressed on. "I will not be the king that stands aside while he sends his soldiers to war."

"Send me in your stead," Josie argued. "I can fight just as well."

"Which is why I trust you to protect Rinnia in my absence," Aidon retorted.

"Majesty…" Aleissande's voice held a subtle warning, but Aidon ignored it.

"This is not a suggestion," he growled to the room. "This is a command from your king." To Aleissande, he said, "Ready the Visya unit. I will meet you at the departing bay in two hours."

Aleissande looked as if she were preparing to argue. Her jaw shifted, her features seeming to grow even sharper with that challenging glint in her eyes. But then she nodded curtly and exited the room.

Josie wasted no time in rounding on him the moment she was gone. "You cannot go," she hissed. "And you know why."

Their mother frowned as she looked between them.

"He's lost control of his affinity," Josie said in response to her questioning look. "He's increased his tonic dosage, but he's not sure it will help. Are you?"

Frustration rose in Aidon like a tidal wave. "Thank you for your discretion, Josie," he snapped.

"I am trying to protect you!"

"Are you? Or are you angry that I've sent the Visya force and you don't qualify?" His words were coated with a bitterness he didn't know was waiting to erupt from him. His sister reeled back, a ringing silence filling the room.

"That is quite enough," Zuri said quietly.

Aidon pinched the bridge of his nose, inhaling deeply as

he tried to steady himself. Guilt had replaced the bitterness instantaneously, and it only intensified as he said, "I will take precautions, Josie. I'll even increase the dose of the tonic again. With that, I should be fine."

It wasn't necessarily a lie, but it wasn't the truth either. Natali didn't know when his power would consume the tonic entirely—and him. If he could get through this battle, if they could stop Kakos before they grew even stronger...

Josie shook her head in resignation. She didn't bother to say goodbye as she left the room.

Aidon sighed as he braced his hands on the table, his mother's gaze like a weight on him.

He expected a lecture. Or at the very least, some show of emotion that he had kept this from her. After all, it threatened his claim to the throne. His family's claim to the throne. He wasn't the only one defying the gods. No one would think his family had been unaware of his powers.

But Zuri merely sighed, the sound heavy with exhaustion. "I cannot advise you if I do not know the truths of what we face," she murmured. "This was a foolish secret to keep, especially in light of the threats surrounding us."

Aidon nodded, his gaze fixed unseeingly on the map. "You can lecture me fully when I return," he quipped, forcing a smile to his face as he looked at her. "I'll even go to bed without dinner."

The joke was hollow, his grin more a half grimace that flickered and faded as Zuri put a hand on his arm. "You are sure the tonic will suffice?"

Aidon's throat went dry.

His family deserved the truth.

And yet the steady tick of the clock on the wall reminded him of what was at stake. This was bigger than Aidon. Bigger than his family. This was about the realm and its continued existence. "Yes."

The lie was as smooth as his mother's soft fingers as she

527

cupped his face. "You may not make it in time," she warned him, nodding at the map.

"I know."

And it was that fear alone that had him pulling himself from the comfort of her hold. "I'll issue a formal proclamation of what's to come." His people would need to be informed. He'd also need to increase the protection on the palace and the bay.

He paused as he reached the door. "And raise the flag," he added, looking over his shoulder at where his mother stood. Trahir's flag, emerald green and marked with a golden ship, always waved from atop the palace. But the spear and sword hadn't been raised in over two hundred years. Not even when petty skirmishes had called their troops to sea or land in defense of their borders.

Aidon held his mother's gaze, his voice low and commanding as he said, "Let the realm know that Trahir is at war."

76

A NGER QUICKENED JOSIE'S STRIDE AS SHE STORMED INTO the Maraciana and scanned the main library for one of the Saj. Luckily, her frustration was palpable, because a young man came to greet her immediately.

"Can I help you, my—"

"Natali. Where are they?"

The man's throat bobbed. "I believe they are researching on the lower level, my lady. But they have asked not to be disturb—"

Josie pushed past the man, her hands tightening into fists as she found the staircase and jogged down to the lower floor. It looked much like the first, except its bookshelves were smaller, stretching only to the ceiling instead of several stories high. The floor was carpeted, and it added to the musty odor of the ancient books that made the air smell stale.

Josie found Natali in the fourth row, their silver hair masking their face as they peered at the book in their hands. She opened her mouth, but Natali spoke first.

"If you're here to ask after Viviane," they muttered, not bothering to look up from the text they were immersed in. "I have nothing to tell you that you don't already know yourself.

She is reluctant to do anything—even take the tonic that saves her. But we force it anyway."

"Did you force it down my brother's throat too?" Josie asked darkly. "Or was increasing his dosage his idea?"

That got Natali's full attention.

The Saj snapped their book closed, their amber eyes narrowing slightly as they met Josie's. "On the contrary, Princess, I told him the opposite." They stalked toward her, peering down the narrow hall. "And you would do well to remember that listening ears are *everywhere*."

"What do you mean, the opposite?" Josie pressed.

Natali's mouth twitched with annoyance. "Follow me," they ordered, pushing past Josie and heading down the hall in the opposite direction to the staircase. Josie bit back her own frustration. She didn't have time to waste. A half hour had already passed since she'd left the palace. Aidon and the Visya unit would be leaving soon. If she were going to stop him, she needed to hurry.

She let out an aggravated noise, but followed Natali, who ducked into a small study room at the end of the hall. They closed the door, peering out the small window to ensure they were well and truly alone before turning to face Josie.

"I take it your brother did not give you the full story," they muttered, a judgmental look that only set Josie's teeth further on edge sweeping across their face. "I told him to stop taking the tonic so that we can train his power."

Josie frowned. "But then he risks discovery. The tonic masks his power."

"And the longer he continues to take it, the more he risks death." Natali's words were simply stated, their tone matter-of-fact. But they stole the air out of Josie's lungs, transforming her voice into a strangled rasp as she said, "What?"

Natali pursed their lips, their arms twining behind their back, as if they were preparing for a lesson. "It's a theory, as all things are until proven. But I believe that by suppressing his power, Aidon's affinity has become unstable. It's overriding the tonic, and it will do the same to a higher dose until it cannot be contained."

Josie's ears were ringing, her throat growing dry, but she managed to ask, "And that will kill him?" She wasn't as familiar with the inner workings of Visya power as her brother was. She knew Visya had different levels of strength in their affinities, and that children had to learn how to manage their power lest it overtake them, but the specifics were detailed in a way Josie hadn't had to learn.

Natali made a contemplative sound. "I suspect it will. If his affinity continues to grow unruly under the tonic, it may be too late by the time the tonic is rendered completely ineffective. It may overtake him entirely."

Josie rubbed her chest, her breath feeling tight. He hadn't told her this. He hadn't told her that he was dying. And now, he was going off to battle, and increasing his dosage because he wanted...

To fight.

The realization was incredibly clear in her mind. Of course he wanted to fight. Josie and her brother were different in so many regards, but in this, they had always been the same. They were warriors, and it had nothing to do with whatever titles they held throughout their life. General, princess, king, soldier—they were fighters, and she knew Aidon would rather die than not be able to defend his people.

"Thank you, Natali." Josie's voice sounded distant to her own ears. She pushed past the Saj, her mind hazy as she made her way out of the room and down the hall. She wouldn't be able to stop him. She should've known better than to even try. But that did not mean she was going to leave Aidon to die.

Slipping out of the palace was far easier than Josie had expected. Then again, she and Aidon had been doing it for years, as had Josie and her mother on those nights Zuri would drag Josie to the abandoned paddock to train.

But that had been in the dark. It was daylight, and Josie, dressed in fighting leathers and with a sword strapped on her back, wasn't exactly inconspicuous. But the attendants were busy rushing around, readying their king for battle and their advisor—regent, now—for war. Anyone who did happen to give Josie a passing glance didn't pay her any mind, though she supposed she could just be off to train.

She had made it halfway down the hill before hitting her first impediment.

Cole was coming from the opposite direction, his face red and breath short, as if he'd run up the first half of the hill. "I was just coming to find you!" he exclaimed. "Did you see the flag?"

Josie glanced over her shoulder at the palace. Sure enough, beneath the emerald green flag of their kingdom, another had taken its place: the spear and sword.

"It's true then? We're sending aid to Milsaio?" Cole pressed, his mouth twitching in pain as he rubbed a stitch in his side. How news of violence traveled so fast was something that Josie was always astounded by, even unchanging as it was over the years.

"The Visya unit, yes," Josie informed him as she started back down the path, silently swearing as Cole fell into step beside her, giving her a quizzical glance.

"Are you off to train?" he asked with a frown. Josie's jaw shifted. If she was, she was heading the wrong way.

"In a little while," she replied, forcing a cheery smile to her face. "I have to take care of a few things in town first. I'll meet you there."

Cole waved her off. "I can come with you. I was going early anyway, but I'll just stay after for extra practice."

"No," Josie cut in, drawing to a stop. "You should go now."

Cole cocked his head, his honey eyes blinking rapidly in the bright sun. They narrowed suddenly, his mouth dropping into a surprised *O* as he said, "You're sneaking onto the ship."

Some other time, in some other place, she would've been warmed by the fact that she had a friend who knew her well enough to realize this. But for now, she shushed him heatedly, her head whipping in either direction to ensure no one had overhead his accusation.

"How do you know I haven't been asked to fight?" she hissed, taking a step toward him so he knew to keep his voice down.

"Because you're not Visya and Aleissande hates you," Cole remarked in the same matter-of-fact tone Natali had used when speaking of her brother's death.

"Fucking hells," Josie swore under her breath. And then, slightly louder, she said to Cole, "You cannot tell anyone. Promise me you won't tell anyone." She wasn't sure why his face lit up then, but she already dreaded whatever he was about to say next.

"Why would I tell anyone?" Cole asked incredulously. "I'm coming with you."

If Josie were the devout sort, she would see this as a sign from the gods that she should not go. "No, you're not," she replied fiercely. "This isn't a game, Cole. This is war. You can't just—"

"Sneak on to a ship with a unit you're not qualified to join?" She knew he didn't mean it as any sort of insult, but the words stung anyway. Josie ground her teeth as she shook her head, but she knew her friend. Cole did not back down from a fight.

Even one he would lose.

"Cole," Josie tried to reason. "This is dangerous. I'm only going because Aidon is, and I can't… I won't…" She sucked in a frustrated breath. "Please. Don't do this."

She didn't want to use force. She *wouldn't* use force. But

Cole's face was grim. "If you're going, I'm going. And if you want to stop me, you'll have to injure me, because I will go straight to Aleissande and tell her your plan."

Josie's fingers twitched, as if longing to reach for her sword. Seven hells, she did not have *time* for this. The ship was leaving in under an hour, and she needed to get to the bay before the soldiers did.

She let out an aggravated breath and looked to the water, where the warship was anchored. On the far end of the beach, some of the Visya unit had already gathered. She looked beyond them to the docks where the small boats that ferried merchants to their ships were located.

"I hope you know how to row," Josie muttered, looking back to Cole. "We're going to have to steal a skiff."

77

Present

THE SCENT OF DEATH HAD VANISHED.

It was the first thing Will noticed when he realized he was breathing.

The rot of flesh had been replaced with the rich smell of soil, damp with rain he hadn't remembered falling. The sounds of the sea were also gone, but he could hear evidence of a small creek, or perhaps a waterfall, nearby.

He cracked an eye open, his head aching with the sudden brightness of *life*.

Will groaned, every muscle in his body aching as he shielded his eyes with his arm. It took him a few moments to adjust, to register the ceiling above his head and the mattress beneath his back.

He was in a modest bedroom, the space subtly decorated in hints of silver. But the main beauty was left to the window, which looked out upon a large expanse of jungle. It was open to let in the sounds of the birds and the water trickling down a small fall that seemed to be part of the structure's wall, as if they'd built the home into the nature surrounding them.

Will turned his head to the door and found Akeeta lying on the floor between it and the bed, her eyes locked on his prone form. Her leg was wrapped, but she appeared unbothered by it.

"I take it we made it to the third island," he croaked to his wolf.

"That you did," a voice said from the doorway. He hadn't heard the door click open, and the unexpected visitor had Will sitting up far too quickly. His head swam with the movement, and a deep chuckle came from the man who stepped further into the room. "Easy, Son. Wait to catch your bearings."

Perhaps Will wasn't alive at all. Because standing before him, looking tired and worn but very much *not* dead, was Sarhash, King of Milsaio.

"You're alive?" Will couldn't tell if it was disbelief or exhaustion that made his voice sound like gravel. King Sarhash smiled.

"As are you. A close call for us both, I hear."

Will ran a hand through his hair, his skin damp with sweat and moisture from the humid air. "What happened?"

"Burnout," Sarhash explained as he pulled up a chair next to Will's bed. "It appears you drained your affinity entirely. And here I thought they trained you Dyminara to pace yourselves."

The king's deep baritone dipped into a teasing drawl, his thick arms folding over his chest as he smirked at Will. Sarhash was several inches taller than Will when standing, and while his hulking figure was still long and lean, the wrinkles in his brown skin had deepened. His hazel eyes were bloodshot, but his crown still sat proudly atop his long braided brown hair.

"I am indebted to you and your warriors," Sarhash remarked quietly. "Your second unit was crucial in helping me escape the capital."

"They're here?" Will asked, his throat aching as he forced out the words. The king reached a pitcher of water that stood on the small table and poured Will a cup. He waited until Will drained it before nodding.

"Indeed. All twenty-five of them. Without them, I, and the citizens who were protecting me, would be dead. As would a significant number of warriors who remained on the second island, had you not called for aid."

Will's jaw shifted as he fought off the phantom grip around his neck. Had Aidon been more than a moment later, he likely wouldn't be sitting here. And still, so many lives were lost. Like Leanora. Will held the king's gaze, his fist finding his heart as he vowed, "No condolence would be enough to soothe the agony you must feel about your wife. So instead, I offer you my sword and my power in the name of justice, Your Majesty."

It was a warrior's oath, sealed with the symbol of a Dyminara vow, and Sarhash, his face stoic and firm, accepted it with a solitary nod.

Will glanced around the room before asking, "Where are we?"

Sarhash followed his gaze, a fondness softening his features as he took in the room. "My family has dwellings on each of the islands. The palace in the capital is the largest, but this has always been my favorite. To the west is the jungle that makes up most of the island. To the east, the sea. The palace is built into the mountains that serve as a natural barrier to the southern tip of the island." His smile was sad as he looked back to Will. "Milsaion history says this was to be our capital, but the remote nature and rugged terrain made it unfriendly. Interesting how it is what saves us now."

"How long have I been out?" Will asked with a frown. He tried to remember arriving here, but his mind was blank.

"Two days," Sarhash replied. Will let out a low curse. He'd never lost that much time before.

"Kakos hasn't made an attempt on the island?"

Sarhash shook his head. "Not yet. It seems that the arrival of King Aidon's forces stayed their hand, at least for now.

We've assembled our naval defense. When they come, they'll be forced to come through the southern port."

Will drained the rest of his water. "Have reinforcements arrived from Tala?"

"No." The answer didn't come from Sarhash, but from Aidon, who was leaning against the doorframe. His arms were folded, his posture loose, but there was an air of regality to him that Will had never seen before.

Not a prince anymore, but a king.

Aidon grinned at him. "Gods, you look like shit."

Will barked a laugh. "And yet I still manage to look better than you."

Sarhash gave a bemused shake of his head as he stood. "I'll let you two catch up. Try to pace yourself, Enforcer. We need you healthy." The kings nodded at each other, and Aidon settled into the chair Sarhash had abandoned as the door closed behind him.

"I sent some of my troops to inspect the route alongside the third and fourth islands," Aidon explained, his voice suddenly serious. "There were no signs of wreckage or attack."

Will rubbed a hand over his jaw. They should be here by now. If they'd received his call for aid, they should have arrived.

Unless...

His hand dropped to the mattress, a bitter thought taking hold. Unless Gianna had refused to send any additional soldiers.

"Has there been any news from the continent?" he asked sharply. Aidon frowned at his sudden intensity.

"None that we've heard, but as you're well aware, we've been a little tied up here. Why? You don't think..." Something must have clicked for Aidon then, because his eyes sharpened as he said, "You don't think Kakos made a move on Tala as well?"

"You're the general," Will muttered. He pushed himself

off the mattress, his teeth bared as the room tilted with the movement. His insides felt raw, as if he'd taken a beating not just on his body, but on his affinity as well.

He supposed he had.

"Former general," Aidon was saying as he stood, holding out an arm to steady Will. Pride kept Will from grabbing it immediately, but Aidon rolled his eyes and muttered something under his breath that soundly an awful lot like *fucking impossible*, and the room was *still* swaying, so pride be damned.

Will gripped Aidon's arm, inhaling a shaking breath as he made his way slowly toward the bathing chamber. "I suspect Kakos has concentrated the bulk of their forces here, with the rutting we just took," Aidon mused as he walked with Will. "It could be that your queen is anticipating that once they take Milsaio, they'll head straight for Tala. If her reinforcements fell here, it would only further weaken her forces."

Will let go of his arm, catching himself on the porcelain sink as he sucked in a few steadying breaths. "Perhaps," he muttered as he turned the faucet to the coldest setting.

Something didn't quite add up, and the frustration of it was not soothed by the water Will splashed on his face. He frowned as it ran clear in the sink and glanced at his reflection in the mirror. He looked utterly wrecked, but someone had washed the blood from his face.

"That would be Josie's doing," Aidon remarked, watching from over his shoulder. "She was insistent that we at least clean the blood off the visible parts of you. Said it was good for healing or something."

"I'm surprised you sent her here," Will confessed, dousing his face with water again. It might not be easing the rapidly spinning cogs of his mind, but it was helping to jar him awake, and that was something.

"I didn't." There was enough of an edge to Aidon's reply that Will glanced at him in the mirror. He waited for a further explanation, but Aidon remained resolutely silent, so Will let it lie.

He'd get the story from Josie, surely.

"So two days, no movement," Will remarked to change the subject.

"I know." Aidon sighed, a dark look crossing over his face. "I don't like it either. Something doesn't feel right." So he felt it, too. But before Will could press him on it, Aidon continued. "But if you think something's wrong in Tala, you should be focused on going *home*."

His words were heavy with implication: Will should be focused on getting back to Aya.

"You think I want to be here?" Will muttered. "This is Gianna's form of punishment."

"What did you do now?" Aidon asked, his arms folding as he leaned against the doorframe. "Aren't you the queen's favored of the Dyminara? The most trusted and all of that nonsense?" Will shot Aidon a look. The exaggeration was clear in Aidon's voice, and Will didn't take well to it. It rubbed at a sore spot in him, the same one that he pretended didn't exist whenever he heard the murmurs about his position as Gianna's plaything.

Besides, Aidon had no idea just how far out of favor Will had fallen.

Aidon held up his hands in an appeasing gesture, no hint of disparagement on his face at all. "I jest, Will. Tell me, honestly, what did you do?"

Will focused on the sink, his hands gripping the edges of the basin. "I wanted too much." His words were soft, and bitter, and perhaps the most honest he'd ever been with Aidon. And maybe that was why the king did not respond immediately. But when he did, it was with a squeeze on Will's shoulder and a quiet rumble equal to his own as he said, "It's the wanting that hurts the most." Will met Aidon's gaze in the mirror, his brown eyes wide with understanding. Aidon let out a long breath. "But I suppose it's also the wanting that makes life worth living. Without it, I don't know if I'd like to be here."

Will huffed a laugh, or perhaps more a noise of agreement, because *yes*, the wanting did hurt the most and *yes* it made his life hells as it had been at times, but it was worth it.

"I see spending all that time with Zuri has made you smarter," Will said finally as he straightened. Aidon let out a laugh of his own as he backed away.

"Remind me to let you die next time."

"Remind me to let you," Will shot back. But even he couldn't fight off the grin that was working its way onto his face. Gods, it felt good to see Aidon, much as it pained Will to admit it to himself.

Aidon barked another laugh. "Right. Well, I'll leave you to bathe. That water splashing did nothing to make you look less on the brink of death. Come down to the meeting room on the first floor when you're done. I'd like you to meet my general. She can catch you up on all you've missed while you were taking your beauty rest." He rapped the doorframe with his knuckles in goodbye, but Will called him back.

"Thank you," he stated, giving Aidon a nod. "That's twice you saved my life."

Aidon grinned. "Are we not counting the throne room debacle? I suppose that was more Aya's doing than mine, but I deserve some credit," he said lightly.

Will's scoff was dark and low. "Get out."

78

THERE WAS AN UNNATURAL STILLNESS TO THE FIRST ISLAND of Milsaio. Aya scanned the shore with a telescope, her frown deepening as she took in the emptiness. The *silence*.

It wasn't heavy, like death. It was strained. Wary.

This wasn't an island that had fallen. A *kingdom* that had fallen.

"What do you reckon?" Tova murmured from beside her, the wind whipping tendrils of her hair around her face.

"Something isn't right," Aya replied, dropping the scope. This wasn't the silence of war, or even surrender. This was the silence of an island bracing for impact. But where, then, were the Milsaion forces? Why were they not lining the ports, ready to defend their people? Where was Kakos?

"Push on to the next island," she ordered. Tova echoed her, calling back to the man Mathias had provided to captain the ship.

"We should be prepared for a fight," Tova remarked privately to Aya. "If the forces aren't here, they're likely engaged elsewhere. We'll be sailing directly into battle."

Aya nodded her agreement. "Ready your troops, General."

Tova's laugh was a quiet rasp, as if they both knew they

were burying their fears. Just as they had been the last four days they'd spent sailing toward war. The Caeli had exhausted themselves, using every bit of their affinity to manipulate the winds to accelerate their journey. It had been dangerous, the seas rough and the winds harsh with their modifications. But Aya hadn't cared. Because every second they spent looking at that endless horizon, not a piece of land in sight, was another second she spent wondering if Will was alive, or if they were too late.

The jostling of people across the ship's deck soothed Aya's frayed nerves. Finally, they were *doing* something. She pushed away from the vessel's edge, her steps steady and sure as she jogged down to the lower level, where a large room was fitted with hammocks. Will's spare sword lay beside her hammock, braced against one of the wooden polls. She sheathed it at her back before she went about checking her knives.

And then she stood, her eyes closing as she inhaled a long, deep breath.

He's not dead.

He's not dead.

He's not dead.

This little sliver of each day was the only chance she gave herself to wish so fervently—to *feel* her desperation as it writhed in her stomach and twisted around her heart. Just a few moments, carved out for this. A few breaths to hope, and pray, and beg the gods who had chosen her.

It would not do to be entirely lost to her desperation. To let it cloud her judgment more than it already had or muddy her thoughts on the precipice of battle. So instead, she took it out each day, not to examine it, but to simply feel it. To remember the burn of it, and how it tasted both sweet and bitter on her tongue. And then she tucked it away again, just as she did now, her eyes fluttering open to meet the dank wood of the vessel's wall.

Footsteps sounded on the stairs behind her, and Aya

turned to find Tova, her face grim, her jaw set. "You're needed above deck," Tova muttered. The thundering of boots above rumbled like the beginnings of a storm as their soldiers rushed about.

A warrior's song of preparation before a battle.

"What is it?" Aya asked as she stalked toward Tova, her shoulders automatically rolling back as her body primed itself for a fight.

"We have company," Tova replied, her gaze dark. "And not the friendly kind."

The bath, Will had realized after seeing the dirt and blood-soaked water, had certainly been necessary. As had the visit from one of the Anima, a healer who handed him a tonic to help replenish his well.

"Think of it like nutrients for your affinity," the healer said. "It won't work immediately, but it will accelerate the healing."

Thank the gods for that, Will had thought, because right now he felt aches deep within him that he swore no tonic or healer's light could touch.

Except, perhaps, Aya's.

Aleissande, Aidon's new general, debriefed Will on the days he'd missed, and had just finished when a Milsaion soldier rushed into their war room. "Majesty," he said, addressing Sarhash with a quick bow. "A ship has been apprehended on the border of the northern patrol. They claim to be Talan reinforcements, but they bear no crest, nor sigil."

Will straightened in his seat, meeting Aidon's gaze across the driftwood table. "Is it possible?" Aidon asked him.

Will frowned, his jaw tight as he ran through the options. It *was* possible Gianna had sent reinforcements, and they were just now arriving. Milsaio was closer to Trahir than it was to Tala, especially Dunmeaden. But he couldn't shake the doubts that had settled over him, the nagging feeling that they should have been here already, and not like this. Not unmarked.

"I don't know," he finally conceded. "It wouldn't make sense to arrive unmarked, unless they were trying to throw off the Kakos soldiers. But they would have taken into account that we wouldn't know if they were friends or foe. I don't see the Talan forces making such a mistake."

"Where are they?" Sarhash demanded.

"Being held offshore, Your Majesty," the warrior replied. "They've made no move against our ship, but we're aware it could be a trap to get inside the fortress."

King Sarhash rested his chin on his fist, his eyes narrowed in contemplation as he turned over his options. "Send word to bring them inside the portcullis," he finally ordered his soldier. "And get General Kiara. I want her down there with the guards we have stationed at the base of the cave." To Will, he said, "I trust you'll accompany me to identify them?"

"Certainly," Will nodded.

"I'll come as well," Aidon chimed in, even as Aleissande shot him a look of contempt. Clearly, his general did not agree with Aidon's thirst for adrenaline. But the king's mind was made up as he looked at Will and winked. "Given you haven't fully recovered, I'm happy to lend you a hand should a skirmish break out."

Gods. If Will had known Aidon would be this smug about saving his life, he might have chosen death over facing that godsdamn smirk.

"I'm coming as well," Aleissande remarked in the firm tone that Will was learning was simply the general's voice. She shot Aidon another exasperated look that Will noticed Aidon chose to ignore. He tucked that away for later, along with his questions about Josie and whatever had befallen the two siblings.

"Alright then," Sarhash said as he stood. "Let's greet these visitors of ours."

545

"I don't like this," Tova muttered from beside Aya, her eyes tracking the rising portcullis. Aya didn't respond. She'd barely spoken since the Milsaion ship had come alongside them, cannons at the ready. They didn't seem keen to believe that they were Talan reinforcements, and Aya supposed she could not blame them.

They were an army of rebels and crooks and thieves.

"Are the other Talan troops alive?" Aya had asked one of the soldiers desperately after she boarded their ship. She and Tova had agreed to parlay, leaving the rest of their unit anchored alongside their vessel. But the Milsaion troops refused to answer. Their silence had grated on Aya, but it was Tova who snapped, "Is this a negotiation or not?"

They didn't answer that either.

They'd barely spoken, even when they'd received the orders to bring them to the cave, which was apparently a hidden upriver entrance beneath the fortress that towered atop the mountains.

Aya scanned the cave now, the space lit with torches and spots of sunlight from the holes in the granite cave top. Two Milsaion soldiers stood guard on the rocky shore, their backs facing a line of steps carved into the stone.

Aya glanced over the edge of the ship, reassuring herself for the hundredth time that their vessel was being towed by the Milsaion ship. The fighters stood at the ready, weapons not visible, but easily within reach. Aya had to hand it to Mathias. He had chosen his people well.

Her fingers tapped an unknown rhythm against the side of her leg as she waited for the ship to anchor and the crew to ready the gangway. She and Tova were escorted off the ship, their fellow Talans forced to wait on their vessel while they walked up the stony shore. The sound of the portcullis closing behind them felt eerily similar to a dungeon door closing.

"Wait here," a Milsaion solider ordered curtly.

"For what?" Tova demanded, her arms folding as she glared at his retreating back. "Why the fuck did we come here again?" she mumbled to Aya. "They obviously don't need our help."

But Aya was focused on their surroundings, her fingers dancing within reach of the one knife they hadn't taken from her, unseen and unsurrendered. There were voices coming down the stairs, but the echoes of the cave made it impossible to distinguish them, or to pick apart the footsteps and know how many people approached. But it didn't stop them from trying.

"Three?" Tova murmured from the side of her mouth, her feet bracing apart in a subtle fighter's stance.

"Four," Aya answered, her jaw shifting in frustration as she tried to pick apart the voices.

He is not dead.

She shoved the thought away. Now was not the time to be seized by desperation's vise grip.

Finally, a shadow spilled across the stone shore they stood on. Aya felt Tova shift beside her, her hand reaching for her concealed blade just as Aya reached for her own.

But then she froze as a rich baritone spilled from the mouth of the stairs, her heart seizing in disbelief as its soothing tones washed over her, her shock so severe she couldn't even parse through his words.

But she knew that voice.

And as Aidon stepped out of the stairwell, a gasp escaped Aya's lungs, her body moving before her mind could warn her not to, not with the soldiers standing at the ready, fully prepared to strike her down.

But then Aidon was shouting, extending a hand to the guards who turned their swords on Aya, and he was running toward her, and Aya was meeting him in the middle of the melee, throwing her arms around him, his laugh joyous and bright and so *Aidon* that Aya couldn't help but hug him harder.

"You're here," she gasped into his shoulder.

"Of course I'm here," Aidon replied, drawing back so he could see her face. "I couldn't let Will have all the fun, could I?"

Aya's heart seized at Will's name, her breath catching as she tried to force out the question she was afraid to ask. "Is he—"

"Aya?"

The realm slowed as Aya looked past Aidon.

Will was standing at the base of the stairwell. And while he was dressed in clothes that clearly didn't belong to him—tan linen pants and a loose white linen shirt—and while there were circles under his eyes and bruises around his neck and a gash on his cheek that had clearly seen the healing touch of an Anima, he was whole, and *here*, and a broken sound was wrenching itself from somewhere deep within Aya.

And then she was moving, her body colliding with his so hard that Will staggered backward, but his arms wrapped just as tightly around her waist as he lifted her from the ground, her head burying in the crook of his neck. He let out a long breath that sounded something like relief, and Aya inhaled his woodsmoke and spiced honey scent deep into her lungs, not bothering to try to hold back the tears that slipped down her face.

"How are you here?" Will murmured, the question a rumble against her throat as he pressed his lips against her skin. He asked the question again, her feet touching the ground just as his lips captured hers, as if he didn't truly care about how they were together again, just that they were.

Aya was glad for it, glad to have something to anchor her to the realm as her head went spinning, her heart hammering in her chest as she kissed him just as fervently, her mouth opening at the slightest brush of his tongue.

He was alive. He was alive, and she could *feel* him, and gods, her heart was mending itself and shattering all over again but in the sweetest sort of pain.

I love you. The words were on the tip of her tongue, but someone cleared their throat, and Aya pulled herself away from Will's kiss, his eyes blazing with heat and reluctance as he shot the woman who had stepped up beside him a glare.

"I take it you know them, then?" she asked pointedly.

"Gods above, Aleissande," Aidon cursed from behind them. "Obviously."

Will kept an arm firmly around Aya's waist as he looked past her, taking in Tova and the anchored boat filled with Mathias's rogues, recognition flickering in his eyes as he realized that this hadn't been an officially sanctioned mission.

"I cannot thank your queen enough," a deep voice said from behind Will. Aya marked the crown on the man's head. "Her first two units were instrumental in ensuring Milsaio did not fall entirely."

"She sends her apologies she could not send more, Your Majesty." Tova was stepping forward, her chin held high in that easy confidence that came so naturally to her. "But she hoped that sending a carefully assembled team of fighters would do."

The lie fell easily from Tova's lips. A necessary one, given all that was unfolding. It would not gain them any allies to make it clear that Gianna had refused aid.

"We will take all the help we can get," the king replied. It was beneficial, Aya supposed, that war was too consuming to allow one to look too closely at anything but survival.

"Aya, Tova," Will said, his hold on Aya unmoving as he turned to face the man, "this is Sarhash, King of Milsaio and ruler of the seas. Your Majesty, this is our general, Tova. And this is Aya, the…"

Will's voice trailed off, the words dying on his lips as he looked down at her.

I hate it when you call me that.

He remembered. Even in the midst of fucking war, he remembered.

It warmed the coldest places of Aya, enough that she gave him a small, understanding smile before stepping out of his hold to face the king.

"A pleasure, Your Majesty," Aya said, giving Sarhash a bow. "Our fighters are at your service." It was effortless to create a ripple of lightning across her skin, effortless to call those affinities forward in tandem, creating something raw and powerful that she had previously only been able to call forward in fear or grief.

Murmurs rippled through the cave as her light illuminated her skin. But Aya held Sarhash's gaze as she straightened and added, "As is the Second Saint."

79

WILL HAD NEVER CONSIDERED HIMSELF AN IMPATIENT man. But as they reconvened in the war room, Aya and Tova now joining them, he found his focus drifting, a restlessness coursing through him as Kiara briefed Aya and Tova on the situation with Kakos.

He was all too aware of how Aya's arm brushed against his as she shifted, and how it sent a ripple of flame through his blood. She was *here*, and Tova had come, too, and there was no way Gianna had sent them, and he wanted her alone to get answers, but only after he had reacquainted himself with every inch of her.

Tasting death had clearly solidified his priorities. Let the world fucking burn. As long as he was with her when the flames consumed them. That was the only death he would settle for.

But Aya's face was one of concentration, that firm set of her jaw indicative of the rapidity of the thoughts moving through her mind.

"Two days since your retreat, and there hasn't been any movement?" she finally asked, a small crease forming between her brows as she looked to Kiara.

Aidon shot him a knowing glance from across the table, as if to say, *Of course she sees it, too.*

"We believe the arrival of King Aidon's forces was enough to stay them. And once they become aware the Second Saint is here…"

"No," Will interjected. It was the first word he'd spoken, and his abruptness attracted more than one raised brow. "Announcing Aya's presence only puts a larger target on these islands. And with all due respect, Majesty, even with the additional forces, that would be a blow I do not think Milsaio would survive."

It was sound reasoning. Even Aleissande was nodding her agreement, and Will hadn't seen the general express anything other than disdain or displeasure. But Aya cut him a look, her lips pressed together as she bit back an argument he was sure he would hear later.

"What are the odds of retaking the capital?" Tova asked from her place on Aya's left. The impact of the three of them sitting here together, against Gianna's orders, hit Will with unexpected force. This was the Tría they could have been, the Tría Gianna could have had at her disposal. It made something in him ache as he realized the loss of some desire he hadn't even realized he'd had.

"If Kakos doesn't have reinforcements to send for? I'd say there's a sixty-five percent chance we could retake the capital," Kiara answered.

"I like those odds," Tova and Aidon said simultaneously. They looked at each other with matching grins, and Will watched as Aya bit her lip, as if she were trying to contain her own amusement.

"The odds improve if we remain here," Kiara muttered. "This terrain is far better suited for our army's advantage."

"And if Kakos brings additional warriors?" Aleissande asked.

Kiara's face was grim. "That is a game of hypotheticals."

War was a game of hypotheticals, but Will could see her point. No one knew just how large Kakos had grown their army in the years since the embargo. Clearly, they'd had numbers when they attacked Sitya, and they'd shown just how powerful they were when they took the capital.

He supposed they could have reinforcements on the way. Or those reinforcements could be biding their time, waiting to use the spoils of these battles to launch a larger-scale attack.

Will had spent years attuning himself to Aya. And so it was no surprise that he felt her tension as soon as it seized her, her mind likely conjuring up the same scenarios. And still, they didn't have answers. About Gianna, about the prophecy.

"We hold position for now," King Sarhash said decidedly. To Aya and Tova, he added, "My home is your home. I'll have spare rooms for you two made up immediately, and your soldiers are more than welcome to share the barracks with my forces. Anything you need, you let us know."

"Thank you," Aya murmured. "Your hospitality, especially given the circumstances, is not taken lightly."

"I'll go brief our soldiers," Tova said as she stood. To Aya, beneath the rustling of the rest of the room standing and readying to leave, she muttered, "Remind them of *decorum* and to keep their thieving hands to themselves."

Aya's lips twitched, but any response was drowned out by an overly eager Aidon, who had pushed his way to their side of the table. "I'll escort you. Someone will need to show you where the barracks are."

"Subtle," Will remarked beneath his breath, but Aidon shot him a look.

"Aya," he continued, pointedly changing the subject. "Josie is here. I'm sure she'd love to see you. I'll track her down after I show Tova the barracks."

That had a rare true smile breaking through Aya's careful composure, and Will wasn't sure he would ever get used to seeing the way it lit not just her face, but everything in the vicinity. As if that light she had shown them in the cave was woven in her very spirit.

"She came with your forces?" Aya asked, pride evident in her tone.

"Unfortunately," Aleissande muttered as she passed them. Aya stared after the general, clearly affronted on her friend's behalf.

"It was an unsanctioned mission for her," Aidon said by way of explanation. Ah, so *that* explained the look he'd had in Will's chambers. It tightened his features once more as he said to Aya, "We can discuss it later."

Because clearly, there was more than Aidon was letting on. Even Will could see that. Aidon gestured for Tova to follow him, nodding to Will and Aya in dismissal. And then, finally, *finally*, they were alone, the only sound in the room the soft click of the door as it shut behind Aidon.

Will allowed himself a selfish moment to drink her in. To rememorize the slope of her nose, and length of her lashes, and the crystal blue of her eyes. The image he'd conjured, the one he'd tried to hold in those moments he thought were his last...

It did not do her justice. Not in the slightest.

Aya took a step toward him, her hands cupping his cheeks as she tilted his head down to hers. Her eyes darted across his face, a quiet hunger in them, as if she were soaking in all of him, too.

"She said you were dead." It took a moment for her words to sink through the haze of simply being near her. And while her comment was jarring enough to send him reeling, Will's hands found her hips and he tugged her in to him, unwilling to let even the shock of her revelation drive a sliver of space between them. "I thought you were dead."

Questions were on his tongue, but he swallowed them down at the tremor in her voice. This wasn't a debriefing. She wasn't telling him to answer the burning questions he'd had since she showed up with a group of fighters he knew weren't part of the forces.

Will gently grabbed her chin between his thumb and forefinger, tilting her head up slightly as he kissed her, deep and slow. "I'm here, *mi couera*," he muttered against her lips. A shudder raked through her, as if the vibration of his voice went all the way down her spine.

She pulled back slightly, her nose grazing his as she whispered, "I was afraid to hope."

Gods, did he know what that was like. But the corner of his mouth lifted, his head tilting back so he could see her fully. "Would it make it better if I told you I *was* almost close to death?"

It was his favorite way of pulling her from the tangle of her mind, if only because he got to hear her beautiful laugh, which was mixed with an incredulous scoff as she released his face and landed a hard smack to his chest.

"I hate you," she said, chuckling.

Will's grin only grew, and he pulled her impossibly closer. "No," he muttered. "You don't."

"No," Aya breathed. "I don't."

Her grin melted into a smile he hadn't seen on her before. It was another variation of that rare, unbridled one, but softer. Shyer. She gripped the fabric of his shirt around her fingers, pressing up on her toes to make their eyes level. "I love you."

The words were quiet but certain, edged with a fierceness that was so utterly like Aya that it cracked something in Will in the most beautiful of ways.

"I loved you in the paddock in Rinnia. I loved you in the desert of Trahir. I loved you in the middle of the ocean, and in the mountains, and in the thousands of breaths and moments we've somehow woven together to make *this*," she breathed, tugging on his shirt. "I love you, and I hope I get a thousand more of those moments so I can tell you over and over until you're sick of hearing me say it."

Will's breath was shallow, his throat thick and his eyes wet, and it would be *impossible* to ever grow tired of hearing those words come from her mouth, and he tried to tell her just that, but it came out as a jumble of syllables as he crushed his lips against hers, his hip clipping a chair as he pushed Aya back into the wall.

"I love you," he murmured, the words a whispered prayer against the skin of her throat. "I love you." Again, against her collarbone. Her fingers tangled in his hair, and she tugged his head back up to hers, her lips finding his as he continued to murmur the words over and over on every inhale he took when his lungs became desperate enough for air for him to pull away from her, only to dive back in again.

Their lips were red and swollen by the time Aya stayed him with a hand to his chest. His leg had ended up between hers, his hand digging into her hip and well on its way to encouraging her to move against him in the way he knew she wanted to. He could see it in the brightness of her eyes and the flush of her cheeks.

"I don't know that this is what Sarhash meant when he said his home is our home," Aya teased breathlessly. Will chuckled, and Aya bit her lip as the sound vibrated through every part where they were pressed together.

"Are you saying such things are better fit for a bed, Aya love? Because I have one ready and waiting."

Her nose scrunched, even as Will trailed the lightest of kisses and nips up her jaw. "I need to bathe," she replied, squirming against him and sucking in a sharp breath at how it pushed her core harder against his leg. Will sucked on the spot beneath her ear, relishing the steady thud of her head falling back against the wall. "I've...I've been on a ship for days."

"Don't care," Will muttered. He couldn't stop tasting her, and touching her, and feeling the hammering of her heart against his chest, a reminder that they were both alive to experience this. Aya's fingers raked through his hair again, and this time, her touch was gentle. Soothing. As if she could feel the fire coursing through his veins, could feel the way he could *die* from wanting her, his love so intense it twisted his lungs until he could hardly breathe.

He let his head fall against her shoulder, let himself be soothed by the soft touch of someone who only showed her sharp edges to the world. And when his breath was finally steadier, he pulled himself away from her and held out his hand.

"Come on," he said. "You can wash up in mine."

80

AYA COULDN'T RECALL THE LAST TIME SINKING INTO HOT water felt this good. She let her eyes close, her head tilting back to rest on the edge of the tub as her aching muscles finally unclenched. "I didn't expect this was a luxury I'd be walking into when we arrived," she confessed quietly.

Will's deep chuckle bounced off the tiled floor, reaching her like an echo from where he stood leaning back against the sink. "One could forget there's a war going on at all," he agreed. It was a quiet reflection, but it was wrought with all that was waiting for them outside these walls.

Aya turned her head, her eyes opening as she took him in. Her gaze lingered on the bruises on his neck.

One could forget there was a war going on, except that Will bore the physical reminders.

"How are you here?" he murmured. It was the same question he'd rasped against her skin on the shore of the cave, and while it was tinged with the same awe, the same relief, he wanted answers now. She could tell by the sharpness in his gaze and the concentration that pulled his lips into a straight line.

Gods, where to even begin? Had he truly only been

gone two weeks? All that had transpired in that time felt overwhelming when she was faced with recounting it now.

Mathias and his attack on her father and his hiding of the supplier and Gianna's knowledge of Dominic's heresy and—

Aya ducked her head beneath the water, breathing out in a stream of tiny bubbles before resurfacing. Will was exactly where she'd left him, his focus fully on her. Aya scratched a nail against the metal of the tub and began.

She started with finding her father's attacker, and she spared Will none of the detail, nor the lengths she went to ensure Eryx would work with them. She detailed her partnership with Liam, and their plan to kill Mathias, and how they'd been given the supplier instead.

Will was quiet as she recounted how the supplier had gone to Gianna first, but he swore viciously when Aya mentioned Lena's involvement, his hands gripping the edge of the sink so tightly, she was surprised it didn't break.

"Every time I've turned around, she's been there," he spat out. "She's been in Gianna's pocket this whole fucking time."

Aya stood from the tub, something in her warming slightly as Will instinctively reached for a towel and handed it to her, even in the midst of his rage. Aya sucked in a breath as she dried herself off, turning over another suspicion she'd been mulling over during the journey here.

"She was in the dungeons when I found you," Aya remarked as she wrapped the towel around herself. "It's not a stretch to believe that she was the one who told Gianna about us."

But Will shook his head, a muscle in his jaw twitching as he bit back his anger. "She knew the whole time. Lena may have confirmed it, or shared that you reciprocated the feelings, which may be why Gianna finally decided to rid herself of me, but she knew before then."

Which brought them to how, exactly, Aya was here. "Gianna received your call for aid. But she said it was news that Milsaio had fallen. That all in the unit were presumed dead." Aya bit her bottom lip, an echo of that agony she had felt in the forest aching somewhere inside her as she approached him. Lightly, she trailed a finger across the bruises on his throat, goose bumps rising on his skin as she did so. She felt the bob of his throat against her finger, and she lifted her gaze to find his eyes dark in a wholly different way than just moments ago.

"She was nearly right," Will remarked, the truth vibrating against her finger. "Aidon arrived just in time. And even then, I completely burned my affinity out. Even now, I doubt I could muster much of anything in my well."

Aya slid her hand down to where the base of his throat met his collarbone, laying her hand flat against the space there. His skin was warm beneath her palm. "I'm sorry I didn't get here in time," she breathed. "When Tova found the truth, I–I went straight to Mathias and demanded he give me fighters."

Will curled a piece of her wet hair around his finger, his lips tipping into a smirk. "I thought a few of them looked familiar. I *am* curious as to how you managed to convince him to lend you his cronies."

Aya gave an innocent shrug. "I might have threatened to kill everyone in his home."

Will blinked at her, a brief look of surprise flashing across his face, and then his hand was curling around her hip, his grip firm even through the towel, and his forehead was pressing against hers as he growled, "I should *not* find that as attractive as I do."

Aya's laugh was breathless, her inhale sharpening as he dipped his head to kiss her neck. "Which part? Gathering an army for you, or threatening to kill people for you?" she joked, her throat going dry as Will's hands slid to the top of her towel.

"All of it," he muttered against her jaw, the backs of his fingers brushing against the swell of her breasts as he undid the towel. The coarse fabric tickled her sensitive skin as it skimmed down her body and dropped to the floor.

Slowly, Aya undid the buttons on his shirt, her eyes locked on his as she murmured, "I suppose I do love you," as if it were the only logical explanation for all she had done.

She supposed it was.

Her words snapped whatever tether Will was keeping on his control. He tugged her roughly in to him and captured her lips in a bruising kiss, and it was enough to have Aya pushing his shirt off his shoulders, desperate for the feel of his skin against hers. Will released her only to tug his shirt off completely, and then his hands were back on her, stroking and grabbing and *memorizing* every single bit of her skin, her curves, and gods, she wanted him, she wanted him, she would never ever *not* want him.

Aya nipped at Will's lip, and he sucked in a breath as he turned and slammed her back against the wall, that godsforsaken thigh shoving *exactly* where she was aching.

"Right back where we started," Will mused, his teeth grazing the shell of her ear and his laugh low and dark and sinful when it made her jerk her hips. Aya gasped, her lungs tightening as pleasure zipped through her, and gods, it had never felt like *this*.

Aya's hands trembled as she found his belt, her breath punching from her lungs as Will's hand gripped her hip once more and *tugged*, encouraging her to move her core against his leg.

"Fucking hells," Will groaned, as if he were in the sweetest sort of pain. "I can feel how wet you are through my godsdamn pants."

And perhaps that should have embarrassed Aya, but her skin was on fire, and her heart was hammering, and it was filthy and lewd, but she didn't fucking care. She *finally* managed to get his belt undone, and then she flipped open the button on his pants and her hand was reaching inside, desperate to feel him. She closed her hand around his rock-hard cock, a soft moan escaping her at the warmth and smoothness of him, but in the next moment, Will had her wrist pinned against the wall, and then the other, and he was looking at her with a wicked grin as he dipped his head and dragged his teeth across the peak of her breast. Aya's head slammed back against the wall, another breath rushing from her lungs as she writhed, the muscle of Will's thigh providing the *perfect* friction against her throbbing core, and gods, he was going to kill her.

"Please," she begged as he went to work on her other breast, all tongue and teeth and *fuck*, she couldn't *breathe* from how badly she wanted him, couldn't form words besides *Will* and *please* and *gods*.

Will let out another dark chuckle as he moved his lips to her ear. "Beg all you want, Aya love. I'm not letting up until you ruin these ridiculous pants they gave me."

Oh fucking *gods*. Aya was so utterly lost in the sound of his voice and the feeling of his lips and teeth that she hadn't even realized he'd released one of her wrists so he could guide her hip once more, encouraging her to rock back and forth, his breath hot on her neck as he laid a trail of kisses there. And then his hand was on her breast, and his mouth was back against her ear, and his leg was moving from between hers as he said, "On second thought…"

Will dropped to his knees, a dark smile playing on his lips as he looked up at her. "Let's let them hear what it sounds like when a saint is properly worshipped."

And then his mouth was on her, his tongue licking her slit as he slid her leg over his shoulder and pinned her hips to the wall with his other hand. Aya's hands tangled in his hair, her hips jerking despite his hold as his tongue dipped into her. His fingers followed, and her breaths became mere pants as desperate, high-pitched noises escaped her throat. Will groaned against her, the sound vibrating through the very core of her, and his tongue circled that bundle of nerves as he curled his fingers inside her.

It was enough to shove Aya off the precipice he'd dragged her on, and she grabbed Will's shoulder as she shuddered, her hips jerking as she came. She tried to pull away from him, but Will held her there, his mouth drawing out her pleasure like a starving man at his first meal in weeks.

He pressed a chaste kiss to the inside of her thigh, his hand stroking her leg as he lowered it from his shoulder before he stood. He was smirking, his eyes glinting with satisfaction, but Aya twisted his hair in her fingers as she pushed up on her toes and kissed him before he could speak.

She grinned into it, using her body to move him backward, out of the bathing chamber and to the bed, where she pushed him down on to the mattress and made quick work of the pants he'd so desperately wanted her to ruin.

Aya wasted no time lowering herself onto him, their moans intermixing as Aya's eyes fluttered shut. He felt better than she remembered, something she hadn't even known was possible.

Perhaps it was the desperation that came with war. Or perhaps it was the relief that they had not lost each other. Or perhaps it was simply that they were madly, irrevocably, fucking devastatingly in love.

An expected swell of emotion stole her breath, and Aya opened her eyes to find Will's locked on her, his lips parted in something like awe. He pushed himself up, his arms curling around her and his forehead pressing against hers as they moved in tandem.

"You feel..." Will's words were tight with pleasure, and he cut himself off with a groan as Aya rolled her hips.

"Like home," she finished for him, the words an exhale against his mouth. Will sucked in a shuddering breath, his eyes bright with pleasure and love as he tangled a hand in her wet hair, his palm cupping the back of her head as he speared his hips upward, pushing even deeper, dragging another gasp out of Aya.

She could die right here and be happy, she decided.

Aya blinked back the burning in her eyes, desperate for him to keep moving, to keep fueling that fire that he had poured into her very blood, but it was impossible to hide herself from Will. He stilled, one hand tangled in her hair, the other clutching her waist, his fingers gripping her tight enough that she wouldn't be surprised if she had bruises in the shape of his fingertips.

And yet his voice was heartbreakingly gentle as he rasped, "What is it?"

Aya shook her head, her nose brushing his with the movement. "Too many words," she breathed. "Too many things I—" She rocked her hips against his, hoping he knew what she was trying to say.

She was feeling too much. The swell of emotion, of pleasure, of love, was too much.

But for once, she didn't care.

Slowly, she pressed a hand to his chest, right over the hammering rhythm of his heart. She stared at Will for a moment longer, waiting for recognition to dawn on his face, before she closed her eyes and let her shield fall, leaving herself open, and exposed, and utterly at his mercy.

They had never done this before. It had always seemed like their power didn't belong here. But now, Aya saw it for what it was:

Sharing that last part of themselves with each other.

Letting that final wall fall.

Will let out a low curse, his fingers gripping her even tighter as his own shield fell and their sensations, their emotions, met in the middle. Love and pleasure and desperation and longing, all wrapping together in a mix of magic and movement as Will began to rock his hips again, their lips not quite touching, but hovering *right there* as they exchanged breaths.

"I only need three words," he gritted out as he began to pick up his pace, his forehead pressing against hers. The pleasure inside of her was building, pulling so tight she swore that when it snapped, she'd break with it. It intensified with every thrust of Will's hips, every brush of his sensations against hers, his motions sharp and hard, as if he knew the exact way to pull the most ecstasy from her body.

He captured her lips in a searing kiss, swallowing her gasps and her moans and pulling away only to say, "I love you."

That pleasure inside her snapped, her muscles clamping down on Will and dragging him into bliss with her as she came. Will's shout was hoarse, his lips still pressed against hers as they trembled and shook and clung to each other as if daring the world to try to tear them apart.

And when they finally came down, their breaths still shallow and bodies still tangled, Aya pressed a soft, slow kiss to his lips and gave him those three words, too.

81

"THIS FEELS A BIT PERFUNCTORY, DOESN'T IT?" COLE'S question rang out from across the dungeon cell. Josie wiped her brow, leaning her weight on her mop as she shot her friend a look.

"I'm fairly certain that's the point," she retorted. They'd been relegated to cleaning the dungeons, and the bathing chambers, and the weaponry, and anything else that needed a rag or a mop or soapy water ever since they'd made it to the third island. The punishment hadn't even come from Aleissande. Not directly, at least. One of the senior-ranking Visya on the elite unit had delivered it.

Aleissande hadn't said a word to either of them—not since they were discovered by her and Aidon just as the ship was approaching battle. It was amazing they'd managed to go undetected for three days.

Impressive, really.

But Aleissande's gaze had been anything but impressed. And Aidon…Josie had never seen Aidon this angry at her. Sure, they'd fought over the years as all siblings did. But this… this was a fury she hadn't met in her brother before.

He'd waited until after the battle to chew her out, unable

to get all his words in when they were approaching the port under siege. But once they'd gotten Will and the others to safety—once they had settled into the palace—Aidon had grabbed her arm and pulled her into an abandoned room.

"What the *fuck* were you thinking?" he'd snarled. "Do you realize the danger that you put yourself in? That you put *Cole* in?"

"You don't get to talk to me about danger," Josie had shot back. "Not when you are willing to let yourself *die* or risk discovery simply by fighting." A flicker of realization passed over Aidon's face then, and Josie latched on to it viciously. "Yes. I went to see Natali. Imagine my surprise when I found you in *another* lie, Brother."

"Godsdammit," Aidon had hissed, taking a step toward her. "I am not just your brother. I am your *fucking* king! When I tell you that you cannot join a mission, you *cannot join a mission*. I trusted you to defend our capital. To defend the people I left behind to answer this call for help. And you took that trust, and you threw it back in my fucking face."

Aidon rubbed a hand across his jaw, anger sharpening his features as he stalked away from her. "If Aleissande decides to expel you from the force for disobeying a direct order from both your general and king, do not come to me to advocate on your behalf," he spat out.

And then he had left, his words ringing in the empty space for far longer than Josie cared to admit.

Footsteps sounded in the dungeon hall, pulling her from her thoughts. One of the Zeluus from the Visya unit stopped outside the cell. "The general wants to see you," she said curtly. Dread curled in Josie's gut. Would Aleissande truly dismiss her from the force?

Would this be yet another thing she had failed at?

But despite the way her pulse had picked up, Josie squared her shoulders and kept her chin high as she stepped out of the cell to follow the Zeluus, who had already started back down the hall. She cut a glance at Cole, who mouthed, *Good luck,* with an enthusiasm that was never far away, even in the direst of circumstances.

Josie rolled her eyes, but she made sure he saw the upward tilt of the smile she forced, and hoped looked genuine, before she followed the Zeluus. They walked in silence for several minutes, and it was enough to have Josie's chest tightening as her thoughts whirled. The woman finally stopped at a door that led to a long terrace overlooking the jungle. She jerked her head toward it and turned and left Josie without another word.

Aleissande was waiting against the balustrade, her arms folded over her chest. Her blond hair was down for once, its gentle waves brushing her shoulders. Josie had never seen it like that, and her first thought was that it made Aleissande look softer.

But then there was the severe line of her mouth, which tightened as she laid eyes on Josie.

They stared each other down for a moment, the heavy silence of the jungle that stretched beyond them seeping into every crevice of the terrace.

"Explain yourself," Aleissande finally ordered. She stayed leaning against the clay balustrade, as if it were physically anchoring her to the spot and preventing her from launching herself at Josie and showing her, with her fists, just how angry she was.

Josie braced her feet apart, her jaw shifting as she considered what she could possibly say to clear her name but not condemn her brother.

There was nothing.

"You truly have nothing to say?" Aleissande pressed.

Josie clasped her hands behind her back, her chin dipping slightly. But she kept eye contact with Aleissande as she said, "I thought I could help." It was the closest to the truth she could get. And she *had* helped. She had held the line and protected their method of retreat, and it had changed the outcome of what would have been a massacre on that beach.

Aleissande's sharp jaw shifted, a rare breeze making it over the fortress wall, into the mountains, and across the terrace. "That's all?"

"What do you want me to say, Aleissande?" Josie asked, frustration pricking at her skin. "What is it that you'd like to hear? That it was reckless? Fine. It was reckless, as is the fucking king going into battle, but I'm sure you had your words with him, right?" The words spilled from Josie before she could even think about how this was the last person she wanted to break down in front of, but now that she'd started, she couldn't stop.

"Or perhaps you want to hear that I put Cole at risk? He's a grown man and makes his own choices, but yes, by merely befriending him, I have put him at risk. Because *that* is what happens when anyone gets close to this godsdamn family, but apparently, I have yet to learn that. It was either let him come or strike him down, and I was not about to do the latter. I was not about to fail *another person* I cared about!"

Josie's words were hoarse and loaded with months and months of anger, and frustration, and fucking *hurt*. It dawned on her then, as she shouted the words into the endless abyss of the jungle, that this was the best place Aleissande could have chosen for this conversation. That perhaps, the general was smart enough to know that Josie was on the precipice of shattering.

But Aleissande just blinked at her, impassive and stoic as always, and her steadiness in the wake of Josie's unraveling made Josie want to scream.

"But you did," Aleissande replied, her voice even and quiet and, *gods*, Josie was going to pummel her if she didn't show some godsdamn emotion. "Your king trusted you with the protection of our people, and you failed him by coming out here because of some self-important—"

"Do not"—Josie cut her off, taking a single step toward the general—"presume to know anything about what motivated me to be here."

"Then *tell* me," Aleissande pressed.

But Josie was done. She let out a breath, that spark of anger still there, but smothered by her duty.

Responsibility.

Loyalty.

She took a step back.

"Just get on with it," she said warily. "Cut me loose and be done with it."

Aleissande's lips pursed as she considered Josie for a long moment. "I know," she finally said. "About his power." Even in privacy, Aleissande did not identify Aidon. But it didn't stop Josie from reaching for ignorance and denial automatically, the last seventeen years preparing her for a moment just like this.

"I don't know what you're talking about."

"I've seen it. In the dungeons—and I swore never to speak of it, even though he was hellsbent on making me. Stubbornness is a family trait, I see," Aleissande retorted.

Josie bit back the hundreds of questions she wanted to hurl at Aleissande, and the bitter betrayal she felt that Aidon had told his general—his second choice of a Second—before his own sister.

"If you've sworn not to speak of it, then you should stop speaking," Josie hissed, her eyes scanning the balcony.

"We're alone out here," Aleissande replied. "I've been promised privacy."

Josie choked on an incredulous laugh. As if a promise meant *anything*. As if a promise prevented someone from doing whatever was in their own best interest.

Something like understanding flitted across Aleissande's face, her lips parting as if she were carefully choosing her words. "I would rather fall on my sword than betray my king."

Betray her king, like Viviane had.

The implication was there, and it was worsened by the—*Fuck*, was that pity in Aleissande's eyes? Josie shook her head, her hands curling into fists at her sides. "I am so glad my brother has found such a trusted confidante," she seethed. "Did he also tell you about how that godsforsaken tonic he takes is killing him slowly, because every day he shoves his power down, the stronger and more unpredictable it grows, until one day it will devour him entirely?"

Aleissande's face went slack, and Josie felt a sick rush of victory at that. "Did he tell you how he has chosen death or certain discovery by being *here*? By taking more tonic so that he can fight in this war? Did you know, General? Did you agree to let your king sign his early death sentence?"

Josie was in Aleissande's face now, her chest brushing against the general's as she spat out, "Because if you did, you might as well fall on that sword right now, because *you've* failed him."

Josie wasn't sure when she'd shoved Aleissande, but suddenly Aleissande was gripping her wrist, her face a breath from hers as she growled, "Do that again. I *dare* you."

Her breath was hot against Josie's mouth, her blue eyes bright with anger and something else, something Josie couldn't place because her own heart was thundering, or perhaps it was Aleissande's heart racing against her chest, and all she could think was that *finally*, finally something had broken through that stern, cold, mask that Josie had been wanting to put her fist through.

Aleissande shoved her backward, her eyes blinking hard, as if she were coming back to herself. She inhaled, long and sharp, through her nose before shaking her head. "You're fucking infuriating."

"Then cut me loose," Josie shot back quietly. It was risky to goad Aleissande like this. She very well might do just as Josie dared her to. But there was something zipping through

Josie's blood, some adrenaline she hadn't felt in quite some time, and she had a feeling, especially as Aleissande's jaw tightened, a small muscle in her cheek flickering with the force of it, that Aleissande would not.

"That's why you snuck on board," Aleissande finally remarked. "To try to protect him."

Josie nodded once, and she swore that beneath the irritation, the frustration, hells, even the exhaustion on Aleissande's face, there was a hint of respect in her eyes.

They had something in common, after all.

Aleissande nodded once, as if confirming something to herself, before she straightened, her chin lifting in that aggravating way of hers. "You'll be given additional attendant duties when we return and restricted to City Guard patrol only for three weeks." It was a demotion of sorts, but at least she wasn't expelled from the force entirely. Aleissande didn't bother to wait for Josie's agreement before she stalked past her.

The general paused, her hand sliding up Josie's arm to grip her bicep. The soft waves of Aleissande's hair brushed Josie's cheek, sending a shiver down her spine as Aleissande dipped her head and murmured, "And if you ever disobey an order from me again, I'll ensure your punishment actually fits such a crime."

She squeezed Josie's arm once, and then she was gone, ducking through the door at the back of the terrace.

Josie stared at the place Aleissande had just been, her bergamot scent lingering in the air.

"Well, *that* was interesting," a soft, smooth, *familiar* voice drawled from the doorway. Josie turned, a laugh escaping her on an exhale as she took in the woman standing there, her blue eyes crinkled in subtle amusement as she shot Josie a smirk. "Aidon told me you were in trouble, but he didn't mention it was *that* sort of trouble."

Seven hells, how Josie had missed her.

It was enough to shake her from her surprise and send her hurtling toward her friend, a shout of disbelief, of *joy* bursting from her as she threw her arms around the woman, a grin on her face and lightness in her heart as she finally greeted her.

"Fuck you, Aya."

82

WILL HAD BEEN RIGHT, AYA THOUGHT AS SHE SAT ON the rug in the room Tova was occupying, her back against the bed and a goblet of wine in hand. With Tova sprawled out on top of the mattress, and Aidon sitting cross-legged on the floor, and Josie beside Aya, and Will with his legs outstretched in a wooden chair and three bottles of wine they'd snagged from the kitchens, it was easy to forget they were in the middle of a war, waiting for the enemy to attack.

It felt so like those nights in Rinnia, when Aya, Will, Aidon, and Josie would eat in their family's informal dining chamber, laughing as Zuri regaled them with tales of Josie and Aidon's childhood antics.

Aya took a deep sip of her wine, her gaze darting between the two siblings. Josie had filled her in earlier on the divide between her and Aidon, and then made Aya swear on their friendship that she wouldn't tell Aidon she knew about the issues with his power.

But Will, it seemed, had had no such briefing.

"Alright," he drawled, taking a deep sip from his own goblet as he looked between Josie and Aidon. "Are you two going to tell us what the hells has you so at odds?"

Aidon managed to look affronted. "We're being perfectly cordial. We don't parade our problems around like some people I know," he retorted, looking meaningfully between Aya and Will.

Will ignored him and zeroed in on Josie instead. "Josie?"

"Do you want to tell them, or should I?" Josie asked her brother. Just like that, the easiness vanished from Aidon's face. "They deserve to know," Josie pressed. Aya felt Tova shift on the bed above them as she propped her chin on her hands.

"Well, now I'm certainly curious," Tova chimed in.

But Aidon wasn't amused. His shoulders had gone tense, his gaze calculating as he looked at Tova. "She's trustworthy," Aya assured him.

Aidon rolled his eyes, accusation written in the firm line of his jaw as he said, "Fucking hells, Josie, you already told Aya, didn't you?"

"And here I thought we were finally bonding, Your Majesty," Will remarked with an exaggerated wave of his goblet. Aidon looked like he wasn't sure who he wanted to murder first—his sister or Will.

"The tonic has made his affinity unpredictable," Aya explained to Will, her gaze fixed on Aidon. "And the longer he uses it, the worse it gets." Aidon looked like he was going to kill *her* now, and she gave him a small shrug. "I thought we were done keeping secrets from one another."

Josie nudged her arm, her wine dangerously close to sloshing all over them. "That's what I said!"

But Aya kept her focus on Aidon, letting him see the concern on her face as she said, "You're playing with your life."

"We're all playing with our lives. It's war, Aya."

"Wait a minute," Tova interjected from the bed. "Are you saying what I think you're saying?" She'd pushed up on to her knees, an incredulous look on her face as she stared at Aidon. "You're Visya?" Tova shot Aya a look. "You left this out of your tales of Trahir."

Aidon's throat bobbed as a heavy silence filled the room.

Of course Aya had kept his secret. She wasn't about to betray Aidon to anyone. But now they were here, and with another battle imminent, and Aidon risking his life to fight with them, and *Tova* betraying Gianna just by being here...

Well, hiding it seemed rather pointless.

"So," Tova drawled. "What's your affinity?"

And gods, Aya had never been more grateful for her friend's ability to completely shatter tension with a well-timed quip. Even Aidon was fighting off a grin while Will snorted a laugh into his goblet.

"I'm an Incend like you," Aidon replied, his grin turning sly. "Didn't you wonder why you were so immediately drawn to me?"

This time, it was Aya choking back a laugh as Josie rolled her eyes and Tova cooed, "Must be your humility."

Aya found Will looking at her, his lips tipping up in a knowing smile as he took a sip of his drink. Perhaps he was thinking what Aya was—that introducing Aidon and Tova was either the best or the worst thing to ever happen to all of them.

"Seriously, though," Aya said to Aidon once she'd recovered herself. "Why not train with Natali?"

Aidon cocked a brow. "Because you enjoyed the experience so much?" He let out a sigh. "I will not ask my troops to go to war and die while I sit in a palace. After everything, this gets to be my choice. This gets to be the type of king I *choose* to be."

He was looking at her intently, and she knew he was remembering their discussion in her room in Rinnia.

Haven't you ever wanted something for yourself?

This was his choice. And Aya hated it.

"Speaking of powers," Aidon continued, his gaze heavy on Aya. "How is untangling the prophecy coming? I assume you've made great progress if Gianna's allowed you to be here."

Aya drained her wine and grimaced. "Like Josie, my mission here is unsanctioned."

"No need to remind him," Josie muttered as she refilled Aya's goblet.

"Gianna wasn't going to send reinforcements at all," Aya continued. "She told us the islands had fallen, and that everyone was presumed dead."

Aidon blinked in confusion. "Why the hells would she do that?"

"You do recall how she tried to barter with Aya as if she were no more than cattle, yes?" Will muttered darkly.

"Still," Aidon pressed, disbelief woven in his voice. "Political alliances are made in such ways all the time. That's not the same as sentencing an entire unit of your army to death. And to what end? Was there news of movement toward Tala?" he asked Tova. "Was she intent on keeping troops there in that case?"

Tova shot him an affronted look. "If there was movement toward Tala, do you think I'd be here? And even if that was the case, why lie about the situation here?"

Why indeed. It was a question that had kept Aya circling in her own mind, and she hadn't been able to answer. It was one thing to want Will killed for his crimes against the crown. But if Aya knew one thing to be true about Gianna, it was that she was utterly devoted to the gods. Why, then, would she allow the heretics a single chance to gain a foothold? She had done it with Dominic, too. She knew he was aiding Kakos and let it play out...

Will had gone still, a faraway look in his eyes that told Aya he was turning something over in his mind. "Perhaps," he said slowly, as if searching for the words as he spoke them. "Perhaps she wants Kakos to be an actual threat."

Aya frowned, her head cocking as she considered it.

"Why the hells would she want that?" Josie asked.

Silence fell between the lot of them, but Aya's mind had begun to race, her spine straightening as she held Will's gaze.

The supplier. Dominic. Milsaio.

Hells, maybe even Sitya…

Gianna had stood by as Kakos grew stronger and stronger. She had done nothing to prevent them from becoming a viable threat, a threat that no one could ignore, that *Aya* would soon not be able to ignore…

"She thinks that's what it'll take for me to open the veil."

The words were out of Aya's mouth before she even *knew* she had come to the realization, but as it registered fully in her mind, her grip went slack on her goblet, the metal bottom clanking against the floor just beneath the chorus of questions that Tova, Aidon, and Josie pelted them with.

And just like that, they were drawn back into the reality that they were at war, the anxiety of it hanging heavily in the room.

"That's what the heretics want, isn't it? To war with the gods? You think she's partnering with Kakos?" Aidon asked sharply.

Aya and Will exchanged another look, coming to a silent agreement. *No more secrets.*

So Will told them everything. His mother's faked death. Her residence in Trahir. Her vision of the veil and suspicions of Gianna. Will's own desperate attempts to learn the truth from the queen directly, and how she had played him.

"Seven hells," Aidon swore. "Why haven't you *killed* her?"

"You think it's easy to kill the ruler of a kingdom?" Will snapped.

Aidon's gaze darkened with his stiff retort. "No. I don't."

It was the worst possible thing Will could have said. His face paled, his lips parting to apologize, but Tova was sliding off the bed, her brow furrowed as she began to pace. "That's why you think she planted the papers on me," she murmured to Will. "So that Aya would show her power."

Pain and guilt flickered across Will's face. "Yes. I was hoping when we returned that I could get back into her good graces.

That between Aya and me, we could uncover exactly what Gianna truly is trying to achieve." His eyes were wide as he looked to Aidon. "There's a possibility Lorna isn't even correct."

The explanation was intended for Aidon, but it had a shiver of dread snaking down Aya's spine as she remembered what Evie had said in her dream.

"The veil might not even be torn yet," Aya breathed. "But if she thinks that she can corner me into it, it's possible that *I'm* the one who—"

Her revelation was cut short as Tova held up a hand, her pacing coming to an abrupt stop as she turned toward the window. "Do you hear that?" she asked sharply.

The room fell silent immediately, and for a moment, Aya could hear nothing, not even their breaths. But then…

"Shouting," Josie remarked. "Someone is shouting."

They were instantly in motion, one of the bottles of wine tipping over as they rushed toward the door. Will got there first, and he was halfway into the hall before they realized Kiara was sprinting down it. Dread curled in Aya's stomach, dread and adrenaline as she calculated how quickly she could get to her fighting leathers and knives.

"There's more," Kiara gasped as she skidded to a halt outside the room. "There's *more*."

Will was pushing past her, his eyes fixed on the door of his room, ready to grab his weapons, but Kiara grabbed his arm and dragged him back.

"Not here," she panted, trying to catch her breath. "A scout. He saw them."

"Saw *what*?" Tova ground out.

Kiara's eyes were wide—with fear, with *sympathy*, with desolation—as she said, "Kakos is moving on Tala."

83

IT WAS TOVA'S MOTHER WHO HAD FIRST PUT THE IDEA OF aspiring to be a general in Tova's mind, during one of Tova and Caleigh's sisterly squabbles. Tova had devised the perfect strategy to catch Caleigh unaware, complete with diversions and all.

Their parents had grounded Tova on account of setting Caleigh's favorite dress on fire (it wasn't like she was *wearing* it at the time, alas), and her mother had had to hide her amusement when Tova argued that it wasn't her fault Caleigh couldn't think strategically.

Okay, little general, her mother had said. *Go to your room.*

Tova supposed it had just stuck after that.

She loved that her brain worked this way. That it could see several steps ahead, that it could calculate likely and unlikely moves. Which she supposed was why, as they raced back in the same godsdamn vessel they'd uselessly stolen to get here, she was *furious* that she hadn't seen this coming sooner.

It could have been a diversionary tactic, she supposed— attacking Milsaio and hoping to draw some of their forces here to assist. But there had been *no* reports of Kakos moving on Tala. None. Not a hint, nor a whisper.

It was why they'd fucking come in the first place. Kakos's forces were supposed to be concentrated in Milsaio. And yes, war was like gambling in the Rouline, but instead of copper they used their lives, and so she supposed she'd taken a gamble and lost, but she couldn't help but replay Will's theory in her mind.

What if this was what Gianna wanted?

What if their queen had *allowed* Kakos to march to force Aya's hand, so that she might call down the gods?

"Would she sacrifice her own kingdom?" Aidon had asked with a frown, his hands bracing on the table as he scanned the map he and Tova had been studying in the captain's quarters. He had insisted on coming, and lending what he could afford of his Visya unit. Who they could fit, mostly. The rest, including Aleissande and Josie, remained at the ready in Milsaio, as Kakos continued to wait in the capital.

"I don't know what she would do," Tova admitted quietly.

She couldn't imagine Gianna would leave her own people to die. But then again, she couldn't imagine Gianna would lie about the fall of an entire kingdom either.

And now Milsaio's forces were decimated and Aidon's divided, his unit in Milsaio exhausted, and fucking hells, she thought she might kill someone she was so angry.

Gianna.

She would kill Gianna.

That she knew for sure.

She didn't fault Aya, not one bit. And they couldn't possibly have known that Kakos hadn't hit Milsaio with all their might. Not with the calls for aid.

And yes, it felt like taking a little bit of herself back from Gianna, but if Gianna had indeed let Kakos march and hadn't prepared them for this fight…

Then what did it matter?

Either way, Tova ended up spending the time ruminating on ways to kill Gianna. Except for last night, when she'd found Will standing at the back of the ship staring off into the night.

"Will you tell me?" Tova had asked him hesitantly. "Will you tell me again what you said to me when you came into the cell?"

It was acceptance. An apology. And Will's own had come to her in the form of a patient retelling of every detail she couldn't remember, but believed did in fact exist somewhere forgotten in her mind.

And then you realized what I'd managed to hide from everyone. That I loved her. That I love her.

Tova had cried. So had he. And while they both vowed they'd never like each other, and this changed nothing, she thought it was okay that they lied then. That they did what they needed to keep themselves whole in that moment.

Or at least, as whole as they could be, with all that Gianna had forced them to do.

Akeeta had lain between them as they sat on the deck in silence, Tova's fingers seeking reassurance in the coarseness of the wolf's fur.

"She doesn't have the answer to the prophecy, does she?" Tova hadn't planned to ask Will that, but the question had fallen from her lips without her even giving it permission to do so.

Will had frowned at the sky, as if he were trying to decipher the intent of the gods themselves. "I wouldn't be surprised if Gianna has been ensuring she doesn't find it this whole time," he had finally confessed—another accidental admission she suspected he had never said aloud.

Tova was going to kill her.

If it was the last thing she did, Tova was going to kill their queen.

84

THE CRY OF WAR IN TALA DOESN'T START WITH THE WOMAN who is being tortured on the docks of the Rouline, a Diaforaté filling her lungs with blood while the water of the port drowns her on dry land. Nor does it start with the screams of those being burned alive in their homes, or butchered by those they trusted to protect them, but who serve a queen who has decided to let chaos reign.

The cry of war in Tala starts with the howl of a lone wolf on a boat that sails into a harbor, and the answering caw of a raven that settles on the mast of the ship, as if it knows carrion awaits.

85

Aya has known terror. It has looked like a young boy beside a grown man who reads her mother's name off a list of goods lost, reporting her death as if she's an item. It has looked like a broken bone protruding through an arm while the same boy lies in a puddle of blood. It has looked like her father, unresponsive on the floor of her childhood home.

Aya has known terror. But she has never known terror like arriving in the port of Dunmeaden to the utter destruction and chaos of war.

Chunks of brick blown apart from taverns and gambling halls of the Rouline littered the docks, and bodies floated in the harbor, and *screams* seemed to stretch from the port to the Relija to the Merchant Borough to the winding paths of the Malas.

Kakos was here. And Dunmeaden was falling.

Their feet had barely hit the planks of the docks before they were swarmed, but that, at least, they were ready for. Swords drawn, affinities at the ready, they met the attack head on.

"Where are the godsdamn Dyminara?" Will's question was a shout across a bloodied path, hardly heard over the clanging of Aya's sword as she fought off a Kakos solider. She extended a hand and tightened her fist, her affinity collapsing the man's lungs instantly.

She risked a quick glance around.

She didn't see the elite guard anywhere.

Perhaps they were further into the city.

"We need to get to higher ground!" Tova ordered.

Because right now, citizens were running into the mountains, and Kakos soldiers were everywhere, and the Talan force was between it all, trying desperately to stop the push of Kakos, which appeared to be heading toward the palace.

How had Kakos's forces grown so large? So powerful? How the hells was this possible?

The questions circled in Aya's mind as they fought their way steadily to the streets of the Merchant Borough. Sword, knife, affinity. Sword, knife, affinity. It was like a dance, a cadence all of her own as she carved a bloody path through the chaos.

"My gods," Tova breathed as she looked around them.

It was on fire. The restaurants, the offices, the apartments and gilded town houses. It was all on fire, flames stretching as far as Aya could see.

And the horror of it was enough to still Aya, just for a moment, just long enough for someone to grab her from behind, their arm hooking around her neck with unnatural strength. A Zeluus or a Diaforaté, she didn't know. She didn't care. She reached behind her, lightning dancing across her skin as she grabbed their head and sent a pulse of that raw, *raging* power into their very brain.

They were dead before they hit the ground, smoke pouring out of their ears and blood streaming from their eyes like tears.

Aya dropped to her knees, her breath coming in choked gasps as she braced her hand in a puddle of blood. Her power was churning inside her, begging for a drastic release, but there was too much chaos, too much risk of hurting one of their own. They needed an organized front. They needed *help*.

She glanced at the dead soldier next to her, sweat dripping down as her face as she realized they weren't wearing the uniform of the Kakos soldiers.

"Move!" Tova yelled.

Aya rolled instinctively, her back feeling the heat of Tova's fire as she sent a stream of it directly over her head. Another man dropped to the ground, his body charred beyond recognition. Tova yanked Aya off the ground, her face streaked with blood as she dragged Aya forward.

"They're not from Kakos," Aya croaked, her throat still sore from where the attacker's hold had been.

"I know," Tova said tightly. "They're prisoners from Chamen."

Tova's words registered slowly as dread crept over Aya like vines.

Gods above. Kakos had freed the prisoners. They had freed them, and now they were *here*, fighting with the heretics.

Aya shoved the thought away, her grip tightening on her sword as she grabbed a knife and flung it at a soldier that was chasing a terrified family fleeing to the mountains.

She scanned the scene, fear rising in her when she realized she couldn't see Will. She caught sight of Akeeta, a mere flash of white fur as she tackled a soldier to the ground and ripped into them. Aya hacked her way in that direction, blood flying from her sword. A flash of flame soared by her head, and then Tova was beside her, pulses of fire coming from her outstretched hand as she took down soldier after soldier.

Where is he where is he where is he?

"There," Tova barked, her voice already hoarse. She nodded to the right, where Will and Aidon stood back-to-back, a whirl of silver swords as they fought off a swarm of Kakos troops.

Aya grunted as she cut down an attacker in her way before she extended a hand, a steady stream of fire blasting into the troops advancing on Aidon and Will.

From beside her, Tova gave a small laugh of disbelief. "Mine are still prettier," she croaked.

Aya's relief was brief, a mere flicker, because as Aidon and Will raced in her direction, her eyes snagged on a familiar face.

Ophelle.

The Auqin was decked in her Dyminara battle black. And she was sending a wave of water toward some citizens.

Their citizens.

Aya was on her in the next moment, the knife from the sheath at her hip in her hand and at Ophelle's throat as she grabbed her from behind. "You fucking traitor," Aya snarled. Ophelle tilted her head away from Aya's knife, her eyes wide and wild as she strained to see Aya.

"She's waiting for you," Ophelle rasped, a small grin twisting her lips. "She asked us to bring you to her."

"Who?" Aya demanded.

"Gianna."

Cold snaked down Aya's spine, such an inconceivable contrast to the heat of the fire blazing around them. "*Bullshit*," she snarled. But Ophelle laughed, the sound crazed. "She has a Diaforaté friend, you know. The one who persuaded the Athatis when all thought it was impossible. I wonder what he can persuade *you* to do."

Aya paused, horror twisting around her insides like vines. "He's dead," she breathed. Another wild laugh from Ophelle.

"So easily fooled," she crooned.

Was that what had happened to Ophelle? Had the Diaforaté forced her to do this?

"How many of you are working with her?" Aya asked, wrapping her persuasion affinity so tightly around Ophelle that it forced the truth from her.

"Twenty."

Gods above. Aya was shaking, but she kept her knife steady, her grip tight as she snarled, "Where are the rest of the Dyminara?"

"Dead," Ophelle rasped. "Burned alive in the Quarter. Took care of the wolves, too. She said it could have been avoided if you had stayed—"

Aya didn't think as she sliced her blade across Ophelle's throat.

"You have to get out of here," Will insisted, his hand latching on to Aya's arm. But she couldn't move as she saw another member of the Dyminara appear. He beheaded a Talan soldier fighting off one of the Chamen prisoners.

And then there was another, attacking a young mother as she ran with her child.

And another, their knife finding the back of a Talan soldier's head.

Her fellow warriors—*traitors*, or dead.

Tyr, dead.

He could have been safe. She could have brought him with her to Milsaio, and he'd still be...

Aya's body shook so hard her teeth clacked painfully, her mind hazy as she tried to stay above her grief, to reconcile what she was seeing. Will swung her around to face him, his grip tight on her arms as he shook her slightly. "*Aya. You have to get out of here.*"

"I have to stop her," Aya breathed.

"No," Will started.

"I have to stop her!"

Because *this*...this had to be what Gianna wanted. Aya desperate and ready to do anything, *anything*, if it meant saving the people she loved.

Aya gripped Will's face. "Let me end this. I can end this." Her power was far greater than Gianna's. Greater than her Diaforaté's. Perhaps she could overpower him. Force *him* to change the tide of this attack.

"I'll kill her," Aya promised.

"She's mine!" Tova snarled from where she struck down a Kakos soldier.

"See? Tova will be with me. And I'll have the higher ground," Aya said to Will, jerking her chin toward the section of the towering Wall of Dunmeaden. The same section where Will had once stood, dancing across the edge, a smug king overlooking his kingdom.

"I can't use my power here. Not in the way it can help. But from there, I can see."

If Aya could get to the Wall, she could use her power more widely, could attempt to wipe out rows and rows of Kakos soldiers, but not like this. Not with the blur of bodies rushing about, not when she could hardly tell who was friend and who was foe.

"I'm coming with you," he insisted.

"No." Aya shook her head, tears streaming down her cheeks. "Organize the lines. Save our city. Save our people."

Because perhaps, by some miracle, they still could.

Will looked as if he were going to argue. His jaw tensed, his teeth grinding as he physically fought back his retort. He pressed a searing kiss to her lips instead, and for the briefest moment, Aya let herself lean into it, let herself breathe him deep into her lungs, let herself remember exactly what it felt like.

"I love you," he muttered as he pulled away, his hand grabbing hers, thumb pressed against the scar of their oath.

"No matter how far the fall," Aya whispered back. And then she grabbed Tova and ran, her feet carrying her faster than they ever had before as they raced toward the palace.

Aya's legs ached the further they sprinted into the mountains, her breath short and sharp as she rotated between her sword, her knives, and her affinities, trying everything she could to reserve the power in her well, just in case.

They reached the palace gates, two Dyminara standing guard, and she and Tova lunged without a second thought.

Yet something shattered in Aya as they struck their fellow warriors down. But they kept going, sprinting across the palace grounds, smoke from the Quarter billowing through the trees like a thick haunted mist. Aya looked toward the path that would take them to their home.

She could put the fire out. She could use her Auqin affinity and—

"No," Tova said, following her gaze. "It's too late. Come on." There were tear tracks on her round cheeks, but her face was set in fierce determination as she grabbed Aya and tugged.

She killed them. She killed them all.

Aya buried her agony beneath her rage, letting her hatred for Gianna add on a burst of speed.

They reached the palace doors to find them unguarded. Tova threw an arm out, blocking Aya before she could enter. "The Royal Guard should be here," Tova remarked, a frown marring her brow. "This could be a trap."

Aya's teeth ground together so tightly, she thought her jaw might snap. The screams of the dying echoed off the granite of the mountains, a chorus of *go, go, go* that had Aya shaking her head as she ducked under Tova's arm and through the door.

She would not stand by while her people were murdered. Not anymore.

"Aya!" Tova yelled, racing after her. She didn't have to go far. Aya had stopped just inside the entrance hall, her sword hanging limply at her side as she took in the carnage.

They had found the Royal Guard. At least ten lay dead by Aya's count, but gods, there was so much blood; blood and scraps of uniform and gore that made even Aya's stomach turn.

"Will told me about this," Aya breathed as she reached the center and turned a small circle. "The Diaforaté he faced in Kaksos…they have the strength of at least nine Visya. He saw one overcome by her own power."

"Do you think Gianna was behind this?" Tova asked. Aya turned back toward her, a *yes* primed on her lips, but the door behind Tova was opening, and Aya was reaching for her knife faster than she could say Tova's name and flinging it as hard as she could as Lena wrapped an arm around her friend.

Lena yanked Tova sideways, and Aya screamed as Lena's knife found Tova's chest.

# 86

WILL HAD REFLECTED ON DYING MORE IN THE LAST several days than he had ever wished to. But the thoughts came creeping back in as he and Aidon fought side by side in the Merchant Borough, their swords glinting in the firelight.

Had his father been burned to death?

Did he care?

Would he die here, too, reduced to no more than ash?

"We need to re-form the lines," he choked out, smoke and dust coating his lungs. "We need an organized approach."

A muscle in Aidon's jaw twitched. "Any ideas?"

"You're the general," Will retorted. Aidon had just enough time to shoot him a look of disdain before they were lifting their swords once more. Gods, the Kakos force seemed endless. And with the turned Dyminara…

"Fuck!" Will swore, his sword coming down again and again as he channeled his rage into something visceral, something *useful*. He found a weak spot in the man's armor, and he fell, but then an affinity was slamming into him from the back, his shield buckling under the force of it.

Will stumbled forward, his body screaming in pain as he

turned to face the attacker. It was Cleo, the young Sensainos, her eyes dazed. "Cleo," Will bit out. "This isn't you."

But Cleo kept coming for him, her sword twirling in her hand as she sent lash after lash of agony into him. Will dropped to his knees, one hand braced on the ground. "Cleo!"

He couldn't kill her. He had *trained* her. He *knew* her. Cleo was not a traitor. Not by her own regard.

But she was stalking toward him, and it was her or him, and gods, he didn't want to die—

Cleo paused as a hair-raising howl ripped through the air. She had just enough time to turn her head in the direction from which it came before a mass of gray fur and teeth barreled into her, ripping into her shoulder.

"Tyr," Will breathed.

Tyr, it seemed, had no hesitation in ending Cleo's life. He lifted his head, his maw dripping with blood, brown eyes alight with fury as he tilted his head back and let out another vicious howl.

It was a battle cry.

A promise of vengeance.

A roar of pain and fury as their home *burned* around them.

As their own betrayed them.

And it was answered. First by Akeeta, and then, by a howl coming from the mountains. And another. And another. It reverberated throughout the Malas until the cry of the Athatis was all Will could hear as he pushed himself up. It pricked his skin and set fire to his heart as he sucked in a breath, readying himself to reenter the fray.

But the Kakos soldier heading toward him suddenly dropped to the ground, a knife sticking out of their neck. Behind him, blood soaked and soot covered, was Liam.

Liam, with a group of Dyminara at his back.

"Sorry we're late," Liam drawled as he reached Will. "Escaping a burning house is a bitch. As is saving this lot of beasts," he said as he jerked his head toward Tyr.

Tyr merely growled and lunged to assist a Talan solider.

Will sent a pulse of his power into an oncoming Chamen prisoner. She clenched her throat, her eyes bugging as she dropped to her knees. Liam's knife lodged itself in her skull.

"Fuck, I never thought I would be this happy to see you," Will croaked as he turned to Liam.

"Always so ungrateful," Liam retorted with a grim smile.

"I mean, he offered me a kiss. So clearly, I'm the favored of the two of us," Aidon chimed in from his other side as he shoved his sword into a warrior's chest. He kicked the man away, dislodging his blade, and flashed Liam a smile. "King Aidon of Trahir. A pleasure."

And then Aidon was sprinting ahead to where one of his Visya fought with a Diaforaté.

"How did you escape?" Will asked Liam.

"No time," Liam said with a shake of his head as he scanned the melee. "I'll regale you with the tale when you buy me a drink for saving your ass."

Will couldn't believe he could manage a laugh. "We need to organize some sort of front," he said. "Get them to retreat. How many Dyminara are left?"

"I didn't have time for a head count. Thirty, if I had to guess."

Not nearly enough. And the look on Liam's face confirmed that he knew it. But at least they outnumbered those turned traitor.

"Fuck it," Will breathed as he flipped his sword and squared his shoulders. "Can you take care of this while we organize?"

Liam flipped his knife. "I'll do my best."

Will nodded. "Aidon!" The king turned to him. "We need organization, now!"

Aidon grinned. "Good thing I'm a general."

87

"Please." Aya's voice broke as she raised her hands, her eyes fixed on Tova, who was slumped in Lena's hold. "Please let me heal her. I'll do whatever you want, Lena, just let me heal her."

Lena made a noise of contemplation and looked down at Tova with a grim smile. "What do you say, Tova? Should I let her?"

"Fuck you," Tova rasped beneath shallow breaths, her face pale.

"*Please*," Aya begged, lowering herself to her knees.

"Who's to say you don't use this as an excuse to strike me down?" Lena asked. She withdrew a knife from her sheath and held it to Tova's neck. "I should just slit her throat—make it easier for her."

"No!" Aya pleaded, her hand reaching toward Lena. "I swear it, I won't use my power. You can keep the knife there as assurance, just don't...don't use it."

Lena's lips pursed. "I'll compromise with you. I'll keep the blade in. Less chance she bleeds out," she said. "And *you* persuade her not to use her affinity."

"Like hells," Tova spat out.

"I would do it," Lena continued as if Tova hadn't even spoken. "But you might be more…forceful." Aya's stomach turned as she realized what Lena wanted her to do. "Compromise, Aya," Lena urged, her voice lilting. "Gianna may even let her live if you behave."

Aya looked at her friend, her hands shaking as she noted the fear in Tova's eyes. Aya sucked in a steadying breath. "Tova," she began, her voice trembling as she forced back tears.

"Aya, don't."

"Tova," she continued, taking a small step toward her friend as her power reached out. It met Tova's shield, stubborn and resolute. "It's going to be okay," Aya said, her power wrapping around her shield.

Let me in. Please let me in.

"But you can't use your power, okay?"

Aya found a crack in the shield. A weakness. She sent her power through it.

Tova's eyes closed as she let out a frustrated groan between gritted teeth, as if she could force Aya to stop.

She couldn't.

"Tell me you won't use your power," Aya pressed, tears streaming down her cheeks. That resistance gave, and Aya felt the moment her persuasion, her *compulsion*, was complete.

"I won't use my power," Tova repeated in a broken voice.

Aya let her hand fall, her tears coming faster. "I'm sorry," she whispered to her friend. "I'm so sorry."

Lena rolled her eyes and forced Tova forward, keeping that blade nestled against her throat. "Gianna is waiting for you in the throne room," she said to Aya. "Shall we?"

"Aya. You certainly kept me waiting."

Gianna was seated on her iron throne in a dress of pure white, and as Aya stopped before the dais, she couldn't help but feel as though she'd been here before.

She supposed she had.

A different crazed monarch.

A different throne room that reeked of death.

A different person she loved dying beside her.

"How could you do this?" Aya seethed as Gianna stepped down the stairs, her crown of iron glinting on her head. "*Your own people.*"

"People you have the ability to help, Aya," Gianna corrected as she stopped before her. "You see it now, don't you? Kakos is too strong to defeat. Not without the help of the Divine."

Gianna nodded to Lena, who dropped the knife at Tova's throat, gripping the one in her chest instead.

"As long as you obey me, Aya, Tova will live," Gianna instructed.

"Obey *what?*" Aya snarled. But she already knew, didn't she? The suspicions she and Will had voiced in that room in Milsaio had been all but confirmed the minute she watched the Dyminara turn on their own people.

There was only one reason Gianna would let things go this far, and she was looking at Aya as if she knew that she finally understood. But that didn't stop her queen from giving her a small smile as she admitted, "You are going to open the veil and call down the Divine."

"Go to hells," Aya bit out.

"Come now, Aya, you've been so obedient thus far," Gianna said as she motioned to the throne room, as if Aya's presence was evidence of her compliance. "I thought I'd have to make more use of my Diaforaté to fetch you from the fray."

She waved a hand to the corner of the room, where the door to the antechamber was. A man stepped through it, his skin decayed in patches, but his clothes clean and sturdy. Well cared for.

"I thought…"

Gianna's laugh was light. Airy. "You thought I risked my

own Diaforaté in the entrance hall? What a waste that would have been. No, that was another that Andras procured for me." She looked at the man—the Diaforaté—as if he were no more than a pet. "I couldn't part with Andras before we had a moment to chat, could I? Not when he's been so useful in *persuading* people to do things," Gianna continued as she looked at Tova.

"You," Tova breathed, her voice trembling with rage. "You *made* me forget."

"Too much, it seemed. I didn't realize you'd forget the information you gave *me* when I questioned you, but that ended up being a pleasant little twist," Gianna said. "All the more reason for Aya to distrust you."

Aya thought she might be sick.

"And the Dyminara?" she asked. She needed to keep Gianna talking, to keep the queen focused on *her* while she came up with some sort of plan. She would not lose Tova. She would *not* lose Tova. "You used your Diaforaté to turn them?"

A steely glint entered Gianna's eyes. "Those that I could, yes. Unfortunately, I couldn't achieve my plans for them all. But the rest met their end. Did you see the present I left you on your way here?"

Aya took a step toward Gianna, her rage a living thing inside her, but Tova's sharp inhale of pain had her freezing, her gaze darting to where Lena had begun to pull on the knife.

"One move against me, Aya, and Tova dies," Gianna said steadily.

"Do it, Aya," Tova gritted out. "Fucking kill her."

Gianna raised her brows. "You could. But then Andras here has been instructed to attack. And, well, you saw how that went for the Royal Guard in the entrance hall. Is that the fate you wish to leave Aya to, Tova? Perhaps her power would overcome his, but do you want to leave her survival to chance?"

Aya's mind was racing, her breath coming in shallow pants as she looked at her queen. It did not matter if she could overpower

Andras. She would not let Tova die. They needed help. *Someone* had to come. Surely they would, wouldn't they? If she delayed long enough, Will would know something was wrong.

"You would kill the Second Saint?" Aya tried to keep her voice lofty. Sure of herself. "Are you sure you aren't on Kakos's side, Majesty?"

Gianna's brow furrowed as she stepped toward Aya, her hand warm and soft against her cheek. "I am trying to *defeat* Kakos, Aya. The longer you delay calling down the gods, the more Kakos's success is on *your* conscience."

"And yet you were the one who did all of this, just so I would do your bidding. How long, Gianna?" Aya spat out, daring to use her name. "How long have you been letting this go on?"

Gianna sighed as she stepped back and began to pace. "We could have saved some time had you shown your power when I originally intended. Poor Andras here nearly persuaded the Athatis for *nothing*."

Aya's blood went cold. This whole time. It had been Gianna this *whole* time. How had she captured a Diaforaté? When?

Aya didn't have the chance to ask, because Gianna was continuing, her hands twining behind her back. "I realized after the failed Dawning attack that you would need more incentive to show your power. Luckily, I knew just who could motivate you," Gianna continued, cutting a glance at Tova. "I must admit, I didn't expect your journey in Trahir to take so long. And then, when you returned, I knew that you would not do what I asked unless the threat was dire. That was clear enough with Hyacinth's reports. So yes. I let Kakos advance, first in Sitya, and then in Milsaio, so you could see the *true* threat. Each death at their hand lies with you. You, and your refusal to do what you know the gods have asked you to do."

"You're sick," Aya hissed. "You know the gods do not want the veil opened. They do not want to come here!"

"You don't know what the gods want!" Gianna yelled.

Her face was flushed, her eyes widening slightly. "They speak to me. *Me*. Their loyal servant! They have instructed me for years in my dreams. The power they blessed you with is *wasted* on you! But *I*...I will be loyal. The Decachiré is the greatest wrong, and only the gods can abolish it for good! I will not let their desires go to waste!"

"They will kill *everyone*," Aya argued, desperation creeping into her tone. "That was their promise when they closed the veil five hundred years ago."

"They will NOT kill the devout! I have been obedient! They will reward those loyal to them beyond measure!" Gianna's fervor was enough to have Aya stepping back, her heart thudding in her chest so hard, she swore she could hear it.

Help me. Someone help me. Please someone help me.

"You and I both know you, as the Second Saint, are the only one powerful enough to open the veil," Gianna continued. She nodded to Lena, who moved the knife in Tova's chest just slightly. It was enough to have a noise of pain escape Tova's lips. "You can delay further if you like, Aya. But it just means more deaths when Kakos's reinforcements arrive."

Aya's throat was closing, her hands shaking as she stared at Gianna. Could there truly be more soldiers from Kakos on the way? Was this another truth Gianna had hidden from them, or was it a lie to get Aya to act?

Help me. Help me. Please help me.

"In the meantime...you can watch Tova bleed," Gianna murmured.

"Wait!" Aya called desperately. She would do anything. *Anything* to save her friends. To save her *home*.

Promise me you will do anything to stop her.

Aya's eyes widened slightly as she looked to Gianna.

She didn't need to open the veil. Not fully. The gods wouldn't help her. But someone else *could*. Someone else they had sent to her before.

"I'll do it," she breathed. "I'll call down the gods."

88

AYA HAD NO IDEA IF IT WOULD ACTUALLY WORK. IN THE desert with the Vaguer, she hadn't known *how* she summoned the veil. She had touched Evie's sword, and then it was there. But Evie had said that there was a likeness to their power and the gods-created barrier.

The way bondeds find each other.

The way souls attract.

And Aya supposed that was what it all came back to in the end: her soul. She just hoped that this wouldn't be the thing to destroy it as she reached in deep, the furthest she'd ever gone into her well, and extended her arms out wide, her hands grasping for air, and *pulled*.

She pulled, the same way she'd *pulled* when searching for Viviane's essence and latching on to it. And just like then, Aya found it somewhere that wasn't here in the throne room but wasn't Beyond either. It was vast and wide and so powerful that she could taste it on her tongue and see it before her eyes, and she was in the throne room, but she was lost in her head as well as she pulled and pulled and pulled, light dancing on her skin, flashing through the room while the air swirled, just like that storm she'd conjured in the desert.

Gianna was shouting praises, her fervent prayers lost in a cacophony of noise that Aya couldn't even place. She tried to focus, but she felt like she was splitting at the seams, right down to her very soul.

Please. Help me. Help me.

She was screaming it in her head, or perhaps she was screaming it aloud, and it didn't matter, because someone, somewhere, was listening to her prayer. Because there, right *there*, something shone before her, a mist, or a haze, or a vision, because perhaps she had gone mad at last, had lost herself in her power entirely, but Aya reached for it anyway, her fingers brushing against something *other*, a hand on the other side reaching toward her.

A hand, a woman, with raven hair and cobalt eyes, and Aya channeled that light on her skin into a thin line that sliced through the veil. She grabbed the hand and *pulled*, sobs racking her with the effort, with the way her power thrashed as it met the veil, as it held it open and Aya tugged Evie through.

"Get Tova," was the only thing Aya could say as she fell backward, Evie's hand falling from hers as her power burst from her, that thin line of the veil sucking it straight from her very soul. The veil vanished as Aya hit the ground, but Aya threw a hand out and sent one last pulse of power across the room, to where Gianna was on her knees, her arms outstretched before what she thought was a god, screams of reverence filling the air.

"Deikosi! Deikosi! Deikos—"

Aya's power hit Gianna directly in the heart.

The queen stilled, her lips parted in a reverent cry, frozen in a moment of worship. And then she fell sideways, her eyes blank before she even hit the ground.

Dead.

Aya whirled to see Evie, with a flick of her wrist, sending Lena dropping to the floor too, and then the saint was catching Tova, her friend weak and ashen and limp in Evie's arms.

For a moment, all was silent.

Aya took in the two dead bodies, her heart hammering and her head swimming. She staggered to her feet, weak and clammy and like her limbs weren't her own. She turned and looked toward the Diaforaté, who was standing with his eyes wide. He began to reach for her, and Aya lifted her hand, ready to put an end to him before he could even think about using his power, but something was stopping her, forcing her arms down, forcing the Diaforaté's down.

Aya turned to look at Evie. She was still holding up Tova, her free hand outstretched toward Aya and Andras. "What are you doing?" Aya rasped. "We have to get rid of him. We have to get to the Wall. I'll have the advantage there, I can help eliminate Kakos's lines."

The saint cocked her head, her raven hair slipping over her shoulder. "Why would we do that?" she asked.

In one quick motion, she pulled back her outstretched hand.

And she snapped Tova's neck.

89

EVERY SOLDIER WAS TAUGHT THAT DEFEAT DIDN'T HAPPEN until death. That hope lived while swords still swung. But as Aidon's body ached, his sword arm growing heavy, and as Kakos pummeled and pummeled the loose lines they had managed to form and continued to form, the more their people dropped, the more defeat seemed imminent.

The more death seemed imminent. Even with the arrival of the Athatis and the Dyminara.

And as a horn blew from the port, a long, piercing sound of war, Aidon felt his last vestiges of hope slip and slide away. Because if Kakos's reinforcements had arrived...

Then Aidon, and his troops, and Will and Tala and the remaining Dyminara might as well be dead.

But Aidon kept going, kept hacking, kept pushing, his throat raw as he barked orders to troops he had never met but who had decided, by some miracle of the gods, to trust in him.

On his left, leading a flank of his own, Aidon saw Will fall. But then he was up again, his sword still swinging, blood coating every inch of his skin.

"Incoming!" Liam yelled from Aidon's right, his gaze

fixed on the port. Aidon sucked in a shuddering breath, his armor feeling impossible heavy. But then Liam was yelling again, and there was a clear note of hope in his voice as he said, "Hold the line! Hold the line!"

And inexplicably, the warriors they were pushing against were backing up, first a step, and then a second, and Aidon couldn't understand why, couldn't figure out what had changed, until another voice was screaming over the din, "Fall in! Fall in! Fall in!"

And suddenly there were uniforms of emerald green folding into the Talan lines, their swords brandished and affinities flowing, and fucking hells, it was Aleissande, and she had brought the rest of the Visya unit.

"I ordered you to stay in Milsaio!" Aidon barked to Aleissande, his throat utterly raw.

"And I made a different decision!" Aleissande yelled back.

"Thank the gods for her better judgment," another voice chimed from beside him.

Josie.

Aidon looked at his Second and his sister, his spine straightening as he forced his breath to steady. "Forward!" Aidon proclaimed, his command received with a mighty roar that swelled up from the Trahirian Visya, from the remaining Dyminara, from the Talan forces.

And together they pressed on.

There is a moment when one knows a battle changes hands. When the tide shifts and suddenly, things change.

That moment was happening now.

Aidon could feel it as surely as he could feel his energy draining, his legs growing weak the further they pushed on. But Kakos…Kakos had started to retreat.

Slowly, at first. A few steps back. A few more.

And then faster. A line falling. A flank crumbling.

They were going to win.

They were going to *win.*

He repeated it to himself over and over and over as they pushed on, forcing Kakos back, and back, and back. He was exhausted, and bloody, and a metallic taste was in his mouth, but still, Aidon fought on.

They were going to win.

They were going to *win.*

Another line down.

Another.

And suddenly, they were breaking *through* Kakos's ranks, and the warriors were scattering, and even then Aidon pressed forward, his sword swinging viciously as he cut down anyone he could reach.

Aleissande was there, and she was yanking him back. "Don't be foolish," she spat out before ordering the next line forward. "You are our king. Have some self-preservation."

Aidon looked around at the lines of Talan and Trahirian forces moving forward. Perhaps she was right. Perhaps he wasn't needed in the front.

"Aya should have been at the Wall by now," Will rasped as he reached them, his sword soaked with blood. How the hells he was still standing, especially after his recent burnout, Aidon had no idea. He supposed it had something to do with the way Will cut a glance at that Wall, his face growing graver.

He had survived for Aya. He was *still* surviving for Aya.

"Go," Aidon commanded, jerking his chin toward the palace. "We have this."

Will hesitated only for a moment before he nodded and took off.

Aidon let out a grunt as he chopped down another prisoner from Chamen, and gods, they were *running* now, their backs turned as they lost the tide of the battle. And just as Aidon went to raise his sword and let out a cry of victory, he caught sight of Josie, her sword locked with a Diaforaté.

The Diaforaté shoved her back and Josie stumbled, and Aidon lunged, because the Diaforaté was gaining on Josie, her power setting her skin awash in bright light.

"No!"

Aidon wasn't sure if the scream came from him or from Aleissande. But he knew neither of them were going to reach Josie.

And so he did the only thing he knew to do.

He threw out a hand, his long-buried fire bursting from the center of his palm.

And he burned the Diaforaté to ash.

90

Later, Aya wouldn't remember if she screamed, or how she got to Tova's body, or whether her friend's eyes were open or closed in death.

But she would remember the broken angle of Tova's neck, and the coldness of her skin, and the way her own sobs echoed off the walls of the throne room.

She wouldn't remember how long it was before something snapped in her and she threw her hand out at Evie, a blast of raw power, dwindling after she'd summoned the veil, aimed straight toward the First Saint.

But she would remember how Evie brushed it away as if it were nothing more than smoke. And that Evie laughed, and laughed, and laughed.

"You…" It was the only word Aya could manage, and she said it again and again as she stared at the saint, at the woman she had desperately thought would save them.

"I cannot tell you how long I have been waiting for this moment," Evie said as she rolled her neck and flexed her hands. "I have been trapped in that veil for over five hundred years."

Aya was shaking, her hand still uselessly outstretched

toward Evie as she tried to rally more of her power, as she tried to clear the fog in her mind.

She would kill her. She would *kill* her.

"It is no use," Evie muttered with a dismissive wave of her hand. "You'll only burn yourself out."

"I have just as much power as you do," Aya spat out. "The gods chose me, too."

Evie's face twisted at the mention of the Divine. "No, Aya. *I* chose you." She inspected her hand, her tone casual, as if they were discussing the weather. "A kernel of my power latched on to you when I sent a ripple through the veil. I guess you could thank your goddess of fate for that, but I don't think Mora would take kindly to your bringing me here."

"You're lying," Aya rasped, one hand still gripping Tova's shirt. It was the only thing she could think to say. The only thing she *would* say, because that couldn't be true, she had finally accepted what the gods had given her. "The prophecy—"

"Oh, how history loves to twist the truth." Evie cut her off, her sigh deep. She grinned at the shock on Aya's face. "Let me tell you a story, Aya, about a girl who would do anything to save her people. The people who rescued her from the Decachiré practitioners after her parents were killed trying to become immortal. The people who raised her as if she was their own.

"Let me tell you a story about a war with no end and a girl who hiked to the highest point in the Malas, where the gods first created the Visya, and used the power she never asked for to destroy the veil so that the gods she prayed to might grant them salvation from darkness.

"Let me tell you a story of how she was successful in calling down the gods, but when they saw she had their power, they *killed* her."

Aya's body trembled harder, her throat constricting as she shook her head. "You're lying," she repeated. But this time, it was a mere whimper.

"It would be nice, wouldn't it? To believe the gods you cling to are as *divine* as you think? To believe they wouldn't kill the one person trying to save this realm? But no." Evie sighed. "They are selfish, and power hungry, and they killed me and shoved me in the veil, to spend eternity not in the Beyond and not in the hells, but in a prison of their own making."

Evie's face twisted with anger, her cheeks darkening as she took a step toward Aya. "But I made sure to damage their precious veil. I tore it, and I spent five hundred years continuing to worsen that tear until one day, a kernel of that power landed with you."

Evie began to pace, her hands twining behind her back. "It is fascinating how prophecies work. The Seer obviously had known I would create another saint. And so, it was easy enough for me to devise a plan once I realized *I* was the one the prophecy spoke of."

She paused, a small smile on her face as she raised her brows. "Do you know what the gods didn't account for when they trapped me in that damn veil? That I would be able to commune with those who worship me, the same way the gods could if they gave a damn. But you...you rarely thought of me. You were too focused on the death of your mother, and the *fear* of your power. But imagine my luck when I discovered a pious young princess with a mind fixated on me and my prophecy. It took much less power for me to reach her in her dreams, thanks to only having part of the veil between us. Plus, human minds are so *malleable*."

Aya could feel the blood drain from her face as she looked to where Gianna lay, her brown eyes blank in death.

No. Gianna couldn't be another victim in this, not after all she had done. Aya couldn't have killed her for *nothing*.

"Convincing her to kill her father was relatively easy when I realized all I had to do was assure her she was acting in the name of her gods. And making sure *you* were in close proximity to her was even easier once she was persuaded to form her own Tría."

Aya's hands were shaking as she braced them on the floor. She was going to faint, or vomit, or *die*, she was sure of it.

Gianna couldn't have been innocent. This couldn't be happening.

"By the time your queen began to suspect you were the Second Saint, I found I had almost full control of her mind, what with my constant presence in her dreams. Perhaps some of my power even managed to slip through and curl itself around her agency. Either way, I hardly needed it once you *finally* opened yourself to me this year. All that studying in the Synastysi worked *wonders* for our connection."

Aya's throat clenched, her lungs spasming as she tried to fight against the panic racing through her. This couldn't be true. This couldn't be possible.

"What do you want with me?" Aya breathed as she looked up at Evie.

The saint crouched down before her, a gentle smile on her face as she brushed a piece of Aya's hair out of her face. "Why, to help me right the greatest wrong, of course." Her hand was warm and smooth as it cupped Aya's face. "You're going to come with me. To Kakos. And together, we're going to form an army that can truly defeat the gods."

"I would rather die," Aya swore, yanking her head from Evie's touch. "Besides, why wait? Why not just tear open the veil and attack them now?"

Evie chuckled. "I may be powerful, Aya, but that doesn't mean tearing down the entire veil is an easy endeavor. It would drain me, and I would be no match for nine gods alone." Evie seemed unperturbed as Aya remained silent. "I figured you'd need some convincing. So allow me to give you the chance to change your mind. You come with me, or so help me, I will destroy this town, and every single person left that you love. I'll even save your precious William for last. And I will make you cut him into pieces."

And then, as if to prove to Aya that she could, indeed, force Aya to do just that, Evie laid a hand on her, and Aya screamed as Evie sent a pulse of white-hot power into her. It shattered her shield, leaving her raw and defenseless, and unable to stop her as Evie said, "Take the knife from Tova's chest."

Aya tried to fight it. She tried and tried, Galda's relentlessness about shielding ringing in the back of her mind, but Evie's power wasn't persuasion, it was compulsion, and it was one hundred times stronger than her own, and so she grabbed the knife, a sob escaping her as she wrenched it from Tova's chest.

"Wipe it clean," Evie said gently.

Aya did.

"Good. Now shove it in your own. You know where." Gods, did she try to fight.

And gods, did she fail. Aya screamed as her hand acted of its own accord, as it shoved the blade into where her scar marked home.

Another throne room. Another brush with death.

Let me die. Please let me die.

But she knew Evie wouldn't. Evie was sick. She was sick, and Aya was weak, especially after the veil. And Evie knew it.

"Pull out the knife, Aya."

Aya did.

"Heal yourself."

Aya did.

Even though it took every last bit of her strength. Even though it had her lying on her side, in a mix of her blood and maybe Tova's, her breaths coming in wet rasps. Evie crouched down beside her.

"Why not just force me to follow you then?" Aya panted, her whole body trembling and jerking.

Evie shrugged. "I was hoping you and I would remain friends. We have a lot of work ahead of us, Aya. Besides, I want you to remember that I spared your city because you *behaved*. I can't reward good behavior if it's forced, can I?"

"Go to hells," Aya spat out breathlessly.

Evie sighed. "I see this is going to take us some time," she said sadly. "How about this: I shall spare your town. And you remember that when you wake up, alright?"

Aya frowned, but Evie was already standing. "Do not move," she called back to Aya as she approached Andras.

The Diaforaté stared at Evie, eyes wide, as she gave him a small bow. "Can I count on you to assist me in returning to your kingdom, so that I may offer my services to your king?"

Slowly, as if overwhelmed by honor, Andras nodded. "Excellent," Evie said. "Knock her out. The old-fashioned way, if you wish."

It seemed Andras didn't even need the motivation of Evie's compulsion; his grin was a slash of yellow and black decay. Aya tried to move but her body was frozen in place, shaking, and gods, this was some sort of nightmare; this couldn't possibly be real.

Help me. Someone help me.

Andras stepped forward.

"Quickly though," Evie chimed.

The first kick he aimed was to Aya's stomach.

The second to her ribs.

And the last, to her head.

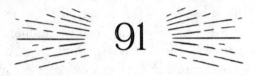

91

WILL WASN'T A PRAYING MAN. BUT AS HE RACED UP THE winding path to the palace, Tyr at his heels, he didn't just pray.

He begged.

Not her. Not her. Please, gods, not her.

Time was impossible to keep in battle, but he knew Aya had been gone too long. Something wasn't right, and gods, it made his throat burn as he wondered what had happened, as he tried to keep the worst of the possibilities from clouding his mind.

He and Tyr reached the palace gates.

The Quarter still burned, and by now, the flames had reached the forest. He could hear the shouts of some of the Auqin trying to prevent it from spreading, but Will didn't spare them another glance.

Where were the guards?

Why was it empty?

He and Tyr burst through the palace doors, and Will came skidding to a stop, a vicious curse erupting from him. There was blood everywhere. Blood, and bodies, and pieces of uniform, and flesh, and fucking hells, he had seen this type of monstrosity before; he knew what had caused this.

Will swallowed, his ears ringing as fear, true fear, turned his blood cold.

He didn't care if it was a trap—he screamed her name anyway.

He screamed it in the entrance hall.

He screamed it in the corridor.

He screamed it when he stepped into the throne room and saw three bodies on the ground.

Not her. Not her.

Please, gods, not her.

Lena.

Gianna.

"Tova," Will choked, dropping to his knees beside the woman. Her head was cocked at an unnatural angle, her neck clearly broken, and Will couldn't stop the sob that ripped from him as he bowed over her broken body.

What had happened here?

"Fuck," Will swore, tears streaming down his cheeks as he looked around the room. Aya wasn't here. Will forced himself away from Tova's body, forced his grief down as he raced to the antechamber, still screaming Aya's name.

It was empty.

He tore the palace apart room by fucking room. The chambers, the library, the ballroom, the prison. Tyr raced ahead of him, but it didn't stop Will from pushing on, from calling out for her.

Where is she? Where is she? Where is she?

And then they were back in the throne room, and Tyr was circling the room once. Twice. A third time, and Will was standing helplessly in the middle of it, his breath coming in jagged pants, his mind blank, because she was *gone*.

Aya was gone, and he knew it as certainly as he knew Tova was dead. Someone had taken her. It was the only explanation. Someone had taken her, because only death or something worse would have been able to drag her from Tova's body.

As if to confirm it, Tyr finished his final pass of the room. He stopped next to Will, his head wrenching back as he let out a heart-shattering howl.

Again.

Again.

Again.

Aya was gone.

And Tyr continued to cry.

Glossary

Anima: Visya with life and death affinity

Aquine: God of water

the Athatis: The sacred wolves who protect the Dyminara and the Kingdom of Tala

Auqin: Visya with water affinity

the Bellare: Rebel group in Trahir that resists the modernization of the kingdom

Caeli: Visya with air affinity

Cero: God of earth

the Conoscenza: The book of the gods, used by Visya to worship the Nine Divine

Dark Science: A dark-magic practice that had Visya corrupting their well of power so that it would be limitless, in order to bestow power on humans and seek immortality

the Dawning: Celebration of Saint Evie and her sacrifice that rid the realm of the Dark Science

Decachiré: The dark-affinity work that strives for limitless power

Diaforaté: Visya who siphon power to create the raw power they had before the War

Dyminara: The Crown's elite force of Visya warriors, scholars, and spies who serve the Kingdom of Tala

Genemai: Birth of Magic festival

Hepha: Goddess of flame

Incend: Visya with fire affinity

Maraciana: Home of the Saj, where the knowledge keepers study the affinities

mi couera: Term of endearment in the Old Language, "my heart"

Mora: Goddess of fate

Nikatos: God of war

Order of the Corpsoma: Visya with physical affinities

Order of the Dultra: Visya with elemental affinities

Order of the Espri: Visya with mind, emotion, and sensation affinities

Pathos: God of sensation

Persi: Visya with persuasion affinity

Phanmata: In the Old Language, "the lingering ghosts of nightmares"

Pysar: Trahir celebration of the coming spring and the delicacies that established the kingdom's place in trade

Sage: Goddess of wisdom

Saj: Visya who study magic

Saudra: Goddess of persuasion

Sensainos: Visya with sensation and emotion affinity

Terra: Visya with earth affinity

the Tría: Crown's three most trusted Dyminara

the Vaguer: Devout worshippers of Saint Evie who were excommunicated from the Maraciana

Velos: God of wind

the Ventaleh: Bitter winter wind of the north; said to be a reminder from the gods that they hold the power to cleanse the world

Visya: Mortal with a kernel of godlike power

Zeluus: Visya with strength affinity

Acknowledgments

I OFTEN SAY THAT *SINS* WAS MY DRAGON OF SORTS. I KNEW exactly how it was going to end as I went into it, but making sure all of the pieces came together was such a huge feat and would not have been possible without so many people.

First and foremost, thank you to the readers who have made this possible. Your excitement, support, and reception of *SAINTS* made me all the more eager to write *SINS*, and I cannot tell you how grateful I am that Aya and Will have found an audience that loves them and wants to be on their journey with them. I am forever indebted to you.

Thank you, from the bottom of my heart to my agent, Jessica. Not just for sitting with me for hours on end on a cold London day and pulling this book from me, but for always being my rock. You have believed in Aya and me from the very beginning, and I would be lost without you. You meet every wild, unrealistic dream I throw at you with, "Okay, let's try it!" and you are ALWAYS in my corner. I love you endlessly. Thank you to the entire bks Agency team for championing my work!

To the amazing Becks and Jorgie at Penguin Michael Joseph, the editorial duo that elevated this book to the best it can be, thank you for your thoughtful feedback, your passion for Aya and Will, and your willingness to always listen to me ramble my way to what I'm actually trying to say in a certain scene we're working through. You two are incredible. Thank you, Steph, for your marketing brilliance, and to the entire team at Penguin Michael Joseph for your support in sharing Aya and Will with the world!

To Mary and Alyssa, my powerhouse U.S. team at Sourcebooks Casablanca, thank you for bringing *SINS* to my home country and giving it your everything. I appreciate every Zoom call, every strategy session, and every extra thirty minutes we spend just chatting away. Thank you to the entire team at Sourcebooks for welcoming me with open arms and sharing Aya and Will across North America!

To the incredible team of sensitivity readers who gave me such detailed feedback, thank you for helping me represent our beautifully diverse world in an accurate and respectful way.

To the incredible authors who welcomed me into the author community and talked me down from the hundreds of spirals I had while debuting *SAINTS* and simultaneously taking on *SINS*—Barbara, Nic, Claire, Piper, Evan, Jill, Kendall—I love you all so much. Thank you for feeling like a slice of home, always.

And speaking of home…

Thank you endlessly to my friends and family. You all have been my biggest cheerleaders, and I truly could not imagine this wild ride without you. I love each and every one of you to the moon and back. Mom and Dad and Julie and Billy and Court and Mollie and Morgan and Bubbie and Squish—I'm the luckiest girl in the world to be surrounded by your love. Mollie, thank you especially for being my right hand, our Author Event Mom, and the best sister in the world.

Cassie, I love you endlessly, and there are not enough pages allowed to express my gratitude for all that you are.

Thank you for being you. Also sorry for... well, no spoilers. But you get it. 😔

To my fur babies, Clara, Duke, and Tilly, thank you for your snuggles and the laughs you always pull out of me, even when I'm deep in a plot hole.

And to Po, who crossed the Rainbow Bridge just as I was finishing proofs of *SINS*—thank you for loving me for ten years, even in the times when I didn't love myself. Thank you for fighting for extra time, for lying on my laptop so I'd have to take a break, for being the truest depiction of what a *bonded* could be. You are, and always will be, my sunshine. Rest easy, little man. Mommy loves you always.

About the Author

KATE DRAMIS is an Atlanta-based writer whose obsession with fantasy worlds and escaping into a good love story eventually drove her to chase her dreams of being an author.

When she's not busy writing banter that makes her laugh in an embarrassingly loud fashion, you can find her impulse-booking her latest travel adventure, snuggling with her dogs and cat, or tormenting her growing legion of readers on TikTok and Instagram with vague book teasers.

You can connect with Kate on her social media sites for behind-the-scenes content about the realm of Eteryium, such as character profiles, a glossary, and more.

Website: katedramis.com
Facebook: Katedramis
Instagram: @Katedramis
TikTok: @Katedramis